NOTHING WILL COME BETWEEN US

BY

JOSIAH JAY STARR

NOTHING WILL COME BETWEEN US

BY

JOSIAH JAY STARR

SPIRIT OF 1811 PUBLISHING
NEW ORLEANS, LOUISIANA
www.spiritof1811publishing.com

Spirit of 1811 Publishing

New Orleans, Louisiana

www.spiritof1811publishing.com

Library of Congress Control Number: 2021921256

Paperback ISBN: 978-1-953102-05-8

Hardback ISBN: 978-1-953102-04-1

eBook ISBN: 978-1-953102-06-5

Audiobook ISBN: 978-1-953102-07-2

Editors: Kimberly Rose

Interior Design: Loopa

Cover Design: Loopa

Dedicated to Azariah Starr
"Lil" Naomi Starr
Lil Jeremiah Starr
Shanice Johnson
Artanza Starr
Nyla Starr
And to the future generations to come.
Always follow the Lord and pray for discernment.

CONTENTS

PROLOGUE

THIS IS MY FIRST VISIT TO Miami and I'm unprepared. Everything about this place just feels so foreign to me. When I was a little girl, my bombastic grandfather often regaled me with vivid stories of his younger days, partying on South Beach. After a few sips of his ice-cold malt liquor, he would describe how much he loved feeling the ocean breeze cool his sweaty brown skin. Yet in the midst of reliving earlier times, my loving grandfather would always caution that everything he experienced in Miami had this deceptive allure to it. To be sure, Miami was the polar opposite of my Reparations Colony that comfortably sat among the rolling brown hills of Oakland. Nothing about this South Florida city was remotely similar to the life I had grown accustomed to back in California. I witnessed that this totally foreign habitat had a unique ability to magically change even the most sheltered visitor. In Miami, there was absolutely no cautions and worries of tomorrow. Life seemed to only matter within each passing second in this sunny paradise adorned with its sandy beaches and brightly colored palm trees.

Now, as a grown black woman, I found myself making the very same conclusions as my boastful grandfather. This whole experience felt so poetic and a tad bit ironic. Here I was, enjoying my time in Miami and making my own memories. My embarrassing adventures would be tales that I dare not share with my future grandchildren. These memories would certainly have to remain private. Given the harm they could cause, I would never openly relish nor celebrate them.

The driver of my hover taxi guided his car over the packed walkways near downtown Fort Lauderdale. When we cleared the mass of high rises, he turned southwest, facing the clear flat plains near Opa-Locka Airfield. Then, I felt him throttle up the taxi's small ramjet engine to a blistering pace. The airfield's bright floodlights grew in size as we closed on them. My driver was carelessly speeding along, blasting us well beyond allowable airspeed limits for the city. Part of me wanted to tell his ass to slow it down a tad since I wasn't in a hurry. Resisting the natural inclination to mouth off, I decided to bite my tongue and instead nervously adjusted my ponytail that still smelled of cigar smoke and sweat. Barely hanging on to consciousness after two measly hours of drunken sleep, I could feel the harsh effects of last night's tequila shots erupting within my foggy skull.

Below my taxi, young party-goers lined the powder-grey walkways. They were heading towards the scores of nightclubs in the downtown area. For them, their only goal was to make the night as memorable as possible. In the uniqueness of fate, none of them had any idea that in the taxi cruising above, rode a Foundational Black American that was on her way to making history. Tonight, we Foundationals will deliver sweet revenge upon a mortal enemy. It was my assignment to administer God's justice to a White Extremist named Bradley Wood, the blood-thirsty leader of a group called The Vanguard. In three deadly years, Bradley and The Vanguard had killed hundreds of Foundationals and terrorized God-loving Black Americans beyond measure.

My colony in Oakland had fallen victim to three of Bradley Wood's well-trained active shooters. The three white men were fanatics, and intent on becoming White Sacrifices in a racist jihad against Black

Empowerment. The active shooters carried out their suicidal ambitions with deadly precision. Dozens of Foundationals were violently murdered in their demonic assault, which targeted women, children, and elderly men. For three long years, my Force Protection unit investigated Bradley Wood, sewing together every shred of evidence we could find in the hopes of ascertaining his well-hidden whereabouts. As my FP unit's Chief Intelligence Officer, this entire manhunt boiled down to my ability to correctly interpret raw intelligence data. For three years, the investigation had taken the better part of me, but I was sure that my team had located Bradley's secret headquarters in the Dry Tortugas of the Florida Keys. I discovered he was managing his terror operations from a condemned museum named Fort Jefferson. Now it was our turn to deliver death upon this murderous white man. A white demon who thought nothing of bombing black children as they innocently rode in school buses.

Out of the corner of my eye, I caught my taxi driver using his rearview mirror to sneak peeks at me in the back seat. The distinct wrinkles on his forehead, his well-lotion dark skin, and overly aggressive perfume told me that he was a Haitian immigrant. From his awkward silence, I knew he was trying to figure out if I was a Foundational or just another Zebra living her life in White Miami. After catching him in mid-glance several times, I began to worry if he might recognize my face from the news reports about my fiancé, Quinton Sellers. Sensing he was about to ask if I was indeed Quinton's fiancée, I beat him to the punch with a distraction.

"How long have you been in Miami?" I asked while staring outside of the passenger side window.

"I've been here about four years now," he responded with a heavy accent. "I'm from Haiti and I'm still working on my citizenship."

The driver applied the air brakes, slowing the taxi down until we came to a still hover over the front gate of the airfield. Below us were three armed white men wearing blue U.S. Navy uniforms. All three men coldly stared at our taxi as it lowered down to earth, softly landing several dozen feet away from their checkpoint. The sight of the white men distracted my Haitian driver, sending him into a nervous panic. From my back seat, I could sense the intimidation swelling up in his wobbly spirit.

"I can't go any further, Ma'am," he said. "You have to get out and walk the rest of the way to the hanger," he instructed with concern in his voice.

He lowered his window, displaying an innocent smile at the security guards as I opened my door to exit. One of the white men beamed a handheld flashlight in the driver's face before sarcastically instructing him to get moving. Pretending to be ignorant, the driver displayed a wider smile while nodding his head in humble obedience. The arrogant chuckles that proceeded from the lips of these white bastards pissed me off. To them, black immigrants are less than trash and certainly not deserving of any respect nor consideration. In defiance, I took my sweet ass time getting out of the back seat. After pulling my bags out of the trunk, I gave the driver my monetary card and watched him scan it. After thanking the Haitian driver, I reached into my pocket and gave him a generous tip.

"Black First, brother." I relayed after giving him a five hundred dollar bill.

As the driver gazed down at his money, I saw him smile when he recognized the green face of Dr. Frances Cress Welsing adorning the bill. Realizing that I was indeed a Foundational Black American, the fear within him disappeared. He looked up at me and our eyes met one final time. I gave him a wink before turning around to walk away, purposely leaving him without words.

In the background, I heard the taxi lift skyward and take off into the distance as I neared the gate. One white security guard walked towards me and immediately began scanning my bags with his sensor, looking at me suspiciously as he sized me up. Reaching down into my bra, I quickly pulled out my Force Protection badge, displaying it for all three men to examine.

"Agent Nuria Phillips. Oakland Colony Force Protection Unit Six," I calmly stated.

The white man's eyes widened. He took a deliberate step away before turning off his sensor and smiling as though he had stumbled upon free money. He was tall, with a perfect military-style crew cut and an undersized uniform that exposed his muscular frame. In my mind, I had no doubt that this sailor was one of those white boys who had languishing hopes of being some badass special forces hero. Instead, he was just badass enough to become a gun-toting security guard at an obscure Naval Base in South Florida.

"Agent Phillips, we've been looking for you, Ma'am."

"Your partner, Donovan Reid, has been calling us all night. He ordered us to comb this base looking for you," he explained.

As the white man's words sunk in, I realized that my mentor and boss had already arrived at the base before me. That could've only meant one thing; it could be that Donovan hadn't slept well, and if he hadn't, then something about our mission was certainly worrying him.

"How long has Agent Reid been on the base?" I asked. "He's been here for several hours already, Ma'am," the white man explained. "He mentioned something about you being late or whatever."

Jolted and confused by his words, I immediately grabbed my watch and re-checked the time. As expected, it read 8:15 PM. We weren't supposed to report to Opa-Locka until nine, so I was early. Why the hell would Donovan think I was late?

"It's 8:15 PM. Why would he tell you that I'm late?" I cautiously asked.

A self-confident grin washed across the white man's face, and his boastful spirit immediately bothered me. It was obvious that he knew something that I was unaware of. Deep inside, I knew that he was quietly relishing this moment of superiority over a Foundational, and that alone was enough to piss me off.

"Opa-Locka Airfield did a time tick last night, Ma'am," he eagerly explained. "We reset the bases clocks to plus two hours Greenwich Time, so your watch is three hours behind."

"Shit," I vented. "I fucking forgot about the time tick."

"Can you please drive me to the hanger? I'm super late and I need to get geared up for our mission."

Satisfied with my sudden vulnerability, the security guard slowly turned towards his colleagues and lightly waved for them to open up their gate. I followed him as he directed me towards a small shuttle parked just inside the base's perimeter. The other two guards opened the shuttle's trunk and placed my bags inside the loading compartment.

"Your hanger is on the other side of the base Agent Phillips," one of the men said as he sat himself down behind the controls. "The base speed limit is only 20 MPH. It will probably take us five minutes to get you over there."

The man pushed the ignition button, and our shuttles electric motor came to life. The shuttle crept forward and we slowly made our way down a lonely airfield road. In the isolation of the back seat, I felt the nervous chills roll down my spine. The apprehension only worsened my pounding hangover. In my mind, I could already see the painful look of disgust on Donovan's face. He would probably roll his eyes right out of his head before blazing into me with a few choice words. We were a few hours away from the most important counter-terrorist operation in Foundational Black American History, and I had started the damn mission off by showing up on colored people's time. Feeling embarrassed, I pensively looked down at my watch as the two white men silently sat in the front compartment with gated smiles.

The Anti-Black jokes regarding my tardiness would certainly create themselves. I quietly knew that these white bastards would have a field day laughing at me. When the U.S. government paid us reparations and designated our territorial colonies, the Dominant Society had made it their business to highlight our every mistake. As expected, White America was certainly bitter about having to pay reparations for the moral cost of centuries of White oppression. The Great Recompense, as it was coined, was a vast political movement geared towards providing Foundational Black Americans full compensation for the evils of Systemic Racism. Black Americans whose ancestry stretched back to concentration camps or slave plantations in the United States, were eligible to receive restorative benefits and restitution under the Great Recompense initiative. The first corrective measure of the Great Recompense was the Reparations Bill of 2054.

One of the well-noted articles within the Reparations Bill, was the Joint Force Protection Clause. Due to the clause, the U.S. government was obligated to provide combat support to Foundational Anti-Terrorist operations. My Force Protection unit had been deployed to Miami and we were working with a U.S. Navy SEAL team to fulfill this specific clause.

Finally, after what seemed like thirty minutes, we made it to the hanger and the shuttle parked in front of a well-lit entrance. Above the entrance was a large sign that read, 'Skunk Works Hanger," undoubtedly a tribute to Lockheed Martin's infamous aeronautical engineer, Kelly Johnson. I exited the shuttle and unloaded my bags before offering the two security guards a humble wave goodbye. As I began walking towards the entrance, the front door flew open and I saw Donovan Reid walking towards me. His long dreadlocks swung menacingly with his every step. His pace was deliberate and his cutting stare was icy as our eyes met. Donovan was justifiably pissed and he had every reason to be irate. In anticipation of his ensuing tirade, I prepared my already tender pride to consume his verbal blows.

"Nuria! What the Fuck!" he cursed. "We've been after Bradley Wood for three whole years and you're gonna piss it all away in one damn night!"

"I fought my ass off to get you assigned to this mission and you decide to embarrass our people."

"You told me you were ready for this Nuria," Donovan barked.

"You told me you were locked in. You said your situation with Quinton wasn't going to be an issue and I believed your lying ass."

"Now you show up late after partying all night with some low-down Negro Zebra...I can't believe you did that shit Nuria. We look really foolish and unprofessional right now."

"We can't defend our colonies against these people if you're out here fuckin'em!"

Donovan's words were harsh and I felt each letter as they cut me to the bone. Not only was I late, but somehow Donovan knew I had spent the night with Jeremy Woodson. Now my forbidden little outing in Miami had become common knowledge. Looking into his intense eyes, I felt a cold blanket of shame and embarrassment wrap itself around my soul.

"Damnit, Nuria," he continued. "Your fiancés' little escapade with a white stripper already has your name trending for all the wrong damn reasons."

"Why do this to yourself? Why expose your personal life to even more white media scrutiny? Especially when we have Bradley Wood cornered and ready for the taking."

I stood in front of Donovan, trapped in inner silence, totally paralyzed in the midst of my own embarrassment as I let him vent. Unlike my grandfather's glorious adventures in Miami, mine would be nothing to remotely boast about. This whole situation had become a complete mess, and it was all my fault.

Donovan took one of my bags from my hand and gave a dramatic nod towards the hanger's entrance, ordering me into the building. He had said his piece and I knew that it was not the right time to argue with him. I had worked with Donovan for years and I knew him well. He was a great boss but an even better mentor for me as a newbie in the Force Protection Agency. Donovan Reid was the main reason I was selected for the job. Out of a competitive group of thirty applicants, Donovan had personally selected me to be a part of his FP team. Being the only woman in the applicant pool, I had thought my chances of selection were next to nothing. I wasn't the fastest nor the strongest out of the bunch. To be honest, I wasn't even the smartest, but Donovan had seen something within me that he coveted. At the time, he didn't know that I was the fiancée of a famous Foundational who would become the Heavyweight Champion of the World. To him, I was just the stubborn-minded little heifer who struggled through every obstacle course, lagged during every 7-mile run, and fought my way through every written exam.

I knew that Donovan's anger truly came from a place of love and disappointment. The thought that I had failed him hurt me to my core. This man believed in me and I had let him down in a moment of personal weakness. Walking into the building, I saw the final member of our team standing outside of the locker room. Pernell Jones was already dressed in a dark black combat bodysuit, wielding his long gun. His helmet and night vision glasses hung from his neck, as did his communications earpiece, which dangled just below his earlobe. I watched as Pernell's rifle swung on its sling while he meticulously loaded spare magazines into his gun belt. Unlike the Texas-born Donovan, I had known Pernell for years and we were both local products of the Oakland Reparations Colony. Growing up in the same neighborhood, Pernell had been a middle school classmate of mine. Pernell and Quinton were close friends, as both had this obsession with boxing and martial combat. If my mentor Donovan had played the role of my adopted father, Pernell would most certainly have been my adopted brother. Working alongside both never truly felt like a job to me, as they always made my task easier. These two black men were my family, and it was this family's job to protect Foundationals at all costs.

"Nuria... you have really lost your mind," Pernell loudly proclaimed.

"I warned you about this Zebra, Jeremy Woodson. I saw it all in his eyes. That damn Zebra couldn't stop staring at you. I knew it was only a matter of time before he made a pass. That Zebra's been looking to get in your panties from day one."

"I bet it was them white folks that put that Zebra up to this shit," Pernell murmured.

Pernell's eyes grew wide and his nostrils flared with every word he spoke. I noticed that small beads of sweat had formed on the top of his freshly shaven head. It was obvious that Pernell was stressed, but it wasn't because of the anticipation of combat. Rather, it was me and my hurtful situation. My internal cloud of remorse began to consume me, so I purposely took my eyes away from Pernell, hoping to find some emotional reprieve in the tan-colored walls of the hanger.

"You and Quinton are both really fucking up so bad right now," he murmured. "First, Quinton and now, you. Y'all are both being childish. This is not how we, as Foundationals, are supposed to behave."

"I love and care about both of you, Nuria. What y'all are doing is putting me in a bad position, where I'm gonna have to choose between the both of you."

"You're my partner and my teammate out here. Quinton is my homie... there's no damn way I can win."

"I mean, you two are such a great couple...but now you're both risking it all over some white prostitute in New York and a Zebra who denied his Foundational roots to live with white people."

"I didn't start this," I shot back. "Quinton is the one who chose to disrespect the sanctity of our relationship, not me."

"Are you sure about that, Nuria?" Pernell interrupted.

"Because I know for a fact that you ain't the type of woman who is comfortable just waking up next to any ole man."

"What happened between you and Jeremy Woodson has been building for a long time. The hard truth is that you allowed it to build. Jeremy has been giving you all kinds of attention, even before Quinton screwed around. You have to be honest, Nuria. You enjoyed his attention and I could see that you were. You and Quinton have both been losing focus. That's all I'm saying."

"Well, you can save the lecture. Especially if it didn't work on your bestie Quinton." I offered with purposeful sting.

"I don't wanna hear a damn thing about my personal affairs from you, and I'm not going to allow you to blame me for Quinton's infidelity. Quinton did what he did, so you can go fuck yourself."

Pernell shook his head wildly and let out a loud sigh that echoed throughout the narrow hallway. I could see him holding back his boiling hot fury while trying to find words that wouldn't further escalate our loggerhead. His visible frustration caused me to regret my mean-spirited assault. I knew Pernell didn't deserve it. He was just trying his best to be a friend to both me and Quinton. Unfortunately, at the moment, Pernell had the hardest job in the world.

"You two are so stubborn," he quietly lamented. "You two will be ripped apart by your bull-headedness."

"I saw you sneaking Jeremy Woodson into your hotel room last night."

"I saw you two and knew what was going on. The sad truth is, right after I saw you guys, Quinton called me from New York."

"He asked about you and told me that you've been ignoring his calls and messages," he explained with wet eyes. "He sounded like he's really in a bad space."

"I'm not trying to get involved in your relationship Nuria, but I do think you and Quinton should at least talk, especially since we are embarking on this mission. Who knows what could happen out there tonight?"

Pernell used his palm to wipe his face, then looked over my shoulder at Donovan. This was their intervention, and I could feel the trepidation oozing out of both men's spirits. Their genuine concern was touching; they truly cared about me. Yet, there was no way I would talk to Quinton right now, not after what he had done. I needed time, and if my timeline didn't match Quinton's needs, then to hell with him.

"Well, I'm glad that shits outta the way," Donovan mocked. "We have the other half of your issue to deal with now."

"Nuria, some filthy White media tabloid named the Kingfish took photos of you and Jeremy Woodson at a bar in Las Olas Beach yesterday."

"The damn photos show you two drinking, cuddling, and making out in public...amongst other things."

"The Kingfish contacted both the Navy and our Colonial Leadership Council, asking them to comment on you and Jeremy's alleged affair."

"The Kingfish was about to publish those photos, along with a nasty hit piece about your sexual liaison. Somehow, Rear Admiral Judith Bean and Secretary Patrice Williams have invoked the National

Urgency Clause. Because of the clause, the Kingfish are now under a gag order that has prevented them from publishing the items."

My heart skipped when Donovan mentioned Secretary Williams. Now, I was certain that details of my affair were being consumed among Foundational Leadership circles. On one of the biggest stages of our existence, I had let down my people and proven to be just as untrustworthy as Quinton. If Patrice Williams knew about all of this, I knew for sure that I'd be dismissed from the Force Protection Team when all the smoke cleared. Donovan looked towards Pernell and pointed towards the hanger. Obediently, Pernell's eyes instantly filled with recognition and he dutifully walked away, giving Donovan and I a moment of privacy.

"Nuria, they had to invoke the clause because if this went public, a lot of Top Secret matters would be compromised."

"The Navy doesn't want it disclosed that there are Special Forces teams located here in Miami, and our Colonial Leadership Council wants the fact that we have been training and sharing Intel with these military units to remain a secret."

"Due to the threat of you and Quinton Sellers being exposed as cheaters... Secretary Williams had no choice but to beg these White folks to invoke a gag order to protect you two," Donovan lamented.

Donovan gently placed his hands on my shoulders and slowly turned me around towards the locker room entrance. There was a moment of silence between us as Donovan opened the door while plastering me with a stare filled with anger.

"Apparently, Admiral Bean has already reprimanded Jeremy Woodson for fuckin around with you," Donovan explained.

"Inappropriate professional relationships are forbidden in the Navy, and they violate U.S. military protocol."

"Jeremy is in the locker room waiting for you. I will allow him to talk to you so you both can bury this mess once and for all."

"I'm sorry, Donovan," I softly pleaded. "All this drama with Quinton... seeing all the reports about his affair in the news... all got to me. I thought I could handle it, but it all just overwhelmed me yesterday." "I wasn't thinking, and I fucked up."

"You know what you need to do for your people, Nuria?" Donovan interjected, cutting me off in mid-thought.

"Jeremy is a Zebra and you are a proud Foundational Black woman. He isn't one of us. There ain't a bit of difference between these white folks and their Zebra lackies, and you know that."

"Clean this trashy mess up and save your marriage, Nuria. I'll talk to Secretary Williams about delaying the mission and sending a replacement for you. I've already called our colony over in Mobile, Alabama, and their Senior FP Intel analyst is standing by to come out here and relieve you."

"Donovan, I don't want to leave. Please let me finish this mission."

"This ain't up for debate," he shot back. "You are my priority Nuria, not Bradley Wood."

Donovan held the door open in silence and I knew he was done talking. I walked past him while attempting to avoid his disgusted stare. Both Donovan and Pernell despised black Zebras almost as much as they loathed White Supremacists. In Donovan's mind, any black person who decided to forgo their reparations benefits so they could live in White Society, was a traitor. Unfortunately for Jeremy Woodson, he fell into that category.

"You got five minutes," Donovan barked while slamming the door behind him.

I heard the locker room door shut and before me sat a nervous-looking Jeremy. He looked emotionally exhausted and his spirit gave off the aura of a wounded man still determined to fight his opponent until the bitter end. Without words, I walked to the bench and sat next to him. Jeremy gave me a welcoming stare that highlighted his beautiful brown eyes. Sensing his need for support, I gently rubbed his knee, offering him a wordless moment of comfort. His eyes softened at the touch of my hand and right then I knew that whatever the Navy had done to him must have weighed on him heavily.

"They reprimanded you," I softly asked?

"Hell yeah," he admitted. "They're fucking pissed."

"When this mission is over, I'll probably be busted down and kicked out of my SEAL unit. My Commanding Officer made me sign some legal non-disclosure agreements today. Now I'm obligated to lie if anyone asks me about all this."

Jeremy shook his head and chuckled to himself. I wrapped my arms around his hard-muscular body, pulling him close to me. Jeremy was a good man. He didn't deserve any of this mess he was currently facing. Now Jeremy, a man who truly loved me, would become the fall guy for my own mistake. He reciprocated my hug by caressing my forearms as I held him tight in heart-speaking silence.

"I'm so sorry, Jeremy," I let out while erasing the tears from my face.

"I made a big mistake, and now you're in all kinds of trouble. I feel like such a terrible person right now. I hope you can forgive me."

"Big mistake?" Jeremy shot back with concern in his eyes. "What do you mean by that, Nuria?"

"I had no business being with you last night. I'm a Foundational Woman, Jeremy. To boot, I'm engaged. I'm supposed to be getting married in less than four months, remember. Quinton and I...Our virtual wedding has more than 15 million RSVPs. We've already received thousands of wedding gifts."

"The whole damn world is set to watch us tie the knot. For months, the Colonial Leadership Council has been promoting it. But now all of this has gotten so much bigger than me and Quinton just getting married."

"Quinton Sellers, the Heavyweight Champion of the World and his lovely wife, the officiator of Foundational Justice. It's one of the biggest PR campaigns we Foundationals have undertaken since we received our reparations, Jeremy.

"Quinton and I have been made into this perfect idealistic image of Foundational values."

"We were supposed to be a public demonstration of the success of our Black Reparations Agenda. I mean we were promoted as the conquering power of black love."

"Seeing all of that crumble around me after I found that Quinton was cheating caused me to start questioning a lot of things."

"Everything that happened between us, I don't know if it was real, or if it was just my way of searching for my own truth."

I felt Jeremy beginning to lift himself from the bench, so I released my hug. He towered over me, looking down with his beautiful eyes that pulsed with urgency. I may have been confused, but I knew Jeremy had no doubts about his own feelings.

"You can't look me in my eyes and tell me you didn't feel something special between us last night, can you, Nuria?"

A streak of confusion hit my wobbly spirit, so I turned away from Jeremy's eyes. I didn't want to find the answer to his question. I didn't truly have the strength nor the courage to look for the truth. After an uncomfortable silence, I felt Jeremy's hand gently pull up my chin, guiding my eyes to look up at him.

"That's what I thought."

"You know what your heart is telling you. Maybe this doesn't have anything to do with Quinton. Maybe what we're both feeling right now is real," Jeremy explained.

"I know Donovan and Pernell hate me," he continued loudly. "They put you up to this... to have you come in here to kill me softly."

"I understand I'm not a Foundational Nuria. In Donovan's eyes, I'm a mindless Zebra who likes being the token negro for white folks. No matter what I do to help your Foundational cause, to Donovan and Pernell, I will forever be an outsider... but that doesn't matter to me, Nuria."

"What matters to me is what you think. To me, you're not just some public relations ploy. You're the woman I love. The black woman I cherish. Looking into your beautiful brown eyes defines my purpose in this fucked up world."

"Plus," he continued with a hushed whisper.

"How could either of us walk away? You remember all that hollering you did last night."

"You know you loved taking that shit, just as much as I loved giving it to your ass. Deep down, you damn well know you want more of it too. Don't you, Nuria?" he asked with a cheesy smile.

I delivered a playful punch to Jeremy's thigh before pushing the vivid images of our steamy night out of my mind. After limping around mocking an injury, Jeremy calmly retook his seat next to me and reached down into his pocket. Before he could reveal what was in his hand, I heard the distinct rattle that gave me a clue on what he was holding. I felt a childish smile instinctively form on my face as I reached my hand out in front of him. Jeremy immediately smiled back at me before pulling out the candy box and pouring a couple of pieces into my palm. After he finished pouring, I swiftly reached out with my other hand and snatched the entire box away from him. His boyish smile disappeared from his face and I laughed loudly at his expense.

"You just said what I want matters, right?" I playfully teased. "Yeah, I guess so, Nuria," he murmured.

We sat on the bench playfully joking with each other. It was good to see Jeremy's whole mood improve. Out of nowhere, Jeremy reached over and held my hand. I received his tight grip with my own light squeeze as a spirit of seriousness came over us.

"Nuria, I've been thinking about something for a while," he began.

"Now, it seems like the time for thinking about this is over and I have to get right into actions."

"To be honest, even before all of this, I was getting tired of the Navy. It isn't the lifestyle I want to live anymore. I'm planning on getting out after this Bradley Wood mission is finished."

"I'll be applying for residency at the Oakland Reparations Colony," he explained. "I have distant relatives that run a distillery in your colony."

I was shocked hearing those words. Instantly, I felt my stomach flutter as I processed Jeremy's words. This man was about to give up everything he ever knew and had. He didn't have to say it, but I knew he was doing it because of me. Embarrassed, I let his hand go and pulled away from him. This was all too much and not what either of us needed.

"No, Jeremy," I replied. "You can't do this, not for me anyway. I won't let you."

"I'm doing it," he interrupted. "I believe in you."

"Look, I'm not trying to pressure you. I ain't Quinton Sellers. I'm not the Heavyweight Champion of the World. I know you still care about that guy, but I also know that he can't possibly love you like I can."

"I'm willing to do whatever it takes to prove that I'm the one for you. Even if that means starting at the very bottom of Foundational

Black Society. If I have to scrub toilets or mop floors until I work my way up the ladder, then so be it."

"No, Jeremy," I yelled. "This is crazy. You can't just throw everything in your life away just because of me."

Ignoring me, Jeremy rose from his seat and stubbornly gazed into my eyes with a motivated spirit. At this point, my tears were flowing. I was filled with so many mixed emotions that I was having trouble finding the right words that could convey my feelings. Deep inside, I felt trapped and everything I did to free myself only seemed to tighten the noose around my soul.

"We can talk more about this after the mission," Jeremy relayed. "I'll be requesting a discharge when we return. I'll claim its due to stress or something, and I'm sure my command will happily accommodate me."

"Jeremy, we just need to focus on the mission right now," I blurted out. "We don't need to be focusing on us."

"I know, my love," Jeremy answered. "That's one reason I'm about to leave. We both need to get ready for this mission tonight. I know how much stopping Bradley Wood means to you and I won't let you down."

"Not to mention, the five minutes they gave me is almost up, and I'm sure Donovan will be more than happy to run in here to remind me about it."

Jeremy walked towards the locker room door and pushed it open before entering the hallway. The door slowly closed behind him, leaving me alone with my thoughts and confusion. After cleaning my face, I reached into my pocket and pulled out my handheld computer. Scrolling through the menu, I opened my mailbox and saw the dozens of unread messages from Quinton. Part of me wanted to read each of them, but I wasn't sure if I was emotionally ready for all of that mess. Until this situation with Jeremy, Quinton had been the only man that had ever known me intimately. Since our days of youthful innocence back at Neely Fuller Middle School, Quinton Sellers had been the center of my universe. We grew up together. We both lived on the same colony street and our parents attended the same church. When Quinton went to the summer Olympics in Singapore and won the gold medal, I was there right next to his family, cheering him on.

A lot of my childhood memories were all wrapped around being Quinton Sellers' longtime girlfriend. Even before our relationship got all this media attention, I had known that we had something special. Yet, after Quinton won the Heavyweight belt, I felt something began to change between us. At the time, I couldn't quite put my finger on it and part of me didn't want to try to figure it out. So, I denied it, hoping in my soul that it was just my imagination. When the news of Quinton's cheating was revealed to me, it cut me deep. He wasn't just some wayward boyfriend to be discarded like tainted trash. Quinton was my fiancé. A Black man that had been a major figure in my life.

The fear churning inside of me caused me to put away my handheld computer. As I buried the computer in the bottom of my duffle bag, I quietly knew that Pernell had been right. I needed to address this, Quinton and I both needed to address this shit. There would most definitely be a time when I would have to confront my fears, but that time would have to wait. Right now, I needed to refocus myself. Bradley Wood was still out there and if he wasn't stopped, more Foundationals would certainly die at his hand.

I reached into my bag and pulled out all of my gear. As I dressed, the familiar feeling of the flexible titanium armored combat suit gave me a temporary surge of invincibility. The unique clicking sound each bullet made when I loaded them into my spare ammo clip was empowering and all too intoxicating. In my moment of self-mediation, I heard the locker room door swing open.

I turned around to see Donovan and Dennis walk in towards me. Dennis was our team's technical expert. With his elaborately braided hair, muscular physique, and self-confident swagger, Dennis looked more the part of a professional athlete than a computer engineer. Dennis, a nerd at heart, was responsible for managing all of our advanced weaponry. He was literally a genius and his street-hardened exterior could easily deceive anyone who wasn't familiar with him. I saw a virtual meeting phone in Dennis's hand. Its glowing green light told me that someone was on hold on the other end.

"What up, Nuria," a stoic Dennis stated as he sat down next to me.

I waved my hand at Dennis and nodded at him while he placed the phone on the floor below me and began to calibrate the hologram image that hovered above it. Donovan also sat down on the bench, gently tapping my leg in an attempt to get my attention.

"Secretary Williams wants to have a conversation with you before tonight's mission," he coyly stated.

"The Colonial Leadership Council wants to personally make sure this whole Jeremy Woodson affair is a non-issue before we move forward tonight."

"Secretary Williams is insisting that you stay on this mission. So, I won't be replacing you."

I could see the agitated look in Donovan's eyes and knew that he had been on the receiving end of an enormous amount of political pressure. Here we were, on the cusp of launching a mission to attack one of the world's most dangerous terrorists and my mentor seemed more worried about pleasing elected officials in the Foundational community.

"I'll make sure Secretary Williams understands this is a non-issue," I reassured Donovan.

Both Donovan and Dennis departed the room, leaving me alone as the hologram image of Force Protection Secretary Patrice Williams slowly came into focus. Patrice Williams calmly sat behind her desk, looking polished and professional in her expensive yet simple-looking crème colored cape shoulder top. Patrice's family lineage was littered with prominent and outspoken black advocates for reparations. Her influential grandfather had been viciously assassinated while raising money to investigate ties between law enforcement and white extremist groups. So, Patrice's family name was held in high esteem in the Foundational community, earning her exclusive opportunities to climb up bureaucratic ladders.

We all understood that Patrice's nomination as the Foundational Force Protection Secretary was only a temporary gig. Working with us was merely a steppingstone in this woman's bright future. Unlike us, she wasn't a working class stiff and knew next to nothing about securing thirty-two Foundational colonies that are under constant threat from White Supremacists. Patrice came from the rich oil fields of colonial Texas, where she had been responsible for ensuring that all Foundational Oil refineries followed EPA regulations. What Patrice lacked in professional knowledge, she made up for with her excellent leadership skills. Unlike most political figures, she had a knack for knowing when it was best to listen. When the moment required it, she was always able to cleverly find ways to come across as humble, even though she was indeed the boss. Patrice Williams was going places and her leadership style and attitude had easily won us over. We would fight to the bitter end to ensure Patrice would never be labeled a failure. She was the future of Foundational politics and was sure to one day become a powerful heavyweight in her own right.

'I know it's been a tough few weeks for you, Nuria. How are you doing, girl?" Patrice asked. "Madam Secretary, I'm doing well. Just ready to start this mission," I deflected.

"Drop all the Madam Secretary shit," she intentionally shot back. "The Colonial Leadership Council and our entire community have invested heavily in your virtual wedding girl. We need no bullshit answers right now."

"Given that brain-dead stunt your dumb ass fiancé pulled in New York and the shit Kingfish wants to publish, we need to know if your wedding is still gonna happen."

"As you well know, we have world leaders that are supposed to attend the event. We just wanna make sure that the both of you still plan on walking down the aisle together....it would be a major embarrassment if either of you got cold feet in front of the entire world community, Nuria."

"Telling the truth and being honest would spare us a lot of pain."

"Whichever way you wanna go with this, Nuria, just know that we can spin it into a positive for you and our community," she relayed.

I caught the quiet underlying message Patrice was clearly sending. She was lowkey informing me that Foundational leadership would protect me if I decided that marrying Quinton was no longer an option. They had chosen to protect me over a disgraced Foundational Heavyweight Champion who had shamed our community by sleeping with a coke head white stripper. To my shock, after hearing Patrice's words, my laboring heart sank for Quinton. The streak of compassion for Quinton felt strange as it made its presence known within my soul. Quinton had wounded me deeply and betrayed me in the worst way possible. Yet, I didn't want to hurt him, not like this anyway.

By publicly protecting me, the Foundational community would all but exile Quinton from our society. He would become a pariah to his own people and I just couldn't allow that to happen to him. Despite

Quinton's selfishness, I knew that casting him out of the society we had both grown up in would be too much for him to bear. The alienation would destroy him.

"Thank you, Patrice." I humbly began.

"I really appreciate the support from the Foundational community, and I understand the magnitude of the situation for all involved. But right now, Quinton and I would simply like a little privacy while we address our issues."

"Yes, we are having relationship issues, but they are issues that we are fighting through," I relayed as Patrice soaked it all in.

"So, this Jeremy Woodson affair is nothing?" she pointedly asked. Without hesitation, I looked her image straight in the eyes and gave Patrice the answer I knew she wanted to hear. "No, Patrice," I confidently explained. "My one night with Jeremy was exactly that, one night. We both understand that there can be nothing between us."

From the look on her face, I knew my words had pleased her and would surely comfort nervous members of the Colonial Leadership Council. For now, they would have to protect all of us, and that's what I needed them to do. I had bought us time.

Patrice thanked me for my honesty and offered me the best of luck and prayers for tonight's mission before ending the virtual call. As her hologram image disappeared into nothing, the thought of what would occur if I happened to get killed tonight suddenly dawned on me. The somber thoughts of my own larger-than-life state funeral replaced the lively mental images of my huge virtual wedding. In my mind, I could already see the visuals of a grieving Quinton Sellers dressed in all black and using a white handkerchief to wipe underneath his dark sunglasses. My funeral would be just as strong of a public relations message as my wedding.

"No one was going to die tonight," I quickly told myself as I laughed off the possibility of death. Besides, this mission is quite literally a layup. My team had secretly rehearsed this exact mission alongside the Navy SEAL's dozens of times. Tonight, we would be performing a classic special operations maneuver called the Drop and Hop. Within a matter of seconds, we would drop from the heavens and hop right on top of our opponents, engaging them in lethal close-quarters combat. Bradley Wood and his associates on Fort Jefferson would be surrounded, outnumbered, and overwhelmed by our firepower. All of my Intel told me that Bradley had no idea that we knew of his whereabouts or that we were in Miami preparing to attack him.

I rose from the locker room bench and walked out into the hallway where Donovan, Pernell, and Dennis all stood outside waiting for me in silence. Upon seeing me, Pernell dramatically turned towards the hanger and walked away. He was still angry and his body language spoke volumes. Ignoring Pernell, I walked over to Donovan and hugged him. Even if he didn't want me on this mission, I understood why he felt I needed to be replaced. For him, it wasn't just about breaking the rules. Donovan genuinely cared about me.

"You ready Nuria?" Donovan softly asked. "Yeah, Donovan. Let's go get this asshole."

Donovan and I walked down towards the hanger entrance, leaving Dennis alone in the narrow hallway. I followed Donovan into the aircraft hangar and was greeted by the familiar smell of lubricated metal and warm electronics. The hangar was huge and spacious, as dim lights hung from a ceiling that was more than several stories high. In front of us sat three diamond-shaped U.S. Navy assault rovers quietly humming as their stealth pulse jet engines idled. Each top-secret rover looked menacing and invincible, as the hanger lights from above made them look like ghostly shadows. The outer hulls of the rovers were painted dark blue and were reinforced with a special version of titanium alloy. Donovan looked at me and pointed towards our rover, which was marked with bright yellow bands painted on its wingtips. I walked over to my rover and started to climb up the accommodation ladder before I felt someone aggressively tap my leg.

"Nuria, you and your team all need your night vision contacts," Dr. Hernandez explained with a light smile.

Looking back down at Dr. Hernandez, I saw he was carrying several small boxes. Each box had names stenciled on them. I quickly noticed my last name labeled on the top box and climbed back down to the ground.

A second-generation Mexican American whose grandparents immigrated to El Paso during the Texas Border Run of 2037, Dr. Hernandez always made it a point to tell us stories about his family's struggle to gain citizenship. To me, it seemed like his own little way of trying to identify with us as Foundationals on a level he thought we would understand. Oftentimes, Dr. Hernandez would instead come off as disingenuous, demonstrating a profound lack of knowledge and respect for black people's unique struggle.

Dr. Javier Hernandez was the lead physician for the Joint Special Operations Unit. He was a good Doctor and went out of his way to make us feel comfortable and accepted in a unit that hardly wanted to deal with us as Foundationals.

"Here you go," he stated, as he happily handed me my box of contacts.

"I also have a blood agent I'll need to administer to you. The agent will help the SEAL team distinguish you from the enemy."

"Fuck no," Donovan barked from behind Dr. Hernandez.

A rattled Dr. Hernandez turned around and looked up at Donovan as he towered over him. After handing Donovan his box, Dr. Hernandez waved his hand in the air in frustration. I could tell his mind was searching for the right words to try and calm Donovan.

"Donovan, it's a requirement that all JSO operators take this injection before going into combat," he insisted.

Donovan's piercing eyes seemed to make Dr. Hernandez melt as he stared him up and down. I knew what was about to come next and I felt sorry for him. "You're not about to inject any of my folks with that bullshit cooked up in some white lab," he pounded.

"You can take your needles and whatever's in them and go to hell. This is your last warning, doctor...get the hell away from my team or you gonna need medical help yourself."

Severely shaken by Donovan's aggression, Dr. Hernandez nervously nodded his head and quickly jolted away from us. As he left, I looked at Donovan and watched as a lighthearted snicker flashed across his face. I laughed to myself and climbed up the accommodation ladder into the rover's crew compartment. Once onboard, I found Pernell already buckled into his seat, quietly looking out of the window in his own world. I took my seat beside him, and my noisy presence didn't seem to register as he continued to gaze out into the nothingness.

"Come on now, please get seated. We must leave," the pilot stated impatiently, looking at his wristwatch.

Our pilot was a Chinese American named Travis Wu. His family was from the Bay Area, not too far from our colony. Wu joined the Navy and earned an officer's commission after graduating from Berkeley. We worked a lot with Wu on many training missions, so we were used to his high-strung style of communicating. Once we were all buckled in, Wu taxied our rover out of the dim hangar and into the darkness of the night. The Miami sky was clear and the full moon hanging over the city was beautiful. The glowing moon seemed to make the dark black tarmac below us sparkle like a diamond as our wheels rolled over it.

Wu brought our rover to a stop at a fairway. We watched the other two rovers each accelerate down the runaway and take flight. In my earpiece, I could hear the air traffic controllers and pilots having a conversation. After a few final mechanical checks, Wu pushed down on the accelerator and the rover sped down the tarmac before lifting its nose towards the heavens. Wu climbed to altitude and banked the rover east towards the Atlantic Ocean. Within seconds, we had broken through the sound barrier and the lights of Miami were left in the distance behind us.

"Turning to starboard. New course two-four-five," Wu relayed before banking right towards the Dry Tortugas.

I looked over at Pernell and our eyes finally met. I could sense his spirit relent as he bit down on his lower lip while reaching over and giving my hand a light squeeze. Despite it all, we cared about each other and this was a moment that neither of us wanted to spoil with our petty differences. The other two rovers went into a steep dive towards lower altitude. When it was our turn, Wu followed them down and we plummeted towards the dark ocean.

As our rover descended, I went through the various steps of our mission, making sure that they were absolutely committed to memory. The other two rovers would deploy their SEAL teams on the small beach in front of Fort Jefferson's entrance while our rover would deploy us near the shallow water boat dock. Our job was to plant explosives on Bradley Wood's motor yacht, so as to destroy his only means of escape. Therefore, he would be stranded on Dry Tortugas, making him easy prey.

As the rover's altitude dropped, I was able to see the Rebecca Shoals yellow navigational light blinking below us. We were minutes away from H-hour now and I could feel the adrenaline pulsing within me. Overanxious, I watched as Donovan loaded a live round into his rifle before looking over at Pernell and I, giving us the non-verbal order to do the same.

'Stay ready and you won't have to land and get ready," he instructed.

"Thirty seconds," a panicked Wu yelled into his microphone.

We all unbuckled from our seats and shuffled over to the deployment area. After we hooked into our safety repelling line, Donovan hit the ready button and the green light flashed over the deployment door. Wu brought the rover to a stop and we silently hovered about 80 feet above the small sandy beach.

'Let's go, Wu! Get us the hell outta here," Donovan screamed over the radio.

Obediently, Wu pushed the button and the rover's door fell. Donovan stepped out first and hit the beach. I swallowed my fear and said a short prayer before following him to the ground. As I fell towards the beach, it felt like I was falling into a dark bottomless pit. The weight of earth's gravity pulling me down, made that internal spirit of fear grab my thoughts. What if I fell in the water? What if I flipped over and landed on my head?

Suddenly, the repelling line tightened around my mid-section and my descent rapidly slowed. To my blessed relief, my boots landed softly on the sandy beach. On instinct, I unhooked from the line and ran from the hovering rover, positioning myself next to a kneeling Donovan. At that moment, I could almost hear my heart pounding away within my chest. Seconds later, I heard Pernell's feet touch earth behind us. After confirming we had all landed safely, Wu maneuvered the rover away from the dark fort. Out of the corner of my eye, I saw Jeremy Woodson and his SEAL team gathered near the large wooden door that was Fort Jefferson's entrance.

The old fort was pitch dark and looked ghostly. During the Civil

War, this fort was once a Union prison. The black outline of its walls contrasted with the moon lite night sky and the sight of it gave me an ominous feeling. Everything on this small island felt eerie. Not even one light could be seen from within the fort, giving the appearance that no one was home. My mind was briefly flooded with self-doubt. What if Bradley Wood wasn't here? What if I was wrong and he caught wind of our operation and had already left? What if I was the reason he had caught wind of the mission? It only would take one person at the Kingfish to be a White Supremacist sympathizer. In that instant, I heard the sound of the SEAL team leader's loud whisper blast through my earpiece.

"All clear. Yellow team. You're a go." He instructed.

Donovan slapped our shoulders before sprinting towards the wooden boat dock near the beach. Pernell and I obediently followed, struggling to keep up with Donovan as the uneven sand shifted beneath our boots. When we reached the dock, I climbed into the yacht tied up at the pier. It was my assignment to salvage anything inside that could be of use for intelligence purposes. While I collected Intel, Donovan and Pernell slipped into the shallow water and placed their explosive satchels underneath the boat's outer hull. Within three minutes, I had confiscated the vessel's GPS monitors, charts, satellite communications equipment, and several small hard drives. Satisfied with my bounty, I hopped back to the pier and helped Donovan and Pernell climb out of the warm water.

"The boat dock is clear. We are making our way to the front entrance," Donovan murmured into his microphone.

We sprinted to the SEAL team positioned near the front entrance and concealed ourselves behind a large concrete walkway that was raised above the beach. In the darkness, I could see Jeremy's probing eyes looking at me as I lay in the sand next to him. He was wearing a pleased smirk on his face and he playfully winked before he rose to follow two of his teammates to the fort's entrance. We all anxiously watched as Jeremy and his teammates placed breaching explosives on the outer hinges of the fort's door.

"Something isn't right here," I heard Donovan whisper. "This is way too quiet."

I felt Pernell crawl his way behind me, trying to find the SEAL team leader. When he located him, both men pulled remote detonators from their pockets and activated them. Jeremy and his teammates ran back to our concealed position and took cover in anticipation of the volley of explosions. In the intense silence, I could hear the SEAL team leader begin his countdown and braced myself for the coming percussions of two simultaneous blasts.

The countdown ended and I felt two shock waves that made my insides shake. A brief flash of heat warmed the sweaty skin hiding within my thick combat suit, and an ear-piercing rattle accompanied the sudden warmth. I looked up and saw the fort's large wooden door missing as the sight and smell of smoke overwhelmed my senses. Behind me, I saw the burning wreckage of the Yacht giving off a spectacular display of bright fire in the midst of our total darkness. The first part of the mission was a success and had gone off without a hitch. In that moment of victory, I mentally prepared myself for the subsequent objective. Next, we would finally face Bradley Wood head-to-head, and this would be a matter of life or death.

The SEAL team leader jolted up from the beach and ran to the open exit, leading the way for his squad of subordinates. As the SEAL's disappeared into the smokey darkness before us, I felt Donovan aggressively slap me on the shoulder.

"Come on, damnit! Move forward," he screamed.

Donovan and I rose from the sandy beach and ran toward the fort's open entrance. Before we met the hanging cloud of smoke, out of the corner of my eye, I saw Pernell following us with his rifle gripped tightly in his hands. I instinctively flipped the safety of my rifle to the off position and placed my finger inside the trigger guard as I entered the fort. It was then that I heard the unmistakable sounds of gunfire and I knew I had to quickly find cover. Running through the entrance put us directly in the fatal funnel. We would have to force our way past the kill zone.

I entered the fort and felt pieces of exploded door sliding underneath my feet, which almost caused me to slip and fall to the ground. I stumbled my way out of the fatal funnel, finding cover behind a large brick pillar that upheld a balcony walkway. It was then that I noticed the bullets peppering the concrete floor in my area. Attempting to move from behind the security of my brick pillar would be suicidal, so I decided to stay pinned down. I looked back at the entrance and noticed several bodies among the rubble of the wooden door just below the layer of smoke. It was then that I saw Pernell lying motionless among them. The sight of Pernell's dead body grabbed my spirit. This wasn't some training mission; this was real life. We weren't attacking some sleepy old fort ripe for our taking. There were real-life racists here, who were all eager to fight back. We had walked right into their well-planned ambush and Pernell Jones had paid the ultimate price for my miscalculation.

I knew I couldn't stay behind this pillar forever. I needed to find a way to advance and bring the fight to these White Supremacists. Searching for a solution, I looked across the fort and I saw Donovan firing his rifle as he and Jeremy slowly advanced towards the concealed machine gun nest, pinning us down. Their covering fire caused the rain of bullets exploding around me to cease briefly. I bolted from behind the brick pillar and ran to a concrete wall in the middle of the fort, ducking behind it once I arrived. The machine-gun fire once again erupted. I looked over and saw

Jeremy and Donovan cowering behind a small brick building opposite of me. Now they were being raked with machine-gun fire and were totally pinned down. My training told me it was now my turn to advance on the machine gun nest, returning the favor to Donovan and Jeremy.

I took a deep breath and put my finger on the trigger before springing from behind the safety of the well and running towards the nest. Aiming, I cited my rifle while in a dead sprint, concentrating on the dark silhouette firing from behind the machine gun. It seemed like the world shrunk as I aimed in on my target. Everything was blurred except for my rifle sight. When my finger touched the trigger, the noise around me melted away, disappearing into nothingness. Slowly, I applied pressure to the trigger and the report of my rifle surprised me with its first discharge. I again aimed at the moving silhouette and shot twice more. The machine gun suddenly stopped firing and I watched the silhouette slowly crumble to the ground. I continued running towards the machine gun and kicked it off its mount atop several layers of sandbags.

"All clear," I shouted into my microphone.

Looking down over the pile of sandbags, I saw the mortally wounded young man lying in a pool of his own blood. The strange blue-colored blood seemed like a glowing ooze under the moon in the night sky. I was stunned and shaken by the sight of this young black child. He looked to be barely in his teenage years and his low-cut hair with its impeccably manicured lineup and naked chin confirmed his tender age. His body was riddled with bullets and my final few rounds appeared to have been the shots that were his undoing. The sight of it all stopped me dead in my tracks and I stared down at him, searing the image of what I had done into my spirit forever.

From out of nowhere, the SEAL team leader appeared out of the shadows. I watched him limp towards me as his bloody hand pressed against a wound near his kidney while his other hand wielded a pistol.

"We gotta get the fuck outta here. There are more of them on the second floor. We're sitting ducks down here," he shouted after grabbing me and pulling me away from the nest in a mad panic.

Just as I was about to object, I noticed the rounds ricocheting around us and heard the loud pops pouring down from above. We both ran along the wall of the fort, stopping briefly to find cover behind thin pillars as bullets from the second-floor balcony chased our every step. Within thirty feet of the exit, we found cover behind a long wall and the SEAL team leader grabbed his radio.

"Hot evac, I say again. Hot evac," he shouted into his microphone. "Broken dancer. Broken dancer."

"Roger Broken Dancer," Travis Wu replied. "We are two minutes out—rally on the beach. Yellow Rover will land. Blue and Red Rover will provide covering fire."

Their conversation sent waves of shame cascading through my spirit. The term Broken Dancer was the code for an ambushed or pinned down special operations unit. Per U.S. Navy protocol, after any Broken Dancer radio transmission, the navy would immediately send every nearby military asset to come to our aid. Now, there was no earthly way for us to hide our failure from the world. Everyone on the planet would know that the Foundationals had faced White Supremacists in armed combat and had been soundly defeated.

"Get the hell outta here. I'll cover you," the SEAL team leader yelled while pointing at the exit.

He leaned out from behind the pillar and shot a volley of rounds up into the balcony. I moved past him and ran towards the exit, leaping over the bodies of several of his SEAL team members along the way. Just as I was about to exit, I saw Donovan approaching the exit from the other side of the fort. He was carrying a wounded Jeremy who was sporting a white battle dressing around his thigh on his back. As Donovan ran towards the exit, Jeremy was shooting his service pistol into the balcony while cussing loudly in anger.

"Mercury Auroa. Mercury Auroa," Donovan screamed over the radio. "Tally one for Jeremy Woodson!'

His words boosted my spirit and I felt the warmth of ultimate victory console me as I stood by the open fort entrance. The coded term Mercury Auroa meant that the notorious White Supremacist terrorist Bradley Wood had been identified and killed. It also meant that physical evidence of his demise was in our possession. In that instant, I felt a surge of renewed confidence, and I didn't give a damn if I was vulnerable and out in the open. Instead of leaving the fort and finding cover to hide behind, I pointed my rifle skyward and wildly sprayed the second-story balcony as Donovan and Jeremy approached the exit. I could see dozens of silhouettes above me ducking for cover as my bullets raked them.

Donovan ran past me, exiting the fort, while an excited Jeremy yelled in jubilance, proclaiming his victory for the hearing world to consume. As they left, I heard the horrifying click of my rifle's empty magazine. Immediately, I dropped my rifle and I quickly transitioned to my service pistol. As I squeezed off two shots, I felt the SEAL team leader shove me towards the exit before dropping to his knee and firing his own bursts into the balcony.

"The rovers will be here in thirty seconds. Get the fuck outta here and don't wait," he instructed.

I turned and ran out of the fort. As I made it outside, I saw Donovan kneeling and looking down at Jeremy who was lying in the sand. Donovan was using both of his hands to push down on Jeremy's chest while screaming loudly for him to stay awake. I made it to the beach and kneeled next to Donovan. Jeremy was bleeding from a small exit wound near his heart. The body armor around his chest had been punctured in several areas like swiss cheese. From the glassy look in his eyes and the clammy feel of his skin, I knew Jeremy was about to lose consciousness.

"Come on, Jeremy. Stay with me," I yelled in panic.

Jeremy's looked up faintly, searching for the sound of my voice. I could almost feel him mustering his strength to speak, fighting valiantly to reply. Instead, I was forced to watch his eyes fade away and feel his spirit relent as he departed from us. In frustration, Donovan cursed loudly and drove the palms of his hands into Jeremy's chest harder.

"Wake ya Zebra ass up, man," he shouted angrily. "One of us has to make it damnit!"

Looking up, I could see the three small lights descending from the heavens and I knew they were the rovers. Resigned with Jeremy's death, Donovan pulled an evidence bag from his pocket and handed it to me. In it were a severed hand, a wallet, and a lock of bloody blonde hair. As I tied the evidence bag to my wrist, I noticed how fatigued Donovan looked and saw blood running from his stomach.

"You take this, Nuria," he ordered. "I ain't gonna make it either."

Scared and shocked, I grabbed a battle dressing from my first aid pack and leaned towards Donovan. As I attempted to stop his bleeding, I heard three loud pops from within the fort walls followed by loud explosions occurring above. I was immediately blinded by a series of bright flashes coming from the sky. Looking up, I saw all three rovers burning in balls of flames. The sight of the burning rovers falling helplessly into the ocean forced me to accept my impending mortality. At that moment, I knew I was about to die on this island.

Looking back at the entrance, I saw the SEAL team leader limping towards us, grimacing with every step. Several shots from within the fort rang out and I watched the SEAL team leader's body fall to the earth. He went motionless and I knew he had been fatally hit. For several seconds, the loud gunfire stopped and a weird sense of silence fell over the island. Trying to remain calm, I refocused myself on Donovan and taped the battle dressing over his bloody wound.

Suddenly, I experienced a painful crack near my left elbow and felt my body fall to the ground. As I lay on the warm coarse sand, I tasted my own blood and could hear my heart pounding away within me. I felt the many bullet holes that riddled my body armor as I searched for the wound with my right hand. Donovan picked up my handgun and crawled on top of my chest. He fired several rounds towards the fort while screaming for close air support into his radio. The powerful recoil of my gun and Donovan's weight on top of my chest made it difficult for me to breathe. I knew I would lose consciousness if I didn't force myself to inhale some air.

As Donovan continued to shoot, I saw the cloudy images of two white men approaching in our direction from the fort. Donovan fired at the men, struggling mightily to strive off exhaustion and keep himself in the fight. As Donovan fired wildly, he missed the men as they calmly continued to walk towards us with weapons in hand. Out of bullets, I felt Donovan anxiously reach into my ammo pack, searching for another magazine. My spare magazines were in my hip pocket and I fought to cook up the energy to deliver Donovan the bullets he needed. I tried to move my left arm and reach down into my pocket, but the more I tried, the closer the white men came. In the panic of it all, everything went black. I felt my heart pounding uncontrollably and I was now unable to move.

"Fuck all you white bastards," Donovan murmured in eternal defiance.

We both shook as a violent hail of bullets rained down on us. Donovan's once tense body went limp on top of me. I felt my human spirit begin to fade. Mustering up a burst of will power, I made one last attempt to breathe but instead experienced the incredible pain of human failure. My physical body was exhausted and weak. The wounds were too much for me to overcome. I was done fighting the cold blackness that was now consuming me. In my ultimate moment of self-realization, I just let it all go and humbly petitioned the Lord to take me.

CHAPTER ONE

ICE COLD

THE WHITE NOISE BLASTING OUT OF the hospital's air conditioning system was loud and annoying as hell. The constant hiss coming from the ceiling vents above could only deliver soul-crushingly cold air and not the inner comfort I truly desired. In my rush to make this appointment, I had forgotten to grab my light jacket. Amid my chilly frustration, I suddenly remembered exactly where I had left the darn thing. The damn jacket was at home, on my wooden stool, right in front of the coffee machine. As the freezing air harassed my brown skin, scores of goosebumps began to populate my lonely forearm. I couldn't help but feel angry. I knew that this bitch was going to sit her ass behind that desk and pepper me with stupid questions for every damn minute of our hour-long session. I had known this, yet somehow, I had still come here woefully unprepared for today's battle.

Attempting to distract myself, I readjusted my hair while turning to look out of the large window beside the cheap couch. The beaming yellow sun that hung among the puffy white clouds never looked more comforting. It was a warm Oakland afternoon without any hint of rain or bone-chilling wind. On beautiful days like this, my dad would pick me up early from school. Before we made it home, he would sneak by the corner store and buy us both a few scoops of ice cream before mama served us dinner. The forbidden ritual was our quiet little secret that we both made sure to keep from my strict mother. As the warm childhood memories distracted me, I was brought back to my cold reality when Dr. Wiseman grabbed her pen and jotted down a few words on her long notepad.

"Why are you so quiet, Nuria?" Dr. Wiseman stoically asked.

A part of me wanted to relent and admit the truth to her. God knows that I wasn't exactly on my pee's and que's today. I was certain that Dr. Wiseman had caught on to my outward act of bravado. Keeping up the front for this long had begun to exhaust me, but who the hell could I truly trust? During prior sessions, Dr. Wiseman made it a point to tell me that I needed to work on my communication skills. So, feeling the need to vent, I decided it was time for her to personally witness my ability to communicate effectively.

"I'm not saying much today because it's so freakin cold in here," I started. "I mean...I can't even think right now; it's so cold. How the hell do you survive in this place?"

Dr. Wiseman jotted down a few more words on her notepad before looking at me with that same old familiar stare. Behind the thick glasses she wore, her eyes probed my every mannerism and movement. This over-educated moron enjoyed studying me, like I was some weird science experiment about to go fatally wrong.

"This is a hospital," she calmly began.

"Per Foundational health standards, we are required to maintain the building's sterile condition. Hence, we can't exceed certain temperature levels for the safety of our patients."

"Nuria, when you arrived today, I noticed you weren't wearing your jacket. You usually bring your light jacket with you to all of our sessions."

"Why no jacket? Did something happen this morning?"

"I just forgot it, I guess," I quickly answered. "I left it at home on a stool."

That strangely familiar expression continued to dominate Dr. Wiseman's face as she carefully considered my excuse. She began to stare me down with her undecipherable brown eyes. It was almost impossible for me to predict what angle this woman would try to subdue me from next. Yet, I instinctively knew she was about to engage me in another round of mental and emotional combat.

"Did you really forget your jacket Nuria, or you just didn't want your husband to help you put it on this morning?" she boldly asked.

Dr. Wiseman had gone for the jugular. As the blunt intentions of her bold question bounced around in my spirit, I tried my damnedest to put on my best poker face. "If I told you I forgot it, Dr. Wiseman, what earthly reason would you have to assume I might be purposely lying to you," I shot back.

"Well, Nuria", she began. "Maybe it's not me you're lying too right now. Maybe you might actually be lying to yourself about something you don't want to recognize or confront."

"Or maybe you should shut the hell up and just believe me when I'm trying to be honest with you, Doctor," I forcefully interrupted.

"You asked for honesty... You asked for openness... You want me to communicate better."

"Well, I'm communicating with you and you're sitting there behind your desk calling me a liar to my face. That's not playing nice, Dr. Wiseman."

A slight flinch washed across Dr. Wiseman's face. Realizing that she had struck a nerve, she sympathetically nodded, took her pen, and stared down at her notepad before writing out several thought-filled sentences. I was so over this woman's bullshit tactics. Looking at my watch, I noticed that my hour-long session had mercifully reached its time limit. Excited to get my cold ass out of this freezer and finally feel the warmth of the California sun, I grabbed my purse and quickly rose to my feet.

"Alright, Dr. Wiseman, our session is over... and I need to leave."

"My husband asked me to pick up our daughter from school, so I actually have a real life I need to attend to...if you don't mind."

Sensing my sarcasm, Dr. Wiseman flashed a shrewd smile as she embedded her biosignature into my prescription card. "Here's your card for your medication. Be sure to stop at the pharmacy dispenser and refill your prescription before you leave."

"See you next week, Agent Sellers," she stated with sting.

I snatched the prescription card out of her hand with purposeful rudeness before hastily exiting the room. I truly hated these torturous sessions, but attending them was the only way I could keep my job. According to Foundational Law, the severity of my physical and mental disabilities was supposed to prohibit me from employment in our government. I was designated as a one armed crippled, so a lot of strings had been pulled to keep me employed at the Force Protection Agency. Governor Patrice Williams had personally assured me that I would be able to maintain my employment-ready status if I could handle it emotionally. These mind-numbing mental evaluations were the Foundational leadership's way of ensuring my frequent bouts of PTSD were kept at bay.

I took the long elevator ride down to the hospital's ground floor. As the elevator doors opened, I made my way past the reception area and walked up to the pharmacy machine to fill my prescription. Sliding open the scan guard, I inserted my card and watched as the machines pulsing green light examined Dr. Wiseman's biosignature. After a few seconds, the screen displayed a list of my medications. Below the list, I was forced to read a name that harkened my thoughts back to better times. As the name sunk into my spirit, my eyes began to water, and I felt my bottom lip quiver as the memories flooded my soul.

"Pernell Jones Medical Center," I mumbled to myself.

Below his name was a gripping narrative on how Pernell was killed in action at Fort Jefferson during the Dry Tortugas assault. Every detail about their narrative sounded courageous and heroic. Anyone reading that screen would be filled with pride and fully support the hospital being named after him. As I wiped a tear from my eye, I felt myself reliving the bitter truth of Pernell's demise. Unlike the screen's false narrative, Pernell Jones hadn't been killed in some furious shoot-out with the racist archfiend Bradley Wood. In fact, Pernell didn't even have the chance to fire his own rifle in anger.

He was killed doing what he had always done. Pernell was doing what defined him as a black man. Without prompting or even needing to be asked, Pernell was right there to back us up. He ran into a cloud of smoke and hail of gunfire simply because he was concerned about me and Donovan. That was the real Pernell I knew. He didn't need to be shot by Bradley Wood to become anybody's hero because he had spent every day of his short life being one.

Standing there in my internal emotions, I felt a hand lightly tap my lonely shoulder. The feel of another person's unexpected touch snapped me out of my intimate thoughts. I turned around only to see one of the hospital's young receptionists. Her youthful smile was pretty and filled with solemn reverence as she humbly requested my attention.

"Agent Sellers," she whispered. "Your partner Ed is out front waiting on you, Ma'am."

Pushing away my thoughts, I discretely cleaned away a tear before snatching my bag of pills from the machine dispensary. With a curious grin, the receptionist led me to the large sliding glass doors and typed in the access code to remotely open the entranceway. After a few electronic chimes and a flashing strobe light, the doors slowly began to part, and the pressurized cold air of the hospital rushed out ahead of me.

"Agent Sellers, thank you so much for all you've sacrificed for us," the receptionist stated. "Everyone here admires you and as a black woman, you have been my role model."

I looked at the receptionist and noticed the overflowing admiration that filled her brown eyes. In the fallout of the Fort Jefferson assault, I had become some sort of celebrity. The Foundational Media had turned me into a conquering hero, the strong black woman who was the lone survivor of the blood bath on the Dry Tortugas. A loyal Foundational who willingly gave up one of her arms to pursue racial justice. Young black girls in every Foundational colony gave me that same adoring look that this receptionist was now flashing. Seeing that look of black girl pride somehow made me feel guilty. If anyone found out the truth, they'd discover that I was nobody's hero.

Moved by the receptionist's quiet respect, I made sure to offer her a phony smile before walking out of the hospital. In my youth, I too was once a naïve black woman. I was an idealist that believed everything this cruel world told me. Now, I knew better. This thing called life was no flowery romance novel. It was more like a gut-punching horror story.

I walked out of the icy hospital and into the warmth of a sunny afternoon. The feel of sunlight against my skin instantly thawed my icy demeanor. Looking up towards the blue sky, I noticed the full parking area floating above me. After a few seconds, I found Ed's car and watched as it descended to the ground and landed. The passenger side door opened and to my surprise, Dennis hopped out wearing a giant-sized smile.

It had been almost ten years since Dennis Winslow and I were in Miami together, preparing for that fatal mission. After that infamous day, a lot had changed for the both of us. Dennis was now a happily married man with a young son. No longer resembling a well-built athlete, he now looked the part of the well-manicured professional with his low-cut fade, flabby belly, and graying beard. Time and maturity had seen fit to mold Dennis into a quiet family man. After Fort Jefferson, Dennis was chosen to be the Director of Technology for all of our West Coast colonies. The job paid well, and it sure as hell kept Dennis at home way more than supporting Force Protection units. From time to time, I would bump into Dennis at the local food market and he always made it a point to tell me how much he enjoyed his new gig. Since we both were no longer deployable members of the FP units, I would play along with him, pretending to agree. Yet, unlike Dennis, a big part of my soul missed all the action and relished every thought of reliving it all once more.

Now here stood Dennis, one of the few veterans of the Dry Tortugas raid that was still above ground. He greeted me with a smile that betrayed the joy in his spirit. Since Dennis had come along with Ed to pick me up, I instantly realized that I must have forgotten something important. While I walked towards the car, my mind churned, trying to figure out what I had missed.

"What up, girl," Dennis said while politely opening the backseat for me.

"Oh, hell no, Dennis," I loudly proclaimed. "You get your big black behind in the backseat. Ed is my partner and I get front-seat privileges, not you."

Dennis laughed and shook his head as he squeezed himself into the cramped back seat. I buckled myself in, then looked over at Ed. He looked tired and worn out. From his facial expression, Ed was obviously annoyed with me. Undoubtedly, while I was stuck in the ice freezer with Dr. Wiseman, Ed had been out running countless errands for Governor Williams. I presumed one of those errands was to pick up Dennis, but I could not quite figure out why.

"What's going on today?" I asked him in a low voice while gesturing towards the back seat.

"You forgot, didn't you, Nuria," he replied. "I knew you forgot about it. Patrice didn't want to believe me when I told her, but I knew that you had forgotten."

Ed Carter shook his head in disgust at my ignorance. He angrily pushed down on the throttle without giving me an answer and I felt the car rise into a hover. Ed was mad as hell, and it wasn't the first time Nuria Phillips Sellers, the Foundational hero, had pissed him off. Almost ten years my junior, Ed was still a very young man. After finishing college, Ed had aspirations of earning a spot on the Oakland colonies deployable FP units, just as I had at his age. Unfortunately for Ed, he had a serious problem passing one of the many FP entry-level aptitude exams. Ed had taken this same exam battery three different times, failing each of them with no signs of improvement. Like me, he was on the outside looking in at the Force Protection Agency, so we both had been assigned to Governor Williams private security detail. The security detail was a way of keeping us in the Force Protection realm, but not actually assigned to one of the deployable Anti-Terror FP units.

When Ed was first assigned to Governor Williams, Patrice had discussed his testing issues with me, hoping that I could somehow help Ed get over the hump. After several years of working with Ed, I found out that his issues had nothing to do with his knowledge. He was smart as fuck and knew more about FP than I did. The real issue with Ed was his confidence. For some reason, he would trap himself inside useless details, failing to deliver answers he knew were correct. At the mere sight of a multiple-choice question, Ed would lose his nerve and allow his lack of self-confidence to detour him from what he knew was right. His absolute obsession with chasing after women was another problem. Part of me was convinced that Ed's self-confidence issues stemmed from his consistent desire for approval from the opposite sex.

"OK Ed, you got me. I admit, I forgot... Now tell me what is going on today please?" I ordered.

"Governor Williams is scheduled to go to San Francisco and give a speech," he sarcastically began.

"You know.... That speaking event with Senator Bean from Florida. I can't believe you forgot about this shit, especially since you and Dennis are supposed to be involved in the festivities."

"Yeah, Nuria," Dennis chimed in.

"You and I are on photo-op detail, my friend. Hell, I even trimmed my beard and cut my nose hairs for the cameras. Today our orders are to look dignified, smile gracefully at the happy white liberals, and humbly tell everyone how friendly we Foundationals are."

Dennis's playful jabs jogged my memory and I felt the sting of self-frustration burn my already tender spirit. This evening, we both would attend a mindless political function with Patrice Williams. The mayor of San Francisco had invited Governor Williams and Florida Senator Judith Bean to speak at a rally celebrating the fifth anniversary of the Farmers Treaty. The highly touted treaty between Foundational Farmers and merchants from the Dominant Society was one of the first of its kind in the country. Many in the Dominant Society and the Foundational community viewed the treaty as a giant step towards mutual trust and economic integration.

Senator Judith Bean had been the Navy Admiral in charge of the

Special Operations Command during our assault on Fort Jefferson. She gained national recognition and political respect after the assault at Dry Tortugas. This paved the way for Judith Bean to become a household name throughout the country. Behind the scenes, Senator Bean had also won the trust of Patrice Williams. Her astute handling of my Jeremy Woodson situation and her ability to get the Kingfish not to publish any defamatory articles, won her favor among Foundational leadership circles. The huge voter turnout she received from Foundationals in Florida, gave her the decisive edge in her tight Senate race. Politically, Judith Bean the quintessential white politician, was married to Foundational voters and she knew it.

After the Fort Jefferson assault, my boss, Patrice Williams, had also earned national acclaim. Graduating with honors from Yale, Patrice demanded respect from the elites within the Dominant Society. Her college connections allowed her to seamlessly float among white circles and take advantage of their personal networks. Patrice's hardnosed approach to politics and her reverence for Donovan Reid and Pernell Jones garnered her the respect of every Black Foundational. Assigning me to be alongside her as some makeshift security guard made me feel like a human mascot at times. Yet, I knew people seeing me with her was important political imagery for Patrice. My presence as the one-armed war hero went a long way to bolster her political clout within the Foundational community. Patrice had easily won the election for Colonial Governor of Oakland and was a shoo-in to become the next chairperson on the Colonial Leadership Council. To everyone with half a brain, it was clear that Patrice Williams was the standard-bearer for Foundational Black American politics.

"Damnit," I cussed. "How the hell did I forget all about this?"

"Yeah, I've been asking that same damn question all morning," Ed jabbed. "There is a pre-departure briefing at the capitol in about thirty minutes. We've been out here waiting for you for over an hour, so we are really pressed for time."

Ed turned the car towards the large gray dome that sat atop our colony's capital building. After adjusting his throttle, he propelled us forward. My heart sank as I looked at the timer on his radio, noticing that Lindsey would soon be out of school.

"Ed, before we go to the capitol, I need to go run an errand," I demanded. "Quinton is working at the church today and I promised him that I would pick up Lindsey after school."

"Oh, hell no," Ed vented. "You're putting us in a bind. Can't you just call Quinton and have him go pick up Lindsey?"

"No!" I reflexively shouted, startling Ed.

"Geez," he responded. "You two negroes are a clown show. Is married life really that bad, Nuria?"

"It's a hell of a lot better than running around with those brainless sluts you chase after," I shot back. "Anyway, why can't I meet any of them Ed? Why are you always hiding them from me like funky laundry? Are the women that embarrassing to you?"

"I guarantee that you won't be meeting any of them because I already know you would say things like brainless sluts, Nuria." Ed snapped. "And no, they aren't embarrassing...you on the other hand...might be."

"My wife is at the school waiting to pick up my son," Dennis purposefully broke in. "I can call and have her pick up Lindsey for you if you need it."

"No, Dennis. Today is my day to pick up Lindsey, so that's what's gonna happen."

Frustrated, Ed pulled back on the throttle and put the car into a hover before turning it towards the elementary school. The tension-filled car grew quiet as the large campus seemed to increase in size on the horizon. We sped to the waiting area and Ed put us into a hover. The line of other parents waiting was almost a mile long. I heard Ed let out a loud sigh of exasperation as the line seemed to inch forward at a snail's pace.

"Just drive up near the entrance and let me out," I ordered. "Put on your blue lights and hover near the sidewalk while I go inside to get Lindsey. That's how we'll beat out this traffic."

He drove up near the entrance and lowered down to the ground. I quickly jumped out of the car and rushed into the building. In the lobby, I saw Lindsey's home room teacher wearing a hall monitor badge. He greeted me with a smile that was riddled with surprise. It had been months since we last saw each other. I've been ducking the man after backing out of a Foundational history event, which I had promised to participate in. Feeling cornered and in a hurry, there was no other choice but for me to walk up to him and hold a conversation.

"Hello, Mr. Stewart," I stated with my friendliest smile.

"Mrs. Sellers, it's so good to see you. It's been a minute. How have you been?" he asked with a shocked expression.

"Oh, I'm fine. I really want to thank you for all your extra effort in the classroom. Lindsey tells us every day how you are the best teacher here."

He thanked me and shook my hand graciously. From his impatient spirit and serious stare, I could tell he wanted to have a much deeper conversation. It was obvious that he had something else on his mind that he wanted to address. Before he spoke, Lindsey suddenly appeared from out of the hallway, bouncing towards us with excitement.

"Hey, sweetie," I said while wrapping my arm around her.

"Mrs. Sellers," he stubbornly continued. "I'd like to have a meeting with you about Lindsey's upcoming reading assessment this semester. We'll be hosting a Parent-Teacher Conference in two weeks and I'd really like to have the opportunity to sit down with you."

"Sure. I'll be there," I relented.

"Good. I'll pencil you in to attend," he stated with relief in his spirit.

Taking advantage of the pregnant pause between us, I took Lindsey by her hand and we hurried out of the building. We walked down the block until I found Ed's car. He lowered to earth and quickly landed before Dennis popped open the back door.

"What's up, little Lindsey! How are you today, young lady," Dennis asked in a sweet fatherly voice that made me chuckle to myself.

"Hi, Mister Dennis," Lindsey said with a shy smile. "I'm doing OK."

Ed reached back and playfully tickled Lindsey's arm before pushing down on the throttle and racing towards my house. We arrived at my home and found the landing pad occupied. Quinton hadn't moved his car inside the garage, which told me that he hadn't finished his business for the rest of the day.

"You told me Quinton was at the church," Ed proclaimed. "Why is he at home, Nuria?"

Ignoring Ed's question, I collected Lindsey and her school bag out of the backseat. Lindsey gave both men a childish wave that perfectly matched her adorable smile before we both walked into the house. I closed the front door behind us and followed an excited Lindsey, who rushed into the living room and jumped into her father's lap.

"Hey there, you beautiful little angel," Quinton shouted as he embraced her with a bear hug.

I walked past both of them and went into the kitchen, picking up my light jacket off the stool and tossing it over my shoulder in aggravation. Reaching into my purse, I took my useless bag of prescriptions and tossed the bottles on the kitchen counter. As the bag landed, I noticed Quinton had left his magazine tablet on the counter. His touch screen was unlocked, so I walked over to take a closer look. There was a photo on his screen display showing a government building on fire in El Salvador. The faces of young black teenagers celebrating in front of a hot blaze captured my attention and made my heart stop. Especially when I noticed that one of the black boys in the photo looked eerily like the young man I had killed at Fort Jefferson. The magazine's ominous headline read, "Violent Black Supremacists In El Salvador Kill Dozens During Riot."

"The White Media is reporting that these kids are violent," Quinton explained as he approached from behind.

"Word on the street is that Governor Williams and the rest of our Colonial Leadership Council are gonna allow a few Foundational Blacks to join a U.N. peace-keeping mission down there."

"Why wouldn't they, Quinton," I dismissively shot back. "If they are smart, they'd allow hundreds of us to go down there to monitor the White Hispanics."

"If you really wanna support Black Empowerment, you need to stand behind Patrice's political agenda, Quinton. Violence does not work. It can never work."

Tickled by my words, Quinton came up to me and gave me a soft kiss on the cheek before reaching down towards the table and picking up his heavily stained coffee mug. After all these years, I was amazed that Quinton still had that familiar coolness within him. His face always seemed to be filled with a calming presence that was both attractive yet infuriating. It had been ten years since Quinton last stepped into a boxing ring. He now dedicated all his energy towards being a boring family man and faithful church deacon. Now his body wore a thin layer of fat that covered his once chiseled frame. Quinton's face was noticeably puffy and he proudly sported a long black beard with more than a few grey hairs hanging from it.

"Nuria, I reserved a table for us at Lotus tonight," he proudly proclaimed. "Paster Mitchell and his wife agreed to watch Lindsey for a few hours while we go out and eat."

"Since your home early, maybe I can call the Pastor and see if he minds us dropping off Lindsey a little earlier, so we can go to the theater before dinner."

"No, Quinton," I responded before pointing at the window. "I totally forgot that we had this thing with Patrice in San Fran tonight. Ed and Dennis are out there waiting on me right now."

In silence, Quinton walked over to the window and peered out from behind our thick sun curtains. He gave a courteous wave to Ed's running car that sat on our shiny gray landing pad, then quickly closed the curtain before walking back into the kitchen.

"So, I'm being shunned for the great Governor Patrice Williams once again. Aren't I, Nuria?" He blurted out while pouring a splash of milk into his coffee cup.

"The holy Goddess Patrice Williams and Ed Carter, the insatiably horny bachelor. Both of them are of more interest than washed-up ole Quinton Sellers."

"Quinton, I'm not about to do this with you right now. Not today!" I warned.

"Well, I guess I'll have to get on your calendar then," he replied. "If you are free next week, maybe we can block off some time so we can finally fix this broken marriage."

"Fuck you Quinton!"

"Fuck you, just like you fucked that white coke whore in New York. You remember that!"

"Just like you fucked up your entire damn boxing career and screwed over everybody that was depending on your dumb ignorant ass."

"The only reason we are even married right now, is because of me...so you can take your weak-ass guilt trip and flush it down the toilet like you did your entire life."

The coolness that dominated Quinton's spirit quickly disappeared as he took a rather large sip of his hot coffee. Feeling profoundly satisfied, I resigned myself towards making my exit and continuing on with more important matters. I heard Quinton slam his empty coffee cup on the kitchen counter as I walked through the living room.

"I'm so sick of this bullshit, Nuria," he yelled. "You'll never live that shit down, will you?"

"That's why I called Dr. Wiseman after you left this morning. We can't even have a simple discussion about who's picking up Lindsey from school without you exploding."

"Your night terrors are getting worse, and you refuse to take your medicine. You fall asleep and you have these wild nightmares. I can hear you all the way downstairs calling out to Donovan and Pernell."

"Last week, you were sweating and shivering in your sleep every damn night. Hell, I've had to wash our bedsheets three days in a row now."

"I'm concerned about you, and you ain't even trying to help me fix this."

His words stopped me dead in my tracks. This man had the nerve to bitch at me about picking up our daughter, then went behind my back to talk to my doctor about it. Turning around, I saw Quinton holding my prescription bag and shaking it in his big ashy hand. Pissed, I charged at him, venting my anger with each closing step.

"Don't ever call my doctor again. Understand?"

"If you were really concerned about me or this marriage, you wouldn't have involved anyone else in our damn business," I shouted. "Everything has always been all about you, Quinton. Every damn thing!"

"From the long hours of fight training and traveling to all those boxing competitions. Plus, all the late nights I had to come over to your parents' house to help them look after you when you got your ass beat."

"It was always about you. I put your boxing career ahead of everything else. I also put you and your dreams ahead of mine. Hell, I catered to your every need before I even tended to my own."

"But you threw those sacrifices away. All for one drunken night in a New York City strip club with some nasty ass white whore."

"You go ask Dr. Wiseman about that shit, then have her write your dusty ass a prescription for it!"

As I neared the front door, I saw little Lindsey sitting on the floor. She held on to her favorite teddy bear as a river of tears streamed down her face. The sight of her sitting there looking confused quelled my raging spirit and instantly filled me with regret. I walked over and kneeled down next to her. In the back of my mind, I wished that I could somehow pick her up with two arms and apologize for the words she must have heard. Instead, I reached down with my one arm and wiped the tears from her shining brown cheeks. It was all I could do for her. That would have to be my meager attempt to pass along the inner strength that had sustained me in this brutal world.

"You've forgotten about what we used to have," Quinton shouted from the kitchen. "We both took care of each other. Everything we did was always about us, but now, I've become the selfish one."

Ignoring Quinton, I stood up and walked out of the house. I was done arguing about the past in front of Lindsey. She didn't need to hear the rest of our truth, at least not yet anyway. From his car, Ed gave me a death stare while I locked up the house. As I opened the passenger side door, I could feel the thickness of our uncomfortable silence. Not wanting to worsen my discomfort, I buckled in my safety restraint and didn't utter a word to break the tension. The odd quietness of the two men told me that I had been the topic of their private conversation. Quinton angrily glaring at them from behind the living room curtain had surely caught their attention. I was certain that both men had burning questions they wanted to ask, but the sanctity of my marriage prevented them from meddlesome intrusion.

"We got about five minutes," Ed stated. "To the Capitol building we go."

We rose skyward and turned towards the large gray dome on the horizon. Suddenly, a soul-scratching visual appeared directly below us, pushing my thoughts back to little Lindsey. Not far from my house, I saw children playing at the newly built jungle gym park. I couldn't help but feel a sort of emptiness as I watched the children run and scream with glee. Their mothers looked relaxed and confident as they sat on a long row of wooden benches, obviously engaged in a lively conversation. The women looked proud and secure in the communal moment. Their daily experience was something foreign to me. Yet, for them, it was just another Thursday evening with the kids.

Ed increased his speed and we glided over the picturesque cul-de-sacs of our colony. After passing over the many shopping centers and churches, we made it to the colonial industrial zone. The industrial zone was a well-organized cluster of large factories and luscious farmland that fueled our local economy. Fully laden transportation trucks flew under us as they made their way towards California's Intercoastal airway. As we neared the Capitol Zone, I could also see our colonial airport with its long grey runaways and statuesque orbiter launching pads.

Ed turned us away from the airport's secure airspace and we decreased speed to approach the Capitol building. In haste, Ed pulled back on his throttle, and I felt the car sink like a rock before he used one huge burst from his engines to soften our landing.

"We're already three minutes late, so we need to move as fast as we can," Ed noted as he popped open the doors.

We all scrambled out of the car and rushed towards the double doors, pulling our entrance cards out of our pockets along the way. After piling into the Capitol elevator and launching ourselves up to the 11th floor, we jogged down the wide marble hallway towards the Governor's secure conference room. Ed jetted in front of us and reached out towards the room's large oak doors. As he grabbed the gold-plated door handle, I saw the small beads of sweat covering his shiny forehead. Ed had worried himself into a frenzy about being tardy and was now acting selfishly. His special effort was not to be the last among us to come strolling into our meeting with Governor Williams. Ed wanted to ensure that if there were to be any sort of embarrassment, it would be left for either Dennis or myself.

"And...they're here. Well, I feel much better now," Governor Patrice Williams coolly announced as we all found seats.

Governor Williams looked energized and happy in her comfortable leather chair. Since becoming Governor, she had endured a lot of stress and I had been by Patrice's side to witness it all. From the national energy shortage last summer to an explosive outbreak of raccoon pox several years ago, Governor Williams's first term had been one drowned in unforeseen challenges. Yet today she looked unbothered, sporting a radiant smile and glossy eyes. Governor Williams's lightly graying hair was perfectly styled, presenting the essence of control combined with wisdom. Her brown skin magically appeared to be absent of any wrinkles. Her make-up was perfectly applied, not too much but just enough to highlight her naturally beautiful features.

Seated next to Governor Williams were Colonial Lieutenant Governor Gary Freeman and our Force Protection Secretary, Vincent Towns. Gary Freeman had run several unsuccessful campaigns for colonial office before Governor Williams nominated him to be her second in command. The Freeman family name was a stalwart within the Oakland Foundational community. Gary's great uncle once owned one of the oldest and more popular soul food restaurants in the Bay Area. My partner Ed, happened to be a member of that illustrious family tree, which is likely why I was forced to have to babysit him. Even within this proud colonial community, a small vein of nepotism was always present.

While Gary had an understandable soft spot for his cousin, he had always been dismissive of me. Gary always makes it a point to question my continued presence as a member of the Governor's security team, especially whenever he sees me. Having one arm and being legally termed as disabled, per Colonial Law, I was supposed to be exempt from eligibility to work in the Force Protection field. Gary personally resented the fact that Governor Williams had bypassed that law and kept me in service. I, for one, hated the man. Gary was arrogant, obtuse, and a certified know-it-all. The mere sight of Gary would put me in a bad mood. There was something about his ridiculously big ears and beady brown eyes that just rubbed me the wrong way. Although I abhorred having to work this security detail, keeping Patrice alive and Gary away from the powers of being Governor was enough motivation to keep me on the job.

In the world of politics, access is power and my special relationship with Governor Williams was a threat to the ever-ambitious Gary Freeman. Gary's relationship with Governor Williams was one of abject political necessity, while Patrice and I communicated on a more personal level. At their cores, Gary and Patrice were bitter political rivals. Governor Williams decision to appoint Gary as her second in command was more of a practical choice to silence black hardliners within our colony. The past few years had seen colonial politics become extremely contentious. The hardliner party members pushed aggressively to unseat moderates like Patrice and replace them with more aggressive Foundationals like Gary. Despite their best efforts, Patrice's popularity made it difficult for the hardliners to gain traction among the Foundational electorate. Aware of her growing political vulnerability, Patrice had to appease her hardline opponents, so appointing Gary as her Lieutenant Governor was a proper concession.

The Secretary of Force Protection, Vincent Towns, also had issues with my close relationship with Governor Williams. Originally hailing from the huge colony outside of Philadelphia, Vincent had been assigned to Oakland by high-ranking family members in the Colonial Leadership Council. Having just completed two envoy assignments in Africa, Vincent's tour of duty in Oakland was meant to cut his teeth in the arena of Foundational bureaucratic responsibilities. Only twenty-six years young and more than a bit overweight, Vincent had clearly come from a life of money and extreme privilege. Always wearing the finest designer clothes and sporting the shiniest jewelry, he didn't look the part of a focused leader of an agency that is responsible for hunting down violent White Supremacists. Unlike the dutiful Patrice Williams, Vincent was not valued nor respected within the FP world. Vincent Towns was only punching the clock in his tenure as Oakland's lowly FP Secretary. For him, the long titles and superficial pomp of larger stages of colonial government were his real ambitions.

"Nuria, I hope it was the afternoon traffic that delayed you," Gary hinted with a touch of frustration in his voice.

"No, Gary, it actually wasn't traffic," I immediately shot back.

"I had to go pick up my daughter from school and bring her home. My husband had errands to run, so it was my job to manage my life today."

"How's my little Lindsey doing?" Governor Williams jumped in.

"I really need to swing by to come visit her! It's been a few months since Lindsey's birthday party; please tell her that I have that doll that she asked for."

The smile on Governor Williams face was wide and glowing. Out of the corner of my eye, I could see Gary's ego almost shrink into his squeaky wooden chair. Patrice had sent him a not-so-indirect message. No matter how late I was, Nuria Phillips Sellers was off-limits. The only judgment of formality that mattered in this conference room was that of Patrice Williams. As the Governor and I shared a laugh, I saw Gary bite down on his dry lips, pretending to play along.

"Madam Governor, if I may, the FBI officials from the San Fran field office will be here shortly," Vincent confidently began.

"I'd appreciate it if we'd all review this evening's Force Protection report before they arrive."

"Sure," Governor Williams gladly declared.

Some of the Governor's aides walked to the table and handed us small tablets. I swiped open my tablet and scrolled through the screen until I found the Force Laydown diagram. Governor Williams and Senator Bean would speak to several thousand supporters on Yerba Buena Island. The San Francisco Police Department would handle the outer perimeter of the rally location, while both the California State Police and U.S. Coast Guard handled all waterborne security. A small contingent of Secret Service agents and security personnel from D.C. would provide point security for Senator Bean. Governor Williams point security would consist of Ed and myself, and we would work alongside two FBI agents from the San Francisco office.

As I read the names of the two FBI agents, the mental images of their familiar faces popped up inside my head. They both were a pain in the ass and were sure not to be in the best of moods. Participating in a lowly security detail for an arrogant Foundational politician was not the most desirable assignment for any FBI agent. To their regretful luck, these same two agents seemed to have been drawing these particular security assignments regularly. It had even gotten to the point I couldn't recall the last time I had worked with any other FBI agents besides these two.

After a light chuckle, I scrolled through the screen and found the reports Anti-Black Threat Assessment Summary. Scanning through the summary pages, I noticed the typical Intel-driven warnings and precautions that any prudent Intelligence Officer would present. Low-security threats from liberal environmental protection gangs and right-wing militias. Medium-security threats from White LGBTQPISXYAW lifestyle extremist organizations. Medium-security threats from local White Supremacist Extremist Groups. This entire damn report lacked the imagination and boldness we would need to keep Patrice Williams safe while behind enemy lines. Fully engaging my sense of disappointment, I scrolled down on my screen to the last page of the report and found the Intelligence Officer's name.

"Agent Mary Ann Haskins, Force Protection Intelligence Specialist, Oakland FP Team number 6." I read aloud for all to hear.

Ed cracked a devious smile and tilted his head back in anticipation of the ridicule he knew I was about to unleash. Instantly, I felt Dennis reach over and deliver a light slap to my knee underneath the table. He also knew that I was about to kick a hornet's nest. Ignoring Dennis, I threw the tablet on the well-polished wooden table and leaned back in my chair.

"Damnit Nuria," Vincent vented. "Why can't you let go of this little grudge you have with Mary Ann. She's on the FP teams now...not you. You need to accept that and move on."

"Look," he sighed. "Everyone knows that you were one of the best Intel officers we've ever had, but you ain't on the FP teams anymore, Nuria. Your day has passed."

"I need you to embrace the fact that fighting this war is something you will never do again. You have given us so much. You gave us everything you had within you. Black Foundationals can't ask you to give anymore; just let Mary Ann handle this."

"Nuria, you are a wealth of professional knowledge," Governor Williams began as she picked up my tablet and pushed it back at me.

"This is the point when you need to become the teacher, and not just the sassy critic."

The words from Governor Williams stung. Despite my disposition to disregard Vincent's empty critiques, Governor Williams's assessment hit home. As a black woman, it was my obligation to help Mary Ann get this right. She was a young woman and new to the agency, not too much unlike me when I was at her stage in my career. I first caught wind of Mary Ann Haskins five years earlier when she won the Donovan Reid Force Protection Scholarship. After she graduated from college and began her year-long Force Protection apprenticeship, I met with her several times. Mary Ann impressed me with her vigor and eagerness. She was a black woman that was proud to be a Donovan Reid Scholarship recipient and always told me how much she idolized me as a child. Yet, despite all her promise, Mary Ann had made a habit to constantly disappoint me. It was becoming increasingly hard to ignore her lackluster performance and my gasket was now about to rupture.

"Well, Governor Williams, I can't teach from the Governor's Office. I need to be right there in the classroom with my students. The best way to teach is by example," I shot back.

"No way, Nuria. Like Vincent told you, your days on the FP teams are done, sister."

"You're a Foundational hero. Blacks and Whites across this country admire you a lot. We can't have you out there getting yourself shot to death by drunken rednecks," she explained.

"But I can do security for you, Patrice. Is this how the game works now?" I asked.

"Nuria, you can retire today if you'd like to. I'm not the one keeping you here?" Patrice proclaimed with a tone of seriousness.

"Girl, if you wanna leave, just let me know and I will personally start planning your retirement ceremony tonight."

A hush fell over the room as Governor Williams and I stared each other down. She had called my bluff and we both knew it. Wearing suppressed expressions of victory, both Gary and Vincent leaned back in their chairs, soaking up the satisfaction of the Governor finally putting me in my place. As much as Governor Williams needed me, she also knew that I needed her as well. Patrice was the last link I had to the memories of Donovan and Pernell. Aside from Dennis, she was the only person who could relate to the secret trauma I had to go through on that faithful night. In a sense, we were both crutches for each other's hidden pain.

There was a hard knock on the conference room door. Soon afterward, one of Governor Williams's aides opened the door and ushered in two FBI agents. As the two men walked in, I saw their faces and we all exchanged knowing glances. The first FBI agent to walk in was Riley Simmons, a short white man originally from Salt Lake City, Utah. Riley, a former Marine, joined the FBI after graduating from Berkeley University. I found Riley to be soft-spoken and somewhat delicate in manner. His wimpy demeanor always made me a little bit curious as to how he came to be a criminal investigator, let alone a former Marine.

Next, a tall black man named Clark Bernard followed Riley into the room and hit me with his uncomfortable eyes. He looked shaken and nervous, which was not normal for him. I quickly noticed that a dark patch of unshaven hair hung from his nearly naked chin. Clark was always smooth in appearance and his customary lack of facial hair easily betrayed his well-institutionalized mindset. Clark was a proud Zebra from Connecticut, despite his strong Foundational roots. Sadly, his great-grandparents decided to forgo their reparations package during the Great Recompense and continued to live among the Dominant Society. I could imagine that for Clark Bernard, a black man living among white people, visiting a Reparations colony had to be an emotional experience.

The two men greeted the Governor and sat at the table before presenting us with a quick informal briefing, covering all the events security arrangements. Nothing about the briefing was unusual or out of the ordinary. In the years I had been alongside Governor Williams, I must have seen this same security routine over a hundred times. Constant travel is a major component of being an elected official. Rarely are high-ranking politicians like Patrice Williams afforded the opportunity to sit still for too long. There is always the next election or the new media crisis, or the dreaded campaign fundraiser. All of these occurrences meant that I, as the Governor's head of security, was forced to suffer right alongside Patrice and follow her every step outside of the confines of our secure colony. It would entail spending days, if not weeks, traveling across the country to attend hearings or campaign rallies. Ed An I often joked that working for Governor Williams was, in fact, our real marriage.

'Governor Williams, the FBI can confirm that the rally site at Yerba Buena Island is secure," Riley offered.

'Both you and Senator Bean will be provided with armed escorts to and from the rally."

'If you have any questions or concerns, please let me know and I will do what I can to accommodate your issues."

"Oh, gosh no, Riley," Governor Williams answered. Your plans all sound fine. I'm confident that you have left no stone unturned."

"I just would like to depart the rally a little early so that I could have a private moment with Senator Bean, if it's possible."

"Yes ma'am. We can make that happen Governor," he replied with an assuring smile.

"Great! OK then! If you could, Riley, please give us about thirty minutes and we'll meet you and Clark downstairs."

Riley and Clark rose from their chairs and followed several aides out of the room. As the conference room door shut, Governor Williams slowly stood up and walked over towards the hidden entrance to her private suite. Before she opened her door, Governor Williams looked back and scanned each of us as we sat quietly around the table, curiously watching her.

"I'll be in my suite getting some alone time," she began.

"My aides should have meals arranged for you all downstairs in the galley. I would suggest that each of you put something in your stomach before we leave for San Fran. It's gonna be a long evening."

Governor Williams opened her door and disappeared into her private suite, leaving all of us in the conference room. Believing that I had been left out of something, I looked across the table at Gary and he shrugged his shoulders in bewilderment. Ed and Vincent stood up and made their way towards the exit.

"Well, if they're serving free food, I might as well take my ass downstairs to partake," Ed said with a gleeful smile.

We all took the elevator down to the galley and chatted amongst ourselves while nibbling on our rather large plates of jerk chicken mixed with Caribbean rice. Twenty minutes later, Governor Williams and her aides walked into the galley wearing fine African garments decorated with shiny gold trimming. She informed us that she was ready to leave with a lazy wave of her hand, so we obediently stood up and followed her down to the ground floor.

"Dennis and Nuria, you two come ride with me, please," Governor Williams stated as the stretched limos lowered to the ground outside of the Capitol.

As the aides opened our doors, I noticed Ed, Riley, and Clark climbing into the back of the limo parked in front of ours. Vincent and Gary found a home in the limo behind us. In the sky above, several armed patrol cars from the Colonial Authority Service hovered in position, patiently waiting to escort us to the outer limits of our colony's jurisdiction. Dennis and I climbed into the limo, situating ourselves across from Governor Williams. After several minutes of barely audible radio conversation, our limos finally lifted from the earth and climbed into the clear blue sky. The driver turned the car towards the bay and increased speed, following the armada as we all headed towards the Bay Bridge.

"Nuria and Dennis," Governor Williams began. "I wanna make sure all of this is cool with the both of you before we arrive at the rally."

"I'll be asking both of you to say a few words to the crowd before my presentation this evening. You guys don't have to participate, but having you both supporting me will go a long way in ensuring that our Farmers Treaty with these white folks remains intact."

The energetic glow and coolness that had been on Governor Williams's face in the regal atmosphere of the conference room, immediately disappeared. In the intimacy of the limo's back seat, I could sense the signs of stress and fatigue in Patrice's worried spirit. The strands of gray hair that once looked cosmetic and dignified from a distance, now appeared to dominate her thinning black hair. The layers of brown makeup on her face could no longer conceal the wrinkles hiding beneath them. Her red glossy eyes caused me to worry about her state of sobriety. For some reason, my good friend, Governor Patrice Williams, was exhausted both spiritually and emotionally.

Wanting to help her, Dennis and I both nodded our heads, openly expressing our willingness to contribute to her cause. It was a rarity that Governor Williams ever asked me for any personal favors. Everything about this request told me that Patrice genuinely needed us to support her. Intuitively, I knew that there was much more to this personal request than two old war buddies publicly displaying our support for the Farmers Treaty. Something was troubling Governor Williams, and whatever it was, she needed all hands on deck to address it. Governor Williams leaned down towards the door panel and pushed an orange button. On cue, the limo's small icebox arose from the floor beneath us. Reaching into the icebox, she pulled out three wine glasses and a large bottle of wine. Reading its label, I noticed that it was a bottle of Intercept Chardonnay, one of the oldest and most popular black wineries among the Foundational colonies.

"Does continuing this treaty have anything to do with the violence down in Latin America?" I asked. "And why are we all of a sudden so hellbent on growing food for these white folks?"

"There are a number of reasons why we have to support the Farmers Treaty, Nuria."

"Yes, the United States is about to get involved in this dispute in Latin America, but we need to make sure that this conflict won't spiral out of control and spread to other regions. That's the real reason Senator Bean will be here with us today."

"American power abroad is under serious threat, and it's in our interest as Foundationals to help them maintain a balance of power," she explained while popping open the wine bottle.

After pouring wine for herself, Governor Williams politely handed me and Dennis our wine glasses before she filled them up. I graciously took a small sip and tasted the tender richness of the chilled wine explode in my mouth. Governor Williams took a large gulp from her own glass and seemed to immediately exhale all the tension out of her battered spirit. Before I knew it, Governor Williams had reached into her pocket and pulled out a half-smoked cigar. Dennis and I silently watched as she lit the thick cigar and took a rather large pull.

'So, we're gonna continue with this silly Farmers Treaty and grow food for these liberal whites?" Dennis curiously asked.

'If we wanna survive as a colony, we will," she shot back, looking him directly in his eyes.

We watched as she chuckled to herself while purposely letting us hang. Governor Williams took another big sip from her wine glass and placed her cigar in an ashtray. Looking over at Dennis, I could feel the confused spirit within him mustering up the courage to request an answer to the question we both harbored. A question with an answer we both might fear.

'After the Reparations Bill of 2054 was ratified, our forefathers believed that these white motherfuckers would turn around and take us out with unadulterated violence," she began.

'In their estimation, the demise of our Reparations Agenda would ultimately come from some physical failure on our part. So, we prepared our people to combat violent racists like Bradley Wood and fought through all of their attempts to intimidate us."

'But there was something we overlooked."

'Our forefathers didn't realize the explosion of financial success our Reparations Colonies would experience. That success happened to be just as dangerous as any motivated White Extremist with a hunting rifle."

'For the first fifty years of colonial life, our economy consistently outperformed the Dominant Societies. Using our ingenuity, Foundationals were able to grow our own food, create our own jobs, and build our own schools," Governor Williams expanded.

'Gone were the days of economic deprivation, white dependence, and political neglect. Foundationals had entered a new era of relative comfort, increased opportunity, and self-reliance. We didn't need their jobs, food, police, schools...we had our own."

'On paper, all of that sounds wonderful. It was all something many of our ancestors had dreamed about their entire lives, but there was still one nagging problem that has begun to rear its ugly head during our generation."

'No one could have predicted this overwhelming explosion of black success within our colonies. Our success has been too fuckin prolific for our own benefit. In some cases, the predicted one hundred years to reach a certain percentage rate of growth has been achieved well within thirty years."

Governor Williams paused and swallowed the rest of the wine that remained in her glass. Looking at my own half-empty glass, I put it to my lips in a vain attempt to keep pace with my half-drunk boss. These thoughts of our own success somehow putting us in danger were foreign to me. Donovan and Pernell had given their very lives to ensure we maintained this type of independence. I had devoted my existence to that aim. Now Governor Williams was telling me that the ultimate indication of our productivity was actually a troubling sign.

'I know what you're thinking, girl." She told me, beating me to the punch.

'But please hear me out, Nuria."

'We have been so successful that we have increased the life expectancy of every Foundational by seven years. Our standard of living has increased five times compared to what it was pre-reparations. Foundational families are starting to have more children because we can now afford it." "Every conceivable matrix or indicator of our community's success has increased, except for one essential measure."

"Everything except...Lebensraum. Those tricky white bastards," Dennis interrupted.

Governor Williams glared at Dennis with a grin dripping in the victory of kindred acknowledgment. Dennis, the certified genius, and Patrice Williams, the master politician, were communicating on a level that was certainly above my comprehension. I was completely lost and had no idea what these two were silently agreeing upon.

"What the hell are you both talking about? Someone in this limo better fill me in."

"Lebensraum," she replied. "When Dennis says Lebensraum, he is referring to the Nazi's primary objective during World War II."

"Lebensraum means living space, Nuria," Dennis jumped in. "What Patrice is trying to convey is that during the writing of the Reparations Bill, the Dominant Society gave us almost everything except the needed amount of living space to properly grow our colonies."

"We are experiencing the same issues that Nazi Germany and Imperial Japan faced before World War II. We have a growing economy that is causing a population boom. That's all well and good until you run out of land to grow food or homes for our citizens. God forbid jobs become limited and crime rates rise. Because if that happens, the bubble will burst and every single Foundational, no matter how loyal they are, will run back to the Dominant Society begging to become a Zebra."

"Given the current Reparations Bill," he continued. "Foundationals aren't legally able to own land or obtain employment outside of our thirty-two colonies. They purposely put us in a small economic flowerpot and it was only a matter of time before our powerful roots outgrew the capacity of the tiny pot they gave us."

"The bastards were playing the long game and they've rigged the outcome against us."

'So, the White folks sold us a spoiled bag of lemons. I get it Dennis, but what does that have to do with Bradley Wood and the rest of the violent racists out here trying to harm us?" I asked. 'It has everything to do with them, Nuria," Governor Williams broke in.

"There is a reason why they were so willing to help us kill Bradley Wood at Fort Jefferson. It's no accident that we haven't experienced a terror attack in over six years, girl."

"The Dominant Society has engineered all of this. The last thing they want to happen is the rabid White Extremists attacking us and dampening our success."

"They have gone to extraordinary lengths to keep their extremist-minded cousins and siblings from hindering us on these colonies. Make no mistake, the Dominant Society hates us just as much as the White Extremists do. But the two parties only disagree on how to bring about our oppression, not our oppression itself."

"Throughout this country, there are large rural communities filled with hard-core racists that have been expelled from the more modern cities in the Dominant Society because they are obsessed with violently attacking us."

'On one side, we have the rural White folks who would happily invade our colonies with violence and divorce us of our wealth. On the other side, we have the more modern White folks who also despise us but wish we would accept their cruel dominance willingly."

'One wants to dominate with violence and aggression, the other with the allure of alternative lifestyles and the pipe dream of a color-blind society. Believe me, I am not naïve regarding the composition of the world outside of the comforts of our colonies."

"Which is exactly why I need you both to get up on that stage and pour your hearts out to the attendees at this rally," she explained.

"We can use this Farmer's Treaty as critical leverage to get more land allotments from this sick government. If we continue to build upon this Treaty, the Oakland colony is guaranteed to increase our living space by at least one-third. That's enough new colonial land to keep our Oakland colony viable for at least another eighty to one hundred years."

Sensing her own exhaustion, Governor Williams stopped talking and poured more wine into her glass before taking several puffs from her smoldering cigar. Like a needy child, Dennis waved his hand towards her cigar, non-verbally asking Patrice if he could partake in the smoking session. Governor Williams handed the lit cigar to Dennis with generosity in her spirit and we both watched as he puffed away like a blackjack dealer at a casino.

Our limo reached the outer limits of our colony's territory and we floated past the rolling brown hills into the white-dominated haven near Alameda. The Colonial Patrol Service immediately fell behind us and was replaced by scores of well-lit San Francisco Patrol units. Directly ahead of us sat tiny Yerba Buena Island with its plush green trees and rocky shoreline. A view of downtown San Francisco rose from the skyline in the background next to the rusty Golden Gate Monument. Our driver slowed down and we descended towards an open field near the island's historic lighthouse. Behind the lighthouse, we could see thousands of rally attendees waving American and Foundational flags. Despite flying through the sky above, I could hear the loud roar of their cheers as we glided over them. We landed on the beautiful, well-kept green grass in front of a large three-story mansion with the greatest of ease. The limos engines went silent and a tall well-dressed white man accompanied by several police officers approached us.

As he neared our limo, I noticed that the white man happened to be the Mayor of San Francisco. Remembering that we were no longer within the safety of our colony's territory, I helped Governor Williams put her wine bottle away while Dennis stowed our empty glasses.

"Good evening Governor Williams," the Mayor said with a broad smile. "It is so great to have you here to visit us in San Francisco."

"Thank you for inviting me, Mayor. I absolutely love coming here," she replied.

Governor Williams stepped out of the limo and made small talk with the Mayor as Dennis, Ed, and I gathered our gear. After we had situated our equipment, the Mayor led us towards the three-story mansion that would act as our staging area for the rally. As we walked, the mayor told us that Senator Bean had arrived early and was waiting for us inside the mansion. Pleased with the news, Governor Williams smiled jubilantly and quickened her pace as we all struggled to keep up in the thick sticky grass. Governor Williams made it to the porch of the mansion and stopped just before the steps as Senator Bean walked out of the front door.

Like long-lost college roommates, the two women exchanged warm embraces as lights from the news cameras surrounding them exploded at a blistering pace. I looked over at Ed and we both shared glares of annoyance. This was the political play-acting we had both fostered large amounts of contempt for. Senator Bean was just as seasoned politically as Governor Williams. A very thin white woman with wealthy roots, Judith Bean was a typecast of a powerful liberal white woman. Her career in the Navy had won her instant credibility on Capitol Hill and her connection to the Dry Tortugas assault won her the undying respect of Foundational voters in Florida.

Almost on cue, Senator Bean walked towards us and began putting it on thick for the cameras. It had been almost three years since I last saw former Admiral Judith Bean, but the same phony smile and insincere gaze was not hard to forget. We pretended to make nice and share memories for the media before hugging it out. As we embraced each other, the air around us became bleach white with camera flashes. At that moment, I thought of the last conversation I had with Jeremy Woodson. This was the woman who had forced Jeremy to decide to risk it all in pursuit of my heart. Without knowing it, I began to cry and tears flowed down my cheek.

Senator Bean quickly took notice of my emotion and I could see that selfish thought process began in her sneaky blue eyes. In one sly move, she wrapped her arms around my shoulders, pulled me close to her while cleverly turning me towards the nearest film crew. As the camera crews recorded, Judith Bean decided to launch into an impromptu motivational speech.

"I served with this American hero during one of our country's darkest hours," Senator Bean blurted out.

"When lives are on the line and the bullets are exploding around you, there is no White or Black America. At that moment, there is only one America. There is only love for your fellow soldier or sailor. At our core, despite all our racial differences, we are all Americans. We all stand up for one another when it truly counts and those bonds will last forever!"

The small crowd of media and police officers gathered around us spontaneously erupted in applause and cheering. Amongst them, I could see the stone faces of Ed, Gary, and Vincent trying their damnest to conceal inner disgust. Next to me, Dennis and Governor Williams fared much better in their attempt to play along. Their smiling expressions merely hid absolute amusement. I was certain they would both riddle me with jokes once this whole thing was over.

'Girl...No wine for you next time," Governor Williams playfully whispered while lavishing me with a comforting hug.

Meanwhile, Senator Bean made her way up the steps and onto the porch with Governor Williams in tow. They both stopped in front of the mansion and gave coordinated waves to the cameramen before disappearing inside. The media representatives quickly fanned out towards the rally site, leaving all of us alone outside of the mansion. As Dennis laughed hysterically, Ed walked over and gave me the evil eye.

'So Nuria, we cry in the arms of White politicians now," he quietly vented.

'I just lost my head for a minute Ed," I whispered.

'What that bitch did to one of the Zebras that worked for her still angers the hell outta me. Crying was the best I could do, not to punch her ass in the face."

'We need to head inside and start getting ourselves set up," Riley said as he approached us from behind.

"The police have shut down access onto the island ten minutes ago, so we are already behind schedule."

I watched Riley and Clark walk towards the porch while their handheld radios blasted loudly. Feeling like a fifth wheel, I slapped Ed's shoulder and headed up the porch steps after them. As my left foot touched the first step, I felt an ear-numbing percussion lift me into the air, throwing me backwards. On instinct, my eyes closed and I felt my body tumble and bounce across the soft grass.

My body went still and my bruised muscles screamed out in pain. Everything seemed to be eerily silent, almost like I had lost my hearing. For a few frightening seconds, I couldn't open my eyes and was trapped in pitch darkness. After several moments of pure panic, my eyesight was restored in the form of blurs. Then came that familiar ringing sensation in my ears, followed by the feeling of warm blood trickling down my earlobes. I tried to raise myself from the ground, but my wary legs buckled and I clumsily fell back to the earth.

My heart began to race. I had been in this spacey fog before and this feeling was all too recognizable and ominous. I lifted my head to try and focus on the mansion and what I saw confirmed my worst suspicions. A white man in a paramedic's uniform rushed towards me and fell to his knees.

"You're gonna be fine, Ma'am," he relayed in an unseasoned voice.

He hadn't told me anything that I didn't already know. This wasn't my first rodeo. It was his job to try to keep me calm, so I laid still and allowed him to check my pulse. At that moment, my real concern wasn't about me at all. The once pearly white mansion looked like someone had dropped a bomb on it. Large pieces of the porch were scattered about the dark green grass. All of the windows had been blown out and the first floor of the house had partially collapsed. I could smell the heavy scent of smoke and I saw the burning orange flames bouncing off the walls inside the mansion. As the realization of what I had seen sunk in, my heart swelled with agony. Patrice Williams, our beloved Governor, was inside, and I knew that her fate had been a tragic one.

CHAPTER TWO

SHADY ALLIES

I FELT MYSELF SHAKING AS I woke up from my deep state of darkness. The cold discomfort of the sweat-soaked bedsheets caused me to roll upright, sitting on the side of the bed. My hand began to shake wildly as I reached towards the nightstand to turn on the light. The lamp burst into action, casting its dim glow throughout the lonely bedroom. Looking at my clock, I winced inside. It was only three in the morning and I had once again failed to sleep through the entire night.

My attempt at resting my worn soul had been defeated by the nightmarish images of that dead black teenager laying in a pool of blue blood. Dr. Wiseman told me those night terrors were a major indication that my PTSD was getting progressively worse. Yet, I knew it was best to keep this all to myself and handle it alone. Too afraid to go back to sleep, I stood up and slid into my night slippers.

It was only a matter of time before Quinton heard me moving around. The sound of being up and about would surely cause him to walk upstairs. This pool of sweat on the mattress and my trembling body would only lead to another intense argument.. Deep inside, I knew he didn't want to feel like I was suffering, but this was my issue to handle and I needed him to stay out of my business. The last thing I wanted was to somehow feel obligated to him. Quinton had hurt me once before and I will be damned if I allowed him the opportunity to do so again.

Determined to make up an excuse and throw Quinton off my scent, I stood up from the bed and headed towards the bathroom. When I turned around, I noticed that the bedroom window had been left half-open. It was then I recognized the goosebumps littering my arm and felt the chilly night air. I hadn't opened the window and Quinton knew that I hated sleeping with them open. Angered, I raced down the staircase on a seek and destroy mission. With every step, I could feel the emotions boiling within me. I found Quinton sitting at the dining room table, reading his Bible while scribbling on a notepad. He was still wearing the dark gray suit he had worn to Governor Williams funeral, along with those nerdy-looking reading glasses I absolutely hated.

"Quinton, why the hell did you open the damn bedroom window when you know I'm trying to sleep?"

Caught off guard by my loud verbal assault, Quinton jerked around in his chair, wearing a silly look of confusion. I heard his writing pen drop to the floor as our eyes met. In a scramble of embarrassment, he quickly leaned down and grabbed the pen from the hardwood floor.

"What the hell are you talking about, Nuria," he shot back.

"You left the damn window open. It's cold as dog shit outside and now the whole bedroom is freezing," I erupted,

"I told you to never fuckin do that. You never listen to me. Everything has to always be about you."

Quinton stood up from his chair, tossing his pen on the table before purposely looking away. I could feel the frustration boiling within him. Instead of indulging in his natural inclination, he walked past me and went into the living room. He quietly sat in front of the television and began to scroll through the channels in a vain attempt to occupy his mind. Quinton was trying to ignore me and his cocky dismissiveness only poured more fuel on my already burning anger.

"So, you're just gonna sit on your fat ass and ignore my question," I blasted him.

"Yeah," he softly replied. "I'm not taking it there with you today. Lindsey is upstairs sleeping and I don't wanna wake our baby up. I'm tired of seeing her cry her eyes out because of our arguments. We need to do better for her, Nuria."

"If you hadn't opened the damn window, I'd still be asleep right now, and this wouldn't be an issue," I interrupted. "Why can't you comprehend that!"

"I didn't open the damn window Nuria. You either believe what I'm telling you, or you don't; either way, I'm not arguing with you."

A renewed surge of anger and frustration gripped me as I watched Quinton press down on the volume button. The sound from the television speakers increased and created a loud echo within the walls of the living room. I responded to Quinton, but my futile words were drowned out as he pretended to focus on the screen in front of him. In an angry panic, I rushed over and slapped him in his face. The harsh assault knocked his head back and I felt the unique sting of my own blow ringing throughout my fingers. In complete shock, Quinton immediately reached his hand up to his face and gently rubbed a bloody scratch just below his left eye.

"If you didn't want to wake her up, then why are you blasting the damn TV," I shouted. "You don't care about me.... You don't care about Lindsey. Everything is always about your ass. Quinton Sellers, the weak-ass Heavyweight Champion of the World who sold out his Oakland colony for white sex. You picked them over us."

Quinton looked up at me with a stare I hadn't seen since his last bout in the ring. My hard slap may not have physically hurt him, but I knew my damning words had injured his tender pride. He slowly lifted himself from the lounge chair and towered over me. Sensing his coming aggression, I backed away from him, creating distance while clinching my lonely fist. I felt the tears of hate running down my face in anticipation of our impending combat. Suddenly, Quinton turned towards the steep staircase and began to climb up to the second floor, leaving me in the living room with only my fury to console me.

I heard him open a bedroom door and wildly slam it shut. In my wordless existence, I sat down in his lounge chair and attempted to clean my face. With a stricken heart, I thoughtlessly stared at the wide TV screen in front of me. A snobby white news analyst was delivering false narratives while Congress held a vote on applying sanctions on El Salvador. In my own world, I knew that I had just done the same with my husband and the mixed feelings about my actions were tormenting me. After ten minutes, I heard two sets of footsteps making their way down the staircase. "Where are you going with her Quinton? Why did you wake Lindsey up?" "We need to leave, Nuria," he answered with a focused tone. "We're going by my momma's house."

'So, you're running back home to momma? You weak-ass bastard. You can carry your ass over there, but Lindsey is staying here with me."

'Hell no," Quinton barked. 'She's coming with me. I'm her father and that's final."

"You need some alone time. This whole assassination of Governor Williams has really put you on edge and neither of us can tolerate your shit right now."

'I understand why you are still so resentful. I understand why you keep Lindsey at arm's length, but what I won't tolerate is you putting your hands on anyone in this house."

'I stopped fighting and haven't hit anyone in anger in over ten years. I'll be damned if I start knocking people out again in my own damn home. I've been through too much to go back to that life. No way."

Quinton picked up Lindsey and carried her to the front door. Deep down in my heart, I knew that I should probably put up a defiant protest and pretend to stop them from leaving, but my emotional exhaustion had completely overwhelmed me. The front door opened and closed abruptly, and I found myself alone. The thought sent me back into the horrors of my past. I painfully recalled that suffocating moment in Miami when I turned on the television and watched all the sports channels break the news of Quinton's arrest. Reliving the absolute shock at hearing about Quinton's transgressions, the tears and anger hidden within me came bursting out. The onslaught of emotions upon hearing the horrifying details about a coked-out stripper, the cheap hotel room, dirty syringes, and rape kits came flooding back.

The memories of the death and carnage I witnessed that night at Fort Jefferson followed. Mental images of Pernell's shattered body lying bloody and motionless at the entrance of the fort overwhelmed me. The exhausted look on Jeremy Woodson's face as I gazed into his beautiful brown eyes one last time, weakened my soul. The feeling of Donovan dying as he lay helpless on top of me kept flashing through my mind. Donovan lovingly gave up his own life while using his last earthly moments to protect me. I relived the foggy visions of U.S. Marines pulling me through the sand and loading my semi-conscious body into their small rescue boat. Then followed the agony of undergoing several lifesaving surgeries with months of painful rehab to teach me how to adjust to this new life as a one-armed crippled.

While fighting for my life in the hospital, I remembered hearing Quinton's voice as he begged me not to leave him. When I mustered up the strength to open my eyes, I looked up and see his unshaven and ragged face anxiously looking down at me. Part of me was comforted by Quinton's devotion, but another part wished it could have been Jeremy Woodson instead. I didn't know how I felt about Jeremy until I spent those long nights in the hospital. The regret of losing him the way I did made me hate this life. My hidden remorse streamed down my face, and Quinton dutifully wiped away those tears. He tried his best to comfort me, but there was nothing he could do. I knew telling him the truth about why I was crying would have wounded him deeply. I was missing Jeremy Woodson and looking at Quinton every day only worsened my ordeal.

I pulled myself away from the endless news commentary on Latin America's racial riots and walked into the kitchen. Opening my cabinet, I reached inside to grab my favorite coffee mug, only to be distracted by a loud ring from my virtual phone. I walked over to the call desk and sat down, making sure to calibrate the brightness of my own image before accepting the incoming call. With the push of a button, I answered the ringing phone and the hologram image of Gary Freeman stared back at me.

"Good Morning Nuria."

Gary looked tired and weary. He was dressed in a faded blue sweater and his normally well-kept beard looked a bit ungroomed. The sight of his obvious fatigue eased my concerns about my own disheveled state. In the background, I could see a huge painting of Muhammad Ali hanging on the wall behind him. I had seen that painting plenty of times and knew exactly where Gary was hiding. Gary was calling me from the Governor's secret shelter, a place only a handful of Foundationals knew existed.

"Damn, you look like shit, Gary. How much longer is Vincent Towns gonna hide you away in that damn shelter?

Gary shrugged his shoulders and let out a sigh of frustration before leaning back in his lounge chair. Having been elevated to the position of

Governor, Gary Freeman now found himself an isolated prisoner within the precious colony we both loved.

'Once the judiciary swore me in as Governor," he began. 'Vincent and his FP teams rushed my ass out of the Capitol building and locked me away down here for safe keeping."

'The Colonial Leadership Council called in from Dallas, ordering Vincent to put me under lock and key until we've figured out what we're dealing with out here. They're concerned that there might be more targeted attacks aimed at Foundational leadership."

'They wouldn't even allow me to attend Patrice's memorial service."

'I complained like hell though. After a lot of cursing and begging, the Council relented and arranged for a private viewing for me", Gary lamented. 'Have you heard anything on the status of Senator Bean?" I broke in. 'She's still alive, but she's on a ventilation machine," he admitted.

'Word has it that Judith Bean won't make a full recovery and will be severely impaired if she survives, so her political career is likely finished."

'The Mayor of San Francisco is out of the hospital. He sustained a few non-life-threatening injuries. A broken leg and a fractured hip...but he's expected to make a full recovery."

'Both of your FBI buddies, Riley and Clarke, survived. They walked away from the explosion only suffering a blow to their pride, along with some superficial wounds."

'Patrice and several of Judith Bean's personal aides took the worst of the explosion. The ATF and FBI's crime scene investigators concluded that Patrice and three of Judith's aides were in the living room when the bomb exploded. The FBI believes an IED was hidden inside of a sofa that was recently purchased from a local antique's dealer."

I watched Gary's hologram image reach down and open a cabinet. He pulled out a small stack of papers and sat them on the desk in front of him before briefly combing through the pages with his fingers. Having found the document he was looking for, Gary pulled one white sheet from the stack and moved it closer so I could read the hologram image.

"This is why I'm calling you, Nuria."

"The FBI has set up an Integrated Command Post over in San Francisco," he detailed.

"The FBI has requested that we Foundationals send representatives of colonial law enforcement, so I'm assigning both you and Ed to the case to participate as our criminal investigators."

His words shocked me. Given my disability, Gary had never been a fan of me actively working in the Force Protection world. Now, all of a sudden, he was handing me the responsibility of participating in what would surely be one of the biggest criminal investigations in Foundational history. Feeling confused, thoughts of mistrust swam through my spirit as I stared at the document in front of me.

"Why did you choose me for this assignment, Gary?" I asked. "Doesn't Vincent Towns have FP teams that you could have used for this?"

"The FP teams are staying out of this investigation, Nuria. I need investigators not directly linked to Vincent and the FP teams for this case."

"Look, Nuria," he further explained after finally catching on to my skepticism.

"I need someone I can trust to represent Foundationals in all of this. Yes, Governor Williams was nationally respected, but she also had tons of people who secretly hated her."

"Some of those people are white, and sadly, some of those people are black. Some of those people were close to her and others were not close at all."

"Nuria, you are the only person I have that can dig into this matter without having some sort of axe to grind. We have had our differences between us, but one thing I never questioned was your loyalty to the truth and this colony."

'If I decide to do this," I rebutted.

'It can't just be me and Ed out there all alone. I'm gonna need Dennis to participate, just like the old days. Since you say you need people you can trust, well that same logic should go for me too."

Gary placed the document back on his desk and shook his head in agreement. Grabbing his mobile computer, he swiped it open before pressing a few buttons. Almost immediately, I heard the loud chime of an email arriving in my inbox. Opening the email, I quickly browsed through the official documents Gary had sent. At first blush, the scope of the entire multi-agency organization appeared to be endless. From the FBI to the EPA, almost every agency in the Federal government had representatives assigned to this Incident Command Post.

'What I just sent to you are all the documents pertaining to the ICP. You need to be at the ICP at eight o'clock sharp. The FBI plans on reviewing surveillance footage collected from a camera around the mansion on Yerba Buena Island this morning, so be there to keep an eye on things."

'Ed should be on his way to pick you up right now. I called and talked to him before reaching out to you, so he knows the plan and has been briefed already."

'If you two discover things that are troubling, don't hesitate to reach out to me," Gary offered. 'You both are about to enter into a world of shit. If it looks or feels funny, it probably means it's funny. So, don't doubt the instincts that God gave you, sister."

Gary saluted me with a respectful nod before reaching down to cut off his connection. The bright image of him disappeared, evaporating into nothing right before my eyes. Once again, I found myself alone and filled with emotions. This time, the emotions ablaze within me were much different.

This was an opportunity. I raced back into the kitchen and snatched my coffee cup. After filling my mug, I carefully reviewed every single document that Gary had sent. With every page turn, I could feel that spirit of excitement within me coming back to life. Ed called and said he was about to arrive, so I put away my handheld computer and ran upstairs to get ready. After a quick shower and change of clothes, I walked back down to the living room to find Ed's car sitting in my driveway.

"Good morning, Nuria. I stopped by the coffee shop and grabbed you a cup," Ed happily proclaimed as I climbed into his car.

"Thanks," I replied, taking the cup from him.

"Are you sure you're ready for this shit, Mister Playboy? It's time to put all your women on hold and focus like never before. You've been waiting for this your whole life, and here it is. We're in the big ballgame now."

"I'm more than ready," he confidently replied.

"All I've ever asked for is a chance to prove my worth, and now I have it. The beautiful ladies can wait, they are all well trained anyway, so they can do without big daddy for a little bit."

Ed powered the car into the air and sped towards San Francisco. The morning sun glowed in the car's rear-view mirror, shining a light on our westward path. A thick layer of low-hanging fog blanketed the bay and concealed all but the highest hill tops on Yerba Buena Island. Noticing the hazardous layer of fog in front of us, Ed calmly reached down and engaged the foul weather vision display. Dark-tinted window panels slowly rolled down, covering the car's large front windshield. The car's foul weather navigation systems projected a virtual image on the tinted panels, giving us a perfect depiction of everything surrounding us as we flew through the dense clouds.

We made it to the island and Ed flew a circle around it as we both looked down, taking in the situation beneath us. The island was now filled with the presence of law enforcement and all roadways to the damaged mansion were closed. On the east side of the island sat a large gray complex next to several floating finger piers. A blinking signal sat atop the large square roof, blasting the red letters ICP from a blinking monitor. Ed lowered his car towards the ground and was only able to find one lonely parking space near the boat piers. The parking space seemed like it was miles from the looming complex. Nonetheless, we landed and began the long walk uphill towards the ICP.

After an excruciating hike, Ed and I made it to the front door and we both paused to collect our breath. It had been years since I felt this type of exhaustion. As I struggled to suck in air, the fond memories of my old workout routine came flooding back to me. In the good ole days, both Donovan and Pernell would be here lighting a fire under my ass. Both men would surely yell in my ears, forcing me to keep pace with them and imploring me to never give up. They knew how to motivate me with their fearless presence and encouraging spirit. As I caught my breath, I realized those days were far gone. Now, I was forced to experience something far different in comparison. I looked over at Ed and saw sweat dripping down the back of his neck. He looked mildly panicked. His sweaty button-up shirt made him look as though he was about to have a nervous breakdown. Ed would be the one needing that same encouragement and I was the only person qualified to give it to him.

"Agent Sellers and Agent Carter," a black man said while opening the front door for us.

"Glad you guys finally could make it. Follow me and I'll take you both upstairs so we can get you guys caught up.

After several seconds of staring at the man, I finally recognized him as FBI Agent Clarke Bernard. He held the door wide open, staring down at me with his trademark annoyed and impatient expression. I hadn't seen Clarke since the day Governor Williams was assassinated. For some strange reason, he looked to be tired and weak. His dark brown skin was ashy as hell, and from the state of his short nappy hair, he had definitely missed a haircut appointment. On his wrinkled forehead and underneath his chin, I could see fresh scabs that were still healing. Gauze band-aids bulged from his right hand as it struggled to prop open the heavy door. It was clear that Clarke had just been released from the hospital and was still recovering from the impact of the deadly explosion.

Ed and I walked into the building, nodding our heads at Clarke as we passed by. The inside of the building was stuffy. The first-floor lobby was wide open with shining pearl tiling and egg white painted walls. The few pieces of furniture were cheap and dull. This was the boring look of almost every government building in the Dominant Society. By design, white society had made them plain to a fault, offensive to more sophisticated eyes, and overwhelmingly inhospitable with their uncomfortably humid climates. It was no small wonder why Clarke looked so pissed off. If I had to work in this hell hole, I would be mad at the world too.

We followed Clarke to the elevator and walked inside. Clarke leaned down to look into the eye scanner and inputted the floor number after gaining authorization. The doors quickly closed and we rocketed skyward to the seventh floor. As gravity pulled against our rising elevator, I saw Clarke giving Ed a once over. He chuckled at his drenched shirt, grinning widely at Ed's expense.

'I see you had quite the workout this morning, Ed," he teased.

'If you had called before you arrived, I could've arranged a much better parking situation for you."

"Nice to find that out now...Brother Man," Ed shot back with contempt.

Clarke's playful giggle and smile disappeared. He turned towards Ed with a determined spirit, ready to confront him. Sensing the escalating tension between the men, I grabbed Clarke's arm and gave him a light tug to break his train of thought.

"OK, guys, that's enough," I warned them.

"Naw Nuria," Ed angrily dismissed. "This Zebra ass coon has jokes, so I wanna see what's funny."

"What's funny is you being too damn pro-black to ask for help," Clarke responded.

"All you had to do was swallow your pride and call, but you Foundationals are too ignorant and self-righteous to ask for help from a fellow black man. Especially, if the black man ain't drinking your damn Black Supremacist Kool-Aid. That's why nobody in America likes you damn people."

The elevator's rise came to a halt and the bell chimed. The doors split open and in that instant, I could only watch as Ed's balled fist hammered into Clarke's throat. The sound of the punch hitting Clarke's flesh was loud and heavy. Clarke stumbled backwards before gathering himself and launching forward into Ed's torso. Both men spilled out into the hallway, wrestling each other to the ground in an explosion of loud grunts and personal insults. Alarmed, I chased behind them using my lonely arm in a futile attempt to stop the wild skirmish. Grabbing Ed by his wet shirt, I felt helpless as he slipped through my weak grasp.

Out of nowhere, Clarke's partner Riley arrived. Agent Riley grabbed Clarke and struggled mightily to disengage him from Ed. Even with both of us there to break them up, Ed and Clarke were laser-focused on dominating each other. A group of cops ran over, and with their help, we all were able to finally separate the two angry men.

"What the hell is going on here, Nuria," Riley shouted at me!

"Are you blind, Riley? They're fighting damnit!"

I pulled Ed away from the confused scrum, guiding him towards an empty office to get a moment of privacy. Once I closed the door, Ed sat down in a chair and slammed his fists into a table. In frustration, he cursed loudly, screaming at the top of his lungs about the disrespect Clarke had shown him.

"Calm your ass down," I mumbled to Ed.

Ed went quiet and wiped his cheeks with his hands, erasing any sign of Clarke's punches. We shared a long moment of silence while I patiently allowed Ed time to compose himself.

"I fucked up, didn't I?" he softly asked.

"When Gary finds out about this, he's gonna be pissed. I'll never get my shot at being on the FP teams."

Feeling his need for comfort, I reached over and gently rubbed his back. Being on an FP Team had always been Ed's dream. Aside from his testing skills, Ed was an immature hothead and live wires like Ed weren't particularly well-suited for duty on FP teams. Being on the teams meant you had to be cool and calculating. Making decisions off emotion and personal desire, was a no-go in the FP world. Over the years, I had tried to help Ed with his temper, and we had seen some improvements. Yet, Ed still had this angry streak buried deep within him. An angry streak that always reared its nasty head at the most unfortunate of moments. Looking at Ed, I could almost visualize the words of wisdom Donovan Reid use to deliver to me. Words that gave me a greater perspective on who I needed to be as a Foundational.

"You can't let anyone in the Dominant Society have control over your emotions like that. It's not a good look and it's dangerous."

"You are a Foundational, Ed. As Foundationals, everyone will hate us.

We must accept that fact and learn to deal with it because this is our path and journey."

'From the Liberal Whites like Agent Riley to the White Supremacist Extremists."

"To the Asians, the Hispanics.... hell, even black Zebras like Agent Clarke. They all hate what we truly represent and who we really are. They hate our fundamental truth. A truth that makes them uncomfortable with themselves when they are among us."

'We should not be merely seekers of comfort amongst these other groups. Our journey is truth and justice between us all. That's what makes them uncomfortable with us."

'If we become overly emotional, we must understand that these other groups have always found a form of comfort in our own distress."

'When we are sober and logical, when we are seekers of truth and justice, these Anti-Black groups find themselves having to navigate through some very difficult conversations. These groups want to avoid doing that at all costs. You see, that's why they try to provoke us emotionally."

'Never give those bastards that way out. Don't let them off the hook. Control yourself, and you will control them."

Ed looked up and flashed a bright smile. I reached over and grabbed his hand, squeezing it softly to let him know I still believed in him. Ed stood up from his chair and let out a heavy sigh before slowly pacing the room.

"That sounds like another one of Donovan Reid's legendary lessons," he proclaimed. 'When did he tell you that?"

'He explained this to me whenever I needed to hear it," I admitted.

Ed shook his head in approval before reaching into his pocket and pulling out his handheld computer. He lowered himself back down in his seat before beginning to type an email.

"I'll reach out and contact Gary to let him know what happened," he lamented. "I'm sure he'll be disappointed, but I wanna make sure he hears about all of this from me first."

"Well, Ed," I jokingly began. "Just make sure you're using Gary's number and not one of your little lady friends. This ain't the time to cry on anybody's shoulder. We gotta job to do."

As Ed's thumbs pounded away on his hand-held computer, I heard several loud knocks behind me. Looking over my shoulder, I saw Riley crack open the door and poke his head into the room. His expression portrayed a nervous seriousness that was a bit worrisome to me.

"Nuria, can I see you for a moment, please?" he gently asked.

Without words, I rose from my seat and began preparing myself for the bullshit. Ed looked up at me, and I could see the remorse in his eyes. In a moment of bravado, I smiled at him and slapped his back.

"Tell Gary I said he should get Dennis's ass out here pronto," I jokingly ordered.

I walked outside the small office and followed Riley down a long hallway. We both made our way into a secure area with a huge screen positioned in front of a wall-mounted projector. Riley shut the door behind us and activated the room's sound suppression machine before turning off the recording system. Whatever he had to say to me, it was clear that Riley needed to say it in confidence.

"Look, Nuria," he nervously began. "I talked to Clarke and I want to apologize for his behavior today."

"This entire situation has been a whirlwind, but Agent Clarke let his emotions get the best of him."

"We have seen all the reports coming from Foundational News Media. Your folks are blaming the FBI for the assassination of Governor Williams and it's very hurtful to hear."

"Being bombarded with all of that misinformation got the best of Clarke and he lashed out at you guys."

"Clarke also told me that during past assignments, he overheard you and Ed refer to him as a Zebra. As you know, that is a hurtful slur for the blacks that remain among us in the Dominant Society."

"That said, simply hearing you say that word is no excuse for Clarke blowing up. As an FBI agent, he should have handled himself with more professionalism. I wanted to talk to you and kill all this drama before it really gets out of hand."

His words shocked me. For some reason, Agent Riley was trying to disarm me and I knew it. Historically, the FBI never admits making mistakes, much less directly apologizing to Foundationals for the damage they've caused. Agent Riley was after something more valuable than professional harmony, and in order to find out what the FBI really wanted, I knew what I had to do. Now it was my turn to play along.

"Riley, we accept your apology. Both men were in the wrong. Ed also knows better and he feels awful about his part in the scuffle today."

"As for the use of the term Zebra, I will talk to Ed and make sure he is more respectful in the future. I will also ensure that I am more sensitive with my own words as well."

Riley smiled and nodded his head in approval before pulling up a seat across from me. I could sense that his real objective would soon be revealed, so I braced myself to examine his every word in the hopes of discovering his hidden agenda.

"Good. I'm glad both men are reflective about this," he stated.

"With all the tension between us, we can't have any inkling of this fight getting out to the press."

"If Foundational Media happens to find out about today's fight," I interrupted. "It won't be because Foundational lips passed along any details. As far as I'm concerned, nothing happened here."

"That's what we want to hear, Nuria," Riley confirmed. "In the face of all this chaos, we have to at least maintain the appearance of teamwork, or what we are trying to do here will fall apart real fast."

"Especially since we now have a solid lead on who might have been involved in the assassination," Riley admitted.

I tried to hide my shock, but I knew Riley was able to easily decipher the hidden surprise in my spirit. The FBI was in the know and had gotten ahead of us. At that moment, I knew the surprise Riley had in store for us wasn't going to be good. Riley dramatically reached over and grabbed a remote, flipping through a series of videos before settling upon one.

"His name is Bingo Dorrell."

"He's an errand boy for a White Extremist group in Northern California named Hell's Fury."

Riley started the surveillance video that showed a yellow delivery truck parked outside of the white mansion. I looked down at the date of the video and immediately noticed that the images had been recorded four months ago, which was well before Governor Williams had agreed to participate in the Yerba Buena Island rally. Two men opened the cargo hatches on the truck and slowly unloaded a long sofa from inside. After several minutes of unwrapping the sofas protective cover, the two men carried the sofa up the porch and inside the mansion.

"Our FBI explosives experts concluded that this sofa was the source of the explosion," Riley described after pausing the video.

"It's believed that the device was hidden inside the wooden framing."

"From the pieces of electronics that survived the blast, the battery-powered arming device could have been activated using a Wi-Fi signal."

"Whoever built this bomb was very sophisticated and had a lot of skill. The device had been dormant for months. It takes a certain level of expertise to design a remotely triggered bomb that can maintain viability for the better part of a year."

"Per our Intel, Bingo fits the bill for this type of handy work."

As the video rolled on, both men walked out of the mansion. Riley paused it again, zooming in on the face of a brown-haired white man with a long unkept beard. He looked skinny, homely, and weak in appearance. From the ragged look of his face, the white man was probably in his mid-forties. Nothing about him led me to believe this man was some sort of evil genius, but I knew from prior experiences with these folks that looks could be completely deceiving.

"So, you've known about this guy?" I asked. "Yes," Riley admitted. "We have known about Bingo and we have files on him."

"He first came on our radar when twenty Hell's Fury terrorists firebombed three gay nightclubs in downtown San Francisco."

"During our questioning of the group, Bingo Dorrell's name and address kept coming up...so we had him surveilled."

Riley adjusted the remote and zoomed the image in on the second man walking behind Bingo. The second guy looked much younger, certainly not older than thirty. Yet, that wasn't the man's most surprising attribute. As Riley zoomed in closer, I could immediately tell that the second person was a black man. The angle of the camera and the drowning reflection of the mid-day sun gave the appearance of a deeply tanned white man at first glance. After zooming in and examining the man's unmistakable features, I knew he was indeed of African descent.

My heart skipped a beat. In the back of my mind, I could only hope that this black man was just another Dominant Society Zebra, running around seeking some sick form of white approval. Those hopes were quickly dashed when I looked into Riley's eyes and saw the glee that was hiding within them.

"We haven't been able to identify this second suspect," Riley claimed, clearly lying to me.

"He's a black male, about 5'9 and looks to be 180 pounds."

"None of our facial recognition databases are able to identify this guy. San Francisco PD has nothing on him, so we need to look at other possibilities, Nuria," he cleverly relayed.

"Cut the shit, Riley. Possibilities like what," I shot back?

Riley once again adjusted his remote, fast-forwarding the video to a totally different set of recordings. When he stopped, the footage displayed images of a pizza parlor. Aside from a few lonely patrons, the place was mostly empty as the cashier solemnly cleaned his counter with a white towel. Suddenly the front door opened and another man walked into the parlor. The cashier looked up, greeting the man with a smile before putting away his towel and handing his new customer a menu. It was then that I noticed that the new customer was Bingo Dorrell.

Bingo placed an order and sat at a booth that was positioned close to the parlor's entrance. He looked younger and much cleaner than he had in the previous video. It was almost as if he was expecting to meet someone important. His brown hair was neatly trimmed and his face looked a bit puffier. Riley forwarded the video, skipping past several uneventful minutes of Bingo sipping soda alone in his booth. Satisfied that he had reached the right moment, he pressed play and the video returned to normal speed. The pizza parlor entrance door opened again and another person walked in. This time, it was a black woman. Her dark brown skin was easily distinguishable within the well-lit interior of the parlor. The lady walked over to Bingo's booth and sat across from him. They appeared to engage in a bit of small talk before Bingo pulled a brown envelope out of his pocket and handed it to her.

The cashier walked to Bingo's booth and placed a tray of pizza on his table before talking to his new guest. As the black lady looked up to speak to the cashier, I was finally able to see her face and I immediately felt a chill run down my spine. This was not good at all.

'Bingo Dorrell is seen here meeting with Mary Ann Haskins, Intel Officer and Agent on Oakland FP Team number six," Riley explained with excitement. 'From my file, team six was your old unit, right, Nuria?"

'So, Mary Ann is your protégé, I assume."

Riley leaned back in his chair and crossed his legs, taking a posture of nonverbal confidence as he stared at me. He had me in a deep hole and he knew it. Bingo Dorrell could have very well been an informant for Mary Ann, but given the nature of the video, it was hard to tell. It was reckless for Mary Ann to meet an informant in such a public place, let alone in a pizza parlor outside of colonial territory. I watched the video play on and was sickened as both Bingo and Mary casually chatted while eating pizza. This was a shining example of what a rookie mistake looked like.

I knew instantly that the FBI had known about Mary Ann's damn meeting for a while now. This was their way of sending us Foundationals a veiled message. Riley had initially mentioned the negative press coverage our Foundational News Media had been broadcasting. Many of our most popular media figures had been pummeling the FBI for their security failures during the assassination of Governor Williams. The FBI was not the type of white organization to sit idly by and let threatening narratives develop. When pushed, the FBI would always eliminate threats.

"This video doesn't mean a thing to me," I deflected.

"You know the game, Riley. White Extremists like Bingo are always playing both sides against the other."

"That's how they survive. They do so by causing an equilibrium of chaos. Greedy racists like Bingo will scream all day about hating blacks and white liberal cucks, but they will happily give us both Intel if it means earning a few dollars for themselves."

'Hell, for all I know, Bingo could be a double agent for you guys."

'Like you said, when I did that job, I used to meet with white informants and snitches to get my Intel. It's a dirty little part of our job, Riley, and nothing more. So, stop digging."

'But are you sure this is simply Bingo meeting with his handler?" Riley asked. 'How do you know Mary Ann was not there on orders or for something much more sinister?"

'Nuria, I know you and interim Governor Gary Freeman don't really get along."

"The FBI knows that Gary and Patrice were political rivals with starkly different visions on how your Foundational colonies should be operating. I don't understand why you are so sure that this whole assassination isn't some kind of coup attempt orchestrated by hardliner Foundationals like Gary Freeman."

"That's why the FBI needs access to your colony's electronic database. We need copies of your memory cells so we can find out who this mysterious black man is and arrest him."

There it was, out in the open with all the bullshit removed. This was what the FBI was really after. For them, getting access to our memory cells with all of their records, reports, and secure information would be akin to striking oil. The FBI and Foundationals had been in a counterintelligence war with each other since the day we received our Reparations. Handing our memory cells to the U.S. government would be akin to slitting our own damn throats with a rusty razor.

'You aren't getting our memory cells, Riley. It will be a cold day in hell before I allow that to happen."

'Well, Nuria. We'd rather you Foundationals freely volunteer the memory cells, as opposed to having to go through the circuit courts to compel your colony's cooperation in our investigation."

"This black male isn't one of our guys, and we are 100% sure about that. The only place left to identify him is in the realm of you Foundationals. One way or the other, we intend to find out who this guy is. We are just trying to do what we can to spare you Foundationals a bit of public embarrassment here Nuria."

Riley stood up and walked over to the wall-mounted control panel. He punched in a code and the image on the screen disappeared. After a loud ringing noise, Riley reached for the shiny brass handle and opened the door.

"You and Ed can stay in here and review all the video evidence if you'd like," he began. "Just make sure you're both ready for action tonight."

"Two days ago, San Francisco PD located Bingo Dorrell, and he's living in a hostel in Redwood City."

"Tonight, we move on Bingo. We're going to arrest this guy and bring his ass in for questioning."

"Nuria...when we question Bingo and if he indicates that there is some sort of suspicious activity going on inside your colony, just know that the FBI is going to have all we need to access your damn memory cells. You should prepare yourself for that reality."

Riley gave me a cold stare before walking out of the room and slamming the heavy door behind him. This joint investigation was supposed to be about finding justice for Governor Williams. It was supposed to be a living testament of peaceful co-existence between Black Foundationals and the White Dominant Society. Instead, we were once again engaged in a cold war with an opponent that looked to exploit every advantage for personal gain. As I sat in the empty room staring at the dark TV screen, thoughts of Donovan and Pernell flooded my spirit. At this very moment, I knew my colony needed my old team, but we were all gone. Me and my lonely arm were all that was left after the fiasco at Dry Tortugas, and I could only pray that I still had enough within me to fight this battle.

CHAPTER THREE

INCOMPETENCE

BRIGHT STARS LITTERED THE MOONLESS SKY that hung over the calm waters of the Bay. It was a beautiful night and I could see a mass of cars buzzing over the downtown area of San Francisco. I had no doubts that other families were taking full advantage of the ideal conditions and enjoying a night that was sure to be memorable. As Agent Clarke turned our car towards Redwood City, my thoughts wandered, slipping back to regrets about Quinton and Lindsey. At this time of night, Quinton would be tucking a sleepy Lindsey into her bed. I could almost see him leaning down to kiss her brown forehead, with that cute fatherly look in his eyes. For all of his many faults, I could never accuse Quinton of not being a good father. He had always been good to Lindsey and went out of his way to care for her. After giving it more thought, I realized that Quinton deciding to take Lindsey and leave was a good call on his part. I knew I had gotten out of control and shown Quinton the ultimate disrespect by putting my hands on him.

In fact, Quinton didn't know I was not using this alone time to fully reflect upon my own mental well-being. He didn't know that there were no enlightened conversations with that bitch Dr. Wiseman. There was no long evaluations of our struggles as a married couple. No thoughtful self-assessments of my performance as Lindsey's mother. Instead, I was once again risking it all to dive into the deep end, chasing after another White Supremacist.

I was sure that if Quinton discovered that I was out here hunting down another racist, he would go ape shit. In my mind, I could see him reflexively accusing me of purposely putting up another barrier. This was about the well-being of our people, not the happiness of my shaky marriage. Quinton knew this about me from day one. We were both fighters, and to expect me to somehow change like he had, was a wish destined to remain unmet.

Wanting to purge my broken home from my train of thought, I glanced beside me and saw Ed's ass typing away on his hand-held computer like a busy secretary. His reclusive silence and boyish cheese smile told me that Ed wasn't focused on business. Like most young single men, his mind was undoubtedly elsewhere. Feeling the urge to intrude, I leaned over to spy on him and whispered in his ear.

"When do I get to meet her?" I inquired.

"I'm not ready to introduce her to you, Nuria." He dismissed while turning off his computer.

"She's a little shy, so we're both keeping it on the down low for now."

"What the hell does that even mean?" I asked.

"Is she married or something? You better not be fooling around with a married woman, Ed."

"All it means is we aren't ready for our relationship to be public, that's all. We both want our privacy right now."

"Well, you better get your mind focused and ready to do your job," I advised. "We're both on the clock and the colony ain't paying you to sit here and pursue forbidden romance."

We arrived in Redwood City, and Clarke landed in a municipal parking lot across from the local police station. Ed and I exited the car while Riley and Clarke stayed inside to make a few radio calls. It was my first time visiting Redwood City. I had seen photos and videos of this suburb on the news, but seeing it in person did its beauty much more justice. Even in the darkest hour of the late evening, the entire layout of the city felt roomy. The city was definitely more spacious than anything I had experienced in San Francisco or my own colony.

"This place is really nice," Ed commented as he soaked in the picturesque scenery.

"Yeah, but everything tends to look nice when you've spent most of your life on a reparations colony," I responded. "You know what the old folks use to say. The grass is always greener on the other side of the bay."

"Well, this sure as hell beats having to live right on top of your neighbors and sharing rooms with infectious rats over in San Francisco," Ed responded.

"If there weren't so many liberal ass white people out here, this Redwood City place might be halfway decent," he concluded with a light grin.

"There aren't too many liberals over here, Ed," Agent Clarke jumped in while walking towards us.

"In fact, my ancestors once owned a chain of dry cleaning outlets in this city."

"Redwood City is sort of a gateway suburb between the liberal whites in San Francisco and the conservative rural white folks who live out in the sticks," Clarke explained.

"This place is basically no man's land in the ongoing cultural war within white society, which is why extremists like Bingo Dorrell tend to hide out here."

Clarke pulled a small pack of smokes out of his coat pocket before putting a cigarette in his mouth and sparking a flame. Ed and I glanced at each other while Clarke lazily blew foggy white puffs out of his mouth as a relaxed expression cascaded across his face. I had never known that Agent Clarke was a smoker. Unnerved and suspicious, Ed placed his right hand on his holster and began to re-examine our surroundings. We both were thinking the same thing, and his alarmed spirit instantly triggered mine. Was Clarke trying to send some sort of signal?

"Ed! You need to calm the hell down, man," Clarke laughingly stated. "I'm just freakin smoking. There's no way we drove you all the way out here, just to set you guys up."

"I promise, I'm just burning a stick to get my mind right before we start all of this."

Ed rolled his eyes and let out a light sigh while moving his hand away from his gun. Playfully shaking his head, Ed walked over towards a smiling Clarke and offered him his friendly hand. Both men exchanged dap and I listened as they shared a chuckle.

"You know we Foundational negroes are taught not to trust you, tricky ass people," Ed admitted with a grin. "Old habits die hard. I apologize, my man."

"Do whatever you need to do to get yourself together, Agent Clarke," I jumped in. "We may not agree with your politics, but I'm not so naïve as to forget who the real threat is out here."

Clarke blew the final puff of his cigarette out of his nose and laughed before throwing the butt on the ground. As he stomped it out, Clarke pulled a notepad out of his jacket pocket and flipped through several pages.

"There's no need to explain, Nuria. I'm familiar enough with U.S. History to say I wouldn't blame you guys for that cynical attitude towards the Bureau. But tonight, we are on the same team, so I need you to at least try and trust me."

'Our sources are telling us that Bingo Dorrell is still at his hostel. He'll be leaving there in about twenty minutes or so to go visit a home on Blanchard Road."

'Bingo Dorrell has, shall I say, a very peculiar and repulsive sexual appetite."

'Let's just say that he's not swinging by this home to go share a bottle of wine with adults."

I knew exactly what Clarke was getting at. Bingo Dorrell was not unlike many of the White Supremacist informants that I had worked with during my time on the FP teams. White snitches like Bingo often behaved like chameleons. They would be staunch Neo-Nazis one minute and then loudly claim to be Anti-Racists the next, all depending on what they happened to be after at the moment. It wasn't unusual for us to find out that our White snitches harbored a host of secret sexual perversions. In my experience, most of them were always hiding some sort of sexual fetish or chemical addiction. For people like Bingo, hiding who they truly were was an art form they had mastered. These people were professionals at the act of deception. Even when working with them, it was always prudent for any intelligence officer to always keep them at arm's length.

Which is why that damn video of Mary Ann eating and conversating with this fucker worried the hell outta me. If Bingo Dorrell was indeed one of Mary Ann's informants, she had allowed herself to get way too cozy for comfort. Bingo was not a colleague nor a peer. He was a criminal, a snitch, and a violent supporter of White Supremacy.

'Unfortunately for Bingo, when he arrives at this house tonight, he's going to walk right into an FBI sting," Clarke continued.

'For several months now, Bingo's been chatting with one of our undercover FBI operatives on the dark web. He's been trying to meet our operative offline for a while now, but we've had to stall him. Tonight, Bingo will finally get that meeting his heart desires."

Agent Riley joined us and then walked over to Clarke. Clarke leaned down and Riley softly mumbled a few words in his ear. After springing up straight, Clarke reached into his pocket and again pulled out his box of cigarettes. Opening the box, Clarke handed Riley a smoke and also gave him his lighter.

"Well, I'll be damned." Ed loudly declared. "You clean-cut FBI boys are both out here tearing up your lungs with those cancer sticks. Wait until I tell the Justice Department about you two...."

"Ed," Riley responded while coughing.

"Seasoned perps like Bingo can smell clean-cut cops from a mile away. If I smell like a cheap menthol cigarette instead of an FBI agent, it will be harder for him to spot me."

"We better hit the road, so let's gear up and head out."

We all walked back to Clarke's car and he popped open his trunk. Stored inside was an impressive array of expensive vests, brand-new rifles, shiny handguns, and several non-lethal tasers. As a courtesy, Riley and Clarke offered us firearms, but we respectfully declined. Instead, Ed and I chose to commandeer two bulletproof vests and two small tasers.

We all geared up and loaded ourselves into the car. Clarke drove us south for several minutes before turning west and landing at an empty convenience store parking lot. Surrounding the small store was a robust neighborhood littered with three-story houses sporting pristine yards covered with luscious green grass.

"If the good white residents here see three black people walking around, I'm certain they will call the cops," I lamented.

"Just imagine if Bingo Dorrell sees us. You know he will get suspicious."

"Nuria, that's why we all are staying inside the car."

"The house is just right across the street," he said while pointing.

"There are three other agents in the house. Once he goes inside, they will arrest him. When they detain him, we will all come in and take him away. Easy money, my friend."

"What if he sees us parked here in front of this empty store?" Ed asked. "It won't be hard for him to see a car filled with agents sitting across the street from the house."

Riley shook his head in frustration and glared back at Ed with a look of annoyance. I could tell that he didn't particularly care for our line of questioning. Riley received our legitimate concerns as personal attacks and I could feel him loading his sarcasm to punch back at us.

"Bingo isn't coming all the way out here just to buy candy from a mom & pop convenience store, Ed."

"He's here to have sex with a twelve-year-old girl. That's what he's after and that's what the hell he's gonna try and do."

"Once he walks through the front door, we got his ass. Trust me, this guy is going straight for the door. He's done this sort of thing before. He believes these girls' parents are away from home, so he'll be in a hellva hurry. The FBI is a competent agency and we know what the hell we're doing, guys."

Riley rolled his eyes at us and turned his attention towards the car's service radio. He adjusted the feed signal before pushing the broadcast button and ordering all of us to don our earpieces. I inserted my earpiece and immediately heard the low voices of several other FBI agents peppering us with updates. From the pace of the conversation, I knew that Bingo had to be on foot with two undercovers tailing behind him. The mental image of Bingo walking down the street with two out-of-place white males tailing behind him pissed me off. This was amateur hour and Agent Riley should have known better. A professional White Extremist like Bingo would most certainly notice two strange white men following him.

"Why is the FBI following him on foot Riley," I blasted. "This is dumb as fuck!"

"If Bingo participated in a high-profile assassination...he'd be stupid not to notice he's being followed."

Purposely ignoring me, Riley spoke into his microphone in a hushed tone, dismissing the notion of even responding to my concerns. Sensing my impatience, Clarke looked at me and tried to calm me down with a nervous smile and a gentle knee squeeze. Frustrated, I reached into my pocket and pulled out a pair of handcuffs and tossed them into Ed's lap.

"They're about to fuck this up," I murmured. "Get yourself ready, Ed. I'm literally going to need another hand tonight."

"One block away," a voice spoke into their radio.

The inside of the car went silent and everyone's eyes were focused as we peered out of the front windshield, examining the dark roadway ahead of us. After several tense minutes, a shadowy figure was seen slowly walking down the wide walkway. We all went still inside the car as the figure came closer. It was a man; a white man to be exact. His hands were in his pockets as he strolled at a slow pace. The male figure stopped walking several houses down from the sting location and pulled out a hand-held computer. While typing, I noticed him turning his head and looking behind him, almost as if he was checking his surroundings.

"Bingo's on to us, Riley. We need to move now," I whispered from the back seat.

"We wait, Nuria," he firmly rebuked.

Riley whispered into his microphone, informing everyone that we had a visual on Bingo and ordering the following agents to disengage.

Seconds later, a squeaky female voice blasted through my earpiece. It was one of the agents in the house and I could hear the concern in her voice.

"Bingo just asked if I wanted some beer and chips."

"He says he's about to make a quick stop at the corner store. Where are you guys parked Riley?"

I saw Clarke's eyes widen as Riley began to stutter. The tension-filled stillness that had once dominated the inside of the car quickly devolved into a surge of chaos and nervous movements. Bingo Dorrell put away his hand-held computer and started walking directly towards us. I knew that once Bingo saw that the small store was closed, he would rightfully become suspicious when he noticed our car sitting alone in this parking lot. Riley's incompetence was about to blow apart this whole sting, so I knew I had to take control.

"Clarke give me your pack of cigarettes," I demanded.

Clarke looked back at me with a puzzled stare. I could feel the conflict in his spirit. He knew I was right. Clarke knew we needed to act, but his loyalty and underlaying fear of his white partner had paralyzed him into a state of uselessness. Pissed off, I reached towards his shoulder and pushed him, making my best attempt to shake him out of his inaction.

"Gimme the damn cigarettes, Clarke, come on!"

Filled with apprehension, Clarke reluctantly reached into his pocket and handed over the smokes. For good measure, I snatched Clarke's baseball cap from his nappy head and donned it. I tapped Ed on his leg, telling him to follow my lead before instructing Riley to stay inside the car no matter what happens. Opening my door, I exited the car and Ed cautiously followed as we walked towards the front entrance of the store. We needed a distraction, something wild and crazy that would surely mislead a seasoned White Extremist like Bingo Dorrell. I balled up my lonely fist and began to pound away on the store's front entrance. Amid my manufactured chaos, Bingo turned the corner and I saw him slow his pace as he stared at me with amused confusion. With one final punch, I leaned myself into the blow and felt the cheap glass window blister with cracks.

"Come on, get ya gun ready," I yelled at Ed.

"You know, robbing a corner market in this white neighborhood ain't very smart little lady," Bingo laughingly opined as he drove his hands into his coat pockets.

I turned towards Bingo, smoothly slipping my pistol out of its holster as he came into full view. For a brief second, our eyes met and we examined each other, sizing each other up like two different species of apex predators in the wild. Under the moon-lit night sky, his eyes had a bright blueish tint to them. Unlike the Yerba Buena Island video, Bingo's hair was slicked back and neat. His frame appeared a bit thicker and I could tell he had gained a few pounds since that last pizza parlor video. It was clear that Bingo had come upon money between both videos and now. Whoever had paid Bingo had paid him handsomely.

"Who the hell are you, white boy?" I loudly demanded.

"I own this place, sweetheart," he shot back while revealing his silver handgun.

"If you black junkies think you're about to rob my place, you damn sure got another thing coming, I tell ya."

My distraction was working. Instead of stumbling upon Riley's poorly planned sting, Bingo instead thought he had walked right into an opportunity. An easy opportunity to take advantage of a couple of drug-addicted Zebras.

"I've already notified the cops, little lady," he continued. "And I got both of your black asses on camera, so killing me or running away ain't gonna help."

110

I wasn't at all surprised that he was lying. I was just astonished at the ease and supreme confidence at which the twisted lies left Bingo's lips. He had no idea that this black woman he was trying to con was already on to his scheme. Satisfied that Bingo had taken the bait, I slowly put my gun on the ground and glanced over at Ed. A brief flash of shock blasted from Ed's eyes as he looked down at my gun. I snuffled loudly, pulling Ed's attention away from my vulnerability and refocusing him on his task. Begrudgingly, Ed slowly followed suit and placed his pistol on the ground. It was now time to mislead Bingo into my trap.

"We ain't trying to break in," I offered.

"I'm just pissed the place is closed. This is the only store in this neighborhood and I don't have time to drive all the way downtown to go find a place that's open this late."

"I just need to buy a lighter, a soda, and one Blue Ice cigar, sir. Can you open the door and let us get it? We got the money to pay you for the stuff. I swear, we do."

Bingo smiled before laughing loudly and pointing his silver gun directly at my head. I felt my heart skip a beat as Bingo stared into my surrendering soul from behind his pistol's front site. I knew that Bingo had taken my ridiculous request as an insult to his intelligence. If he were the owner, he'd be an idiot to allow us inside after catching us attempting to break in. I was sure that thought was running through his mind as he aimed his gun at my head.

"Look, we'll just leave, man," Ed jumped in.

"We don't want no trouble."

I coolly reached into my pocket and pulled out Clarke's smokes. Using my only hand, I flipped open the box and used my tongue and mouth to pull out a single cigarette. Bingo continued to fix his gaze on me with curious eyes while maintaining his aim. Feeling his curiosity, I decided to continue and dominate the moment.

'Since you ain't gonna let me buy anything, can you at least light my cigarette for free?"

'How about I let you both live instead," Bingo rang back.

He lowered his gun and the smile on his face disappeared as he fished around in his pocket. Finding a lighter, Bingo held it up so we could examine it before gently tossing it at me. Reaching up with my lonely hand, I caught his gift and snatched it out of the air. Sparking a flame, I lit the cigarette and took a puff. My tender lungs instantly sent my bewildered brain its forceful objections, which made me fight like hell to contain the natural urge to cough.

'We're more than fine with leaving my man. We really are...We just don't want no problems, that's all," Ed responded.

'No one is leaving until I'm reimbursed for that window you broke," Bingo bristled.

'It's either we work something out between all three of us, or I'll wait here and let the cop's figure this mess out. Your choice, little lady."

Bingo glared at me with a devious expression that immediately betrayed his sinister motivations. I knew what was on his mind and the mere thought absolutely repulsed me. If this filthy bastard was capable of raping an underage girl, taking sexual advantage of a black disabled drug addict would be par for the course. For Bingo, sex was a means of exerting some sense of power and dominance. Looking at him as he stared back at me with hidden delight in his eyes sickened me to the core. I took my cigarette out of my mouth and blew smoke at him, passively venting the revengeful thoughts clouding my spirit.

'How much is this shitty window gonna cost me?" I asked. 'All of this is going to cost you something money can't buy," Bingo began. 'But I'm sure your pretty little ass has what it takes to make this all disappear forever."

"By the way....for some reason, you look real familiar to me little lady. Where have we met before?", he half asked.

Bingo once again aimed his gun on me and closed the distance, stopping several feet outside of my reach. Sensing him examining me, I looked down at the ground to avoid his curious eyes. Ed stepped towards us and Bingo pointed his gun at him, causing Ed to go still.

"Come any closer and I'll pop your ass boy."

"This is between me and the smoking beauty here."

"Step back Ed," I ordered. "Stay cool. I got this."

Ed backed away and leaned against the wall. He let out a heavy sigh and I could see the frustration and concern in his body language. Inside of the car, Clarke and Riley looked out at us with mortified expressions. I gave them both an eye wink in the hopes of calming their surging concern. Bingo pointed his gun at a set of trash dumpsters on the other side of the property and began to bark out commands.

"We'll go work this out over there behind those dumpsters, little lady," Bingo instructed.

Nodding my head, I turned towards the smelly dumpsters while Bingo followed close behind with his gun pointed at my back. We walked behind the dumpsters and I heard Bingo unzip his trousers. Immediately, I felt him violently push me with the barrel of his gun. As I fell forward, I lost my balance and landed on the nasty milk-stained concrete. Unable to break the fall using my only arm, my body hit the ground hard and I felt the stinging sensation of scraped skin underneath my chin.

"You'll need to stay on your knees for this payoff, sweetheart."

"The cops will be here any minute now, so you don't have a whole lotta time to give me your best performance. All tongue, no teeth, and not one drop hits the ground, or I'll blow your head clean off."

"Besides... If you do a good job, I may even share a little coke with you."

I could feel the anger inside of me beginning to explode. Bingo's disrespect made me thirst to kill him, but I knew I needed to play along just a little longer. This is exactly where I wanted Bingo, he had fallen for my trap, and he would soon pay a painful price. Forcing tears to fall from my eyes, I crawled up to my knees and shuffled towards Bingo's waist. As I neared him, he smiled down at me, reached into his underwear with his hand and began fondling himself. As my face neared his crotch, I reached into my pocket and pulled out the small hand-held taser.

In one swift motion, I jammed the prongs into his exposed scrotum. In a fit of fury, I mashed down hard on the trigger. His pistol fell on my armless shoulder as the force of the electric jolt caused Bingo to drop his weapon. Hearing Bingo's gun bounce on the concrete behind me, I pressed the taser into his nuts harder and watched the light blue sparks dance around his crotch.

Bingo stumbled backwards before falling flat on his back, causing his head to ricochet off the hard concrete as his body hit the ground. He yelled out in pain while both of his hands held onto his family jewels for dear life. I rose to my feet and picked up his gun before walking towards his collapsed body. Standing over him, I reared back and kicked him in his damn mouth, venting my frustration out on his decaying brown teeth.

"You're lucky I remembered I had the taser, because I was planning on biting your little shit off asshole. My cigarette was bigger than you. You should be embarrassed"

Ed came rushing up to me with his gun in hand, followed by a panic-stricken Riley and an angry Clarke. Noticing that Bingo had already been incapacitated, Ed quickly holstered his gun and pulled out his handcuffs.

Ed and Clarke flipped Bingo over on his stomach before pulling his arms behind his back and applying the cuffs. Riley stood next to me, watching the men as they patted Bingo down, removing several condoms, a stash of erectile enhancement pills, and his hand-held computer.

"Are you OK, Nuria?" he asked. "I'm fine, Riley. Thanks for staying put and trusting me."

"Well, our whole sting operation just failed," he whispered. "We won't be able to arrest Bingo. We don't have anything on him because he didn't go inside the house. So, we'll probably have to let him go for now."

I looked right at Riley and laughed in his fuckin face before purposely rolling my eyes. His desperation was obvious, too damn obvious. The FBI didn't have anything on Bingo, but the Foundational Colony of Oakland, California, sure as hell did. I raised my chin and pointed towards the bleeding strawberry.

"Unfortunately for you, Riley, I do have something on Bingo."

"Bingo assaulted a Foundational. A Foundational that also happens to be a commissioned Force Protection agent."

"Both crimes are a felony under Foundational Law, so I'm hereby requesting that the FBI assist in the extradition of Bingo Dorrell. We need to bring him back to our colony to stand trial for his crimes against Black America."

"Hell, no," Riley objected. "That's not part of the plan."

"Bingo needs to go back to Yerba Buena Island. This is supposed to be an FBI collar....You and Ed are just here to back us up, Nuria."

"Per the Constitutional Amendment in the Reparations Treaty," I rudely rebutted. "The federal government is obligated to accommodate our extradition requests if it involves a felony. Do you really want to take this to the circuit courts, Riley?"

Realizing he had been outmaneuvered, Riley threw his head back in frustration and walked away from me in anger. The sight of Riley being upset and emotional pleased me immensely. Satisfied that we had won, I walked over to Bingo as he stood up with his hands restrained behind his back. He winced in pain as Clarke pulled up his soiled underwear. After zipping up his pants, I calmly read him his rights while he looked down at me with eyes filled with malice.

"Bingo Dorrell, do you understand the rights Foundational Black Americans have afforded you?" I concluded.Without notice, I watched Bingo's mouth open and I felt a warm stream of his spit hit my forehead and began to run down the side of my face. Unbothered by his response, I used the back of my lonely hand to wipe away his nasty offense.

"Take his ass to the car," I instructed.

Pissed off, Ed sucker punched Bingo in his stomach before leading him away. As Clarke and Ed disappeared around the corner with Bingo, Riley approached me while staring into his hand-held computer.

"According to the terms in the Reparations Treaty, your Governor needs to submit an extradition request to the FBI in writing," Riley read aloud.

"So, as of right now, there is no formal request for us to honor."

"Do you really want me to call, Gary Freeman, the hardliner? Gary Freeman, the acting Governor of the Oakland Reparation's Colony," I mockingly asked. "I'll be sure to tell Gary that when he talks to the Director of the FBI, he should inform the Director that your little sting operation failed. I'll also tell him exactly why and that I was about two seconds away from sucking a white dick to save your sorry ass."

"Is that what you want Riley?"

Riley turned off his computer and walked away without saying a word. It was then that I realized why Riley had been permanently assigned to protection details. Riley was an awful FBI agent and a white man, who housed within him, a lot of internal weaknesses. We all piled into the car and I directed Clarke to take us straight to our Foundational Force Protection building.

Ed contacted Dennis to make arrangements to book Bingo and prepare an interrogation room. I called our colony's best hotel to book two rooms for Riley and Clarke. It had already been a long day for all of us, and interrogating Bingo was sure to keep us busy for at least a few more hours. I knew that providing the tired men a place to catch some sleep would go a long way towards maintaining our already tortured peace.

Clarke landed us in front of the Force Protection building and we all looked towards the front entrance. Dennis stood outside with several heavily armed agents at his side. As Ed opened his door, the group of men walked up and helped us pull a yelling Bingo out of the trunk of the car.

"Ed, you and the FBI folks can take Bingo inside and book him," Dennis instructed. "There are agents standing by at the booking station."

"Nuria, I need you to stay out here with me for a minute."

Riley looked at me and Dennis, giving us a stare of mistrust before following the group towards the building. The group escorted a limping Bingo while Dennis and I stood by in silence until they all disappeared from view. Once we were alone, Dennis motioned for me to follow him, and we walked towards a picnic area adjacent to the building.

"I talked to Gary and he had me make some last-minute arrangements."

"He wanted to make sure that you and Mary Ann Haskins had a little chat before you interrogated Bingo tonight," Dennis admitted.

"I also have something I need to tell you, Nuria."

Dennis stopped walking and looked directly into my eyes. He cleared his throat and stuffed his hands into his pockets before aimlessly kicking at a harmless blade of grass in front of him. Dennis was uncomfortable. Whatever he needed to tell me was not going to be good news.

"Before you sink your teeth into all this Nuria, you ought to have some background on what happened."

"Bingo Dorrell is not just one of Mary Ann's paid snitches. Bingo Dorrell is a go-between for us."

"A go-between...for us. What the hell does that mean, Dennis?" I asked

"That means we need to be careful about questioning this guy Nuria."

"When Governor Williams named me the head of technical development, one of the secret objectives she assigned to me was to find ways to spy on the Dominant Society."

"My department has been hacking into their databases and monitoring their secure communications."

"In order to do it, we've been using White Extremists like Bingo not just as paid informants...but also as partners. We exchanged food, transferred money, and shared Intel with Bingo and his White Extremist contacts. We used them for their services outside of our colony, and they used us for our technological savvy."

"Racist mercenaries like Bingo have been our delivery boys. Mary Ann was Bingo's liaison. She would perform pickups and bring back Intel that allowed us to penetrate the Dominant Societies firewalls."

Dennis's admission floored me. It took several seconds to make sure I had interpreted his words correctly. The thought of Foundationals working hand in hand with violent Anti-Black terrorists instantly conjured up feelings of betrayal. Sensing my anger, Dennis quickly raised the palms of his hands in front of me, urging me to stay cool.

"Nuria, I need you to hear me out," he pressured.

"Patrice and Vincent both knew all about this."

"Besides, there was no way I could have done any of this without the approval of the Governor or the FP Secretary."

I turned away from Dennis, ignoring his pleas for me to hear him out.

At that moment, all the years of trust Dennis had built with me washed away. This was treason of the highest order. To work alongside the Dominant Society was hard enough, but to work with the White Extremists themselves was an unforgivable sin. I walked towards a picnic table and my mind raced while I tried to somehow rationalize how Governor Patrice Williams, a woman I respected and loved, had secretly worked with our sworn enemy.

"It sorta stings when you first hear it, doesn't it, Nuria?" A voice from the foliage proclaimed.

Mary Ann Haskins walked from behind a tall row of hedges and sat down on the picnic table in front of me. I saw her silver FP badge on her waist that shined like the North Star under the moonlit sky. Mary Ann had noticeably aged since the last time I saw her. The bright glow of a young black woman, fresh out of college and chomping at the bit to take on the world, had noticeably dimmed. Now the look in her eyes was one of a tortured and well-seasoned soul. Mary Ann's fingers scratched in between her tight braids before pulling out her Chapstick and applying it to her bottom lip. She was still a beautiful black woman, but the stress and commitment this job required were clearly taking it's toll on her.

"It broke my heart when Vincent asked me to work with Bingo Dorrell," Mary Ann explained.

"There was no way I wanted to do something like that, Nuria. I mean...I grew up idolizing what you, Donovan, and Pernell had done at Dry Tortugas."

"I didn't become an FP agent to work with these Extremists."

"Yet, Vincent sat me down and explained why I needed to do this crap. They told me that this was critical to the survival of our colony. So, I agreed to do it despite my own concerns."

I slowly moved to the picnic table and sat next to a despondent Mary

Ann. Dennis came up behind me, leaning against the table while we all quietly trapped ourselves in our inner thoughts. In this damnable game of high-stakes politics, where every group seems to have some hidden motive, Mary Ann's words rung true. Like me, Mary Ann was a loyal servant trying her best to protect her people.

Mary Ann had the unenviable task of looking a mortal enemy in his demonic eyes and having to hold her peace. Each time having to summon courage and using endless rationalizations to face our demon in this quest to meet our godly objective. As a child, Mary Ann may have idolized the notion of me, but now she had begun to realize that behind every heroic narrative was a hidden trail of pain and sacrifice. Wanting to somehow empathize with her, I took Clarke's cigarettes out of my pocket and offered her a smoke. She kindly declined, wearing a polite smile that cleverly distracted from the tears welling in her eyes.

"Who was Bingo getting all this Intel from?" I asked. "Do you know who the source is?"

"No, I never knew," she admitted. "Nuria, I honestly don't know."

"Secretary Vincent doesn't even know, the entire FP Department was kept in the dark."

"The only person who might have known the source was Governor Williams and now she's gone."

"A few weeks after Vincent asked me to start doing this," Mary Ann continued. "Vincent and I made sure we had Bingo followed. We were curious and wanted to make sure we hadn't fallen for some sort of trick bag."

"Before every meeting with me, Bingo would stop at Bernal Heights Park and pick up an envelope of raw data. Usually, the envelopes would have passwords and data drives in them, but sometimes there would be photos and drawings."

"Bingo is a veteran White Extremist mercenary and has accumulated a variety of enemies over the years. For safety reasons, I purposely would meet Bingo at public places in Oakland or Emeryville. San Francisco was simply too risky; black faces tend to stand out on that side of the bay anyway."

"The drops have been occurring randomly for about three years now," she described.

"About two years ago, Dennis discovered cyber Intel that the FBI was actively tracking and monitoring Bingo. At the time, we weren't sure if they had stumbled upon us meeting with Bingo, so we discussed stopping the drops with Governor Williams."

"After a long discussion with her and Secretary Vincent Towns, Governor Williams ordered us to do whatever we could to mitigate the risk and continue with the drops."

Mary Ann's voice cracked and spiked with emotion as the words left her lips. I could almost envision the mental images of that meeting with Governor Williams replaying in her mind as she wiped away her tears. Sensing the importance Mary Ann had placed on that meeting, I began to suspect that Governor Williams decision to continue with the drops had ultimately been a fatal one.

"She was killed because of these drops," I mumbled to myself.

"Mary Ann, do you have any idea why Governor Williams wanted you to continue with the drops?" I calmly asked.

"She didn't explain anything beyond telling us that the information the drops provided was critical and we needed it. Yet, she did mention that even if the FBI were on to Bingo, his operating out of Bernal Heights Park would make the Dominant Society think twice about fucking with him."

Patrice may have been right about that. Bernal Heights Park is a so-called liberated LGBTQXYVER terrorist haven known for its not-so-secret child sex rings. Sick white bastards into all types of child fetishes flocked to Bernal Heights Park to engage in their own disgusting brand of illegal pleasure. Included in this horde of crazies were prominent members of San Francisco's government, business, and media society. During my time on the FP teams, I would routinely come across Intel showing Dominant Society judges and business executives hosting illegal child sex orgy parties at the park.

If I could find evidence like that, then it was almost certain that the vengeful White Extremists living outside of the city had also discovered it. For them, seeing their more liberal white kinsmen live in utter decadence while their own racist families suffered and starved out in the rural outskirts of California had to sting. Getting the dirt on their white liberal cousins was critical to the survival of the White Extremists. For the White Extremist like Bingo, useful blackmail was often the difference between having food to eat or your extremist family going hungry. Having Bingo keep tabs on any and every prominent figure indulging in the sin fest at Bernal Heights Park would have been a matter of routine for us as Foundational intelligence officers. Hence the reason why us having a hired White Extremist merchant walking around that park would not raise any eyebrows at the FBI field office.

What would certainly raise eyebrows was the idea that Foundationals would ally with those same Extremist groups. Not merely paying for information, but engaging in the act of mutual intelligence sharing. It's one thing to simply pay a white informant or mercenary and totally another if two competing entities share intelligence. That means they both have some mutual interest or common goal they have deemed important enough to risk the collaboration.

"Governor Williams was killed because of that source, I know it," I opined. "Keeping those drops going was reckless and Governor

Williams was not the type of person to engage in recklessness."

"We have to do whatever we can to find out who this source is, and we must find out before the FBI does. Something tells me that they could care less about getting justice for Governor Williams. What the FBI is really after is our Intel and our memory cells."

"Well, Nuria," Dennis jumped in. "You and Mary Ann better get inside and start questioning Bingo before the FBI pulls all that information out of his head."

"Other than Governor Williams, Bingo is the only person who could potentially identify our Intel sources."

"Yeah Dennis, but Mary Ann shouldn't come inside with me," I replied.

"If Riley sees her, he'll try and find a way to question her as well."

"The FBI is fixated on gaining access to our memory cells. Hell, this entire murder investigation just seems like a convenient excuse to allow them to steal Intel from us."

"We can't allow the FBI to access our database," Dennis explained. "Besides all the secrets we have on the Dominant Society and the White Extremists, the cells could also contain very damaging Intel on elected officials within our own ranks."

"If any of those secrets got out, there would be unrest within our colony for sure."

"And that's exactly why the FBI desperately wants to access our memory cells," Mary Ann chimed in. "For years, we Foundationals have successfully pitted the White Extremists against their liberal cousins in the Dominant Society."

"Now the Dominant Society is seeking to gain more leverage in this Mexican Standoff. Knowledge is power, and this is all an attempt to grab more power."

Mary Ann stood up from the picnic table and reached into her pocket.

She pulled out a small flash drive and handed it to me before walking over towards Dennis. There was a label on the flash drive that read FP files, Bingo Dorrell, along with several dates printed underneath it.

"Those FBI agents are gonna demand some sort of information on my interactions with Bingo," she explained. "We'll have to provide them with something or risk them going to the courts to get it."

"On this flash drive are dummy files we have on Bingo. Most of the information and documents are useless, but there is enough paperwork saved on this thing to keep the FBI busy for a little while."

Staring at that flash drive as it sat in my hand caused a tide of anger to swell up within me. Disgusted, I took Mary Ann's flash drive and threw it on the ground before stomping it into pieces with the bottom of my foot. If I wasn't playing along with the FBI, I sure as hell wouldn't play along with these two either. In this situation, no one could be trusted. I wasn't here to play either side's spy games. I was here to find out who killed my friend, Patrice Williams.

"I don't want your damn dummy files on Bingo," I began. "I want you to cut the BS and come straight up the middle with me, Mary Ann. I need to see the real files on Bingo, and I wanna see the information he was passing along to Governor Williams."

"When you have all of that, then you can come back to me with a real flash drive and not some time-wasting tactic."

Mary Ann looked at me with a face drenched in quiet fury. I could tell that she hadn't planned on me not playing along. I didn't give a damn about sparing anyone's ass from embarrassment. In my mind, if you worked with the White Extremist, you were suspect as hell.

"Oh, by the way," I added. "The FBI has video of Bingo and a Black suspect delivering a sofa to the mansion four months before Governor Williams was assassinated."

"They believe that the Black suspect is a Foundational and that's another reason they want to access our memory cells. Sooner or later, they are going to find out who this guy is. If they do and they discover that he's indeed a Foundational, the California courts will give the FBI the keys to Fort Knox, so we better get ahead of them."

"God forbid the FBI finds out the man's affiliated with hardliners. If that happens, we are all screwed."

I pulled a disc out of my pocket and handed it to Dennis. He took it and quickly stashed it away inside of his coat while Mary Ann boiled with anger. This was my investigation. Whether they wanted to or not, we were going to find out the truth, no matter how ugly it might be.

I walked away from them both, leaving them in a state of confusion. I wasn't sure if they were on my team and I knew they, in turn, weren't sure if I was on theirs. That was exactly the situation I wanted.

The interior of the FP building was cold and well lit, which gave it a feel of a hospital. Two officers waiting at the front desk walked me down a long hallway towards Bingo's interrogation room. In the room, Bingo sat chained to a heavy metal table, facing Ed and Clarke, who both were sitting across from him. Riley stood behind Bingo, leaning himself up against the wall as the three men talked. I opened the door and walked into the room. They stopped their conversation immediately when they saw me and everyone's eyes examined me as I grabbed a spare stool and planted myself next to Ed.

"How the hell are you allowing her in here to question me," Bingo yelled. "If she's gonna press charges against me, then she can't be in here. What type of fucked up law operation are you people running?"

"We won't have to press any charges if you just cooperate with us," Clarke responded.

'If you tell us what we need to know, there is probably a good chance you leave outta here a free man today."

Bingo burst into laughter before taking a sip out of his smoldering coffee. As Bingo amused himself, I could see the growing annoyance in Riley's body language. We all knew that Bingo Dorrell wasn't going to talk without other influences. The mutual mistrust that filled the interrogation room was omnipresent and Bingo, the well-seasoned criminal, knew the law better than all of the lawyers in San Francisco combined.

"There will be no fuckin cooperation from me, buddy. Not until I talk to my attorney first," Bingo informed Clarke. 'You can make up all these lies about me molesting little girls. If you got evidence of it, you better arrest...otherwise I want my lawyer."

'OK, Bingo," I jumped in. 'Let's cut the shit."

'Everybody in here knows that we ain't here because you like underage girls. As a Foundational, I could care less what you white folks do to each other anyway."

'Plus, the FBI isn't going to condemn you for doing something they routinely turn a blind eye to."

'We are here because everyone wants to know what you were doing at Bernal Heights Park. Everyone here seems to have a vested interest in who you were meeting there."

'We also want to know who helped you deliver that sofa to Yerba Buena Island. We have a video of you and a black man delivering a sofa to the mansion. A sofa that FBI experts tell us was the source of the explosion that killed Governor Williams."

'If you help us with all of this Bingo, we can make sure no one will know about you working with Black people or soliciting sex from little girls online."

'And, of course, we can make it worth your while," I teased.

Bingo's eyes gave me a flicker of shock and discomfort as his mind processed my words. I had thrown everything on the wall and something had stuck. When I looked over Bingo's shoulder, I noticed that Riley had stopped leaning on the wall. His posture was tense as he bit down hard on his bottom lip, almost forcing himself into a state of silence. He, too, had heard words that caused him discomfort.

"So Foundationals are officially admitting to paying White Extremists Nuria," Clarke blasted. "And you hypocrites have the nerve to call me a Zebra."

"It's not like you guys haven't been paying him too Clarke," I shot back. "Am I right, Bingo?"

Bingo reached down and once again grabbed his coffee cup, pretending to ignore my question. His actions confirmed what I suspected. Bingo Dorrell was only loyal to Bingo Dorrell. White Extremists like him had created a market for ideological shapeshifters who would lend support to the highest bidder. In an interrogation room filled with potential paychecks, I knew that Bingo's predictable selfishness would make him fold.

"So, Bingo, you're the man with all the information. How much will it cost to get you to talk to us without your bothersome attorney?"

I took a piece of scratch paper from Ed and borrowed Clarke's pen. After scribbling down a number, I slid it across the table and put it in front of Bingo. I stared him down as he studied the number. His eyes flicked again and he seemed to pause in a moment of deep thought. Then Bingo suddenly brushed the paperback at me in apparent disgust.

"I may be a snitch. Some of my friends living outside of the city may even call me a white traitor. In the end, I'm a white man that is willing to do anything to feed my family. Yet there is one thing I ain't, and that is a cheap white traitor little lady," he confidently responded.

"Well, let me try then," Ed smoothly broke in while taking the paper and pen for himself.

Ed drew a line through my number and proceeded to jot down his own dollar figure before tossing the paperback to Bingo. Bingo eagerly looked down at the number and I saw his eyes widen as he struggled to contain the smile that fought its way on his face. Ed had done it. We had him and Riley knew it as he jammed his fists into his pockets.

"You Foundationals must be really fuckin serious," Bingo stated while folding the proposal in half. "I can't guarantee that I have all the answers you need, but I want a guarantee that if I do cooperate, I will get paid and that the knowledge of my assistance won't leave this room."

Ed took his keys and uncuffed Bingo from the table. A victorious smile swept across Bingo's face. The metal jingling sound of the handcuffs echoed throughout the room as Ed removed his restraints before tossing them on the table.

"Your move Bingo Dorrell," Ed demanded. 'We're all ears."

"First, let's start with this Bernal Heights thing," he began. "I'm sorry to inform you and your gay loving FBI buddies, but I have never seen this source."

"Whoever this person is, they would contact me on the dark web and pose as a juvenile prostitute. On the dark web, they would tell me when to go to Bernal Heights and who to meet there, so that's what I did. I just followed their orders."

"When I arrive, I would look for the child. Maybe they would be Black or Hispanic or Asian depending on what the source told me to look for."

"I gave the kid some money and he, in turn, gave me an envelope. It was that simple."

"How did this source first contact you, Bingo?" I broke in.

128

"They contacted me like all you secret squirrels usually do," he explained with contempt.

"I was just getting out of jail and I needed money. Some low-budget lawyer visited me after I was released and recommended a temp agency his buddy ran."

"I went there and applied for a few jobs, and boom...Out of nowhere, one of them replied and I started working."

"I never got the chance to meet my employer, they would just ask me to run a few errands, and if I did the work, my money would show up in my bank account."

"Did you ever look inside any of those envelopes, Bingo? I find it extremely hard to believe that you didn't get the least bit curious about this new employment that magically fell into your lap."

My question caused Bingo to take a long stare at me, patiently sizing me up in the high-stakes game that was surely playing out inside of his head. I met his eyes with my own focused gaze and without blinking, I quietly waited for my answer. Although a snitch, Bingo Dorrell still sympathized with White Extremism and openly identified as a White Supremacist. It must have been obvious to him that he was illegally transferring something from the Dominant Society to our colony. It would be reasonable to assume that Bingo would try and take advantage of the situation for his own group and I kept that in mind.

Bingo grabbed his coffee and swallowed the entire cup in three large gulps. His right leg nervously twitched underneath the table, which also caught the attention of the ever-observant Riley. My experience told me that Bingo would tell me if he had looked inside the envelopes, but his answer would be a large serving of half-truths, small facts surrounded and concealed by a mountain of lies.

"Yeah, I did once," he softly admitted. "I opened one envelope and all

I found was a picture of farmland up in Napa Valley and a few discs. At first, I thought my employer had hired me as a drug runner, so I opened the envelope to see what kinda drugs I was dealing with."

"All of the envelopes are pneumatically sealed. I didn't realize that until I opened it and punctured the seal. I had a hellva time trying to reseal the damn thing before I was supposed to drop it off," Bingo vented.

"After that, I never opened another damn envelope. It wasn't worth it. There was nothing of value in them. Screwing up an easy payday over some old discs and a picture of farmland wasn't worth it. Hell, I was amused that someone would pay me so much money to deliver a picture that they could have printed online, but hey, you secret squirrel fuckers are weird."

Bingo was full of shit and I could tell that he was playing dumb. White Supremacists are masters at projecting fake ignorance when caught in a jam. It's one of their favorite tactics. I knew there was some truth to his statement, but he had purposely made it hard to distinguish where the truth ended and his misleading lie began. It was better to assume that Bingo had opened every envelope and knew exactly what he was delivering. In all likelihood, that's exactly what he had done.

Correctly sensing the rampant mistrust within the interrogation room, Bingo turned around in his chair and looked up at Riley. He cracked a smile and shook his head as Riley stood quiet in his defiance. The Bingo show was about to really kick-off. He had found the perfect scapegoat and was about to throw the FBI under the bus.

"If you want to know what was in those envelopes, how about you ask this queer loving cuckold," Bingo barked. "The FBI sure as hell knew what was in them and that's why they started following me. I knew you bastards were watchin."

"Kiss my ass, you racist prick," Riley shot back. "We followed you because you like to build bombs meant to kill innocent gay people."

Bingo laughed and grabbed the handcuffs that sat on the table. He raised them towards Riley's face in a mocking effort to try and hand them to him. Clarke shot up from his chair, loudly demanding that Bingo put the handcuffs down and answer our questions.

'If you have all this evidence that I built a bomb and killed faggots, then you need to arrest me. If you can't do that, then accept who you are, gay boy!"

Riley launched forward and slapped the cuffs out of Bingo's hand before kicking out the bottom of his chair. Bingo's body splashed as it hit the cold floor, creating a loud thud upon impact. Clarke jolted over and grabbed Riley, who was angrily punching down at Bingo with balled fists.

'Riley, calm the hell down, man!" Clarke shouted while muscling him away from Bingo.

Ed and I sat in amused silence as Bingo slowly gathered himself from the floor while Clarke feverishly pinned Riley up against the wall. Clarke opened a door and shoved Riley out of the interrogation room and then into the open hallway. Bingo collected himself and retook his seat across from us while blood dripped from his lip.

"You Foundational niggers puzzle me," he commented while wiping away the blood.

"You're filled with so much hate against whites like my buddies and I, simply because we are proud to be white."

"Yet, you work with and trust these liberal dick suckers. The FBI killed your black leaders, not us."

"These liberal cucks are the ones who use you for votes and work to keep you powerless. They are the ones who spy on you and try to control the internal politics of your race. They steal your music and art, then turn around and sell it back to you."

"They con you by pretending to support your reparations goals, but since the very first day you got them, these liberal dictators have constantly tried to undermine you Foundationals."

"Now you're here working with them to jam me up," Bingo blasted with pent-up anger in his voice.

"A defenseless white man that both of you have decided to oppress for no other reason besides the fact that I'm white and straight."

"Liberals like that freak outside come after our lifestyle, while you niggers come after us for money..."

"My question to you is, who is the slave and who is really the master between you two?"

"We aren't anybody's damn slave Bingo," Ed replied.

"Slaves can't set people free, like we just did for you. Those FBI boys you pissed off wanted to lock your white ass away forever."

I stood up from my stool and walked towards the door. Looking out of the window, I saw Clarke and Riley standing in the hallway, talking amongst themselves. Riley was still visibly angry and Clarke was doing his best to calm him down. Bingo's little racial sympathy speech was a clever ploy. He wanted to tell us something important, but needed assurances that we wouldn't share it with the FBI, so I decided to play ball with him. "Alright, Bingo," I proclaimed. "They'll be back in here soon."

"We'll play ball with your racist ass, but if you're lying to us, I promise we'll come to see you."

"Tell us about this black man who helped you deliver that couch and why you think he was FBI."

Bingo smiled and looked straight into my eyes before adjusting himself in his seat. I leaned myself against the door to let Bingo know that his words would stay between the three of us. He noticed me blocking the door, as he coughed into his hand, and cleared his throat before talking in a low voice.

'It's been so long that I don't even remember the guy's name," Bingo began.

'The temp agency reached out to me and asked if I was available for short-fuse work."

'Some damn moving company in San Francisco had a contract with the city to deliver furniture to the Yerba Buena mansion. They didn't have enough drivers on that day, so the temp agency reached out and asked if I needed work. I was broke and needed the cash, so I accepted."

'They gave me an address to some grocery store in South San Fran and told me to be there after lunch. I arrived and found a large moving truck parked all alone in an empty parking lot. Inside the truck sat a funny looking black man wearing shorts and flip flops, which was weird to me."

'Everything about this black man screamed government employee or agent, the Federal kind...or maybe even CIA," Bingo described.

'He was short and very skinny. His haircut was neat and his hands were moisturized and smooth...too smooth to be a man that worked with his hands for a living."

'When he talked, I could tell his accent wasn't from around here. He didn't seem like one of those Bay Area niggers," he lamented with a chuckle.

'His accent screamed East Coast. Probably New York or Philly."

'Despite all the warning signs, I decided to stay," Bingo admitted.

'The black man told me that we had to drive all the way up to Petaluma to pick up a few custom-made couches, so we did just that."

'We didn't talk much on the way up, and I did most of the driving because he admitted to not knowing where he was."

'Other than that, I did notice a sleeve tattoo on his left forearm.

It was a drawing of a fiery skeleton dressed in Army fatigues carrying a rifle. He was weird, really weird. I'd often hear him mumbling to himself while I was driving. It was almost like he was talking into a microphone or something."

"Where did you two pick up the couch?" I asked. "Some old wine farm outside of Petaluma," he replied.

"The place was completely ruined. I was surprised they were still operating. Outside of the property, I remember seeing a billboard of a large grape sitting on a pile of dirt. The billboard stuck out to me since everything around the place looked trashy."

"A white lady ushered us onto the property and several field workers helped us move the three couches into our truck. The only person that spoke to us was the white lady, which was strange."

"Was this white woman some sort of White Extremist like you?" Ed asked. "Hell no," he confidently answered. "She isn't one of us. I know who is on code with us and who isn't."

"With that blue hair and fat nose ring, she was definitely a cock sucking liberal. All those niggers and wetbacks at the farm acted like they were her pets."

"She ordered them around and talked down to them like dogs. It's white traitors like her that get a kick out of beastiality if you know what I mean."

"As soon as we loaded the couches into the truck, I got us the fuck outta there. The place was a real freak show and I wanted no parts of it. All this FBI shit about me planting a bomb in the couch is a big lie. I never did anything besides what I was paid to do that day."

"How about your black friend?" I jumped in. "Did he also find the farm strange?"

Bingo leaned back in his chair and sucked the blood from his busted lip.

I could almost see his mind racing, as he looked for the right words that would convey the sentiments of what he had experienced. After several seconds, he leaned forward and rested his elbows on the desk.

"Hell no. He was quiet the whole time and allowed me to do all the talking."

"On the way to Yerba Buena, he just sat in the car and drew a few diagrams. When he noticed I was looking at them, he hid them away in his pocket. He was one weird nigger."

I leaned down and picked up Ed's handcuffs off the floor before retaking my seat next to Ed. Bingo had told us what he wanted us to know. Although I didn't trust his racist ass, I believed him. Whoever this black man was, we needed to find him and look into his background, along with visiting that wine farm. Whatever was out there was of value to someone, and I needed to find out why.

"No bullshit, Bingo," I began. "Did you do anything to that couch after you guys loaded it into the truck?"

"No way, lady," he answered.

"I ain't involved in killing your Governor, no matter how bad the FBI wants to frame me. If we wanted to kill her black ass, we would have done so a long time ago, and you would have no doubt we did it."

"We loaded that couch into the truck and drove it to Yerba Buena, and that was all. We didn't stop anywhere. As soon as we arrived at the mansion, we carried it inside the house and left. If there was a bomb inside, I'm certain someone else put it there before we picked it up."

"I did what I was paid to do, and once it was done, we drove back to the grocery store parking lot and parted ways. The black man gave me my money and we never saw each other again."

I handed Ed the handcuffs and stood up to offer Bingo a friendly handshake for a job well done. Bingo accommodated and reached out, shaking my extended hand with a suppressed smile. When I felt his grip weaken around my hand, I grasped him tight, yanking him towards me. Ed quickly applied the handcuffs around his wrist and punched Bingo in his already bleeding mouth.

"What the hell, you lying bitch," he screamed as Ed locked his handcuffed hands. "We had a deal!"

"You're under arrest Bingo Dorrell," I dismissively responded. "You can remain silent now."

"To be honest, it's probably in your best interest that you stay here with us since you don't trust the Dominant Society. Who's to say that the FBI doesn't just kill you once you leave our colony?"

Ed drove his knee into Bingo's back as he laid on his stomach with his hands restrained behind his back. Ed's weight was all on Bingo, which caused him to curse loudly.

"Don't worry, Bingo. Our monetary deal with you still stands. We'll pay you once you leave our colony, but as of right now, you are under arrest for saying the word nigger on colonial territory."

"Per Colonial law, it is a class C Felony for any white person to use that word on Foundational controlled land. Class C Felonies are designated as violent hate crimes here. Unfortunately for you, Bingo, you used the word several times and we have it all recorded."

"I'll have our judge deny you bail so we can keep you here just in case I need to question you more. We can't afford to have you come up missing."

Out of the corner of my eye, I saw Riley and Clarke as they burst into the room. Both men stopped dead in their tracks once they noticed Bingo handcuffed on the floor. Ed jumped up and pulled Bingo to his feet, aggressively yanking down on his tight cuffs, causing Bingo's racist ass to wince in pain. Riley broke his stare away from Bingo and looked at me. I could see the fury in his eyes as he figured out what we were about to do.

"Nuria, can I see you outside for a moment?" Riley uttered through his forced calm.

Riley held the interrogation door open and I walked out into the hallway. After I was several steps away from the room, Riley slammed the door shut in frustration and came straight for me. As I saw him coming towards me, I refused to back down and stood myself up straight despite his obvious aggression.

"You're not about to keep Bingo here, Nuria. No fuckin way," he loudly whispered.

"We need to question him, and we intend to take him back to San Francisco. This is the FBI's investigation, not yours. You Foundationals are just here to assist us, so you better start understanding that, Nuria, or I'll personally put your ass in jail for obstruction of justice."

"Bingo violated our territorial laws," I calmly answered. "So, he stays."

"If you need to question him, you can make an appointment and we will allow you to do so."

"What pussy foot law did he break, Nuria? Not kissing enough Foundational ass?" he retorted with tons of sarcasm.

"Bingo Dorrell used the N-Word on colonial property....an offense we don't take lightly in these parts. It's a hate crime and Bingo must be punished for his transgression."

"If the FBI wants to arrest me for obstruction, then go right ahead. But keep in mind that it was our Governor who was killed while Senator Bean is still alive right now. Does the FBI really want to explain to the world why they are arresting Foundationals who are in pursuit of justice?"

I watched as Riley twitched as he failed to answer my question. He couldn't arrest me and he damn well knew it. Arresting me would only add fire to the media circus and automatically delegitimize any outcome the FBI delivered to the public. Not to mention the sharp wedge it would drive in between our leaders' diplomatic efforts.

"That's what I thought, Riley," I asserted.

Emboldened by my victory, I closed the distance with Riley and got right in his face. We were nose to nose, well within boundaries of personal comfort. I wanted this weak white bastard to feel my presence and my words.

"Riley. Next time you raise your voice at me, especially in my own territory...in my own home, you better be ready to defend yourself. Do you understand me?"

"I'm not here to play games. I'm here for the truth, and if you and your FBI buddies had anything to do with the murder of our Governor, your ass is mine. Get it."

Shaken, Riley stepped away from me, wiping my spittle off of his cherry red cheeks. In the background, I noticed Clarke open the door behind him and curiously peer out at us in the hallway. Unmoved, I stood my ground without flinching, waiting for Riley's response.

"So Black Foundationals are in the business of believing White Extremists over their white allies in the Dominant Society. Good to know..."

"We have no allies," I quickly responded. "We only have interests. Our only real ally is truth. I don't trust any of you damn white folks."

I felt a large hand grasp my shoulder, and I turned around to see Dennis standing behind me. He had a photo in his hand and the look on his face was an ominous one. In one motion, Dennis handed the photo to me while waving Ed and Clarke over towards us. I felt the presence of both men staring from behind me as I gazed down at the familiar black face in the photo. It was Bingo's suspicious moving partner, the black half of his couch delivery team. Under his image, I saw a name printed in bold white letters. It read Darius Royal, Foundational Black American, Oakland California Colony. Without words, I looked up at Dennis. It was hard to contain my shock and he easily predicted the questions running through my mind.

'I examined the video you gave me, Nuria. I found the identity of the other suspect, but there is something about this guy that is really weird."

'His name is Darius Royal and he's from our Oakland Colony. He's a Foundational, but there are a lot of missing or incomplete files on this guy."

'I have the address where he lived, but other than that, this guy is like a ghost."

'Lived?" I asked. 'What do you mean by where he lived?"

'Yeah, Nuria," Dennis continued. 'That's what's really troubling about all this."

'According to our records, Darius Royal is deceased. He's been dead for five years now."

CHAPTER FOUR

POT ROAST

RILEY SAT QUIETLY AS HE PENSIVELY twiddled his thumbs while Clarke eagerly recorded every word Darius's mother spoke. The confirmation that Darius Royal was a Foundational seemed to re-energize the pair. For three whole days, we staked out the Royal household, hoping that Darius Royal might show up and reveal himself to the world. Unfortunately for Riley, Darius never came and nothing about the Royal family's daily routine betrayed his hidden presence at the home. After a long conversation with Gary, he finally gave me permission to approach the Royal's and conduct an interview.

This was the exact opportunity the FBI had quietly hoped for. A chance to expose the long-existing divisions that were buried within our Foundational community. A Black Foundational's potential involvement in the assassination of Governor Williams would be big news worldwide. The shame of that accusation would undoubtedly embarrass us globally while at home, weakening us politically. Yet, during this entire interview, nothing seemed out of the ordinary or even remotely suspicious. The more questions Ed and I asked, the more visibly impatient Riley became.

Darius's mother, Martha Royal, was a skinny widow in her late fifties. Her long conservative blue dress, greyish wig, and matching gold jewelry told me that she was a modest woman. Martha's living room was decorated with several large crosses, two depictions of Yeshua, and a beautiful painting of her deceased husband and son. Sitting next to Martha was her youngest daughter, Toni. Toni was five years younger than Darius and was employed as a manager at one of our most popular restaurants in our colony. Both seemed truthful and honest as they gave us straightforward answers to our less than aggressive inquiries.

I grabbed my notepad and reviewed my long list of potential questions. Flipping the page, I saw that it was time to ask questions that would be a bit more direct and potentially offensive. Ed glanced over at me with nervous eyes. He wanted no part in asking the questions he knew would cause this strong black family to suffer more than they already had. Taking a deep breath, I collected my thoughts and tried to find the best way to ask this widow if her only son, Darius, was still alive.

"Mrs. Royal, I need to ask you a very important question and I'm gonna need your complete honesty," I began.

"Lives are in the balance and this is very important for the security of our people."

"I need to know if your son, Darius Royal, is still alive and if he is, can you tell us where to find him?"

Martha Royal adjusted her position in her seat, putting herself into an almost defensive posture as she looked away from me in disgust. Being the Christian woman she was, I could sense the unspoken curse words bouncing around in her soul. If her son was indeed alive, I had asked her to betray him and potentially give up a blessing from God that she had prayed for.

'Mrs. Sellers, I respect the sacrifices that you made for us Foundationals at Dry Tortugas," she calmly replied.

'But you of all people should understand how offensive and uncaring it is to come here and ask me if my dead son is somehow still alive. A son that was killed trying to be faithful to his duties as a Foundational."

'Since the moment the U.S. Army told me that Darius was killed in action, I have been forced to grieve my son's premature life every single day."

'Like you, I have given up so much for all of this," she expanded. 'First, I lost my husband and now my son. Both of those brave men gave up their lives trying to make your damned reparations experiment work."

'And now look what I'm left with Mrs. Sellers. Forgone memories of dead black men that were the center of my world and an ungrateful Black heifer here to remind me how painful it is to be a strong black woman."

Toni placed her hand on her mother's back, gently rubbing her mom into a state of comfort. I watched as tears of anger ran down Martha's face. Deep within me, I understood her tears and saw a bit of myself in her wounded spirit. I too, had spent my life loving the Black men God had provided to me, only to have that love misused or suddenly snatched away by death. The cruelties of life had made both of us cold and numb to the expectations placed upon our lacerated souls. Like me, Martha was a tired black woman. Looking at the tears falling from her eyes made me ponder upon my own spiritual fatigue.

'Mrs. Royal," Riley jumped in.

'I'm sorry for your loss, but we must know if Darius was involved with any hardline elements within the Foundational community. Was he a member of any hardliner groups? Did Darius harbor any resentment towards Governor Patrice Williams or the Dominant Society?"

"Remember whose home you are a guest in, Mr. White Man," Martha jabbed.

"What my son believed or didn't believe is none of your damn business, so don't make me lose my religion up in here today."

"Darius has earned the right to rest in peace. I won't allow you to dig up my son's corpse so that you can make asinine political points."

"Please back off, Riley," Ed mumbled.

Clarke tapped Riley's arm, non-verbally conveying that his line of questioning was disrespectful. Wanting to avoid eye contact with Riley, I looked across the living room into the Royal family's dining area. On the dining room wall hung a large photo of Darius Royal dressed in his U.S. Army Class Bravo uniform. His eyes looked full of life and promise as several bright combat awards shined on his ribbon rack.

Darius had been one of twenty Foundational volunteers selected to augment U.S. Special Forces Units seven years ago. Due to the acceleration of utterly destructive liberal life principles, the Dominant Society began to find it difficult to recruit qualified applicants to fill the ranks of their military Special Operations Units. After promoting the propagandized success of our Dry Tortugas raid, the U.S. Government asked the Foundational community for its assistance in filling critical shortages within their physically demanding Special Ops Units. In return, the Foundational Community received extra land allotments and lower tariffs on imported goods from Africa.

Before it was signed, I discussed this agreement with Governor Williams, as she was one of its authors. She convinced me that the agreement was a win for us. In the short term, we got additional territory and the lower taxes would boost both the African economy and ours. As I sat in Martha Royal's living room, I could now feel the ugly long-term problems the agreement ended up creating. What Governor Williams failed to realize was the fact that in that agreement, someone had to die for the interests of the Dominant Society. It wasn't supposed to be their drug-addicted White male homosexuals or their tree-hugging cousins; rather it would be Black men dying on white battlefields. Young and promising black men like Darius Royal had been heavily recruited by the U.S. government and taken away from our community. I mean, valuable black men that small families like the Royal's household could ill-afford to lose. As I sat there in that uncomfortable moment, I could not help but wonder if his sacrifice had been worth it.

"He was a good boy," Martha Royal proclaimed, looking right at me.

"They said he died in some training accident outside of Umm Qasr, Iraq."

"But I never believed Darius was actually killed in Iraq."

"Darius used to write me old school letters every two weeks. He was always letting me know where he had been and what they had been up to," she explained with a grimace.

"Darius told me about every fight he had with his racist Commanders, White Officers who unfairly targeted him, and his fellow Foundational Soldiers."

"His White Sergeants and NCO's would always give him the hardest and most dangerous duties."

"Yeah, it was pretty bad over there for our young black boys, but your precious Governor Williams didn't give a damn about that. It was all good politics for her and she got to stand next to liberal white folks on TV and look like the Magic Negro."

"Our greedy Colonial Leadership Council sent those black boys straight to a white slaughterhouse. All for a few acres of burnt-up farmland near Walnut Creek."

Toni handed her mother a napkin to wipe her wet eyes. I looked beside me and spied Riley wearing a light smile. He seemed to beam with glee at hearing Martha speak negatively about our people. This was the juicy dirt that he and the FBI were undoubtedly salivating over. Black disharmony is sort of like a drug for liberals like Riley. The endless need for self-validation via black confusion and pain was a white desire as old as White Supremacy itself.

"All of the sudden, the letters stopped and I didn't hear from Darius again," Martha continued.

"For three good months, I didn't hear from him. As the weeks went by without receiving his letters, I tried to convince myself that he was probably busy and didn't have time to write."

"In my soul, I knew better. Darius would always make time to write me, no matter where or how busy he was. I knew something was wrong. So, I prayed to the Lord for strength and then I started having these crazy dreams."

"One day, I got that knock on the front door," she explained with a voice filled with sorrow.

"I opened the door and saw that Zebra Priest standing next to a White Army Chaplain. When I looked into that Zebra's eyes, I had an instant feeling of deja vu. Almost like I had experienced and felt that moment before, in my dreams."

Martha stood to her feet and reflexively brushed imaginary lint off of her dress with her hands. The room was silent as we all reflected in her sorrow. There is nothing more painful to watch than a mother grieving over the life of a lost son. Out of respect, we all stood up with her, catching the non-verbal hint that her patience with our company had officially expired. We had gotten nothing out of our interview, and if we were going to ever locate Darius, we needed to come up with another lead as fast as possible. If his family had lied to us, we could be sure that

Darius would find out we were looking for him the second we left the house. Almost as an afterthought, I pulled a contact card out of my purse and handed it to Toni, who then wore a fake smile as she stored it away in her back pocket.

"If you come across any new information about Darius, please feel free to contact me directly, Toni," I politely instructed.

We followed Martha to her front door and excused ourselves out of her house. In frustrated silence, we all piled into Ed's car and lifted into the sky. Once airborne, Riley melodramatically loosened his tie while diving right into a diatribe.

"That old bitch was fuckin playing us. That's why I hate these homophobic Christians. There all flaming hypocrites and full of lies. Your Lord and Savior, Jesus the Messiah, magically woke up from the dead and is somehow alive...but your hardliner assassin son has to be dead...spare me the bullshit, you old hag!"

"That old church rat knows exactly where the hell Darius is at. Part of me wanted to call her ass out and show her the damn photos of her son. I got my real evidence right here! My science trumps your silly faith in that self-righteous sky tyrant they call God," he blasted with purposeful offense.

Hearing Riley's hateful and offensive outburst towards God, I bit down hard on my tongue, forcing myself into a state of calm. The quiet tension inside the car was only outdone by Riley's loud and hostile spirit. Inside of this white man, was a huge reservoir of hatred and pain just aching to be let loose upon anyone that opposed him or his extreme views.

"Well...she was definitely not straight with us," Clarke astutely interrupted. "When she showed us Darius's old bedroom, did any of you notice that all his stuff was still there like he never left?"

"That's all circumstantial and doesn't mean shit," I lazily shot back at the both of them.

"We have to find hard evidence that will point us to where Darius is hiding. Using an evasive mother and a bedroom memorial as probable cause won't get us anywhere. It's a waste of time to work yourself into a lather about it."

I heard my hand-held computer ring inside my purse. Turning on my screen, I saw that Quinton had sent me a message. It had been days since our fight and we hadn't spoken to each other. In my mind, I could still feel the profound love and raw exhilaration of our younger years, but those days seemed long gone. I had given up so much of my life for Quinton. There were many other men like Jeremy Woodson that could have provided me with love, faithfulness, and promise. My life could have been much better, but my love for Quinton and the Foundational cause had banished me to this life of mistrust and vanity-filled pretentiousness.

While I readjusted my hair into a ponytail, I opened Quinton's message. The inside of the car went stone silent as everyone snook peeks at my computer while pretending to not be nosy. As I began to read his message, I could sense and feel Quinton's frustration and panic. He mentioned that Lindsey was missing me. Quinton and little Lindsey had both come back home and found the house empty. Fearing that I may have hurt myself, Quinton claimed he had contacted everyone in the colony about my whereabouts. He also asked me to come home as soon as I could because we needed to talk.

For me, it was too late for Quinton to be a man and try to talk now. I had more important things to do; he would have to wait and continue to learn the hard lessons of running away from problems he created. I shut down my hand-held computer and put it back into my purse without responding. The last thing I wanted to do was return to my broken home and remind myself how terribly my actual life had turned out.

Ed drove us to one of our colony's finest hotels and we landed near the front entrance. Riley and Clarke collected their belongings before opening their exit doors. I turned around to face the backseat and saw a look of exhaustion on the face of both men. It had been a rough two days that were filled with long stakeouts, mixed in with hours of reviewing surveillance video. Everyone in the car had poured a lot of themselves into investigating any and everything about the Royal family, only to come away empty-handed.

"I hope you two are as tired as I am," Riley declared.

That was Riley's coy way of asking us if Ed and I were going to get some rest or continue to push on with the investigation without them. The mistrustful spirit within Riley was manifesting itself in his nervous movements as he stepped outside of the car. It was time for me to lie to the man and mislead him. I was certain that Ed was just as exhausted as I was. There was no doubt that both of us could have used a long night of rest, but we needed to find a lead on Darius Royal. In my mind, we were absolutely going to press on, but our FBI counterparts didn't need to know what I was planning.

"Yeah, Riley," I insinuated.

"We are all tired. Recharging the batteries sounds like the only thing we all need to be doing right now," I deflected.

"That sounds like a plan, Nuria," Clarke added.

"After we rest up, we can do a deep dive on all the farmland out in Napa Valley and see if we can locate that wine farm Bingo mentioned. The Department of Defense should also be granting us access to their confidential files on Darius Royal, so we should come across another lead on this guy tomorrow."

'I sure as hell hope so," Ed replied. 'Because, if we don't, we will be out here practically chasing a ghost."

'Ghost or not, we're gonna find Darius," I chimed in.

'But first, we all need to take a breather and recharge our batteries."

Satisfied with my answer, Riley nodded his head in agreement before shutting his passenger door. As Clarke and Riley began to walk away from the car, Ed glanced over at me with a suspicious expression. He knew that I had lied through my teeth and I sure as hell intended to continue working on the case through tomorrow morning.

'Nuria," Ed lectured. 'Riley is right on this one."

'We need to chill this evening and slow the damn pace. Burning ourselves out isn't going to get us anywhere."

'We have to stay ahead of them, Ed. That means putting in the work to control where this whole investigation goes. We need to take charge, so we can control the narrative."

'If we don't, they'll get the drop on us."

'No, Nuria," Ed sighed. 'We are doing just fine right now."

'Whatever the facts are, we're gonna find them, no matter what Riley and Clarke are trying to conceal."

'You need to go home tonight. You haven't seen little Lindsey or Quinton since this whole drama began. Family time will do you some good. I promise it will, and I can see you need it all in your face. You definitely should unplug a little partner."

'Plus, I feel like I need a break too," he whispered.

'Ed, do you really mean to say you need to go get some quality time with one of your hot tail girlfriends?" I interjected. 'If that's what you're after, just be honest about it."

'Well, Nuria...besides sleep, I'm gonna get some of that too," he quietly admitted.

Ed turned the car away from the capitol building and drove us towards my neighborhood. My mind raced as I tried to come up with some causable objection to prevent him from taking me home. Quinton would be there waiting and having to hear him whine was the last thing I wanted to endure. Ed pulled into my driveway, and from the stern look on his face, I knew that there was nothing I would say that would change his mind about continuing to work.

"Give little Lindsey a kiss for me and tell her Uncle Ed misses her," Ed instructed.

"How about I tell her what uncle Ed is really about to get into tonight?" I sarcastically shot back. "You thirsty asshole."

In silent frustration, I opened my car door and left Ed without even saying goodbye. As I launched my arm forward wildly slamming his car door, I could almost sense Ed's bewilderment as he stared at me. The anger within me began to boil as I prepared for the emotional warfare that would surely begin when I got home. Reaching into my purse, my lonely hand fished around the bottom while I played out in my mind what I knew would happen when I stepped through the door. Quinton would be pissed and ready to argue. He would surely condemn me for not being the mother and wife he thought I should be. Suddenly the front door slowly swung open and I looked up to see Quinton's solemn face. The bloody scratch wound I had given him had not completely healed. Under his eyes hung baggy skin, I immediately knew that Quinton had been a victim of several sleepless nights. This worn-down version of the man that was supposed to be my husband made me do a double-take and jolted my spirit with a small sliver of sympathy.

Quinton opened the door wide and stepped aside to let me in. I walked into the house and immediately felt the comforts of home. My nose was greeted by the smell of hot food cooking on the stove. The sight of our colorful family pictures hanging from the wall momentarily brought back memories of happier times. Quinton shut the door and grabbed my hand, gently pulling me towards him. He leaned down and delivered a wordless kiss to my forehead before heading towards the kitchen.

Taken off guard by the quiet moment of tenderness, I stood by the door and fought the tears as I tried to figure out what Quinton was up to. What was this new tactic he was employing? If he had been the one that hit me, we certainly would have had a rematch when we saw each other again. Yet, Quinton went out of his way not to show hostility towards me. He had to be setting me up. Curiously, I walked through the living room and began browsing through the kitchen. He had cooked a full meal and a delicious smelling pot roast was simmering inside the oven. I stepped up to the stove and opened one of the large pots to see fluffy garlic mashed potatoes. In another pot were several servings of steamed broccoli and carrots. For some reason, Quinton had cooked my favorite meal.

Instantly, my mouth began to water as the sight of the hot food reminded me that I hadn't eaten a good meal for several days. Ed and I had to make do with greasy takeout in between cat napping on lounge couches while reviewing mountains of evidence at the capitol building. This food in front of me definitely wasn't fast food. It was fresh and cooked to perfection. I could almost taste the mashed potatoes melting in my mouth as I gazed down at them with hunger lust in my soul. I felt Quinton walk up behind me and look over my shoulder in the midst of my longing.

"Gary Freeman called here earlier today. He was looking for you," Quinton began. "I told him you weren't home and I had a discussion with him afterwards."

"That's when I found out that you were alright."

"Gary told me that you were working on the Governor Williams case and that's probably why no one had heard from you. So instead of pouting and making myself angry, I figured that after doing all this investigating, you might be hungry and tired," he explained before walking away.

Quinton opened a cabinet, pulling out two dishes. He handed me a large brown porcelain plate and motioned for me to serve myself. As I purposely tried not to shovel mashed potatoes onto my plate with too much eagerness, my mind wondered why I hadn't seen little Lindsey yet. Reading my wondering eyes, Quinton opened the stove, pulling out the pot roast and placing the hot pan on the counter in front of me.

"Lindsey is at my mother's house," Quinton offered. "My mother volunteered to keep her this weekend so we could have some alone time."

I opened the pot roast pan and my eyes beheld the beautiful sight before me. The meat looked tender and juicy while simmering in a sea of brown gravy. Unable to resist, I dove in with a giant serving fork and piled up several large hunks next to my creamy potatoes. After arranging my plate, I sat down at the kitchen table across from an already-eating Quinton. All of this was too good to be true. Unsure of the new trick Quinton was trying to use, I decided to play along with his scheme to see where he was going with it.

"Thanks for cooking," I softly murmured. "You were right. I am hungry and haven't eaten a good meal for days now."

"Look, Quinton, I'm sorry for hitting you the other night."

"I was angry and I let my emotions overwhelm me. I was wrong and I want you to know that I appreciate you."

Unmoved by my words, Quinton barely acknowledged me while deliberately washing down a fork full of potatoes with a sip of cranberry juice. An awkward silence ruled the moment between us as we both quietly ate our food without exchanging any words. I tried to look into his eyes, but he avoided my gaze. Instead, he focused all his attention on the food in front of him. Unnerved, I finally dropped my fork on my plate and leaned back in my chair.

"Quinton, I just apologized and you don't have anything to say to me?"

"What is there to say, Nuria?" He softly replied.

"I want to believe you're sorry. I really do, but deep down in my heart, I know that even if you are sorry about hitting me, nothing will change between us."

"For years, I have lived with regret. A painful regret that haunts me every time I look into your eyes."

"I promised myself that I would make it right. I dedicated myself to fixing the things that really mattered, but nothing seems to be working for us."

"Nuria, the truth is we have never truly forgiven ourselves or each other for our past mistakes. That's why we stay at each other's throats all the time."

Quinton picked up his fork and shoveled a large piece of pot roast into his mouth. I watched him slowly chew in an attempt to distract himself as the tears built up in his eyes. Disgusted by his utter weakness, I shot up from my chair and stared down at him.

"Any mistake I made happened all because of you and what you did." I began.

"You spoiled our relationship when you had a damn baby with a white woman, Quinton."

"Do you know what it feels like to look at little Lindsey...To look in her eyes and know that my broken womb will never be able to make a life for you?"

"I gave you everything, Quinton. I gave you my heart, my time, all my love and dedication...but I couldn't give you the child you wanted. You had everything I could possibly give, but you went out and found some white whore and she gave you the one thing I couldn't."

'I know you have always wanted children. It's torture, Quinton. Flat out torture to know my absolute best wasn't good enough for you."

'You felt you had to go outside of this special bond we shared. You broke me. I'm broken and tired of fighting to fix this in the hopes that we can get back to what you so easily threw away!"

I turned my back and walked away from the kitchen table, purposely shielding my tears from Quinton. It was a closely guarded secret that Lindsey's mother was actually a white whore from New York City. My role as little Lindsey's mother was purely ceremonial, a tragic arrangement concocted to help blunt the shame Quinton's infidelity had bought upon the Foundational community.

Quinton's sex scandal quickly became a national embarrassment for Foundationals. It was hard for us to tout the moral superiority of Foundational Black culture when one of our most high-profile celebrities had fallen victim to a devious white smile and a bag of drugs. A year and a half after Lindsey's birth, her mother was mysteriously killed in a botched heroine deal outside of Old Harlem. No one was ever arrested for her murder, and after hearing news of her death, Quinton was always a bit emotionless when discussing Lindsey's real mother. In the aftermath of the scandal, Quinton retired from boxing. At the time of Quinton's retirement, I was still bedridden from the many combat injuries I had received at Dry Tortugas. He claimed that he did so to focus more on helping me rehab and make a full recovery. Everyone in our families went along with this well-thought-out lie. It all was a clever distraction to take attention away from the public embarrassment Quinton had delivered upon the Foundational community.

I heard Quinton stand up from his seat and approach me from behind. I braced myself for his harsh response, but instead, I felt his hand gently touch my shoulder and glide down my back. He leaned down and kissed my cheek before walking back to the kitchen table and retaking his seat.

"I'm done fighting this war with you, Nuria," he said.

"All I can do is love you. There is no way I can change what happened back then."

"All I can do is love you and hope that you can believe in us again."

"From the moment I saw you fighting for your life in that hospital, I asked God not to take you away from me."

"Watching you lay there, unconscious and riddled with bullets... Seeing you fight feverishly for every breath struck me in ways I've never felt before."

"I asked God to give me a second chance that day. I made a promise to the Lord that I would submit myself to his will and focus on what's really important in this life he blessed us with. I discovered that boxing didn't matter to me anymore. You mattered."

"I can't control how you feel about me. Hell, I even understand why you still resent me, but you are my blessing."

"From the very first moment I met you, you grabbed my heart. If I lost you, Nuria, I would lose a big part of myself."

In frustration, I turned around to face him. Tears streamed down my face as I clinched my lonely fist, trying my best to control the rage burning within me. Suddenly, the doorbell's loud ring stole my attention. Alarmed, Quinton quickly headed towards the front door.

"Wipe the tears from your eyes, Nuria," he instructed.

"People may think I'm an abusive husband if they see you crying like this."

I wiped my face with the back of my hand and followed Quinton to the front door. Before he could disengage the locks, the doorbell rang again, causing a spirit of impatience to grip us both. Quinton swung the door wide open and before us stood Darius's younger sister, Toni Royal. Her expression was blank as she examined us with her brown eyes. In the wordless moment, I noticed that she was wearing an oversized white baseball cap and a light brown windbreaker with the collar flipped up around her neck. For some reason, she was trying to conceal her identity.

"I'm here, Deacon Sellers," she proclaimed.

Quinton stepped aside and ushered Toni into the house. Toni gently nodded at Quinton before looking into my eyes, flashing a confident smile. Confused, I stepped in front of Toni, physically blocking her.

"What the hell are you doing here, Toni?" I blasted.

"Well, you did give me your business card today," she replied while holding it up. "I took that as an open invitation."

"Plus, your husband, Deacon Sellers, asked me to come here so we could talk in private."

"Come on, ladies. Let's all go in the living room and have a seat," Quinton implored.

Toni and I sat down on the couch while Quinton went into the kitchen. She opened her purse and handed me a photo. I looked down at the photo in my hand and saw that it was a picture of Darius Royal. He was standing next to Toni, their mother, and Quinton at their home. All four of them were wearing their Sunday's best and the photo had the unique feel of a post Church service outing. Everyone in the photo was smiling, with the notable exception of Darius, whose face displayed a tortured frown.

"What is this supposed to mean?" I asked Toni.

"This photo was taken a few years ago. I'm here to tell you that you are correct in your assumption that Darius is still among the living."

Quinton came back into the living room with two cups of hot tea and handed them to us. Toni immediately took the cup from Quinton and began to drink from it. I watched in horrified silence as the hot steam floated up from her cup while she foolishly took a large sip. Toni was nervous and I could tell that her emotional discomfort was overriding her mouth's sensitivity to swallowing such a scolding beverage.

"So, you and your mother lied to us?"

"Yeah," she stuttered as the pain finally started to settle in.

"We don't know who to trust right now, Nuria. You came to talk to us with that crazy-looking white man and his Zebra. There was no way we were going to help the FBI. My mother and I have our reasons to be cautious when discussing Darius."

"Deacon Sellers was the only person we confided in about Darius being alive," she explained.

"About three years ago, a strange black man showed up at our front door. He started telling us that Darius was still alive and that he could take us to him."

"Naturally, we dismissed him as a crackpot, but several days later, he came back again telling us the same story."

"Something told me to hear him out, so I did. Against my mother's objections, he convinced me to follow him to Bodega Bay where I would meet Darius."

"So, I followed him, and when we arrived, he took me to some houseboat and that was where I saw him."

"It was like a miracle from heaven. The moment the shock wore off, I hugged and kissed Darius. We cried in each other's arms. My big brother was still alive. It's a feeling I'll never forget."

Toni paused and took another sip of her hot tea. This time her sip was small and measured. As her eyes watered, Quinton took a seat next to her, offering her a napkin to clean her face. It was obvious that finding her brother had been a profound moment for Toni. Having a loved one ripped away from you, only for that loved one to be strangely gifted back must have been an emotional rollercoaster for the Royal family. Sensing her confusion, I placed my hand on her knee and tried my best to gently squeeze some sort of comfort into her wobbly spirit. After a gentle hug and light whispers of encouragement from Quinton, Toni regained her composure, taking a sip of tea and clearing her throat.

"The black man told me that we needed to hide Darius away...that Darius was part of some military experiment. He said the Dominant Society would be looking for him and we couldn't risk allowing anyone to find out that Darius was alive or bad things would certainly happen."

"At the time, I didn't know what any of that meant. I was just grateful that Darius was back with us, but I still asked the black man lots of questions. Instead of giving us answers, the black man just talked in circles, emphasizing that it was important that we hide Darius away."

"After a few days at home with us, my mother noticed that Darius never slept. He would just stay up all night watching the news channels like he was possessed. Before Darius joined the U.S. military, he was never into the news or politics at all, so it was a bit odd."

"He was different. I mean...his mood swings were wild. One minute he would be the same ole loving Darius, singing gospel music with momma in the kitchen as she cooked. Then the next minute, he would just start pacing in the living room while rambling on and on about traitors among us."

"Darius believed everybody was a traitor, even me and my mother. In the middle of his rants, he would always say how he was trained to kill the enemy."

"When he would say those things, the look in his eyes got scary," she described.

"It was like he was gone and there was nothing left of Darius inside his soul. It was almost like Darius was no longer there and some demon had replaced what was left of him. The whole thing really spooked out my mother, so we called your husband and asked him to come pray for us."

"Darius looked up to Deacon Sellers when he was a child. Our family used to cheer for Deacon Sellers when he boxed. Mr. Sellers was sort of a hero to Darius. We hoped that if he talked to Deacon Sellers, we could get our old Darius back," she explained with a cracking voice.

"I went to visit Darius," Quinton began. "He was a much different person from the young boy I knew from the church mentorship program."

"Whatever happened to Darius in the Army really changed him, and he was deeply wounded by the entire experience."

"No matter how warm Ms. Royal kept the house, Darius was always complaining about being cold. His hands were like ice when I shook them, and his arms were always filled with goosebumps. Even after a hot shower, he would still complain about being cold and would need all the blankets in the house to keep himself warm."

After finishing her cup of tea, Toni reached into her purse again and revealed another photo. In this photo, there was an image of a Darius with his arms wrapped around an odd-looking white woman with blonde and bluish-colored hair. The woman had a noticeable scar under her left eye that was accentuated by the large silver ring that dangled from her nose. Even in the still photo, she looked in control with a shaded grin that betrayed her dominance over Darius. The wide smile on Darius's face was obvious as the couple shared a weirdly intimate embrace. Darius was into this white woman, while his presence merely entertained her. Just looking at her in the photo forced me to recall the strange account Bingo Dorrell had told us during his interrogation.

"One day, this white woman came by our house to visit Darius," Toni explained. "She claimed that Darius didn't want to live with us anymore, but he was too scared to tell my mother he wanted to leave."

"The entire situation shocked us. Despite his issues, we had worked hard to adjust to him and hide the fact that Darius was at home with us."

"I'm not sure how this woman found out where Darius was, but it alarmed us that someone had been able to find Darius so easily. She came to our home several times, always trying to convince us that she could take care of Darius better than we had been."

"Somehow, this woman had the ability to calm Darius down and control his mood swings. He was always smiling around her and the way they interacted with each other was strange."

"Yet, Darius was happier when she was around, so my mother urged the white lady to stay with us for a while in the hopes that she could help us resolve Darius's issues."

"We'd ask the white woman questions like... where she was from or how she came to know Darius, but she would always give us different answers. I got the impression that the white woman looked down on black people."

"The white woman ended up staying at our home for two weeks before we kicked her out."

"Momma got tired of walking in on her and Darius having drunken sex in our living room," she explained with disgust.

"We are salt of the earth church folks, Nuria. Bringing that type of sinful spirit into my mother's home was the last straw for me. All of the sex, taking drugs, and whispering they did when we were around them was too much. Dominic wasn't our type."

"That's when Darius turned violent and punched momma," she added.

"I'll never forget it. He hit her and she collapsed to the ground with blood dripping from her nose. I fought like hell to pull Darius off of her. After several minutes, Darius regained his composure and quietly went and sat in the backyard. He lit up a big bowl of weed and began smoking it like nothing even happened."

"After I told your husband about the incident, Quinton and I agreed it was time to get Darius out of the house. He was becoming too aggressive with us, so we called the white girl and told her she could have him."

"The white woman instructed us to bring Darius back to the beach house in Bodega Bay. She promised to hide him away there and keep him safe, and he's been there ever since."

"Toni, do you remember this white woman's name? 'I asked.

Toni looked away and shot an empty stare into the floor with intensity. As she attempted to recall the woman's name, I motioned for Quinton to grab a pen and my legal pad. If we could locate this white woman, it would go a long way towards making sense of these odd circumstances surrounding Darius Royal. After a long pause, Toni's eyes widened, telling me that the mysterious woman's name had resurfaced in her memory.

"Dominic," Toni softly answered. "I believe her name is Dominic."

"At least, I believe that may have been the woman's real name."

"Darius had several other names he would call her... Bamber, Rosie, Patty, and Angie."

"Every other day, Darius was calling the white lady a new name. It was hard for us to keep up."

Sensing Toni beginning to open the flood gates of honest reflection, I decided to ask the question that had been dominating my curiosity the moment she began to confide in me. My only concern was that her loyalty would prevent her from telling the truth. It's not easy for any sister to seriously consider that their brother might be a crazed murderer, especially amongst us Foundationals. We were all raised to be a proud community of black folks, defensive of even the weakest within our ranks. From our first days of elementary school into the last courses of our college curriculum, we were taught never to forsake one another, no matter the circumstance. Yet the question of Darius's guilt begged to be asked, so I needed to approach it in a way that gave Toni the opportunity to give voice to concerns that she might otherwise instinctively bury.

"Toni, I need your honesty," I pleaded.

"Everything you just told me is critically important to my investigation and it's all on the record."

"What I'm about to ask you, we will need to keep between the three of us here."

"Do you believe that Darius could have been involved in the assassination of Governor Patrice Williams?"

I watched as Toni's eyes briefly widened upon hearing my frank question. Her reaction wasn't one of shock, nor was there any sign of offense. Instead, it was a natural response to a question that I knew she had already deeply considered. The seconds rolled by and Toni leaned forward, placing her elbows on her knees before removing her baseball cat and burying her face in the palms of her hands. As she rose to look at me, a trail of wet tears sparkled against her light brown skin. The sight of Toni crying moved me and shook my hardened spirit. From my own personal experience, I knew it was painful to have to seriously acknowledge the fact that a person you loved could be a monster.

"Yeah, Nuria," she said, mumbling in a low tone. "I do."

"He was obsessed with her for some reason. Both Darius and Dominic were infatuated with anything about Governor Williams that showed up in the news or was published online."

"Anytime Governor Williams gave a speech or spoke at a press conference, both of them would quietly watch her, studying every word she said. It was like they were in a trance."

"If you tried to speak to either one of them when Governor Williams was on TV, they would cuss you out or give you a nasty look that made you instantly apologize for disturbing their ritual."

"One day, the news showed footage of Governor Williams speaking to Congress in D.C., and I overheard Darius and Dominic jokingly talking about giving her a blast."

CHAPTER FIVE

DOCK OF THE BAY

ED MADE A SHARP TURN NORTH as we approached the Golden Gate Bridge Museum, driving us towards the rocky shoals of Bodega Bay. The rusty old bridge was once a hallmark of the Bay Area. Nowadays, the Bridge has become a living testament to a more primitive era of transportation. Back then, drivers were forced to hug the limitations of the earth's soil instead of using the vast freedom of the skies. Looking down at the bridge, I watched as white visitors toured the museum, gleefully taking in its many exhibits and displays that beckoned visitors back to earlier times. It was a time when Foundationals were integrated into a state of back-breaking poverty. These were the glory days of what was once the era of America. It was a time when Foundationals were systemically oppressed as a matter of course. Looking at the bridge filled with scores of spectators only reminded me of one of Donovan's favorite sayings. I could literally hear his deep voice blast out.

"The times may change, but these white people don't."

Back then, I didn't quite grasp the message he was trying to send, but today I fully understand it. If it were left up to me, I would tear down this monument that only served to idealize White Supremacy. Seeing this bridge sink into the dark nothingness of the bay would certainly be a joyous occasion.

A ringing noise from the front seat broke my concentration. I turned my head forward to see Dennis receiving an incoming call on his virtual phone. He pushed down on the bright glowing answer button that floated above his chin. Instantly, a hologram image of Gary Freeman popped into the empty air before us all. Gary sat on a stool in the lounge area of the Governor's hidden compound. I easily recognized the brown antique coffee table that Governor Williams had personally picked out when decorating the compound's living room.

"Good morning, Governor," Dennis greeted in a formal tone.

The image of Gary surveyed the inside of the car before breaking out in a coy grin upon seeing Quinton sitting next to me. In Quinton's boxing days, Gary had admittedly been one of Quinton's biggest fans. Despite Quinton's continuous objections, Gary would publicly lobby to get Quinton to volunteer himself for the Force Protection service. For hardliners like Gary, a world-famous Foundational like Quinton Sellers volunteering to publicly protect the colony would have been a propaganda coup of epic proportions. Governor Williams hated the idea and thought it too aggressive of a posture for our people. That wasn't the message Patrice wanted to send to our young Foundationals. In her mind, not every Foundational needed to aspire to be some celebrity or athlete. We also needed thinkers, builders, and thought leaders. I personally tended to agree with Patrice regarding the matter, as did Quinton, which is why he politely shunned Gary's opportunity. Deep inside, Quinton cared about our cause just as much as Gary did, but he was no hardliner. Instead, he chose to continue living out his own quiet life rather than making himself the face of the entire Foundational movement once again.

"I see you are up and at it early this morning," Gary commented.

"And you even have the Champ with you today, Nuria!"

"All right now. Whoever you're about to go see, they in some real trouble for sure," he stated laughingly.

"Good day Governor Freeman," Quinton awkwardly greeted. "I'm more than happy to assist our people whenever the proper moment presents itself."

"Quinton is with us today because he has visited this suspect's residence before," I broke in.

"Apparently, both Quinton and Toni Royal visited Bodega Bay some time ago. Quinton is here strictly as an advisor...and that's it."

Quinton humbly nodded his head in agreement with my not-so-subtle message. Yet, despite my cautious overtones, Gary's face still wore a delight-filled smile. Covert or not, Quinton Sellers, the undefeated former heavyweight champ, was on the job and taking on White Supremacy. In a community that routinely overvalued its celebrities, stories like these were worth their weight in gold, especially for Gary Freeman and his hardliner constituents.

"Oh, alright, Nuria," Gary dismissively responded.

"No one has to know that Nuria Phillip Sellers and her husband are out here hunting down justice for Governor Williams."

"My lips are sealed. You have my word."

"But I need to ask ya'll for an update whenever you finish with your business out in Bodega Bay," he continued.

"The Colonial Leadership Council wants me to brief them on the progress of your investigation. They are keen to not be surprised by any eventuality and want to stay ahead of the White Media's news cycle."

Annoyed with Gary's intrusion, Ed hit the brakes and the car came to a sudden halt in midair. His eyes blistered with anger as he turned to face the hologram image of this cousin that floated among us.

"Enough with the political games, Gary!"

"Nuria and I aren't about to go around lying to cover up facts. We aren't here to protect anybody," he blasted.

"If we find out that a Foundational broke the law, then we intend to pursue that person until hell freezes over. That's what we all owe Governor Williams."

"We owe her the same justice she fought hard to provide for us," he lamented.

Amused, Gary chuckled to himself before melodramatically clapping his hands together and performing a slow hand rub. Yet, his attempt to pass off his obvious frustration as dismissive humor failed to convince me. I could sense that Ed's indigent anger had touched a nerve with his older cousin. For hardliners like Gary, solidarity in the face of White Supremacist aggression was sacrosanct.

"Yes, Governor Patrice Williams deserves justice....my young cousin," Gary flatly replied.

"But the gold standard of justice for her would be to deny these racist bastards the victory they are really looking to win in all of this."

"Ed, all of this really isn't just about the death of Governor Williams. There are so many different levels at play here."

"For one...Nuria, do you know what your best buddies, agents Riley and Clarke, are up to right now?" he asked. Unsure of how to respond, I slowly shrugged my shoulder while glancing over at Dennis who sat stone-faced in a clear attempt to ignore me. Dennis knew where Gary was going with the question and for some reason, I knew that Dennis had already chosen sides.

"Last night, while you two were at home resting and eating a hot dinner, your esteemed FBI counterparts checked out of their hotel rooms and took the liberty of visiting Bingo at the Force Protection building."

"The officers on duty said they questioned Bingo for several hours before abruptly leaving."

"Intel reports are telling me that agents Riley and Clarke are currently at that wine farm Bingo told you about. My guess is that when you asked Bingo the location of the wine farm, he probably told you two that he couldn't remember where it was."

"It seems like Riley and Clarke may have offered Bingo something that jogged his memory in your absence," Gary cleverly explained. "The FBI now has a lead that we don't have. That should be a matter of concern to every warm body in that car."

Riley's punk ass double-crossed me. I felt a jolt shoot up my spine as the four-letter words spilled out of my mouth before I could catch them. Burning hot in the heat of my anger, I took my notepad and slammed it into the floorboard beneath me. We both had agreed that we would all get some rest, but true to form, we both had planned on using the opportunity to get ahead of each other. I wanted to run the same scheme until I foolishly let Ed's thirsty hormones guilt me out of my better judgment.

Just as I was about to dig into Ed's ass, I felt Quinton's hand grip my leg. Looking over at him, I gazed into the serenity of his brown eyes and immediately felt his calmness. "Don't lose your cool. We are all depending on you and we're all here to support you," he whispered.

Quinton was right. Despite Riley's double-cross, we still were able to find a good lead because of Quinton. Now it was just a matter of whose Intel would get them closer to finding the truth first.

"Don't get too frustrated, Nuria," Dennis quickly jumped in

"Intel reports tell us that the wine farm is abandoned and is up for auction due to foreclosure."

"Riley and Clarke may go out there and snoop around a bit,

but they probably won't find much to hold onto."

"Even if they say they didn't find anything out at the wine farm, how do we believe the F...B...fucking I?" I demanded. "

We have no way of knowing what they really discovered out there."

"We don't believe them," Dennis responded.

"We should never believe anything a racist says, anyway. Their actions will always speak their truth better than any of the lying words that come out of their mouths. Sort of like them agreeing to have a day of rest, then turning around and trying to beat you to the punch, Nuria. We should always plan and account for their manipulation ahead of time."

I caught Dennis's veiled jab at me, and knew he was right. Swallowing his blow, I decided not to press the issue any further. Dennis and Gary definitely knew something I just wasn't aware of at that moment. Yet, I was puzzled as to why they felt they couldn't share it with me. Whatever it was, they were both visibly confident as a moment of confused silence ruled everyone except for the two of them. They had an ace up their sleeve, and somehow, they had managed to keep a close eye on Riley and Clarke.

"What the hell is going on here, Gary?" Ed shot out in frustration.

"We are at war, little cousin," Gary responded loudly. "I don't expect you, Nuria, or Quinton to fully grasp the gravity of everything that is happening. In fact, if you don't trust me or the hardliner movement, that's a good thing. Trust no one, including me."

"I need all of you to pursue the truth. The unbiased, hard to swallow truth."

Gary's hologram image looked down at his pants and reached into his pocket, pulling out a long brown cigar. He put one end in-between his teeth and bit down before spitting the butt out of his mouth. In one smooth motion, Gary lit the cigar and took a pull. The hologram depiction of white haze floated aimlessly in the compartment of Ed's car as Gary blew smoke out of his nose.

"That's why I chose you and Nuria for this assignment," he lamented.

"Nuria has always hated me. When you're in combat, sometimes the person that hates you the most can become your greatest advocate merely by default."

"I never said I hated you, Gary."

"I don't agree with your politics, that's all," I tried to explain.

"No matter our differences, we are Foundational family and nothing will come between us."

Gary gave me a contempt-filled snicker as if he knew better than to put belief into my words. Wanting to move us both beyond the tense moment, Dennis quickly jumped in, thanking Gary before ultimately ushering an end to his call. Gary's hologram image slowly faded away while Ed pushed down on the accelerator, thrusting us towards the rocky beaches of Bodega Bay. As we closed in on our destination, I couldn't help but comb over that conversation with Gary in my mind. I reviewed every word, looking for any hidden clues or hints that he may have given in the process. Part of me wanted to believe Gary already knew the truth he had vainly sent us after. I wanted to believe that all of this was his own little sick game to somehow teach me one of his infamous hardliner lessons, but I instead came away with the only logical assumption I could muster. Gary wasn't the type of Foundational to rely on the morality of his enemies to save him. For Gary to take the risk and hedge all his bets on me meant that something was actually going on that was beyond his control. Something that scared him more than our own personal animus towards each other.

We arrived at Bodega Bay and Ed made a lazy left turn, causing us to circle the city from high above. Looking from the sky, I could see old billboards that were plastered on the rooftops of every building. Renting out your rooftop was an easy way to make a few bucks, but given the crumbling state of these advertisements, it seemed that Bodega Bay's economy had taken a turn for the worst.

"There's the house," Quinton instructed.

"Right there next to the rocky beach."

Ed gave a curious stare downward, inspecting the property while looking for a welcoming place to land. The entire property was fenced all the way up to the water's edge. Whoever owned this property clearly valued their privacy and wanted no dealings with outsiders. The house was a modest-sized home, raised on stilts above the bay's cold blue water. Attached to the home was a private wooden boat dock that looked old and hazardous in its decayed state. A short distance down the beach was a large red boathouse that looked freshly painted and newly remodeled. Given the rotting state of the main house, I found it odd that any owner would prioritize remodeling a boathouse over the main house.

"We can't land on the property," Ed remarked. "It's against the law to land on someone's personal property without their consent."

"We'll have to land the car at a parking area a mile or two east from here and walk to the property by foot."

We made it to the public parking area and parked in the desolate lot. The yellow lines designating the individual parking spaces were faded and barely distinguishable against the pebble-filled tarmac. Ed shut down the car's engines and we all rallied around the trunk after Ed popped it open. Dennis reached inside and grabbed two bulletproof undergarments, handing them to Quinton and I.

"Here you go, guys," he lamented.

"There are only three vests in here for the four of us, and you two are more valuable than me. Gary will never forgive me if either of you don't come back from this."

I took the vest and briefly stared at it before tossing it back to Dennis. Surprised, Dennis caught it with a look of disbelief on his face. I entertained him as he uttered his objections before demanding that he don the vest.

"I'm not wearing the vest, Dennis." I broke in, stopping him in mid-sentence. "You can tell Gary I said that."

"I'm in charge here. It's either you wear the damn vest, or you stay here and guard Ed's car. The choice is yours."

I reached into the trunk and grabbed my service pistol, quickly holstering it in my hidden sleeve underneath my jacket. Ed grabbed his and tucked it away in a holster in the small of his back. With the slam of Ed's trunk, we all quietly set off on our two-mile hike towards the beach house. The road to the house was a long wide dirt path, riddled with large chunks of broken and rotting timber. Every step forward was painstaking and tedious, causing me to fight hard to maintain my balance.

"Someone sure wants to make it hard to get to their house," Ed vented from behind me.

"These damn logs didn't get on the roadway by themselves. It looks like someone put them all here on purpose."

Ed was onto something. His comment brought back memories of training Donovan, Pernell, and I had undertaken with the U.S. Navy. The big logs and heavy stones in our pathway were a perfect deterrent for any specialized heavy military equipment. If anyone were to approach this beach house by land, the occupants of the house would know well ahead of time, as the dirt road was the only path anyone could use to get to the house. This left an approach by air or sea. Given the state of the fresh-looking boathouse, I quickly gathered that it likely doubled as an air and sea defense outpost for the property. If this house indeed belonged to the mysterious Dominic lady, then she was no amateur. Everything about this log-infected road and the unique location of the beach house screamed skill craft. I could tell it was all the handy work of a well-trained operative. Someone with tons of experience and tactical skills.

"Wait," I screamed out.

"Quinton, was this road like this the last time you came out here?"

"No," he admitted while catching his breath.

"I was able to easily park on the road right outside of the property. Toni and I walked Darius to the front gate, said our goodbyes, and then we left. There was literally nothing on this road."

"What are you thinking, partner?" Ed softly asked. "I'm thinking whoever is in that house must be expecting company. I just hope that they're in a welcoming mood."

A loud buzz rang out from inside Dennis's coat pocket. He reached down and pulled out his hand-held computer and quickly scrolled through his menu before squinting his eyes to make out the small words on his screen. All of us watched him in curious silence, waiting to hear what news had been bestowed upon us. As his eyes widened and his mouth opened, I knew whatever Dennis had just read was not good news.

"Senator Judith Bean has died in the hospital," he relayed.

"She was unable to recover from the fatal injuries she sustained in the Yerba Buena explosion and the Dominant Societies media organizations are reporting that she succumbed to her injuries this morning."

"The FBI has officially announced that it is opening an independent probe into Senator Bean's assassination," he continued reading.

"This probe will be separate from the allied investigation into the assassination of Foundational Governor Patrice Williams, who was killed two weeks ago."

"They're gonna come after our memory cells," I mumbled as the shock of the breaking news wore off.

"Yes, they are Nuria," Dennis acknowledged. "This is why we need to find Darius and get to the bottom of who is actually behind all of this shit."

"The Dominant Society may have pulled the plug on Senator Bean for all we know. Her murder may be some strategy to get the ammunition they need to come after our memory cells?" Ed blurted out.

"I wouldn't put it past the Dominant Society. It sounds exactly like something they would do."

"Gary Freeman was right," I interrupted. "The only thing we can do now is find the truth before they come after us."

"I don't know who or what's waiting at the end of this road, but we better find out before the FBI does."

I gathered my strength and leaped on top of a rather large log, pulling myself to the timbers mount with my lonely arm. In silence, I jumped down to the dirt road on the other side before approaching my next obstacle and performing the same draining routine. After surmounting several logs, I looked back and saw all three men following close behind. It was a grueling thirty minutes before the wide road began to narrow and a tall gate entrance came into view ahead. Thankfully, as the road began to shrink, so did the size of the logs on the pathway. I wiped away a pool of sweat from my forehead before brushing my wet hair behind my ears. Beyond the gate, I could make out the outline of the boathouse as it sat above the deep blue water. It was then that I caught the unique smell of the sea, which gave me a sudden burst of renewed motivation. We were definitely close and our objective was now within reach.

"That's the front gate," Quinton declared as he continued forward.

"If I remember correctly, there was a call box with a doorbell at the gate."

We all followed Quinton and we considerably quickened our pace.

Nearing the front entrance, I noticed a large piece of plywood that was leaning up against the metal gate. Painted on the conspicuous plywood were the words, "ENTER AT YOUR OWN RISK." The front gate was chained shut. From the electrical wires that dangled above the chain links, I could tell that the call box Quinton had once seen here had been hastily removed.

"It doesn't look like anyone's at home," Ed remarked as he examined the property.

"There aren't any lights on in the house. No parked cars. Nothing."

"Good," I responded.

"If no one is here, then no one will mind if we give ourselves a little tour."

"Someone has something to hide if they went through this much damn trouble."

I looked over at Dennis and our eyes met. I gave him a slight head nod, non-verbally instructing him to do what we both knew he needed to do. Dennis returned my head nod, adding in eyes that were focused and determined. He knew exactly what I meant and I didn't have to say a single word. After walking up to the chain link, Dennis grabbed the old school locking device before pulling an electric Garmin out of his pocket. With the flick of a button, a mini blade appeared on the leading edge of Dennis's Garmin tool. The power light on his handheld tool blinked green. Dennis pushed down on a small lever and I could hear the mini saw blade spin rapidly as it cut through the ocean air. Scores of bright orange sparks flew from the chain as Dennis's mini saw began the task of cutting the lock in half. The sound of grinding metal echoed among us as we all stood by anxiously waiting for Dennis to finish his work.

What we were doing was against the law and violated several major tenets of our Reparations Treaty. Ed and I were both outside of our jurisdiction as Colonial Law Enforcement Officials. Our status as Foundationals would earn us the harshest penalties that the Dominant Society could offer if we were caught, not to mention the liable lawsuits that would surely be levied against our Colonial government. The bright sparks of hot metal were exploding as Dennis leaned his weight into the stubborn lock with his screaming Garmin.

In the back of my mind, I briefly considered stopping Dennis. What we were doing was insane. It went against everything our society had taught us. It was part of our code of conduct to be respectful of the Dominant Societies laws. Why throw away everything I had earned just to find myself in a white-controlled prison cell? Why expose my innocent husband to that same potential? My nerves began to bother me as Dennis continued to cut the lock. Just as I was forming the words to tell Dennis to hold on, the grinding noise came to a halt. I saw the broken lock fall from the gate bouncing three times as it hit the dirt below Dennis's feet. The time for reconsidering was over and I knew we had to make a quick move. Fate had made my decision for me.

"That lock was a motherfucker," Dennis muttered.

"You got it off though," Quinton reassured Dennis. "Good work brother."

Ed and Dennis both pulled the loose chain from the gate. When the chain was unwrapped, the gate glided open by itself and we all walked onto the property, following a paved walkway towards the boathouse. Halfway to the house, I noticed that the lawn suddenly looked like it had been freshly manicured. There was not one tall blade of grass in sight. I looked to my right and saw a yard tool lying on the ground. Breaking away from the group, I walked over to a shiny object and saw that it was a hand rake. Not far from the rake, I noticed a number of tools scattered about the grass. They were a mixed assortment of shovels, axes, and hammers. If they had all been out in the open like this, exposed to the salty ocean air for even a few days, they would have surely looked the part. Yet, all of them appeared brand new and freshly abandoned with not one ounce of rust on them. A nagging suspicion inside of me began to bubble to the surface. On instinct, I pulled my firearm from its holster and clicked off the safety.

"What is going on, Nuria?" a nervous-sounding Ed asked.

The group cautiously walked up to me as I gazed out and re-examined the property surrounding us. I had felt this all before and it was uncomfortably familiar. The eerie quiet was only interrupted by the rhythmic sound of the waves breaking on the rocky beach. Other than that, there was no other sound. There had to be people here. I tried to convince myself that maybe they had all decided to take a nap before we arrived. As the thought lingered in my spirit, I ultimately came to a more reasonable conclusion. Whoever had been outside working had seen us coming and now we were in the middle of a well-planned ambush. The memories of my Dry Tortugas ordeal caused a streak of fear to pulse down my spine. I closed my eyes to say a quick prayer but only saw flashes of blue blood and a dead black teenager. We had walked into a trap and I could feel that truth in my bones.

"Guys," I whispered.

"We need to fall back and get outta here. Don't turn and run, or we're all dead."

"What!" Dennis replied. "But no one is here Nuria."

Sensing the genuine concern in my spirit, Ed pulled out his service weapon and flanked me as we slowly walked back towards the gate. Dennis began to protest, getting louder and louder with each word. Needing him to pipe the fuck down, I lightly kicked Dennis on his thigh with my foot before motioning for him to lower his voice. Now alarmed by my abrupt seriousness, Dennis instead mumbled his protests, while obediently walking down the light gray walkway.

"Jesus," Quinton shouted!

I jerked myself towards the sound of his voice. In-between us and the comforting salvation of the gated entrance were a pair of large canines. The two vicious-looking German Shepard's were large and muscular. Their sharp yellow stained teeth were menacing and dangerous. Both dogs jetted towards us without so much as a bark or whimper, almost like they were hunting prey.

"Get back!" Ed shouted at Quinton before pushing him out of the way.

Both dogs dove in on Ed. Taking the brunt of their attack, Ed tried kicking them away before resorting to swinging punches at their heads. One of the dogs bit down on his forearm, trying to pull Ed to the ground. The other dog grabbed his leg, swinging its head wildly as its teeth sunk into Ed's flesh. Quinton and Dennis raced over, kicking and punching the dogs in their stomachs, forcing them to release their holds. I ran over and joined in, hitting the canines with my heavy pistol as we tried to keep them at bay and get to the exit.

Pissed off and bloody, Ed brushed us all aside, aiming his pistol at one of the dogs. The loud report of his gunshot made my ears ring, momentarily startling the animals and causing them to slow their pace. One of the dogs slowly collapsed to the ground before letting out an ear-piercing groan. Hit by Ed's gunshot, the dog shook violently as red blood poured out of its abdomen. Seizing the opportunity, I took my pistol and sited in the second dog, aiming for the meaty portion of its chest. My finger gently pulled back on the trigger while I concentrated on the site picture in front of me, trying not to anticipate the guns recoil.

Then I felt the world around me tumble and my pistol fell out of my hand. The green grass shot up and plastered me right in the face. I felt someone drive their weight into my back, pinning me to the ground. Deep voices began to yell in Spanish, mixed with a bit of broken English. I tried to force myself up, but the overwhelming strength of the men holding me down was insurmountable. Tilting my head to the side, I could see two Hispanic men pointing their rifles at my back. The looks in their eyes was cold and scary.

"What the hell is this?" Ed screamed out from underneath a pile of men.

"Silence...Silence!" One of the armed men screamed with a heavy accent.

As best as I could, I turned my head to look around. By my count, there were at least fifteen heavily armed men surrounding us. Most of them were Hispanic, while a few others were white and black. All the men wore work clothes, soiled in dirt and sweat. The seriousness in their body language and manner told me these people meant business. Dennis and Quinton were motionless on their stomachs with their hands cuffed behind their backs. The man on top of me handcuffed my right hand, and I felt his hand reach under my left side in a futile search to grab my non-existent left arm. Surely dumbfounded, he began to whisper to someone in Spanish. After several seconds of a panicked back and forth, I felt the man finally cuff my right wrist into the belt loop near the small of my back.

The man whipped me over on my back before pulling me up to my feet. I could feel the small man's endless strength as he lifted me in the air with ease as if I were a toy. The two men with rifles positioned themselves behind me, almost daring me to make any sudden movement. I curiously watched as Quinton, Dennis, and Ed were also brought up to their feet. The armed men ushered them near me with light shoves and loud barks until all four of us stood together with a platoon of rifles at our backs.

A bald Hispanic man carrying a long silver pickaxe walked up to us as we stood in silence. His shiny forehead glowed as the early morning sun left an ocean of sweat sitting atop his head. It was then I noticed an earpiece hanging from his right ear and a small microphone attached to his wide collar. Unlike the other men, there was a much different aura about this guy. For one, his clothes were much cleaner than the rest of the group. In fact, his brand-new attire was neat and perfectly ironed. Everything about this bald man with a large round bulge under his upper lip said leadership, or more precisely, boss man.

He walked up to me, a few inches from my face and stared down into my eyes. Without blinking, I unflinchingly stared back up at him, content to take his non-verbal aggression head-on. After a few awkward seconds, his mouth began moving and the bulge under his upper lip disappeared. The man started chewing on a piece of gum while flashing a devilish smile at me. I could smell his wintergreen mint gum as he whispered a word of Spanish at me in jest. A word that I understood all too well. The Spanish slang word for Monkey Bitch.

He reached into my pocket, yanking out my Force Protection badge. Holding it up to his face, he read my name aloud while speaking perfect English into the microphone on his collar. The other armed men took Dennis, Ed, and Quinton's wallets away from them. Upon completing his microphone conversation, the boss man slowly walked over to the others, snatching each of their wallets before quickly reading through and tossing them on the ground. Now he knew we were Foundationals and the unhappiness in his sweaty face was apparent.

"What brought you lazy fucking leeches here?" He asked us with fury in his eyes.

"Why do you Foundationals come over to our land and try to take it from us," he yelled!

We remained silent and no one responded to him. I looked over and saw Ed lean his mouth into his shoulder, wiping away blood from the corner of his lips. We weren't here to make any pleas or beg for forgiveness. We were all on code and this bastard wouldn't get anything from us.

"What? You niggers can't speak English now," the boss man barked. "Do you need me to put it in a rap song for you to comprehend?"

"Well, let me start speaking a language I know you can understand then."

He walked back over and looked down at me. Suddenly, I felt the weight of his steel-toed boot pounding into my stomach. While falling to the ground, I felt myself gagging for air. The pain of the surprising blow rippled throughout my crumbling body. I knew the wind had been knocked out of my lungs. I had felt this sensation before. Fighting the natural urge to panic, I told myself to stay calm and look into this fuckers' eyes. Forcing my vision upwards, I gazed at him and the anger took over. Several tears rolled down my cheeks and my lungs reopened, allowing me to suck in air. After several gasps, I mustered my inner strength and launched up a salvo of spit towards his chest.

My blood-stained spit hit his collar, spoiling his microphone and causing a few speckles to land on his bottom lip. Surprised by my actions, Mr. Boss Man wiped the blood from his lip and delivered an open hand slap to my jaw. The weight of his blow made me topple back down to the ground. Next to me, I could hear an enraged Quinton screaming and cursing at the Boss Man as four filthy Hispanic gunmen leaned into him, pinning him on the ground.

Then I heard the distinct click of a handgun's slide slamming forward. Someone was loading a bullet into their chamber. I instinctively looked back up at the Boss Man and saw the barrel of his handgun pointed at my forehead.

"I can see that at least one of you Foundationals speaks good English," he said with a flat expression. "Especially when your wife's life is on the line."

"One of you talks, or somebody's lovely wife dies."

The Boss Man thrust his pistol into my head, driving the barrel into my rough edges with a delight-filled smile. Behind me, I could hear all three men cursing loudly and struggling to break themselves free from the strong grip of the armed men surrounding them. My eyes caught the Boss Man slowly pulling back on the trigger. There was nothing to stop him. My life was in his hands and when that trigger was completely pulled back, I'd be gone. In my mind, I said a short prayer to the Lord, asking him to forgive me.

Then came a blessing from the heavens above. He eased his finger off the trigger and pulled the gun away from my head. The Boss Man stepped backwards then lowered his weapon altogether before pushing his earpiece deeper into his earlobe. In confusion, he tried to whisper a few words into his spit-soaked microphone but instead tossed it away in disgust when it failed to work.

"Get all of these niggers into the house now," he yelled at the armed men.

"There's another car inbound. Hurry up. Move!"

With a powerful jerk upwards, I was lifted to my feet. Several armed men pushed me towards the main house while ordering me to run. In front of me, two men stopped running and pulled open a well-hidden trap door, cleverly covered over with a thick layer of grass. Both men dived inside of an underground tunnel, disappearing beneath the soil. Out of the corner of my eye, I saw the red-painted boathouse we had flown over earlier. Its tall doors were propped open and inside the boathouse was a wide array of air scanners with their powder white domes pointed skyward. Several Hispanic men sat behind remote consoles talking into microphones. Just as I thought, they had seen us coming and now someone else was on their way out here to visit. Whoever that might be, they had unknowingly saved my life.

We were directed towards the front door, where the Boss Man took out an old school metal key and began to unlock three deadbolts. The front exterior of the main house looked ominous with its dilapidated metal siding and rotting plywood. Peering through the windows, I could only see murky darkness inside. Nothing about this house looked even remotely welcoming. It was simply an old decaying vacation home that had sustained decades of neglect.

Finally, the front door was unlocked and the Boss Man impatiently pushed it open. After several hard shoves and raised voices, the armed men led us inside. Within the home, my eyes were greeted by bright LED lights pulsing from a chandelier that hung from a vintage vaulted ceiling. Sounds from an entertainment system created loud echoes within the four walls. The home was decorated with beautiful paintings and timeless art displays from the 1980s and '90s. In one corner of the house hung a life-size painting of Jackee Joyner-Kersey, the all-time great Olympian, leaping over a hurdle. Directly under the painting hung a blue and yellow javelin encased in a see-through glass box. Vintage sofas and Persian rugs adorned a living room area where a white woman quietly sat by herself, watching the large TV display its images. Sipping on a tall glass of Bourbon Whiskey, she sat with her back towards us and barely acknowledged our entrance into the house.

The armed men picked up four folding chairs, commanding us to sit down, then promptly tying us to the chairs with plastic fishing line. The Boss Man gathered our wallets and badges before he gingerly walked up to the white woman, whispering to her as he placed them in her hand. Satisfied that he had done his job, the Boss Man smiled wide at the lady before awkwardly asking her if she needed anything else.

The white woman ignored the Hispanic man's respectful solicitation while deliberately browsing through our possessions with intense curiosity. I saw her as she picked up my badge and examined my name. With a slight chuckle, she tossed my badge on the fine oak coffee table in front of her before effortlessly guzzling down a rather large gulp of her Bourbon. She had recognized me and I had no idea if that would be a good thing.

"Go ahead and set up my interview table in front of them," she barked.

The Boss Man nodded feverishly while waving for the other armed men to get to the task. The men obediently walked into a side room and the sounds of heavy furniture being moved were heard. Meanwhile, the white lady sat there with her back to us, flicking through the channels and calmly sipping her Bourbon Whiskey. An image splashed across the TV screen and she stopped her channel surfing, placing the remote next to her nearly empty cup. It was a news alert. The headline read: Senator Judith Bean pronounced dead.

Several white news anchors and commentators pretended sadness as they conveyed the details of Senator Judith Bean's last moments of life. Then the camera zoomed in on the lone Zebra commentator on the all-white news panel, as the news anchor served up a lead-in question for him to answer. Before the Zebra could utter a single word, he began to cry, whimpering loudly for the world to hear. Thin strands of clear snot fell from his nose and the camera abruptly pulled away as he grabbed white tissue paper to clean his face. It was all political theater and a disgusting affair to witness. Looking over at Dennis, I saw the repulsed look on his face as he also watched the stage play on the TV play out in front of us.

"For God's sakes, lady, if you're gonna kill me, then go ahead and kill me, but please don't force me to watch this buck broken flunky grovel at the feet of his white paymasters," Ed shouted.

The white lady let out a loud clapping laugh that rang throughout the house. Her shoulders bounced while she giggled hysterically, wiping her eyes with the back of her hand. In silence, she leaned towards the coffee table, grabbing the remote and accommodating Ed's request by changing the channel. The next channel was also a news program that showed footage of unrest in Columbia. Columbian soldiers were shown wildly firing their rifles into a gathering of peaceful Afro-Latino protestors.

"I honestly don't know which is more depressing," the lady stated in exasperation.

"A cowardly black man shedding tears of remorse over the death of his mortal enemy, or wannabe white men firing their rifles at children in an effort to win a war that they've already lost."

"Such is the way of the world we now live in."

The armed men came back into the room carrying a long wooden table. They hastily positioned the table in front of us and placed a beautiful-looking purple silk tablecloth on top of it. When everything was perfectly arranged, the Boss Man walked up to the table and examined it several times. Satisfied with his men's work, he pulled a small revolver out of his pocket and gently laid it at the center. Almost on cue, the white lady stood up from her seat on the couch, then turned to face us.

Her blonde hair was colored with a light and faded version of blue. Her silver nose ring shined as the chandelier above us beamed down on it. Small wrinkles cratered the skin below her blue eyes. Underneath her left eye, I noticed a deep scar. It was the same scar that had caught my attention in the photo Toni Royal had shown me. This was Darius's Dominic. The mysterious white woman he had smuggled into our colony.

"Welcome to Bodega Bay," she stated with slurred words.

"For most of you, I'm sure it's your first visit."

"But for one of you...it's a very...very welcome return."

She walked from behind the couch and slowly made her way to the table. Her eyes were filled with excitement as she locked in on Quinton. Standing across from him, she leaned her elbows down on the table, closing within inches of his lips. Her eyes were glossy as she gently eased forward until her lips touched his, stealing a kiss from him. Upset, Quinton quickly turned his head away, giving a curse-filled protest. Dominic giggled to herself before brandishing a knife and putting its sharpened edge against Quinton's throat.

"Move your sexy brown lips back towards me now, Mister," she ordered.

"You're on my property. So, you have to play by my rules."

"Plus, you remember our deal. If you decided you wanted Darius back...well...I get you in return, sexy."

"Lady, you'll have to kill me first," Quinton responded.

"I'll have you dead or alive then," she uttered. "I already got your ass once. So, I know I can get you again."

Feeling the anger erupting, I yelled at the woman, demanding that she leave my husband alone. Upon hearing my verbal attacks, Dominic's blue eyes sparkled with drunken excitement. Ignoring me, she took her knife and slashed open Quinton's thin grey T-Shirt, exposing his bare chest. Leaning down further, she mockingly kissed and licked his nipples while laughing hysterically as my husband's body wildly contorted in protest.

"How about we make a new deal," I relented.

At the sound of my request, Dominic stopped laughing and stood up tall, concentrating her gaze on me as the room fell silent. I knew then she was open to negotiating. Dominic and her armed Hispanic foot soldiers didn't have any plans to kill us. We would have already been shot if she really wanted us dead. Instead, this white woman wanted to play and toy with us for her own pleasure. I got the sense that if we brought her any value, the silly games would come to an abrupt end, and serious business would follow. Now it was only a matter of figuring out her angle. Everything about this fortified property screamed that this Dominic lady was expecting unwelcomed company. The type of company that intended to harm her. Finding out the who and the why was exactly what I needed to do.

"A new deal," I continued.

"We keep you alive and you tell us what you know."

"Agent Nuria Phillips Sellers. The anointed hero of the infamous Dry Tortugas assault," she mockingly responded.

"The angelic Black savior that saved America from that monstrous White terrorist, Bradley Wood."

"You can't possibly keep me alive, my one-armed friend. I'm already dead."

"If you're here for Darius Royal, you're wasting your time. You're looking for the wrong lead."

Something about Dominic's statements struck me. The ease and sarcastic manner in which the words left her mouth made me feel uneasy. She pulled out a seat and sat at the center of the long table. After settling in, she reached into her pocket and pulled out two small baggies. The Boss Man rushed over, handing her a fat cigar. Without even looking up at him, she took it and tore off its plastic wrapping. After slicing the cigar open, she removed its tobacco before replacing it with weed and a powdery substance. As she lit up her joint, the Boss Man brought her a small glass and her half-drunken bottle of Whiskey Bourbon. On the bottle was a familiar label and brand that immediately caught my attention. The manufacturer of this particular brand of Whiskey was a popular Foundational that operated exclusively within my very own Oakland colony. The bottle's label read Woodson Bourbon & Whiskey, batch number 0224. Dominic removed the bottle's cork and poured herself several shots before swallowing them with discomforting ease.

I knew she was sending me a coded message. Looking at the name on the bottle forced my repressed thoughts of Jeremy Woodson to resurface in my soul. Jeremy had told me that he had family in our colony; somehow, Dominic knew this as well. The inner quandary knocked me off my game, taking the words right out of my mouth, which was long enough for Dominic to notice. Clearly satisfied with my indecision, Dominic blew a heavy white cloud out of her lungs and poured herself another shot of warm Whiskey.

"Why are you dead Dominic?" I forced myself to ask. "I can't stop anything if I don't know who or what is coming."

"Nuria, that's the insidious thing about this tragic arrangement between us Whites and you Foundational Blacks."

"You people will never know who is really orchestrating your doom," she explained. "Hell, I don't even know at this point. Contrary to what you want to believe, neither does your snitch, Bingo Dorrell. We're all just loyal foot soldiers in this race war of attrition."

"Like you, we're just taking our orders...just like Patrice Williams gave you your orders at the Dry Tortugas. Just like Gary Freeman gave you your orders to come out here and find a dead man, Darius Royal."

"In this battle for power between our races, sometimes your sworn enemies become allies of mere convenience and circumstance...On the flip side, sometimes fellow brothers in arms can become more vindictive and dangerous than mortal enemies."

"Life is a fucked-up ride, isn't it, Nuria Phillip Sellers?"

Dominic let out a girlish laugh that wiped away the seriousness of her statement. She took a rather strong pull from her burning joint, and its cloud of lazy smoke hovered towards my unprotected nose. I felt the knowing tingle in my throat as I inhaled its scent into my lungs. The distinct smell of the powerful plant seemed to intoxicate me on contact. I tried my best to fend off the all-consuming effects of the fog, forcing my spirit into a steady state of focus.

"Are you trying to tell me that it was Gary Freeman who killed Governor Williams?" I broached.

Dominic looked at me with her bloodshot blue eyes that were frustratingly disorientated and filled with drunken riddles. She gave me silence in response to my direct question, seeming to instead engross herself with the menial task of cleaning her joint of its long hanging ash. Out of the corner of my eye, I noticed Dennis biting down on his bottom lip as he leaned back in his chair, slowly shaking his head in frustrated protest. Clearly intrigued by it all, Ed fixed his eyes on Dominic, trying his best to decipher her coded messages.

"If Gary Freeman and his hardliners are the ones that killed Governor Williams," I pushed on. "They couldn't have done it without outsiders, right?"

"Is this where you come into play, Dominic?"

"Are you their White contact on the outside?"

"Is that why you're held up in this little armed fortress?"

"You confessed that your already dead, so...that must mean that whoever is helping Gary Freeman is a loose end. A loose end that needs to be cut away and discarded in order to conceal the identity of the real culprits."

"Are you and Darius Royal the loose ends, Dominic?"

"You really believe you can save me, don't you Nuria?" She asked in a state of astonishment.

"You are so close to the answers you seek but still so far away from the truth."

Dominic picked up the revolver at the center of the table and leaned back in her chair. Opening it, she took out five bullets before spinning the revolver and slamming it back into place with a drunken flick of her wrist. Dominic pointed the gun underneath her chin, pressing it upward into her mouth.

"There are five empty chambers in this pistol. Only one is loaded."

"You've got five questions if luck is on your side," she remarked with a solemn expression.

"It's either this gun will have the final say and all the answers your heart desires die along with me, or I live to tell you my truth."

"Why are you doing this lady?" Ed blasted. "This is a stupid little game you're playing. If you can help us, we will do everything we can to keep you alive. Just fuckin trust us."

Without hesitation, Dominic looked Ed right in his eyes before pulling the trigger. The sound of her gun's click echoed throughout the tension-filled room. Dominic was emotionless as Dennis, and I watched the two of them stare down each other, petrified that Ed would again open his damn mouth to ask a silly ass question.

"That, Mr. Foundational Black Agent Man...was question number one."

"I'm doing this because I want to."

"That's one of the big problems with you people. You don't understand us or even care to try and learn about White people...all the while, I know any and everything about you. You are pathetic..."

"We study you. We know your likes and dislikes. Your strengths and all your weaknesses. Your desirous motivations and your deeply seeded fears. We are your God. You worship at our feet without even thinking to ask any questions."

"You relish interacting with us from a position of abject ignorance and confusion while we control you with the advantages of knowledge, clarity, and purpose."

"That's why you asked that stupid ass question. You see me, a white woman that has you tied up and bound...and you assume that I'm playing some fucking game with you."

"No, this ain't a game for me. I've been playing Russian Roulette with you blacks for my whole damn existence on this planet. I have devoted my entire life to the task of controlling who among you will be allowed to eat and who among you people will starve to death."

"Being God is so tiresome," she sighed.

"Now, I feel the need to let fate decide, instead of exhausting myself in my final moments."

"We aren't as ignorant or confused as you think we are," Dennis angrily shot back.

"I know who and what you are, Ma'am. Rebecca St. Vincent from Newport, Rhode Island, alias Dominic Bamber. CIA Code name Black Dawn."

"Graduate of Yale. Doctorate from Berkley. Speaks several languages fluently. Expert in human psychology and international business."

"All of that made you one of Langley, Virginia's most prized female recruits."

"The CIA sent you overseas to cut your teeth...Africa, England, Haiti, Panama. Anywhere your blonde hair, blue eyes, and diverse sexual appetite could put a pretty face on white oppression and murder."

"You take advantage of Non-White males' thirst for a little interracial sexual access. Dooming them with your innocent smile and sexual curiosity."

"You moved up to the big leagues when the CIA shipped you back home and made you corporate executive of the Sour Grapes Winery in Napa Valley."

"The Winery itself was nothing more than a front business. It helped launder money and make connections for the CIA in the business world. Its main purpose was to be some sort of twisted boarding house for trained assassins on the CIA's payroll. A place where professional killers like the gang of illegal immigrant farmers you have out here, could hide under your shadow."

"Dominic Bamber, AKA Black Dawn, that's who and what you really are," Dennis explained.

"You are the White Man's kiss of death. Lethally efficient, cleverly deceptive, endlessly motivated, and absolutely ruthless...or at least, that's what you once were."

Dennis's words were surprising. The seriousness and certainty by which he made his statement confirmed that he definitely knew more about all of this and hadn't been honest with me. Up until this moment, I had known Dennis for years. Now I quickly realized that there were a few things about Dennis I had yet to discover.

Dominic smiled at Dennis with admiration before facing me and shrugging her shoulders. She pulled the revolver away from her chin, slowly placing it back on the table in front of her, before taking another huge pull from her smoldering joint.

"At least one of you seems to have figured out a few things," she laughingly admitted.

"And I'm not at all surprised that it's Dennis's big brain that was able to put things together. God knows your sassy little Force Protection Secretary, Vincent Towns, is out to lunch...or is it that he's always out chasing underage black boys?"

"But hey, you didn't hear it from me," she chuckled. "That's your problem, not mine. If you blacks aren't even the least bit interested in protecting your own children, then there is no reason for white people to care about your kids either."

The look on Ed's face was one of deep concern, while Dennis and Quinton seemed unmoved by her revelation. My mind raced as the room went silent while we all soaked in Dominic's cleverly delivered admission. Sensing that she had us all under her spell, Dominic shifted in her chair, placing her elbows on the table and leaning her chin into the palms of her hands. Looking at Dennis, she smiled while trying her damnedest to break through his emotionless façade.

'Dennis Marcus Winslow from the Foundational colony in Oakland."

'National Foundational Black Student of the year award recipient eighteen years ago. Earned scholarship offers to every Ivy League school in America, but chose to attend Grambling State University in buttfuck Louisiana."

'You eventually came to your senses and finally relented, accepting a prestigious scholarship to attend MIT for post-graduate...only to disenroll after a half of a semester."

'Let Dennis tell it; he will say he got homesick...but the truth is Dennis Winslow hated the white people at MIT."

'He hated the threatened white men that were intimidated by his mere presence. He hated the cock horny white women that threw themselves at his feet. He hated the insecure white professors that weren't as smart as advertised."

Dominic paused to pour herself another shot of bourbon whiskey, playfully blowing weed out of her lungs, before effortlessly consuming the alcohol. Dennis sat quiet, looking at Dominic with eyes that were crazed and ready to kill. I had never seen this in Dennis's spirit. His anger was all too revealing, and I knew it was best to sit back and soak in the truth these two were hell-bent on exposing to us all.

"Most of all," Dominic reengaged. "Dennis Winslow hated the Black Zebras at MIT."

"Black people Dennis considered useless and pathetic. They looked the part of Black, but in their souls, they were just as White as any hardened White Supremacist."

"In the eyes of black hardliners like Dennis Marcus Winslow and Gary Freeman, there is only one thing that's scarier than a White Supremacist.... and that's any Black person that desires any part of Whiteness. Isn't that right, Dennis?"

"If you're gonna start asking me questions, then you should give me your pistol," Dennis mockingly replied.

"Not a chance in hell," Dominic retorted.

"Like I told you before, I know what you people think, before you think it. I wouldn't trust Dennis with a gun if my life depended on it. You'd kill me in a second if I gave you the damn opportunity."

"Dennis," I interrupted. "Did you and Gary kill Governor Williams?"

"Just tell us the damn truth man! Fess up so we can end this shit," Ed jumped in!

Dennis turned his head away from us, pointing his aim into a faraway corner. His confusing reaction made my heart drop as the thoughts of Dennis's surprising betrayal flooded my consciousness. Governor Williams trusted him. I trusted him. Now to find out that Dennis's true allegiances were with Gary Freeman, I could feel my spirit withering up inside of me.

"Since we are being honest, how about we open the whole damn can of worms and tell Nuria and Quinton all about Dry Tortugas," Dennis snapped back.

"Is that a question or a request, Mister?" Dominic inquired.

"Because it sorta sounded like a question to me."

She snatched the revolver from the table, this time jamming it into the dry river of wrinkles on her pale forehead. I could see her white skin turn strawberry red around the gun barrel as she pressed it hard into her temple. The gun's hammer surged forward and a loud click followed. A small feeling of relief coursed through my veins and I saw a momentary gaze of relief in Dominic's suicidal eyes. Quickly gathering herself, she removed her finger from the trigger and tossed the gun back down before pouring the last swig of her Woodson Bourbon Whiskey into her shot glass.

"Gary Freeman and the hardliners didn't kill Patrice Williams or Judith Bean," Dominic admitted. "They just watched it all happen and didn't do a damn thing to stop it."

"Just like they watched when the first love of your life, Quinton Sellers Heavyweight Champ of the world, had his illicit affair that forever ruined his reputation."

"Just like they watched when Nuria Phillips Sellers, Queen of the Colonial Community, forsook her decency and hopped into bed with a black Zebra. Then fell in love with a man she would never have."

"Just like...they silently watched when Patrice sent Nuria, Donovan, and Pernell to die in that ambush at Dry Tortuga's," Dominic teased with a slight smile.

"Sometimes silence is just as damning as actually pulling the trigger yourself."

"I told you earlier. I know you people. I know you people better than you even know yourselves."

"That's the reason you asked me the wrong question, Nuria."

"You think you understand, but you don't have the slightest clue."

Her statements stunned me. How did she know all of this? I had so many questions running in my head, but I forced myself into silence, not wanting Dominic to try her luck again. I heard a light moan and looked beside me to discover that it was Quinton. Tears were streaming down his face as he looked at me with a vulnerable gaze. I knew the question that was burning in his heart, so I braced myself to give him the honest answer.

"You're in love with another man, Nuria?" he softly asked. "Oh, dear... I'm so sorry. Excuse me...The Champ didn't know about your secret lover, Jeremy. Did he, Nuria?" Dominic laughingly mocked while waving her empty Woodson Whiskey bottle.

"What a hellva way to find out... right Quinton."

"Nuria's lover was a Navy SEAL. An absolutely handsome black man and quite magical in between the sheets, if you know what I mean," she teased.

"That's all it takes for a Black Foundational woman to second guess her entire life... A little bit of naughty loving, mixed with emotional confusion was what got Eve to bite the apple and Nuria Phillip Sellers to lower her standards."

"Just imagine it Champ."

"A hot night on Miami Beach. The unique smell of tequila and warm beer fills the hotel room. The glass door leading to the balcony is left halfway open and the sweet sound of Latin music pulses from the sandy beaches below."

"Then there's your fiancé in the king-sized bed. Beads of sweat have gathered on Nuria's soft brown skin. Her wet hair roughly pulled back in a stringy ponytail. Nuria's bloodshot eyes are only outdone by her curious lips and erect nipples."

"She's bobbing up and down...up and down, slowly taking this Zebra in, while she fights to muffle her moans of lust and passion."

"Can you hear her moans, Quinton?"

"Can you imagine that look in her eyes as she stares down at this guy who isn't you? Because I can, Quinton. I can do more than imagine it all, because I have the video."

Dominic pulled out a memory stick, tossing it on the table next to the revolver. In an eruption of laughter, she looked at me with eyes beaming in victory. Now I knew I had to speak. I had to defend myself...somehow.

'I was hurt, Quinton." I blurted out.

'I was hurt and I thought a lot of things that I shouldn't have been thinking. I did some things and I haven't...I haven't been myself for a long time now."

'I'm sorry."

'So, are you still with me because you love me, Nuria, or because us staying married is good for the colony?" Quinton barked.

'Nuria's a good woman, Quinton," Dennis interjected. 'And you're a good man."

'Don't let Dominic mind fuck the both of you. She is the one behind all of this mess anyway."

Amused, Dominic leaped up from her seat and walked behind Dennis. In a moment of awkwardness, she placed her hands on his shoulders and began to massage him before leaning down to playfully nibble at the bottom of his ear. Annoyed by the intrusion, Dennis struggled to spare his poor ear from Dominic's probing mouth.

'Finally, after all these years, I get to find out exactly what you Foundational hardliners know," she proclaimed.

'I've been honest with them, Dennis the menace. How about you and Gary Freeman?"

Dennis looked at me and Ed, giving us uncomfortable stares. I knew he was debating within himself while I cringed at the thought of this going any deeper than he already had. Goading him, Dominic wrapped her arms around Dennis and squeezed him like a loving mother.

'Come on, Dennis, I'm about to die anyway and your secrets will go to the grave with me. At least give me the courtesy of finding out what I've been searching for all these years. Tell me, Dennis. Tell me."

"The Hardliners have been running a counter-Intel program named Surge. The Colonial Leadership Council doesn't know about it. Patrice Williams didn't know about it; only a select few are aware of its existence."

"The purpose of Surge is to infiltrate the ranks of the Dominant Society and Foundational Leadership itself," he explained. 'It is our mission to root out any threats to the Foundational agenda."

This was why Gary never trusted me or Patrice. He had been spying on us the whole time. Dominic listened attentively as she slowly made her way back to her seat. The look on her face was one of wonderment. She enjoyed the secrets. These games of cat and mouse were all engrossing for her.

"Through our sources, we were able to find out that Dominic had been assigned to an Op involving Quinton Sellers and Nuria Phillips," he continued.

'Having such a high-profile black couple like you two celebrated around the world was an embarrassment to the white folks. An embarrassment that only highlighted the overall success of our reparations project. That success could not be tolerated."

'So, the CIA sent Dominic and her operatives after Quinton."

"What do you mean the CIA sent their operatives after me?" Quinton asked.

I watched Dominic's hand shake as she poured the final drops of whiskey into her cup. This time, the stinging burn of the warm alcohol overwhelmed her throat, causing Dominic to let out an audible sigh upon swallowing.

'He means we targeted you for destruction, Champ," she interjected.

"Your baby momma worked for me. I chose her specifically for you.

It was her assignment to destroy you publicly, and she did a great job."

"Believe me, Champ...it was hard finding the right woman to trip you up."

"You didn't like the pretty blondes. You rejected the voluptuous southern belles. You absolutely hated the Latinas, but with the help of a strong sedative, you turned out to be more than a little partial to dirty brunettes."

Alive with anger, Quinton strained against the restraints holding him back. He yelled and cursed at Dominic, who just smiled glowingly back at him.

"You bitch," Quinton murmured in frustration.

"Come on now, Mr. Bible Thumper," she mocked.

"Nobody made you get high or pay for that lap dance. You did that because deep down inside, you wanted that white woman. You needed to experience her touch and feel. You enjoyed grinding yourself against her. You wanted to control her and treat her like a dirty little whore. You knew your fiancée would never do the things she did to you. Just the thought alone excited you, didn't it, Champ?"

"You and the hardliners knew about all this, Dennis?" I asked. "Yeah. We did Nuria."

"Did Donovan and Pernell know about this too?" I followed up. "Trying to stop it would have exposed our sources," he deflected. "

Sources that we needed to keep safe, Nuria. But it turns out Dominic was already on to us and that's where Jeremy Woodson enters the story."

"What Dennis really means to say," Dominic corrected. "That's where your infamous heroics at Dry Tortugas and Bradley Wood comes into play." "Your teammates, Donovan and Pernell, knew that you had been fooling around with Jeremy Woodson, even before that hot and steamy night in Miami."

"In fact, your mentor, Donovan, secretly lobbied Patrice Williams to have you removed from your Force Protection Team before you even went to Miami. He cited a potential conflict of interest given you were sleeping with Jeremy."

The revelation struck me hard. Donovan had lost faith in me. Part of my spirit wanted to continue to live in denial. I tried to find some way to dismiss her admission as another white lie, but in my soul, I knew she was right. The pain of it all brought me back to one of my grandfather's favorite little sayings. Sometimes, telling the gut-wrenching truth to a person you care about is the boldest act of love. On the other hand, the greatest act of hate is intentionally denying that same person a painful truth that could save them from themselves. In my mind, I wondered if Donovan resented me for what I had done. Yet, I had to consider the painful decisions I drove him to.

With tears in my eyes, I looked over at Quinton. No longer able to hide my shame behind useless pride, I sobbed loudly as the spirit of the Lord's realization overwhelmed me. I had been trying my best to live a lie, and the burdensome weight of living that lie had finally begun to cripple my weak shoulders. Thoughts of Donovan devoting his last dying breath to saving me flooded my memories. The act of giving his life up to become my forgiving battle shield in this gruesome war humbled me. I knew I didn't deserve it. I didn't understand it up until this very moment. Now, I understood and the truth was as clear as the cloudless blue sky above.

"He loved you, Nuria." Quinton jumped in.

"Donovan loved you, just like I do."

Dominic sparked a flame, relighting her half-smoked joint before taking in a small pull. I blinked the blurry tears from my eyes and saw she was also crying. Her hands shook as she took the burning joint away from her mouth and smashed it into pieces inside of her long glass ashtray.

"How sweet," she relented.

"It's amazing that we have tried to be like God for so long, yet, it comes naturally to you people."

"Donovan believed in you and gave up his life to prove it. While I have served my greedy masters faithfully without hesitation, they will still erase me from this world like bad handwriting."

"This whole thing is just a machine. A death cult... and now it's my turn."

"Tell us who's playing us all like puppets, Dominic?" I curiously asked "Who is behind the assassination of Governor Williams?"

Without acknowledging me, Dominic picked up the revolver from the table. She slid open the bolt, reloading five bullets before slowly closing it. Rising from her seat, she walked over towards me with the weapon. Bracing myself for God's will, I mustered the courage to look her dead in her eyes without blinking. As she neared me, Dominic sat the gun in my lap without uttering a word. She then lowered herself to one knee and I felt the fishing line restraining me beginning to give way as she loosened the tight knots.

Free to move my arm, I quickly grabbed the pistol, pointing it at Dominic's head. I watched as she carefully rose from her knee without even a notion of fear in her eyes. Backing away slowly, she reached across the table and grabbed her memory cell, softly tossing it into my lap.

"Now you're asking the right questions," she said as a tear rolled down her face.

"That memory card ought to help you find the right answers. Good luck."

Out of the corner of my eye, I noticed the Hispanic Boss Man push his finger against his earpiece, straining to hear. After a few seconds, he jolted over to Dominic and leaned in, whispering a few muffled sentences in her ears. A teary-eyed Dominic nodded her head before instructing the Boss Man to unlock a closet door. The Boss Man walked over to the closet and rummaged through several sets of keys before finding the right one and unlocking the door.

'Looks like your FBI friends have found out about our little get-together out here," Dominic cryptically stated. 'Now, they're outside, wanting to join in on all the fun we're having."

'Nuria and Ed, I don't think I need to tell either of you that Riley and Clarke aren't the most trustworthy of FBI agents."

'Like the both of you, they seek the truth, but their truth is a truth that is profoundly different from yours. Best of luck to you both."

Dominic looked me dead in my eyes, almost expecting and wanting me to pull the trigger. Sensing her non-verbal request, I stared back at her without blinking and lowered the gun back to my lap. Dominic's face contorted and a river of tears streamed down her cheek.

Then I heard a door burst open. Looking towards the noise, I saw the Boss Man's body in midflight. His body plowed into the hardwood floor and ceased to move. Blood poured out of his ears, as his skull had been cracked in half. Behind him, I saw a dark brown figure and immediately knew who the man was.

'Darius," Quinton screamed out! 'You alright boy."

Unmoved by Quinton's question, Darius zeroed his angry gaze in on Dominic, who stood shivering in petrified silence. Without mumbling a word, Darius calmly walked over to the portrait of Jackee Joyner Kersee, looking up at her with a blank stare while pulling the javelin out of its mount on the wall. In an instant, the brightly colored javelin sailed through the air towards us. The sound it made as it whistled in the air was terrifying. Then came the impact and the feel of Dominic's warm blood as it soiled my clothes. Her body bounced off the hardwood table and hit the floor. Looking down at her, we were all forced to watch as she fought for her final gasps of air. Dominic forced a smile, but it wasn't hard to see the look of regret hidden within her eyes. Then came her death stare and the end of Dominic Bamber, the CIA operative, AKA Black Dawn.

"Darius, what the hell you doing, man?" Quinton blasted.

Unconcerned with us, Darius calmly walked towards the front door and exited the boathouse. I knew we needed to follow him. It was critical to quickly get Darius back to the colony. Murdering a CIA agent would certainly warrant his own death and eliminate our potential to garner any possible information he could provide. I jumped up from the chair and quickly untied all three men before we jetted out of the boathouse after Darius. Outside, Clarke and Riley were held at gunpoint by a large group of Hispanic men at the property's front gate. Both men's hands were up in the air, pleading with their captors to be allowed to chase after Darius. Noticing us exiting the house, Riley waved at me and pointed towards the direction Darius had gone, screaming for us to give chase.

In the distance, I saw Darius was sprinting towards a tall metal fence, part of which had been sliced open in a perfect square. All four of us bolted from the porch to run him down. Darius was fast and I knew immediately he would make it to the opening before we could even try to get close. We all stopped our chase in exhaustion, resigned to the fact we would never catch him. With the gun in my hand, I had the momentary thought of stopping to gather my aim and shooting him in the leg. I collected my breath and aimed for pumping thighs just below his waist. Alarmed, Dennis quickly knocked the gun from my hand, giving me a look of bewilderment. Quinton, Dennis, and Ed began yelling at Darius, pleading with him to stop. Instead, Darius turned to look back at us with a stale expression before leaning forward and galloping faster towards the opening in the fence.

As he neared the fence, he began to low crawl, preparing to dive through to the other side. Then a dark flash came diving into our view. Out of nowhere, a black male figure ran up to Darius, tackling him before he could make it through the fence. We watched as both men wildly tussled with each other, exchanging violent punches and elbow shivers in angry silence. Sensing an opportunity, we all took off towards the fighting men. As we closed, Darius tossed the other black man to the ground, kicking him in the stomach before reaching into his back pocket.

It wasn't the sight of the sharp knife in his hand that alarmed me. Instead, it was the cold stare that he gave us as we slowly tried encircling him. Feeling cornered, Darius backed up towards the opening in the fence like a possessed animal focused on survival.

"Darius, what are you doing," Quinton pleaded. "We are just trying to get you back home, son."

Quinton's words didn't seem to register with Darius. It was almost like he didn't even recognize his childhood hero. Ed bolted towards Darius in a futile attempt to knock the blade from Darius's hands. Outmaneuvering him, Darius swung the blade towards Ed's neck, nearly hitting his target and causing Ed to stumble backwards. I pointed my gun at Darius's shoulder, ordering him to throw the knife to the ground. Quinton stepped in front of me and blocked my aim. He put his hands out to his side in a sign of non-aggression before slowly walking towards Darius.

"Look man, we mean no harm," he softly conveyed. "Your mother and your sister miss you. We are all concerned about you. Just come with us and everything will be OK. I promise."

From behind Quinton, I could see Darius cock his arm back, preparing to throw his knife. He bit down hard on his lower lip while aiming at Quinton's chest. Upon realizing what was about to happen,

Quinton turned to me with fear in his eyes, diving towards me and knocking us both to the ground. As the weight of Quinton's body drove me into the soft grass, I heard several loud claps that nearly burst my eardrums. Using my arm to push Quinton aside, I looked up and saw Darius falling to his knees with his mouth wide open. His body shook for what seemed like an eternity before he collapsed to the ground, falling flat on his stomach.

Riley and Clarke ran up from behind me, kicking the knife out of Darius's hand before placing him in handcuffs and rolling him over on his back. I jumped to my feet and ran over to Clarke, who stared down at Darius with a look of absolute confusion.

"Why did you fucking kill him," I barked.

Unbothered by my question, Clarke continued to stare down at Darius in a state of shock. The chaos in my mind settled and I instinctively followed Clarke's eyes. Darius had been shot center mass. The bullet wounds formed a small cluster just below his heart. Riley and Clarke's aim had been perfect. Then the obvious dawned on me and gave me chills. At first, it was what I didn't see that grabbed my spirit and caused sweat to trickle down my neck. Then the reality of what I was looking at registered. The suppressed memories of Dry Tortugas and the young black teenager I had killed resurfaced.

"Why is his blood...blue?" Ed asked in astonishment.

"I don't know," Clarke responded.

Next to us, the mysterious man who stopped Darius from escaping coughed loudly as he picked himself up from the ground. Finally rising to his feet, he wiped the dirt from his pants and adjusted his shirt before looking into my eyes. While examining him, I felt my heart widen and that all too familiar feeling course through my soul. Unsure about what I should do, I jumped away from him, yet I found myself unable to take my eyes off the man. For some reason, I knew I didn't want to stop looking.

'Hi Nuria," He mumbled with a voice filled with both trepidation and unspoken yearning.

CHAPTER SIX

LOST & FOUND

GARY FREEMAN CONFIDENTLY SAT AT THE table looking like a brand-new man, sporting his freshly shaven head and his neatly groomed greyish beard. After being hidden away in our colony's underground fortress, having the opportunity to once again meet with actual human beings certainly must have felt like an occasion to put on his Sunday's best. Next to him sat our ever-aloof Force Protection Secretary, Vincent Towns, who was reviewing a stack of photos with a dismissive grin. Both men were silent as our FBI counterparts, Ed, Dennis, and myself, all watched anxiously from across the table.

Vincent handed Gary two photos and softly whispered to him while pointing his index finger at a few small details hidden in the image. Obviously agreeable to Vincent's observations, Gary adjusted his reading glasses and focused his gaze before leaning in close. After several hushed whispers, Gary nodded his head in a non-verbal display of understanding. Satisfied, Gary tossed the photos on the table and let out a heavy sigh. Leaning back in his luxurious chair to gather his thoughts, Gary ripped his reading glasses from his eyes and quickly retired them inside his coat pocket. As the conference room fell back into a thought-filled silence, I looked down at the photos and saw the ghostly look on Bingo Dorrell's face. His half-dressed body hung from the high steel bars of his detention cell door. Bingo's toes were inches above the floor; it was almost like he was magically floating in mid-air. His bruised arms were zipped tied behind his back and his dry red tongue dangled from his mouth, in between his two busted lips. Around his neck was the makeshift noose made from thick manilla rope. Dark purple abrasions surrounded the rope that was clinched in tight around the skin on his neck. It had surely been a horribly painful death for Bingo Dorrell. He had fought like hell to save himself, but ultimately, justice was not on his side.

"Well," Gary relented.

"I can say without a doubt that I don't know how this could've happened."

"It was my strict orders to keep this man safe and alive, which is why we kept him here on the colony in the first place... so this sort of thing couldn't happen to him."

Frustrated, Gary leaned forward in his chair, looked down at the photos in front of him, and shook his head in a very convincing display of disgust. Next to me, I could see the burning fire in Riley's eyes. Gary's words didn't convince Riley at all and I knew that he would soon dive into his typical FBI interrogation tactics. Suddenly, I heard the front door of the conference room creep open. Looking over my shoulder, I watched as my protégé, Mary Ann Haskins, walked through the door. She smiled at her boss, Vincent Towns, upon entering the room before quickly turning her eyes towards me. Mary Ann walked up behind my seat and gave me a folded note before finding her own seat at the table. I opened the note and read her words before folding it back up and shoving it into the palm of my hand. Nosy onlookers examined me, trying to gauge my reaction, so I purposely remained stone-faced and unbothered.

On the other hand, Mary Ann flashed a bubbly smile, ensuring that everyone in the room noticed her. She coolly crossed her freshly shaven legs and let out a light giggle as a tempted Clarke lustfully stared at her thighs. Pissed at Mary Ann's grand entrance, Riley exhaled loudly and instead focused in on Gary Freeman.

"If you really gave strict orders, Governor Freeman, then why were they not followed to the letter?" he blasted.

"Bingo Dorrell was not a citizen of this colony, sir. He was a white man. Per our Reparations Treaty, that would officially classify him as a guest under your legal purview."

"To have Bingo somehow...murdered under your jurisdiction begs for an outside investigation to be initiated. Does it not, Governor Freeman?"

The disrespectful tone hidden underneath Riley's question spurred Gary's dark brown face to frown. Riley's subtle accusation was bold and aggressive, but it also gave me a clue of how desperately these bastards wanted to control our colony. Ironically, Dominic, the slutty CIA operative, had been right about her own kind. These people would use anything to advance their agenda. For them, it was not about justice; but only about winning.

Forcing myself to stay calm, I balled my fist tight, hoping that I could somehow hold in the raging fury within my soul. In my imagination, I envisioned myself letting loose a barrage of personal expletives at Riley. My weak fleshly emotions wanted to punch back at this devious bastard, but within my teetering spirit, an inner voice told me to hold my peace. While I was winning the war within my soul, the room around me remained uncomfortably quiet. Everyone seemed to be waiting on someone else to make the first move or play their hand.

After hearing someone clear their throat, I looked down the table and saw that Ed was visibly beginning to lose his own inner battle. For Ed, Gary was a family member and I was sure that having some arrogant federal agent question his cousin's integrity was beyond tolerable. On top of that, due to Dominic's memory cell, we all knew more of the truth than Riley and Clarke. Hearing Riley continuing to manufacture some rationale to incriminate Gary and dig into our colonial business, was predictable but no less infuriating.

Not able to contain himself any further, Ed's eyes turned red and began to well up with tears. As he stood up from his seat and blasted a hellish glare at Riley and Clarke, I knew the wetness in his eyes wasn't caused by remorse or regret.

"You presumptuous little piece of shit," he let loose.

"If you people are after our colonies memory cells, you'll have to find them over my dead body, you hateful damn demons."

Dennis quickly reached up, grabbing Ed's arm and pulling him back to his seat in an effort to reel him in. Next to Riley, an offended Clarke threw his pen down on the table and began to bark back at Ed.

"Whatever you Foundationals are hiding from us, you best believe we're gonna find it! One way or the other, we are gonna find out the truth, Ed," Clarke explained.

"And when we find it, I promise you that your jail cell won't magically become some coffin...like you Black Supremacist assholes made it for Bingo Dorrell."

"So, you're defending the honor of these White Extremists now, brother," Ed shot back.

"I'm defending fairness and equality, you Hotep loving hypocrite," Clarke quickly responded.

"Two virtues you dusty Foundationals aren't familiar with given your inhumane treatment of Bingo Dorrell, a human being."

"You're right, Agent Clarke," Dennis calmly broke in. "You're absolutely correct."

"Bingo Dorrell was indeed a human being."

"No matter how much he promoted the oppression of our people, he didn't deserve to die in such an unjust manner. That's exactly why we Foundationals are dedicated towards the task of arresting those responsible for his extrajudicial execution."

Next to Clarke, Mary Ann uncrossed her legs and slowly stood up from her chair. Everyone in the room curiously watched as she playfully brushed a few small strands of whitish lint away before reaching into the small of her back and pulling out a set of handcuffs. I took the balled-up note out of my hand and slid it across the table to Gary. Without hesitation, he grabbed the note and peered down at the message enclosed within it. I watched as Gary's face went limp, then his eye seemed to flicker in disbelief. Having fully digested the weight and ramifications of the message, Gary looked over at Dennis, and both men shared a non-verbal exchange of quiet disappointment. Mary Ann had played our hand and now my time in the purgatory of inner silence had come to a merciful end.

"Vincent Towns, you're under arrest for the murder of Bingo Dorrell," I stated while rising from my seat.

"You're also being charged with conspiracy, treason, carnal knowledge of a child, unlawful sodomy, and failure to uphold your oath of office as a Foundational Black American."

Ed jumped from his seat and grabbed Vincent's shoulder. He pulled him down to the carpet from his luxurious chair next to Gary Freeman. Awoken from his state of comfort, Vincent began to scream at me, calling me a Zebra-loving whore while pleading with Gary to have me fired due to my affair with Jeremy Woodson. I looked over at Gary to gauge his reaction. He was stoic and unmoved by Vincent's pleas, so I waved at Mary Ann, ushering her over to place Vincent in handcuffs.

"We've found hard evidence that you are working with the FBI and you gave them details about the inner workings of our colony," I explained while purposely looking into Riley's wide eyes.

"You and the FBI have been targeting Gary Freeman and trying to set him up. Now you've been caught."

"Vincent Towns was actually Bingo Dorrell's secret source," I explained.

"The FBI was using Bingo as an Intel mule to deliver useless information to our colony, in the hopes of discovering hardliner spies in the Dominant Society."

"What you bastards did is against every damn agreement in the Reparations Treaty," I reminded Riley.

"But breaking treaties and agreements is par for the course with you damn people. Lies and deception are your way of life."

Without words, Mary Ann and Ed yanked Vincent's arms behind his back, slamming his wrists into the shiny metal handcuffs. After whispering a few ill meant words into Vincent's ear, Mary lifted his body up from the carpet, standing him on his feet. As Vincent stood before me, looking into my eyes, I could see that he was crying. For him, it was the instant realization that his act of treason had been exposed. "It's traitors like you that allow the Agent Riley's and Clarke's of the world to walk right into our peaceful colony and believe we are all as corrupted as you are," I let out.

"By no means am I perfect, Vincent. I have my issues. I can admit that. In some way, we are all flawed vessels pushing this irredeemable world towards the ultimate arch of God's righteousness."

"But there is one big difference between you and I."

Pausing for effect, I pulled out a small photo from my jacket pocket and held it up in front of Vincent's puffy face. His eyes bucked and I could immediately sense the spirit of shame washing over him. Vincent had allowed the FBI to blackmail him. They had taken his vulnerability and used it against us. When he should have come to us for aid, he instead chose to deny us the opportunity to help him because he decided to preserve his pride first. Self-preservation is at the heart of every act of black treason. Unfortunately, Vincent Towns wasn't an exception to the rule.

"Vincent, you sold out your people to advance the interests of groups that hate Foundational Americans."

"Groups that hold contempt for the mere notion of our colony's continued existence. Contempt for the fundamental ideals of Black Empowerment and Universal Justice. Contempt for our enduring faith, righteous spirit, and loving black families."

"You sold us out for them, Vincent...all because you were too ashamed to come to your real family and ask for help. Ask us for help and admit that you had a problem."

"Now your problem controlling your urges around underage children has come to light in the worst possible way, and it's haunting all of us that actually care about you."

With a flick of the wrist, I tossed the shameful photo on the table, allowing everyone in the room to see it. The vivid photo was graphic, disgusting, and repulsive. Every God-fearing man in the room glanced down at it and the sight of the disturbing act Vincent Towns had engaged in made their eyes immediately cut away in anger. Visibly disturbed, Gary leaned back in his chair, tilting his head away from the table in an attempt to distance himself from it. An angry Ed placed his large hand around Vincent's neck and squeezed out his frustration while guiding Vincent out of the conference room.

"What the hell is this Nuria," Riley objected.

"You're gonna scapegoat this poor man because of a sexual preference? This is outrageous, even for Nuria. You people are hypocritical bigots and nothing but a bunch of homophobic beasts."

"Homophobic beasts? Fuck you, asshole!" I shot back.

"This damn colony is in the Bay Area you numb skull!"

"A third of our black citizens happily practice some form of alternative lifestyle. Let's be honest Riley, your big problem with those citizens, is that they roundly claim black first. They are loyal to their blackness and not your extreme sexual preferences."

"You were more than ready to arrest Bingo Dorrell for molesting little girls. Now, when a man is abusing boys, you wanna turn the other cheek? What does that say about you?"

"You may allow this type of demonic shit in your community, but here in our Reparations colony, child molestation is a crime. Under our system, your sexual habit does not grant you any sort of special immunity from the law. So, you can take your perverted value system and shove it where the sun don't shine."

"Your silly little colonial laws are misinformed and way too old fashioned," Riley proclaimed. "Legally it is not rape or child molestation if the other party doesn't even fight back or desires the sex."

"None of those little boys fought Vincent or complained, Nuria. They made a decision, and the children should be allowed to express their sexuality as freely as adults."

"That's the difference between you folks and us," Gary broke in.

"We Foundationals value morals while your people value wickedness and self-gratification. Your entire thought process and justification, is that of an unrelenting pedophile."

"We understand that a society that fails to protect its children will inevitably cease to exist. Under White Supremacy, you White folks have made every living child into a sexual item to be hunted down and controlled for the amusement of demented savages."

"As for your false claims of black homophobia....We've heard that white non-sense for centuries now, so you can stop trying to hide your Anti-Black Racism behind false claims of black homophobia Agent Riley."

Emboldened, Gary stood up from his seat and slowly walked towards the exit while exchanging death stares with a seething Riley. For the two men, this was personal. Both men's body language told me they wanted to take a swing and have a go at each other. From my perspective, I would have been more than happy to allow Riley the opportunity to exact his pathetic form of justice. If he had dared to even touch a hair on Gary's head, that would give me more than enough cause to arrest his sorry ass. I stepped to the side, giving both men a clear path towards each other. Sensing the intensity in the air, Clarke quickly jumped up, putting himself in between Riley and his adversary.

"Chill out," Clarke whispered. "He won't get away from us. We'll get his ass. This isn't how we do it."

Mildly amused at Riley's emotional state, Gary left the room and slammed the door behind him, leaving all of us alone. A satisfied Dennis collected all the photos off of the table, neatly putting them away inside a folder while displaying a victorious smile. Out of the corner of my eye, I noticed a look of frustration splash across Clarke's face as his efforts to simmer down Riley vehemently failed.

"One way or the other," Clarke began.

"We are going to get your colonies memory cells. We are going to find out how hardliners like Gary Freeman and Dennis, the fucking comedian here, killed Governor Williams and Senator Bean."

"Cut the bullshit Clarke," I interrupted.

"You know your whole damn investigation has nothing to do with finding assassins."

"The FBI's goal here is to gather intelligence to use against Foundationals. That's what you and Riley are really after, so you can stop all the pious talk."

"You came here in the hopes of finding out who our informant was. You're trying to find a mole within your ranks, not some assassin."

"As fate would have it, instead of finding some traitor in your midst, you've helped me uncover a mole you bastards had among us, and now you're upset that we've outed your source."

I walked over towards Riley and purposely got right in his face. We were close, so close that I could smell the stale scent of cheap coffee in his hot breath. I wanted to invade the confines of his space and tear down his personal boundaries just to let him know I could touch him. If he understood that I could touch him, he would also know that I could hurt him. Undeterred by my presence, Riley braced himself. He balled his little fists, almost like he was preparing to deliver a blow to my head at the slightest notion. Despite his aggression, I decided that it would be my one arm against his two. So, I wasn't backing down.

"You need to carry your ass back to San Francisco and find out which one of your FBI colleagues ordered Vincent Towns, to kill Bingo Dorrell," I relayed.

"You bastards don't get to drop your smelly piles of shit in my colony, then come around and blame us for pooping."

"Oh, by the way, Riley...The next time you try and pin one of your murders on an innocent Foundational, I'll arrest your ass and have you locked away in the darkest cage in Africa."

Turning around, I made my way towards the exit, leaving Riley and Clarke in the conference room. This part of our plan was over and we now had other fish to fry. Mary Ann and Dennis followed, and we all headed downstairs to meet with Ed. Outside of the entrance, Ed was parked in his car awaiting our arrival. Upon seeing us, he quickly landed and we all climbed inside. In the back seat, a handcuffed Vincent sat motionless, staring into his lap in a state of shock as his tears created a wet pool in the crotch area of his expensive designer pants. I opened the front passenger door and fell into the seat next to Ed, while Dennis and Mary Ann squeezed into the back with Vincent.

As we made the quick drive over to the Force Protection building, we were all silent. The only sound that was heard was the turbulent wind and heavy raindrops as Ed fought to navigate us through a windy thunderstorm. After several minutes, we arrived at the Force Protection building and landed next to the holding cells. On the ground, I could see dozens of uniformed men wearing raincoats and carrying long guns. Our prison had beefed up their on-duty staff after Bingo Dorrell's murder, so every correctional officer seemed a bit on edge. They had no idea that many of them would have the duty of standing suicide watches to ensure their former boss, Vincent Towns, didn't kill himself tonight.

We exited the car and headed for the prison cells, yanking a despondent Vincent along with us. Reaching the first checkpoint, several of the armed men on duty approached us with curious gazes.

"Agent Sellers?" one of the guards stated in confusion as he examined a handcuffed Vincent.

"Is everything all right, Ma'am?"

"Everything is fine," Ed jumped in.

"Take Secretary Towns in and book him. After you process him, take Mr. Towns to the suicide cell and make sure he is watched at all times. Once I've finished a few other matters, I'll come down there and tidy up the paperwork."

Not fully comprehending Ed's order, a heavy-set man with a long array of strips on his shoulders stepped forward. His face was filled with apprehension as he shook his head in disapproval, gazing back and forth between me and Mary Ann.

"We can't detain our boss," he explained. "What are you doing to this man?"

"He's not your boss anymore," I cut him off.

"Secretary Towns has been permanently relieved of his duties by the interim Governor, Gary Freeman."

"Take Mr. Vincent in and follow Ed's directives to the letter. Make sure not one word of this matter is leaked to the public. No one outside of this prison facility is to know that Vincent Towns has been arrested. Do you understand?"

All of the men cautiously relented to my order. They gingerly eased over towards Vincent and took him into custody. We watched the group of guards escort Vincent into the processing building before they made their way inside the prison cells. It was a sad sight to witness. Vincent had been a trusted member of our colony's leadership staff. Now this trusted insider had sunk to the level of a traitorous outcast. "Nuria, we better head inside," Dennis stated.

"We have a lot of catching up to do. Vincent Towns's treason has done untold amounts of damage to the colony's entire security apparatus. I have a strong suspicion that arresting him is merely the beginning of our problems...not the end of them."

We all filed into the Force Protection building, making our way down towards the basement area where our secret interrogation rooms were housed. After walking down several flights of stairs, we passed through the armed checkpoint and entered the secure area. At the direction of Dennis, the first interrogation room to our left, had been converted into a makeshift medical examination hub. In the center of the room sat a long metal table on which Darius's corpse rested.

Before entering the room, Ed and I donned protective gloves and face masks. The temperature inside was cold. I felt myself immediately start to shiver upon entering the room. Looking down at the table, the sight of Darius's frozen dark bluish blood once again catapulted my thoughts back to the young black teenager I had killed at Dry Tortugas. I felt my knees weaken and my eyes began to water as I mentally relived the fear, anguish, and pain of my past. Sensing my sudden overflow of emotion, Ed wrapped his arm around me to prop me up while whispering comforting words into my ear. I appreciated his effort, but Ed's heartfelt words barely registered in my consciousness. On the table below me laid a hidden demon of my past. A demon that Nuria Phillip Sellers, the supposed hero of Dry Tortugas, could no longer avoid. Before me was the truth, a truth that would surely challenge everything that I had forced myself to believe about my life.

Dennis walked into the cold room wearing a long plastic coat and thick protective gloves. In his hands, he carried a heavy bag of medical equipment. While studying me, Dennis placed his equipment on the table next to Darius's feet.

"Are you OK, Nuria?" he softly asked.

I erased a tear from my face and re-adjusted the top button on my thin overcoat without answering him. Somehow satisfied with my non-answer, Dennis leaned down towards the body and used his thumb to open each of Darius's eyelids before shining a small flashlight into his pupils. Forcing myself to look beyond Darius's mysterious blue-colored blood, I noticed that his muscle structure seemed abnormal. The muscles on his thigh and arms were huge for a man of his small stature. Darius had huge veins running from his forehead down to his neck. If I hadn't known any better, I would have assumed that Darius had been a professional powerlifter.

Giving us no advance notice, Dennis took a small shiny bone saw and cut open Darius's chest with three violent swipes from his sharp blade. Ed and I simultaneously winced at the grotesque sight. On the other hand, Dennis appeared enthusiastic and intrigued, like a little boy playing with his new Christmas present. Lost in the wonderment of his examination, the ever-curious Dennis gently tossed the bone saw on the table before grabbing an electrical probe out of his tool bag. Whatever he had found, Dennis was thoroughly engrossed by it.

"What are you thinking Dennis?" I softly asked. "I can see where Darius suffered fatal wounds near his heart," he explained.

"These aren't fresh bullet wounds from Riley and Clarke's gunshots. These wounds are definitely old. They have been patched up and sewed together crudely. Almost like prep work done at a morgue."

"Then there's this cancerous funny-looking hump of flesh right here," he further explained.

Using his thumb, Dennis hit the button on his electrical probe and it came to life, giving off a barely audible hum as its metal tip began to beam a light bluish color. Pointing the probe at a small hump of flesh behind Darius's heart, Dennis moved the heart aside and gently pressed the probe down into the strange-looking tissue. The probe delivered a small jolt to Darius's body and we watched as his eyes began to blink and his pupils briefly filled with life. Seconds later, Darius gasped loudly for air and began to choke. Just as quickly as the presence of life filled his eyes, the stare of death quickly returned to his face and his body went cold again.

"This man is a transhuman," Dennis concluded.

"I'm sure Darius was dead before they converted him into this bio-machine. Which is why all this scar tissue hasn't healed properly."

'In fact, these old wounds match what the Department of Defense told his family."

'It looks like Darius died due to massive amounts of blunt force trauma...he probably was killed in some sort of vehicle crash for sure."

'His heart needed to be re-enforced with this strange-looking organ behind it. In fact, his entire chest cavity is pretty cramped."

'Who would do this to a human being?" I asked. 'Someone with the technology, the motivation, and access to dead human candidates," Dennis quickly replied.

'Whoever did this has technology that is way ahead of what I've ever seen before."

'I recently read about this in a science magazine. It's all supposed to be theory and not actually practiced in real life."

'We're talking illegal and unethical science here, guys. I mean, forbidden underground bioscience where actual human beings are the lab rats and test subjects. Nothing about this is remotely ethical or legal."

'So, these people have the power to bring the dead back to life?" Ed asked. 'Well, Ed...that depends on whether you believe that Darius was indeed alive or just a living machine."

'In my professional opinion, Darius is less Jesus of Nazareth and more bio-machine."

Dennis took a white marker and drew lines along the large veins formed on Darius's neck. Afterwards, he picked up the bone saw and cut the skull off the crown of his head. Embedded in Darius's outer brain tissue were small coils of spaghetti-like material. Dennis cut away the outer brain tissues with a few light slices and used his index finger to pull out a rather long coil.

'This right here is bio-tech, my friends," Dennis started.

'It's an organic material built to survive inside the torture chamber of the human body."

'Interestingly enough, this long piece of organic tissue is also designed to perform like computer hardware. Think of this long string as a sort of old school internet router for the human brain."

'With this stuff, Darius could walk among us and access anything on the internet with merely a single thought. He was basically a walking high-speed internet search engine, a superhuman with the entirety of the world's knowledge at his disposal." 'It seems like Darius was less a human being and more of a breathing robot." I jumped in. 'Yep," Dennis agreed.

'What about the other black guy we captured?" Ed asked. 'Is he a transhuman too?"

Hearing Ed's question jogged my memory. It reminded me of another part of my past that was awaiting me in the next room. The fact that he was still alive after I had seen him die, felt surreal. Neither Dennis nor I wanted to answer Ed's question. With Darius Royal, there was this light detachment. We hadn't trained with Darius, shared personal stories with him, or been blessed to see the spectacle of real God-given life burning within his brown eyes. With this next gentleman, we had experienced the uniqueness of his life, and he in turn, had experienced ours. There would be no feelings of detachment with him, just a resurrection of long-forgotten emotions and buried grief.

'Are you gonna be OK doing his interview, Nuria?" Dennis asked sincerely. 'Don't worry yourself Dennis. I'll get it done."

Not wanting him to address the obvious, I turned my back to Dennis and quickly made my way for the exit, leaving him to perform the rest of his duties alone within the icy confines of his makeshift morgue. Ed and I walked down the corridor, about fifty feet before we came upon the entrance to the second interrogation room. Before opening the door, I peered through a small glass window to take a quick peep within.

The inside of the interrogation room was nothing spectacular, with several chairs, a long table, one cleverly hidden recording device, and a long one-way glass mirror. The all too familiar tall, muscular black man sitting alone in his chair, shivering under several layers of thick blankets, immediately stood out to me. It had been a decade since I had last seen Jeremy Woodson. Seeing his soft plush lips and the rough brown skin on his big hands reminded me of our naughty experiences on that long-lost night in Miami. Somehow, I could still taste the warm tequila in my mouth and smell the scent of his Cuban cigar, among other forbidden memories.

Catching my inner inappropriateness, I tried my best to force the longing desires of my drunken night out of my mind. Instead, I focused my attention on opening the tricky locks that secured the entrance of the room. Frustrated, I leaned my one arm into the door with a heavy push, forcing it to slide open slowly. Walking into the room, I found it to be comfortably warm, yet Jeremy still appeared cold. Jeremy looked up at me with his lips shivering, as if he was stranded on the summit of Mt. Everest.

Inside my own soul, I began to hope that whatever they had done to Jeremy hadn't taken away his real beauty. When his eyes finally recognized me, I saw that alluring life deep within him that I had always been attracted to. For a long second, he flashed a wordless smile and his body seemed to suddenly stop shivering as he slowly rose from his chair to greet me. Jeremy Woodson, the secret love of my life, was still alive.

"Mr. Woodson," I initiated while dropping my notepad on the long metal table.

"We have a lot to discuss, so let's get right to it."

"We sure as hell do, Nuria." He responded coyly. "We have a lot of catching up to do between the two of us, my love."

As we both took our seats, Ed glanced at me with a contorted expression filled with intrigue. Trying my best to ignore Ed's silent curiosity, I scooted my chair closer to the edge of the table and began to flip through the pages of my notepad. There were so many questions racing through my mind, but I made myself read a few handwritten ones from my notepad before looking up into Jeremy's entrapping eyes.

"Mr. Woodson, can you tell us how you became involved with Ms. Dominic Bamber?"

"So, you're gonna call me Mr. Woodson now?" he replied with a teasing smile.

"OK...Jeremy. Now can you answer my question?"

"You guys have Darius's body, don't you Nuria. I'm certain our good friend, Dennis, has already told you what we are."

"You should've already figured out how I got involved in Dominic Bamber and Judith Bean's messy scheme," Jeremy continued.

"I was killed out in the Dry Tortugas trying to help you and Donovan assassinate Bradley Wood. You saw me die right before your damn eyes, so let's not play dumb here. If you are gonna sit there and just ask me questions, let's get to the ones that really matter."

Ed's eyes lit up and he leaned back in his chair, quietly taking it all in before shooting another curious glance my way. For me, hearing the name Judith Bean alongside that of the shady CIA operative Dominic Bamber was shocking. I wasn't prepared to hear Jeremy associate the two, but I kept my face straight and sterile, shielding my ignorance.

"That's why I'm asking Jeremy. I need to fill in the gaps. It's been ten years since I last saw you alive."

"I'd hardly define what I am today as alive," he mocked.

"I know damn well I died out there on that island."

"I'm so sorry," I let out.

"I can honestly say I'm happy to see you again. I've spent every day since your death thinking of you and wondering. Wondering a lot..."

"You're not the only one wondering what could have been. Wondering is all I have now." He answered.

Feeling the sadness embedded in Jeremy's voice provoked tears of empathy to well up in my eyes. Sensing the overwhelming emotion within me, I quickly used my index finger to wipe away the wetness before refocusing myself. Finally realizing that Jeremy and I knew each other, Ed leaned forward in his chair, purposely interrupting our moment.

"Why did Darius kill Dominic, sir?" Ed asked.

"It wasn't Darius who did anything out there. Someone programmed Darius to kill her," he answered.

"Who turned you and Darius into transhumans?" I jumped in. "And what are they hiding?"

Jeremy unwrapped the blankets from around his body, letting them fall harmlessly to the floor beneath him. Standing up from his seat, he slowly walked over to the one-way mirror, examining it in angry silence.

"It's just us, Jeremy," I reassured him. "No one else is listening."

With a light laugh, Jeremy looked at me with an unconvinced expression before leaning himself against the glass with the palms of his hands. Clearly unconvinced with my words, he began digging his legs into the tile floor, pushing himself against the window, and straining his body to somehow crack the glass.

"We're alone brother," Ed softly relayed. "Nuria ain't lying to you. I promise."

"You both are so naïve," Jeremy shot back.

"You have no idea what you're in the middle of."

"Well, please feel free to enlighten us then," I interrupted.

"If Dominic gave you her memory cell, then you both are aware that Vincent Towns is an informant for the FBI," he began. "You should also know that he was Bingo Dorrell's fictitious Intel source."

"By now, you should know that the CIA targeted Quinton Sellers and that we were never supposed to survive the Dry Tortugas raid."

"What's not saved on that memory cell is the fact that the CIA was the owner of a news publication named the Kingfish Magazine. They operated out of New York and were nothing more than a salacious gossip column...but I'm sure that name rings a bell with Nuria."

Hearing the name Kingfish brought me back to my last conversation with Donovan, as it reminded me of the shivering anger in his voice when he told me the white media had been spying on me. Somehow, Judith Bean and Patrice Williams were able to convince the Kingfish to not publish their stories about my affair. I looked at Jeremy and could easily see the concealed fury trapped inside of his soul. For Jeremy, it was the CIA that had cost him so much.

"Dominic was the Chief Editor at Kingfish when we had our night in Miami."

"As a high-ranking CIA operative, Dominic was the one person who could approve or choose to bury negative stories about Foundationals," he described.

"When Admiral Judith Bean and Patrice Williams came calling to the Chief Editor at Kingfish, they asked Dominic for a favor and she gave them one."

"The report of our affair was buried and never published. That doesn't happen because the CIA suddenly experiences a change of heart or motives. You have to ask yourself why the CIA suddenly changed course. You have to find out what other priorities the CIA had during that time period."

"So, Judith Bean and Patrice Williams cut a deal with you CIA folks?" Ed asked.

Jeremy looked at Ed while sizing him up and didn't say a word. He had taken Ed's earnest question the wrong way, presuming Ed was implying that Jeremy had been a part of Dominic's CIA operation. Noticing Jeremy's menacing stare, Ed immediately let out a sigh and attempted to clarify his question. For a few seconds, he stumbled over his words in a futile effort to repose the question in a way that didn't sound accusatory.

"Dominic, Judith Bean and Patrice Williams all made a deal with each other", Jeremy mercifully explained.

"Dominic is the type of white person who will make all kinds of deals, as long as her ultimate interests can be obtained. In the wake of that deal lay all of our bodies, Donovan, Pernell, Patrice, and myself."

"How did you end up becoming a transhuman? Do you remember?" I asked.

Jeremy looked away from us and tried to conceal a strike of sadness while emptying his stare at the faded white wall. For several long seconds, the room went quiet. Only the harmonic sound of the mildly warm air blowing from two small vents above us could be heard in the midst of our stifling silence.

"I don't remember much," he let out.

"I can still remember the darkness and ghostly feel of Fort Jefferson that night. Other than that, all I have are these foggy memories of being in some rusty metal shack. A rusty shack with computers that constantly rang out with annoying beeps."

"I remember the weather was humid and hot. So humid that the young black woman that tended after me was always sweating."

"I can still remember the feel of her sweat when it fell on my skin, mixing with the dark blood oozing out of my wounds. She didn't speak much English, but her bright smile seemed to talk to me."

'Her skin was very dark and her hair was cut low. Her eyes were intoxicating, almost like they were inviting me back to life. She was beautiful. I remember wondering if she was an angel or some sort of alluring demon."

'For some reason, that black woman's beauty has been seared into my memories", he lamented.

'Did you know where you were and how you got there?" I asked. 'No. I can't remember Nuria. I just can't. It's frustrating as hell, and I can't. It's been erased or blocked somehow in my brain", he explained. 'The only full memories I have after Dry Tortugas start with me riding in an old school bus through a desert road outside of Juárez, Mexico. I woke up in the front seat. The bus was pitch dark, smelled like tobacco and everyone was quiet."

'The desert road was bumpy as hell and we drove on it with no headlights. All I had was a handwritten letter in my pocket along with several hundred American dollars."

Jeremy leaned forward in his seat and looked me dead in my eyes. The way he closed the distance between our separated souls only brought home the importance of what he was about to tell me. Fully understanding Jeremy's intentions, I braced myself to hear every word he was about to say.

'We got to the Rio Grande, and in the darkness, people filed out of the bus and started swimming over to El Paso.

'My first thought was to not join them. I am an American, and I didn't need to sneak into my own country. Plus, I had no idea why or how I found myself where I was. It was a scary situation for me."

'Yet, a funny thing happened."

'Something inside of me told me that you were on the other side of that river. Something told me that you were still alive."

'Despite the swampy confusion in my mind, I started remembering all the moments we had with each other. In my cloudy thoughts, I could still see that look on your face as I faded into darkness. It was the despair in your eyes that endured in what was left in my soul."

'I knew I needed to find you. So, I read my letter and swam over to El Paso, bound for the Bay Area."

'I've visited your home several times, Nuria. Almost always in the middle of the night. When you finally fall asleep, I would climb up to your fire escape and open up your master bedroom window."

'I've watched you toss and turn in bed, sweating heavily while experiencing nightmares. I've heard you call out names...My name, Donovan and Pernell."

'Something buried deep within me burned to help you. I wanted to crawl into that bedroom and give you some comfort. To kiss your lips and somehow relieve you of this soul-crushing burden. Yet, as soon as I dig up enough nerve to do so, something else inside would force me to walk away."

Pausing, Jeremy coughed loudly, clearing his throat before leaning back in his chair. I noticed the hopeful blaze burning within him as he stared at me. It had been years since his eyes had last inspected me while trying to shield his naughty ambitions. I felt the familiar nerves ripple down my spine, so I forced myself to look away and pretend to fix my hair with my fingers. Jeremy was still in love with me and I knew everything he had told us was true. It all made sense and the seeds of regret that were buried within my spirit began to bloom. Out of the corner of my eye, I saw Ed pull out his notepad and scribble down a few sentences. Deep in thought, he placed the tip of his pen on his bottom lip and looked up at Jeremy, ready to lob another question at him.

"Are you saying someone programmed you to kill Agent Sellers?" he asked. Annoyed with Ed's inability to follow him, Jeremy shook his head in laughter. Ed's patience visibly expired upon seeing Jeremy's clear disrespect. His face began to show his anger as he sat up in his chair. I could tell Ed wanted to curse Jeremy out, so I placed my hand on Ed's arm, signaling for him to stay calm.

"I don't exactly know what they programmed me to do, my man," Jeremy stated. "I don't even know who the hell did it."

"All I know is that for some reason, I made my way up to Napa Valley and Dominic had this weird interest in me. Her ranch in Napa Valley and her estate in Bodega Bay were used to house Hispanic illegals and transhuman assassins."

"Dominic treated the illegals like shit. She was especially harsh to all the transhumans, but for some reason, she had a soft spot for me."

"For some reason, I secretly hated the damn woman. Something inside of me wanted to kill Dominic, but she always treated me better than the rest of her subjects. It almost seemed like she knew what I was truly there for."

"She made it a point that both Darius and I slept in the bed with her. Dominic gave us the best food, drinks, drugs, every damn thing. She would even allow me to visit this colony from time to time. I would come here every now and then in the hopes of catching a glimpse of Nuria."

"Dominic knew that despite this death and transformation, I was still in love with Nuria. Although my feelings frustrated her, Dominic saw fit to use it to her advantage. It made me one of her most prized curiosities."

"Dominic was infatuated with Darius Royal, probably because he was the exact opposite of me. She called him her little black love pony, and Darius worshipped the ground Dominic walked on."

"Darius adored Dominic. Everything she said was the gospel. He was young, and Dominic seemed to relish controlling him with her words and emotions. Seeing the two interact was sickening to watch."

'Dominic also loved to ask me about you, Nuria. She'd let me talk about you for hours. She would always ask me about the daydreams I'd have about you and the regret I felt for never meeting those dreams. She just sat there, listening attentively, like what I was feeling and saying was important to her."

'After each session, she'd tell me that there was still a chance my dream might happen. Dominic would pour encouragement into me with each puff of weed or stiff drink, then solidify our tenuous bonds with drunken kisses. She would inject fresh life into my confusing world with every drug-induced orgy."

'So, I never could bring myself to get rid of her for some reason. I just played along, fighting off the hidden desires to kill her that strangely continued to boil inside of me. I guess I felt some sort of kinship with Dominic. She was the key I felt I needed to somehow open up this new life."

'We'd have these deep conversations about Judith Bean and Governor Williams."

'Dominic was certain that the both of them could bridge the differences between the Dominant Society and Black Foundationals. She talked about reintegrating White America with Foundational Society. That was her main objective and she was hell-bent on convincing me that her plans could work."

'After each discussion, she would get aroused, taking me to bed with her as some sort of twisted culmination between my black skin and her white power."

I didn't want to believe what I was hearing. This wasn't the Jeremy Woodson I knew and cared about. None of this sounded right to me.

Something else had to be at play here because the pain in his words made it all sound so tortured. Sensing my unspoken concern, Jeremy leaned back in his chair, creating some distance between me and his visible anguish. He wiped a tear from his right eye, and I couldn't tell if that tear came from a spirit of remorse, pain, or deceit.

"But as time wore on," he continued.

"Dominic's faith in reintegrating Black and White Society began to wane. Gradually, my daily bedroom chores started disappearing. They were replaced with long hours locked away in a cold underground cellar."

"Strange guests began showing up at her Bodega boathouse. I could tell they were white people with money by the way Dominic catered to them and became extremely submissive in their presence."

"When the white folks left, Dominic would become extremely depressed and almost panic-stricken with disillusionment."

"It was at this point that she began to abuse me and Darius. We quickly became the main targets of her wild fits of hidden frustration."

"That's when I convinced Darius that we should escape," Jeremy lamented.

"One day, we both escaped. We ran off to San Francisco and hid there until Darius's behavior became extremely erratic. So, I decided to take Darius back to Bodega Bay until I could get his family to hide him in this colony. His family was resistant, I guess they probably thought I was some sort of Zebra scam artist."

"After several conversations with his little sister, I was able to convince her to help me sneak Darius away from Bodega Bay. When Darius made it back to this colony, I decided to go south of the border to find out what had happened to me."

'I got pretty far south, making it all the way to Honduras before a group of armed CIA men captured me. When they took me back to Bodega Bay, Darius was already there, and this time, he was a totally different person."

'He was extremely confused about who he was. His mood swings were violent and scary. Darius was dangerous and Dominic was really scared of him at this point."

'One day, Dominic summoned me to her bedroom. She was fully clothed and wasn't high. I could tell from her mood that I wasn't summoned there for sex. So, when she started talking, I just listened. Dominic was rambling on and on about hardliner Foundationals and some memory cell you guys have."

"Then she looked me in my eyes and made a statement that I never forgot. She asked me to do something special for her. She wanted me to grant her one final request in case she ever went missing or got killed."

'Dominic asked me to take Darius Royal and go find you if she died. She said you were the only person who could free me and Darius."

In his eyes, I could see Jeremy replaying the memory of Dominic's request in his mind. From across the table, I could feel the confusion and underlying fear embedded in his emotions. He was trapped in this maze. An innocent black man caught in between life and death, love and war, loyalty and treason, truth and lies. Ed jumped up, asking him a series of rushed questions to which Jeremy completely ignored. He just sat there, silently looking into the nothingness of the small table in-between the both of us. The thirst within his dreams that sought freedom and love had simply been an empty mirage. I knew Jeremy had suddenly realized that the deeply sewn desires that had pushed him along this path were so close to him, yet millions of miles away from reality.

CHAPTER SEVEN

THE COMFORTING VISIT

IT HAD BEEN AGES SINCE MY mouth experienced the unique taste of tequila. The half-empty bottle sitting on the table in front of me brought back memories of yesteryear. My intentions were to only drink a few swallows, but today in this cold lonely house, the warm burn of the alcohol was my only company. The amazement of having looked into Jeremy's beautiful brown eyes had unsettled my spirit. As regret bum-rushed my soul, I found myself refilling this cup a few more times than I originally planned. For years, I had known that my heart hadn't progressed beyond that unforgettable night in Miami. It wouldn't take Dr. Wiseman's fancy little degrees to tell me that this hidden fantasy was unhealthy. The reality of my situation was hurtful. I had surely gotten older as the seconds of this God-given life ticked away. One of my arms had been lost. My marriage was in shambles. My bouts of depression were only worsening. For me, time had moved on, yet my spirit was still stuck in Miami. In Miami, I was still a young woman. I would still be eager to conquer the world and achieve my lofty dreams. Unlike the person I had ultimately grown into, the person in Miami still had value.

I wanted so badly to find a way to go back in time and talk to my younger self. Hoping I might be able to somehow change all this shit for the better and avoid the landmines of life. Maybe Jeremy and I could have run away together, starting our lives anew and making sure to forsake this world's racial war. We could have gotten married, spent the rest of our lives fucking like wild rabbits, and enjoyed mojitos on sandy beaches. Undoubtedly, doing so would have spared us from this painful and torturous existence we were now forced to experience. My internal fantasy felt so damn warm and promising. It was so warm that it weighed down my real-life existence with cold guilt and frosty unfulfillment.

As the warm tequila began to wear off, I could feel that familiar anger bubbling up within me. In the complete silence of my home, that anger diverted my thoughts towards Quinton's absence. At Gary Freeman's insistence, Quinton had packed up little Lindsey, leaving the Oakland colony to stay with distant relatives in the small reparation's colony outside of Phoenix, Arizona. Deep inside, I knew it was the right decision. Our responsibility was to keep little Lindsey safe, yet I felt this lingering resentment about Quinton leaving. Here I was, once again, left to clean up a mess that all stemmed from his one bad decision. If he only had been able to control himself, Donovan and Pernell would still be alive. Patrice would have had no reason to have been killed, and Jeremy Woodson would have been a mere afterthought for me. Life would have gone the way it was supposed to happen.

Pushing away thoughts of Quinton's lack of manhood, I closed the tequila bottle before activating files saved on Dominic's memory cell. As the files began to load, hologram images of videos, documents, and voice recordings popped up all around me. For several minutes, I quickly scrolled my finger through the air, getting rid of an endless amount of junk that ranged from the totally useless to the ridiculous. This was the life of an Intel specialist. Experiencing the mind-numbing boredom of combing through mountains of pure garbage, in the hopes of finding that one shiny nugget that might lead you to the whole damn gold mine. It had only taken me a few hours to find the goods on Vincent Towns. Dominic had squirreled away a rather large folder filled with intelligence the FBI had accumulated on him.

To their credit, the FBI kept detailed notes on every single meeting Vincent had with his White handlers. Every deposit they sent to his bank account. Every disgusting surveillance video they had that captured Vincent Town's raping little black boys. Dominic had saved it all, and it wasn't hard for me to find any of it. All Mary Ann had to do was double-check a lead and we were able to arrest Vincent Towns. Dominic had made collaring him uncomfortably easy. In fact, it was too easy.

Finding any leads pertaining to the assassination of Patrice Williams was a totally different story. In this maze of uncorrelated information, nothing saved on the memory cell seemed to make sense. Determined to solve her white riddle, I started a pot of coffee and began the task of re-reading documents and identifying keywords that would unlock any unwritten secrets. After several hours, my tired eyes began to beg for a reprieve. Most of the documents I read involved bureaucratic nonsense about the Farmer's Treaty. There was absolutely nothing about the documents that remotely screamed smoking gun. This was going nowhere fast.

As I closed one document and moved on to another, the loud sound of the front doorbell ringing, made me shutter. Alarmed at the notion of having an unplanned visitor, I felt the shocking grasp of insecurity consume me as I realized that I looked like a complete mess. My unkept hair was wild and the smell of tequila still reeked from my pores. Not to mention, I hadn't slept the night before and was in desperate need of a hot bath. Curious about who had decided to visit me, I activated my door cameras to find Quinton patiently waiting outside. Immensely relieved that it was only him, I slowly rose from my chair, walked to the entrance and activated the speaker box.

"Quinton. Why are you back?" I asked. "I missed you," he admitted. "Are you gonna let me in my own house, Nuria?"

With a click of a button, I unlocked the front door and the sound of Quinton's labored footsteps followed as he walked into the house. The look on Quinton's face was one of pure disappointment. He dropped his bag on the floor and bit down hard on his bottom lip. I knew Quinton was holding in inner thoughts of frustration. Our house was a mess. Trapped in my total focus on the case, I hadn't bothered to take out the molding trash. To my embarrassment, a noticeable smell of spoiled food filled the house. Looking for some way to vent his silent anger, Quinton walked over to the couch and began to pick up the empty laundry bag I had left on the floor.

"Please leave it there, Quinton," I shouted! "I'll pick up my stuff later."

"Somebody's gotta do something to keep this damn house clean, Nuria," he countered. "You're so focused on this case...Now, this dude you have feelings for is alive...."

"Did you even get the message from little Lindsey's homeroom teacher about the conference today?"

Surprised by his question, I felt my face involuntarily grimace upon suddenly remembering the meeting I was scheduled to attend. I immediately knew this was the real reason why Quinton had come back to the colony. His lying ass didn't miss me. He was here for Lindsey and was trying to take full advantage of the opportunity to throw my faulty memory back in my face.

"So that's why your ass is here?"

"You don't have to lie and pretend like you came to see me because you love me."

'I don't need you to come here and clean up. I can do that by myself."

'I'll just call the school and reschedule the meeting."

'I already met with her teacher," Quinton broke in.

'Lindsey has been bullying other students at school. She's gotten into fights."

'The teacher told me that she is becoming a handful. She's disrespectful and argumentative with school staff."

'The teacher showed me a few essay assignments that Lindsey wrote. She wrote about the constant arguments we are having. I read how she sometimes cries herself to sleep at night. She wrote about seeing you hit me and yell at me, and she feels like you are attacking me because you hate her."

'Bullshit," I snapped. 'I love Lindsey like she was my own."

'Well, act like it then," Quinton loudly interrupted.

'Because I can honestly say that I understand why little Lindsey would have those feelings, Nuria. I'm not the only one in this house that feels put off by you."

'While your mind is stuck in the past...still trying to fight wars you will never win, the family that needs you right now is crumbling."

'Nuria, you're a perfectionist. As much as you want to go back in time and change every fuckin little thing, I don't. I refuse to go back there with you to wallow in the misery of it all."

'Life is about making errors and learning from those errors."

'I regret the mistake I made. It was the most painful error of my life, but I thank God that He saw me through it. It changed me from an arrogant young man seeking fame and fortune into a wise black man who understands that this world's bright spotlight...burns just as hot as hell itself."

'Before, my life was all about boxing. It was all about dominating anybody who dared to step in that ring. As long as I can remember, I've always wanted to be the best boxer alive."

'Now, the lessons of life have allowed me to see things much clearer. This thing called life is bigger than me and my petty desires."

'God has shown me that he doesn't care how great of a boxer I am or how many title belts I won. None of that really mattered when I was arrested and thrown in jail. Instead, it was the world's scorching hot spotlight, leading me away from the real plan God had in store for me. That's all it was."

'You matter to me, Nuria. You are a big part of God's plan for me."

'I love you and nothing in this fucked up world will come between us."

Quinton went silent before turning away and immediately started cleaning up the house. Before I could retort back with my own emotional volley, Quinton picked up a half-eaten plate of food and bolted towards the smelly trash can. Deep inside, I knew he was right. For years, I had been purposely hiding. In my soul, I could feel the cold fatigue of my painful flight from reality starting to wear me down. I was afraid of being hurt and that fear was weighing me down. Life is about trust and faith, and for a long time, my life had been devoid of both. Due to the painful circumstances surrounding Quinton's affair and the assault at Dry Tortugas, fate had seen fit to snatch away every black man I trusted. Both events drained the faith from me and cast away every ounce of trust this tricky world had earned. I thought I had been strong, but my perceived strength had instead become my glaring weakness. Now the aura of this weakened spirit I carried had negatively affected Little Lindsey. I loved her. I cared about her, but she didn't see that. She only saw the bitter fruits and ravage chaos my perceived strength had produced.

Feeling the sting of defeat, I held my tongue while sitting down on the couch. Wiping away the tears, I could feel the pain I had buried within me rising to the surface. In that instant, I decided not to fight this feeling and truly address my own tortured reality. Forcing myself to concentrate, I swallowed hard and focused within. Closing my eyes, I did the only thing I knew would set my broken spirit on a more stable course. During my teenage years, I would often find my mother on her knees praying to the Lord when the windy gales of life engulfed our family. Back then, I thought her devotion was a bit irrational and slavish. Now I had come to realize that her uncompromising faith was, in fact, a source of strength that I was sorely lacking.

Almost as if the hand of God had reached down from above, I felt the spirit within me move. The feeling was as swift as it was unexplainable and completely undeniable. Overwhelmed by this powerful presence, I fell to my knees. Struck by his sudden revelation, my soul was consumed by his grace and I began to burst with emotion. I had never felt such comforting power and precise clarity. In this life moment of ultimate self-realization, I knew God was indeed real. This wasn't some sky God written about in a book of old detached fables. Elohim's Holy Spirit was, in fact, real and it was living within me. It had always been there through all of life's turbulence. Due to the faults of my own understanding, I just never realized nor welcomed God's presence.

I felt a firm hand grasp my lonely shoulder. Broken away from my inner moment, I wiped my face and looked up into Quinton's soft brown eyes. Feeling blessed, I reached up with my lonely hand and caressed his brown cheek.

"I've never heard you talk to the Lord before, Nuria." He said with a gentle smile.

Puzzled by his statement, I stood up and retook my seat on the sofa. A bit embarrassed by my emotional state, I collected my thoughts, putting away the fear of being perceived as weak. Sensing my insecurity, Quinton wrapped his arm around me in a comforting embrace before delivering a soft kiss to my sweaty forehead.

"I don't remember saying anything," I mused.

"I just felt myself fall to the floor and I started crying."

"I know," Quinton chimed in. "I understand. But I definitely heard you calling out to the Lord, asking Him to forgive you." "Then I heard you thanking God; that's when I felt the Holy Spirit's presence. So, I walked into the living room and found you lying here on the floor in tears.

"I've been praying that this day would come, and now, it's here," he lamented.

Quinton released me and stood up from the couch. I watched as he bolted up the stairs, disappearing into our master bedroom. After hearing him open and close our closet door, he came out of the bedroom carrying a small white cardboard box. As he silently sat down beside me, Quinton removed the top of the box and placed it on my lap. I looked down into the box and saw what was concealed inside. My eyes began to water once more as the instant recognition of Quinton's memento sunk in.

"It's your wrist name tag. The one you were wearing when I first came to visit you at the hospital," Quinton described.

"Even the sight of that name tag immediately reminds me of the fear and shame that I was drowning in."

"Back then, my name was mud."

"I went from Heavyweight Champion of the World to cellmate number 9752."

"Before my mistake, I was the most famous Foundational in the world."

"Yet, there was no amount of fighting that could keep me out of jail.

My mistake dominated the headlines of every newspaper the Dominant Society could print up."

"These white folks were more than happy to expose my weaknesses and celebrate my failure with the world. I embarrassed myself. I embarrassed our people. Most of all, I embarrassed you and soiled our relationship."

Quinton wiped his eyes with the back of his hand, then cleared his throat. His demeanor told me that he half expected a rude interruption, but as I remained quiet, Quinton continued.

"The arrest. The New York jail cell, none of that was worse than seeing you unconscious in that hospital bed."

"For weeks, you laid there. Only a few of the doctors thought that you might live. They tried to convince me that if you survived, you would have major brain damage from being in that coma for so long."

"A majority of the doctors believed that you wouldn't survive. I remember them counseling your parents and recommending they authorize the hospital to secure your oxygen and let you pass."

"I begged your mother to give you a chance and pleaded with her to not give up. I told her that I prayed to God, and also made a promise that I would give my life to Him, whether you survived or not."

"I knew that in the back of your mother's mind, she too was upset and disappointed with me, but she patiently sat there and heard me out as I talked through all my emotions."

"Every night, I slept in that stuffy hospital visitors' lobby. I was too afraid to leave, thinking that I might miss your last moments. Some kinda way, I wanted you to know that I was there."

"At first, most of the women that worked at the hospital were disgusted with me. They all knew what I had done, so I wasn't Mister Popular with them by any stretch of the imagination."

"After several weeks of finding me asleep in those uncomfortable wooden chairs, a few of the nurses grew to have some kind of sympathy for me. Two of them brought me an inflatable mattress and gave me a spare key to the workers' shower room."

'One morning, your mother arrived at the hospital and gave me a Bible."

'She handed it to me, and I'll never forget what she said after I took it," Quinton explained.

'She asked me what my most treasured memory of you was."

'And I told her about the time we were in the sixth grade. My parents had just moved to the Oakland colony from Mississippi and I was the new nervous kid at our school."

'The other kids in our class used to tease me. My voice still had a country twang to it, and I was always the butt of their jokes when I spoke in classes."

'Do you still remember that?" Quinton asked with a laugh.

'Yeah, I sure do," I began. 'At first, I thought your accent was funny too."

'But I saw how the jokes were hurting you. During lunch, you would always sit at a back table all by yourself, trying to avoid talking to our classmates. Then one day, I got tired of the other students picking on you, so I just started fighting and yelling at everyone."

Amused, Quinton let out a loud chuckle and wrapped his arm around my waist. With a gentle tug, he pulled me closer to him, holding me in a warm embrace. Feeling comfortable, I leaned my head into his chest, relishing our childhood memory as Quinton ran his fingers through my hair with tenderness and the love I had missed for years.

'From that day in the sixth grade, I knew I loved you, Nuria."

'It would be a few years later before I would gin up enough mannish courage to ask you out on a virtual date. But from that day onward, I had a major crush on you."

"I told your mother that story and she shared a few stories of her own," he explained.

"Before she left me in the lobby, I promised your mother that I would read the Bible to understand it."

"She told me that if I asked for it, God would provide me with the understanding I was seeking, but I needed to be prepared to truly walk that narrow path once I found it. Like hard hitting truth, God's path is not easy or even accepted in a world that's dedicated to separating us from his path."

"And your mother was sure as hell right," Quinton emphasized.

"People thought I was crazy when I retired from boxing. Throwing away fame and millions of dollars to become some lowly Deacon at a small black church."

"When people in the world recognize me, they mostly see a disgraced ex-champion. A black Foundational loser who got caught in a cheating scandal while engaged to a national hero."

"But I began to grow and understand it all. From the corrupting evils of this White Supremacist controlled world to demonic plagues in our black churches that mislead followers away from God."

"In this life, there are a lot of false paths that will lead us to our own destruction. Many of these paths are paved by our own misunderstanding or our deeply wounded spirits."

"What people thought they understood about me wasn't really important. My true purpose and faith was something they would never grasp, even if I tried my damnedest to explain it to them."

"I decided to stop fighting the Lord and obey him, no matter what worldly things were taken away from me. No matter what people of this world thought or how they persecuted me for my belief."

As my head lay against Quinton's chest, I could feel the warmness of his wet tears falling into my hair as he searched for the right words to describe his life-changing experience. The moment had touched him deeply and his words were sincere. Wanting to encourage Quinton, I started rubbing his forearm, offering him a touch of comfort while he bore his soul.

"God had made it a point to show me what was more important," he continued.

"And to this very day, I have submitted to his will. I have been patient with you, Nuria, because God was patient with me. As a black man, it is my obligation to love you the very same way God loves me."

"I came to understand that, as a black man, it's my example of faith that would ultimately lead us both through this world that seeks to tear us away from each other."

Moved by his words, I looked into Quinton's beautiful brown eyes and finally was able to see the same black man that I had fallen in love with so many years ago. Our lips met and the sensation reignited a once forgotten passion to feel the touch of Quinton's long-lost kiss. Quinton and I cuddled on the couch for hours, talking to each other like reunited friends. No fear of arguments. No silly misunderstandings. No concerns about hurt egos or pride, just loving conversation.

As the twilight hour of the early morning engulfed us, we had both fallen asleep on the couch only to be jolted awake by the sound of our virtual phone's loud ring. Half awoke from our peaceful bliss, I tried to blink away the hazy fog before erasing the cold drool from my mouth. It had been a while since I had been able to sleep so peacefully, and I abhorred the sudden interruption of my much-needed sleep. For the first time in a very long time, I had actually fallen asleep and given rest to my wry soul.

My happy moment of self-recognition within me was shoved away as the virtual phone continued to ring. Quickly refocusing, I rose from the couch and walked over to the phone before pushing down hard on the receive button.

'Hello,' I hastily answered while the hologram image of the caller came into focus.

When the image sharpened, an image of Dennis hovered in front of me. His chin looked freshly shaven and his hairline was sharp. Yet, the fatigue in his eyes was obvious as the scenery of the makeshift morgue in our interrogation room flooded into my view. Instantly, I knew Dennis had pulled an all-nighter. He had found something important regarding our case and sank his teeth into it.

'Hey, Nuria. I'm sorry. I didn't mean to interrupt you. Is it a bad time?' He asked.

As my sleepy fog began to clear, I realized that Dennis was also examining my own image. I was certain that my unkempt hair, loose clothing, groggy stare, and the visual of Quinton quietly sleeping behind me made Dennis consider himself a bothersome intruder. Using my fingers, I straightened my hair before pulling out a seat for myself.

'No, you're good, Dennis. You caught me and Quinton in the middle of a nap. That's all,' I reassured.

'Oh. OK...good.' He said with a sigh.

'I think I may have found something big, Nuria,' he continued.

'But first. Were you able to go through all the files on Dominic's memory cell?'

'Yeah, I did,' I answered. 'Aside from the evidence on Vincent Towns and a lot of documents about the Farmer's Treaty, there's not much else on it to speak of.'

'I'm not sure if anything saved on that memory cell is going to lead us to the assassin of Governor Williams.'

"Maybe Dominic is just playing one last cruel joke on us. Giving us Vincent Towns on a platter is a last-ditch effort to distract us from something much more damaging to the Dominant Society."

"Well, I hate to sound macabre, Nuria, but I've been doing some digging around inside of Darius's skull." Dennis began.

"What I'm finding in his brain is astonishing. The Bio-Technology that Darius Royal is wired with is unbelievable stuff. I mean...it is quite literally the perfect marriage between human anatomy and a computer."

"Some sort of POF bio-chemical was injected into Darius's body after his death. The chemical reactivated his brain cells, programming his cellular RNA to produce tissues that are foreign to the human body."

"His brain tissues actively transmit super high-frequency radio waves that are broadcasted via his hair follicles. The frequency is similar to 406 megahertz, which is old and rarely used these days."

"Embedded in those radio wave transmissions are a treasure trove of compressed data that can only be unlocked or deciphered if you have the right coded receiver and password," he relayed with nerdy excitement in his voice.

"All of this information is received by satellites in orbit that relay the transmission. When the satellite receives the data, it is saved, and then the satellite makes calculations to correct for azimuth error, orbit speed, celestial triangulation, and time delays."

"OK, Dennis. I sort of get it," I interrupted.

"Now tell me in simple terms what all this means, please."

Amused by my confusion, Dennis allowed himself a quick smile. After taking a deep breath to ponder a few words he thought I might understand, his hologram image leaned in close. The look on his face was serious as his likeness drew nearer. Whatever he was trying to explain, it undoubtedly worried him.

"Darius and Jeremy are like living breathing unmanned vehicles," he described.

"Their flesh is alive, but with biotech embedded in their brains, someone can easily see everything they see. A person with the right network setup online can hear everything they hear."

"With a stroke of a button, someone can log into their consciousness and manipulate their feelings, desires, and urges."

"A handler could totally control Darius from afar and manipulate him to the extent that he could involuntarily feed a homeless man or instead murder that same homeless man with not one drop of remorse. This is more advanced them simply downloading some program into a robot, this is complete human control."

"Nuria, this type of technology is dangerous. It's a threat to mankind as we know it. This puts us firmly into a new age. A new age of Transhumanism."

For some strange reason, my thoughts went back to the boathouse in Bodega Bay. The sheer depression that dominated Dominic's spirit before she was killed stood out to me for some strange reason. I remembered her rambling on about being in utter exhaustion. Dominic told us that she was tired of having to be God. It was obvious that she was discontent with the CIA's mission. At the time, what she said didn't make much damn sense. To me, her words were simply the rantings of a crazed White Supremacist who wanted to throw stones at the glass house the CIA had built for her. With this new revelation regarding the Dominant Society's use of transhumans, now Dominic's babble about being God made sense.

White Supremacists like Dominic thrive on controlling the world around them, but there is a more addictive element then their need to control or manipulate. It's an element that is as old as time itself. For

Dominic, control is merely a byproduct of her real desire; a desire hardcore White Supremacists like her must quench at every turn. Having slavish transhuman subjects that will undoubtedly obey every beck and call does nothing for people like Dominic. For White Supremacists like her, it is all about the hunt. The never-ending quest for that addictive adrenaline rush when a dangerous adversary has been subdued by your own force or your own gull. For Dominic, the game of life or death was her real addiction.

Transhumanism would take away the element of force. Forever removing the battle of human wills, erasing the contest between earthly minds and competing spirits, and eliminating the mortal struggle between opposing beliefs. Recognizing that we had discovered a key to new clues, I grabbed my hand-held computer and opened Dominic's memory cell files. This had all the signatures of an interagency battle being waged within the CIA itself. Governor William's Farmer's Treaty had surely been the cause of Dominic's death. Someone in the CIA had been controlling Darius Royal and that person wasn't Dominic.

'If we are able to find out who is controlling Darius, that will blow this whole case wide open," I blasted. "

Is there any way we can find out who is logging into Darius's brain?"

'No," Dennis softly responded. 'The signal is heavily encrypted, and even if I tried, there's a good chance it would just lead us into a wild goose chase."

'But there is one crack in the system," he offered.

'The smoking gun is the satellite itself. I was able to hack my way into the satellite and pull up all the data it received from Darius's brain."

'Much of the data I pulled from the satellite is useless, but I was able to retrieve GPS coordinates for every location Darius's brain transmitted from."

I watched as Dennis grabbed a stack of printouts and quickly thumbed through them. If we could retrace where Darius had been, that would surely lead us to another clue. Then the realization hit that Darius could have purposely been sent to our colony. Agent Riley had asked his mother if Darius visited any hardliners or attended hardline events. It dawned on me that Riley already knew Darius had been in our colony, using his unlawful presence here as a backdoor to access memory cells. Whoever the element was within the CIA that controlled Darius had likely tipped off Riley and the FBI. My mind raced as I tried to ascertain if these CIA elements were indeed a rogue element or if it was Dominic herself who had gone rogue. "Here it is," Dennis declared, breaking my train of thought.

"We have location data for the last three years, give or take a few months."

"He spent a lot of time on the move but never ventured out of the Bay Area."

"At first glance, nothing jumped out as suspicious, but when you factor in two dates, things get interesting."

"The day Patrice was killed, the day the couch was delivered to the mansion on Yerba Buena Island, and the day we met Dominic at her boathouse. Before each of those days, Darius visited a Catholic clinic in San Francisco."

"What part of San Fran is this Catholic clinic in?" I asked.

"The Mission District," He replied. "The records indicate that Darius stayed there for hours before the data shows him traveling north to Bodega Bay."

"It sure is strange that a transhuman would have to visit a clinic," I mused. "A human body that can overcome death shouldn't be the least bit concerned with having a bothersome cough."

"What do we know about the Mission District?" I asked. "Is there anything special about that area?"

"Not in particular," he answered.

"There aren't any science labs there and the Mission District is a pretty good ways away from any government buildings in San Fran."

"I've been there," a voice interrupted.

"My pastor and I visited the Mission District a year ago to feed homeless immigrants that illegally entered the country," Quinton groggily explained.

"Unfortunately, we got robbed after visiting a church and handing out several hundred plates of food."

After wiping the coals out of his eyes, Quinton rose to his feet and walked up to Dennis's image. His hand glided over and gently touched my lonely shoulder as he looked down at me, quietly awaiting my permission. I nodded my head, non-verbally asking him to continue before placing my hand on top of his.

"The state of California designated San Francisco as a safe haven for Latino illegal immigrants. About fifteen years ago, all Federal Immigration Services were banned from the city."

"The Mission District is a neighborhood dominated by illegals from South America. There is a lot of poverty in that part of San Francisco and outsiders aren't too welcome, especially Black people."

"If Darius was going there, then someone definitely invited him."

Quinton's words sparked an explosion within me as the muddy details of Governor Williams Farmer's Treaty began to reveal themselves. Once again, I grabbed my hand-held computer off of the desk and quickly scrolled through Dominic's memory cell. My eyes caught a glance at the document I was searching for and I stopped scrolling. The room remained silent as Quinton and Dennis both watched me read. Satisfied that I had found a major clue, I looked up from my hand-held computer and stared straight at Dennis.

"We're gonna go visit this Catholic clinic. Like right now, Dennis," I instructed.

"OK," Dennis said with an unconvinced tone.

"What are we going there to look for exactly, Nuria?"

"The truth," I barked back. "You call Ed and get him up to speed. I'll call Gary Freeman and let him know what we're about to do."

"What about Agent Riley and Clarke?" Dennis interjected. "They won't take too kindly to us intruding into their jurisdiction, especially after what happened with Vincent Towns."

"We'll call the FBI once we arrive," I explained. "That way, they won't spoil our plans."

"I don't know about this Nuria," Dennis lamented.

"You are talking about going into a situation not knowing what to expect."

"Last time we did something like this, a disgruntled CIA agent got the drop on us and we ended up hog-tied and bound by a bunch of Hispanic transhumans. We could have easily been killed."

"I'd trust Nuria if I were you," Quinton chimed in.

"Her instincts have always been sound. But sometimes you have to throw caution to the wind and go for broke, Dennis."

Frustrated at being double-teamed, Dennis shook his head in muted anger. Behind his quiet unease, I could tell that he was too mentally fatigued to protest. He relented to my instructions and we ended the conversation. Once again alone with Quinton, I rose from my seat and looked into his eyes before kissing his lips. The strong hint of his smelly morning breath nor the endless tasks that consumed my thoughts could detour my hunger to kiss and appreciate my husband.

"Thank you for everything," I whispered.

"You just make sure you come back to me, Nuria," he ordered. "You're what's important to me. You're my life. Little Lindsey needs you, and so do I."

I called Governor Freeman, disturbing him from his own comfortable early morning slumber to inform him that the team and I were following a lead in San Francisco. While still in an apparent state of sleepy comatose, Gary struggled to follow me at first but eventually signed off on the plan. Finally, after a quick shower and two cups of black coffee, Ed's car landed in our driveway. On the way to the front door, I felt Quinton grab my hand and tug me towards him.

"Don't forget this," he said while handing me my hand-held computer. "You might need it."

"You tell Lindsey that I'm going to call her tonight," I said, taking it from him. "Tell her mommy misses her."

Seeing Quinton's wide smile caused me to struggle to hold back my own emotions. Refocusing myself, I quickly opened the front door and bolted to Ed's car. Ed was behind the wheel while a still tired-looking Dennis sat alone in the backseat. I buckled in and we lifted into the clear California sky, heading straight for the Bay Bridge.

Before reaching San Francisco's city limits, I called Riley and Clarke's office. Unable to reach either of them, I left a message for both men with their secretary, telling them where they would be able to find us. We flew over the decaying Bay Bridge, crossing the bay's deep blue water into San Francisco's city limits. Ed turned us towards the hilly walkways of the Mission District and circled the neighborhood while Dennis and I scanned the earth below us, trying to locate Darius's Catholic Clinic.

"There it is," Dennis announced.

Ed slowed the car to a hover as Dennis pointed down below, giving us visual instructions. It took several attempts for Ed and I to see the small unambiguous building. Unlike most churches, it was tucked away in-between two tall storage facilities that conveniently obscured the church from view. It was the perfect spot for anyone who wanted to operate in public yet remain discreet. There were no signs or billboards. No huge crosses. Nothing about the church screamed, 'come here to find God.' From its gated fence to the porched windows, this church had CIA remote operations site written all over it.

Surrounding the church, the Mission District was awash with activity. Hispanic children flooded the walkways, pacing the area in ragged clothes and no shoes. Dilapidated mobile homes and makeshift tents dominated the filthy streets. Groups of working-age men threw wood into a large bonfire several blocks south of the church. The fire's hot smoke rose into the air creating a black pillar, causing Ed to maneuver around it. Ed found a large hilly parking area adjacent to a local flea market that was not far from the church. He slowly brought us back to earth and landed in an open spot.

"Well, boss," Ed stated after landing. "We're here. Now, what's on the menu?"

Reaching into Ed's glove compartment, I grabbed his binoculars and put them to my eyes. I zoomed in on the building using the focus lever, examining it for any activity inside and found none. After several more unfruitful scans, I took the binoculars from my eyes and dropped them into my lap.

"We wait and watch," I declared.

Ed glanced around the parking lot with a nervous expression. We weren't alone in this parking area and the sight of his shiny new car had surely grabbed all kinds of attention. Several homely-looking Hispanic men approached our car, waving bags of half-rotten oranges in front of our windshield. Jittery at their presence, I watched as Ed eased his service pistol out of his coat pocket. I heard his safety click and knew wild Ed was getting ready to make a move.

"No, Ed," I cautioned. "You show them that gun and we won't have enough bullets between all three of us to make it outta here alive."

"We are in their territory. As long as they think they can get something out of us, we'll stay alive. The minute they perceive us as anything different, we'll get robbed and end up dead."

To both Ed and Dennis's quiet horror, I rolled down my side door window and bought two bags of fruit. As I handed each man their well-earned Foundational currency, the smiles exploded across their faces. The quiet racists in the dominant society tended to abhor our money, but these hungry Hispanics were rather tickled to be on the receiving end of Foundational currency adorned with the face of Dr. John Henrik Clarke.

The Hispanic men scampered away with their newfound cash, leaving all three of us unbothered. The morning stretched into early afternoon as we staked out the Catholic Clinic from the hilly parking lot. Aside from a few loud snores from a sleeping Dennis in the backseat, things were uneventful. The inside of the Catholic Clinic remained dark and its doors were still locked. In the Mission District, lunchtime was upon us and the smell of warm tortillas filled the air. Looking over at Ed, I could almost sense the hunger within him growing wings as he impatiently tapped his thumb against his thigh.

"Hey, you can go get us all something to eat if you're hungry."

"Yeah, I did miss breakfast this morning." He easily convinced himself while gazing lustfully at a young Hispanic lady making tacos near the flea market entrance. "

I've never wanted to go buy a damn taco so bad in my life."

"Negro, is it a taco that has you slobbering all over the place, or the young Latina woman?" I bluntly asked.

"What do you want, Nuria?" Ed angrily deflected.

"Please go grab a chicken taco for me and two beef tacos for Dennis," I pleaded.

Ed nodded his head while reaching to open the door. As his door swung open, Ed was interrupted by the sudden sight of Agent Riley and Clarke closing in on us. Both men wore plain clothes and their FBI badges were well hidden behind their trousers. From behind his sunglasses, Clarke looked into our car and pulled the handle to open the backseat. Unable to open the locked door, Clarke impatiently tapped his index finger on the window several times in agitation. Ed let out an annoyed sigh and rolled his eyes before pushing down on the unlock button and popping the door open for Clarke.

In short order, Clarke and Riley awoke Dennis and slid into the backseat next to him. Disturbed from blissful rest, Dennis wiped his face with his hands before examining the fresh faces of our annoyed visitors. Burdened by their abrupt arrival in his comfy backseat lounge, I watched as Dennis's face contoured into a scowl.

"Glad you two decided to accompany us. I see you both got the message I sent," I opined.

"We got'em, Nuria," Clarke barked in a hostile tone.

"Now, you tell us why in God's name you and your roadies are out here parked in the Mission District of San Francisco."

"Isn't it obvious, Clarke? We're on a stakeout. Try to keep up, my friend," I replied while pointing at the Catholic Clinic.

"If you guys wanna join us, you can help us out by grabbing lunch. We've been here all morning, and we're past due for a snack."

"How about you tell us who's in the Catholic Clinic?" Riley shot back.Purposely ignoring Riley's question, I picked up my binoculars and focused on the front door of the clinic. As Riley began to demand answers from the back seat, I examined the perimeter of the church. My jaw dropped when an all too familiar face came into view. I took the binoculars from my eyes as the shock settled in. After my second review, I knew undoubtedly that it was him.

I watched as the Hispanic man walked up to the clinic's front entrance. He calmly entered a code and propped open the door, allowing two ladies in nurse uniforms to walk in ahead. Within seconds, lights were bursting through the church's many windows. The clinic had finally opened for business, so it was time for me to catch up with an old comrade.

"Dennis, get your ass ready," I instructed.

"We're about to go say hello to an old acquaintance of ours."

"Ed, you stay here and cover the entrance."

"If you see anyone suspicious, come in hard and heavy. No hesitation, OK."

With a hushed mumble, Ed begrudgingly agreed. He slammed the binoculars to his eyes while an irate Riley began to loudly jabber into his ears. Dennis and I exited the car and started downhill towards the Catholic Clinic. About halfway down the hill, we saw a group of children run into the church, entering the building with playful shouts and giggles. Our open presence in this mostly Hispanic neighborhood began to attract all kinds of unnerving stares. Most of the stares were an all too familiar mix of curiosity, peppered with Anti-Black contempt. Several Hispanic men burning piles of trash near our walkway paused in the midst of their task to utter unflattering words at us in broken English.

Eager to reach the building without being accosted, Dennis and I simultaneously increased our pace. With my hand in my pocket, I clicked off my gun's safety as several teenage Hispanic boys approached us, begging for money. Speaking back to them in crude Spanish, Dennis gently brushed them aside with a smile, allowing us to close in on our objective.

We entered the church, leaving the agitated onlookers outside. Ahead of us stood the church's wide sanctuary. My nose caught the strong scent of the well-polished wooden pews. The pews were arranged on both sides of the main aisle, which sported a cheap red carpet. The pastor's pew was directly in front of us, as was a long white table. Near the table, one of the nurses stood behind a sign that read "Clinic Sign-on," in both English and Spanish. The inside of the building was dim. Dull yellowish lights dangled down from the vaulted ceilings, giving the entire sanctuary an almost majestic feel.

My ears heard the distinct sound of giggling children, so I turned my head towards the commotion. In the corner, I saw a group of kids laughing. They were huddled around the kneeling Hispanic man who wore a gleeful smile. The Hispanic man started playfully tickling each of them, causing their laughing echoes to bounce off the church's inner walls. I immediately stopped walking and stared at them. I felt Dennis lightly bump into my back in confusion at my sudden pause. He began to inquire why I had stopped, but words were removed from his lungs once his eyes followed mine.

"Nuria, is that who I think it is?" he whispered into my ear. "Why are you damned people here!"

"You shouldn't be here. This clinic is not for you. Go spend your reparations money, you lazy freeloaders." The nurse screamed.

I turned and looked the nurse directly in her eyes. Her brown face was filled with fury and hostility. Immediately, I could feel those non-verbal spirits within this woman's soul. Only other women tend to notice this sort of spirit. The aggression in her hasty tone told me she was drunk with envy. Seeing my blackness invading her world probably touched a nerve. For a brief second, I stood motionless, momentarily contemplating giving her some small sign of non-hostile intent. She quickly moved from behind the table, approaching us with blistering racial slurs and wild hand movements. This Hispanic woman was ready to go to blows. I could sense her urge to intimidate me surging in the air around us.

Any thought of giving this taco-loving whore any peaceful gesture disappeared when she used her half-ass English to call me a monkey bitch. I felt my back automatically stiffen as she continued to walk towards me. Now it was game time. In my mind, I was already relishing the feeling my lonely fist would create as it smashed into her pickle-sized nose. As she entered my striking distance, I balanced myself and balled my fist tight while sizing her up. Then the tall frame of Dennis stepped in between us, blocking my target like a solar eclipse.

"Ma'am, I'm gonna need you to calm down," Dennis calmly asked while gently pushing her to a stop.

"We're here to see Dr. Hernandez." I forcefully objected, creating a loud echo throughout the sanctuary.

"If you wanna fight. I'll be more than glad to whip your ass after I finish our business...senorita."

Enraged, the nurse continued yelling and screaming while Dennis did his best to prevent an altercation. In the corner, Dr. Hernandez rose to his feet and began walking towards us. The group of children stood in confused silence, taking in the chaotic scene before them. As he drew nearer, he looked into my eyes and I saw the spark of recognition come alive within his spirit. The corner of his mouth jolted upwards in a fond smile that usually accompanies old memories. Before he could speak, the other nurse came from a back room carrying a fire axe. Seeing her fellow nurse being pushed around by a tall black man caused her to increase her pace and she loudly shouted at Dennis in panicked Spanish.

"Doctor," I declared. "It's Nuria and Dennis...can you please get your nurses under control."

Dr. Hernandez let out an ear-piercing whistle and the two nurses went silent. Almost like trained animals, their eyes obediently found his authoritative gaze and their spirits seemed to quell in that instant. With a quick wave of his hand towards the choir room, both women begrudgingly backed away from us while cutting me with cold looks of disdain. Dr. Hernandez then turned around and instructed the group of young children to go outside. As a short chubby kid walked past him, he grabbed the child's arm and leaned down, whispering undecipherable words in his ear. The chubby kid nodded before putting his small hand out in front of him. Dr. Hernandez stood tall and reached into his pocket, pulling out a small toy. He placed the toy in the kid's hand before urging him to run off and join the others outside.

"Pardon the confusion, Nuria," he explained with his slight accent.

"My nurses seemed to have recognized you before I did."

"Looks like I'm popular for all the wrong reasons around here," I jokingly admitted.

Dr. Hernandez's failure to indulge himself in my humor betrayed the naked truth behind my own mocking words. Instead of telling me a polite lie to soothe my tender ego, Dr. Hernandez quickly ushered Dennis and I over to a long pew stationed in front of a large hanging crucifix. As I eased down on the hard seat, I felt that familiar ping of discomfort pulse up my spine. For some reason, these women had recognized my face and they instantly hated me.

"You will have to forgive my associates," he continued.

"They recognized you from being on TV with Governor Williams and Senator Bean."

"Patrice Williams and Judith Bean are not popular among my people. In fact, a lot of people around here hate them."

Sensing my opportunity to steer this impromptu reunion into the exact conversation I needed, I leaned forward in my pew and closed the distance with Dr. Hernandez. It was then that I noticed the withering thin grey hairs that barely covered his botchy brown scalp. Like me, Dr. Hernandez had gotten older, but his aging was much less graceful. Stress had seemingly consumed every ounce of youth from this man's peeling and wrinkled skin.

"Does this hate have anything to do with the Farmers Treaty, Dr. Hernandez?"

"Is this hate the reason Governor Williams was killed?

"Nuria, you're still as bold as I remember," he deflected with a half-smile.

"Her question is valid, Doc," Dennis followed up. "Darius Royal came here and gave you a visit before Patrice Williams and Judith Bean were assassinated."

"Why would Darius do that? What's going on with this Clinic Doc?"

Dr. Hernandez laughed to himself. He looked away from us to stare at the hanging crucifix before pulling a long hand-rolled joint out of his shirt pocket. In the middle of the damn sanctuary, he sparked a flame, lighting the bitter end of his potion before disrespectfully blowing its hazy smoke towards the heavens. The lack of concern or respect in his demeanor caught my attention. At that moment, I finally realized who it was we were truly sitting with. A Fox was running this henhouse, and now the fox was revealing his furry coat.

"So that's why you two are here," he sighed.

"We're here to find out the truth Doc," I jumped in. "Darius shows up at this church before the assassinations. Darius shows up here again before he executes a high-ranking CIA operative."

"Everything we have points to our assassin operating in this building and I come here and find you. A medical professional that spent years working in the Black Ops world. Hell, you worked for Senator Bean when she was an Admiral. You have no reason to want her dead."

"Who's behind all this, Doc? Is it the CIA? The FBI? The White Extremists?"

Annoyed by my questions, Dr. Hernandez playfully waved me off with his hand. Biting down on my loose tongue, I forced the angry words lingering within into compliance. Instead, I focused my pent-up energy into my eyes. I stared Dr. Hernandez down until his face yielded to me, causing him to look away in frustration.

"You know so much, Nuria," he began. "But yet and still, you don't know a damn thing."

"The fact that you're even here causes all kinds of problems for me. Problems that can't be fixed. You know what I mean?"

"You and Dennis come here to cry your crocodile tears for that white bitch, Judith Bean, and her lap dog, Patrice Williams. Expecting me to give a damn about either of them. Expecting me to care about the truth behind their murders."

"I'm a gentleman, Nuria. I'm not a man to speak ill of the dead...but sometimes it's best to let the dead dogs rot out in the open. The light of day tends to cleanse their souls."

"As for Dominic," he continued. "She knew the game she was playing and she lost. In real life, tough breaks mean real consequences. Even for privileged white whores like her."

"By now, I'm sure you know what she did to your husband. Now you're here doing her bidding?"

"You and Dennis, of all people, should know how the CIA works.

Her death should be a cause for celebration among you Foundational Negroes. You should be here praising me. You should be here looking for a way to return this favor I have given your people."

Catching himself, Dr. Hernandez stopped talking and put the joint in his mouth, taking a rather large pull. The pensive movement in his legs gave away his attempt at maintaining his cool exterior. At this point, I noticed his tired eyes making quick scans around the sanctuary. All of it reminded me of Dominic's last moments. Like her, he was expecting death. Whatever they had involved themselves in was just too deep for the both of them.

'Is someone coming here to kill you, Doc?" I bluntly asked. 'Did Dominic die after you talked to her, Nuria?" he retorted. "

Did Bingo Dorrell die after you questioned him?"

'How long will Vincent Towns live?"

'Hell, how long will I live?"

I sensed the certainty in his tone as he nervously smashed his exhausted joint into the cool wooden pew. His words were just enough to convey the secret message he wanted to send. I was here to discover the truth, yet someone very powerful was determined never to allow me to find the truth I sought. My coming to this place was tantamount to a death sentence for him.

"Well, if your gonna die, Dr. Hernandez, you might as well tell me why the Farmer's Treaty got Patrice Williams killed."

"Who ordered you to kill Dominic?" I pressed.

'Oh, fuck me. I'm fuckin dead now for sure!" He exploded with laughter.

Dr. Hernandez jumped up from the pew. Any pretension of coolness was now completely gone. He paced the floor in front of us while mumbling to himself in garbled Spanish. Dennis stood up and tried to coral him, but Doc was inconsolable. He pushed Dennis away violently, ordering Dennis to leave him alone.

"Why did you have to ask me that, Nuria?" he begged. "Why?"

"Because we're trying to save lives, Doc," Dennis calmly interjected.

"It's either you take a seat and help us or we'll leave you here to your own fate."

I wasn't sure why Dennis decided to say that, but for some reason, it seemed to refocus Dr. Hernandez, and he lowered himself back down to the pew. Again, Doc snuffled his nose and reached back into his shirt pocket, this time only coming away with a lighter. Unnerved, Dr. Hernandez slapped his knee before leaning back on the pew and taking a deep breath.

"The question you asked is a damn riddle. A riddle wrapped in a twisting enigma," he began.

"Who the hell knows who is truly behind all of this?"

"In this shady world, everybody is flipping sides...I mean, one day they'll be White Extremist, you know...or at the very least they are conservative White Extremist sympathizers."

"Then the next day, they fall in line with the liberal Dominant Society. They'll be all about working with Foundationals and creating some twisted ultra-liberal melting pot."

"Out of one side of their mouth, they are all about helping Foundationals, and on the other side, they absolutely despise you."

"This whole thing is nameless, faceless, and emotionless. At the highest levels, nothing is ever plainly spoken or written down. It's all done in vague whispers...there are never firm orders or instructions."

"At the roots of this tree, the trick of plausible deniability is always available for those at the top."

"The Farmer's Treaty is simply a political show pony," he explained.

"It's a meaningless gesture between you Black Foundationals and the Dominant Society. The treaty itself is more symbolic than earth-changing substance."

"Both Senator Bean and Governor Williams would have no doubt benefited politically from the treaty. However, the used-up vineyards offered to your people in the treaty are useless. Droughts, foreign insects, and over-farming have all rendered that once fertile soil unfarmable."

"Given those facts, my people still hate this treaty, and they specifically resent you Foundationals."

"For decades, many hard-working Hispanics farmed those same vineyards before the Dominant Society pushed us out."

"They crammed us into these damn immigration sanctuaries, and now a lot of us must decide between starving here in America or going back home to fight against the Afro-Latinos. That's why my nurses were so hostile towards you today," he explained.

Dr. Hernandez paused, catching himself before he gallivanted further into dangerous political territory. Looking over at Dennis, I could tell by the stoic look on his face that he had caught the same sentiments coming from Doc's lips. Feeling the anger simmering within me, I decided not to give Dr. Hernandez's disrespect a pass.

"On behalf of every Foundational," I softly began. "I'd like to pass on a heartfelt and loud, I don't give a fuck...to your people."

"None of you damn Hispanics raised a finger to help Black people get the reparations we were owed. In fact, the illegal labor you guys provided to the Dominant Society only stole jobs from my Black ancestors. You came to this country selfish and you used our struggle as a springboard to cozy up next to the White folks you Hispanics idolize."

"Hell, the progress my ancestors died for is the only reason the white folks allowed your duplicitous behinds to come here in the first place...

and for that...we get our jobs stolen while you eagerly pretend to be white? Fuck you!"

"I mean, look at you right now, Doctor Hernandez."

"You worked for the U.S. Navy. You were literally part of the Enforcement Arm of White Supremacy and you have the nerve to lecture a Black Foundational about oppression and racism."

"You people need to learn to hold your own nuts and stop undermining Black Americans at every twist and turn."

Far from defensive, Dr. Hernandez dismissively rolled his eyes at me before uttering a few words of mumbled Spanish. After a loud sigh, he crossed his legs and leaned in towards us to reengage.

"Hispanics should look out for ourselves," he said with a serious stare. "We have never promised you Blacks anything. We never asked to be people of color with you."

"If you blacks are stupid enough to help us along the way, that's your problem, not ours."

"Anyway, you totally missed the point I was trying to make."

"My point was that your damn Reparations is the root cause of all this chaos we are experiencing now. It's all your fault."

"I agree with you, Nuria. Smart Black people ought to be more concerned about the interest of their own group. If the Farmer's Treaty is of interest to you people, you are free to explore it."

"As a worldly Hispanic man...I don't particularly care about that silly Farmer's Treaty," he dismissively explained. "Too many of my people only see themselves as laborers and not benefactors of their own labor."

"For folks like that, Judith Bean and Patrice William's Farmer's Treaty is an unforgivable eyesore. It's an easy target to project their pent-up anger and contempt. A convenient distraction that lures them away from the inconvenient truth we all need to address."

'Like your own people Nuria, too many of my people miss the big picture in all this."

"And what does that bigger picture happen to look like Doc?" I interrupted. 'Please feel free to educate me and unburden me from my ignorance."

Annoyed by my sarcasm, he slowly rose from his seat and took several steps towards the crucifix dangling above us. On the crucifix, the white man's blasphemous version of Christ could be seen hanging his head. His long flowing blonde hair appeared to beam against his pale white skin. The look on his face was tortured and his boney frame was defeated in its posture.

"The bigger picture is all around us," Dr. Hernandez commented.

"We Hispanics and you blacks all believe we are fighting for what is right."

'Is it right to play God and transform the dead into weaponized killing machines Doc?" Dennis jumped in.

"That doesn't sound very godly to me. It sorta sounds like something completely opposite of that, to be honest."

'Fuck you, Dennis," he shot back.

"You're a man of science like me, so you ought to know how this twisted cycle goes. Our degrees are useless without funding."

'I won't let you Foundationals pin the practice of transhumanism on the backs of Hispanics. We're just fighting for our lives. Like I said before, too many of us believe in being laborers. You both should be searching for the benefactors in all of this. They are the villains here, not my people."

"So, you think doing the bidding of your European white folks is actually going to make them accept you, Dr. Hernandez?" I countered.

"Accepting this transhuman garbage and attacking Black Freedom

Fighters won't spare you people from their wrath once the White Supremacists are done with us. You Hispanics will be next for sure."

"Look at the Farmers Treaty. They have already abandoned your people. Do you really believe they won't do that again? You aren't any better than them. You're just a selfish tool with no principles."

"You both come here and weep for Judith Bean and Patrice Williams." He responded. "You come here touting the tricky words of Dominic, a world-renowned liar." "You do all of that to avoid confronting your own truth. You people caused this. It was your damn Reparations movement that destroyed the fabric our world was built upon."

"You Foundationals gained your Reparations and the rest of the black world was watching you get them. They want what you lazy assholes were given. Because of you people, they thought they deserved a better life. Now, look at what you've caused! It's all chaos now!"

"Countries like Mexico, Panama, Costa Rico, and Columbia, all experienced their own violent Negro revolutions."

"You forced us and the whites to act. We could not allow your movement to gain momentum elsewhere."

"We have chosen our side, and it isn't their side or your side. I am not your brother, nor am I their brother. My interest is my people."

Angered, Dr. Hernandez turned his back to the crucifix and walked back to his seat. He reached into his pocket and pulled out his hand-held computer. After unlocking it, he loaded a few images and showed us a picture. I saw a young-looking Doc, much younger than when Dennis and I first met him. He was wearing a jungle camouflage uniform while holding a heavy machine gun. His stone gaze betrayed a man in pain. He looked like a young man that was determined and willing to kill.

"My father," he began. "Was the Interior Secretary in El Salvador. He spent his life devoted to holding our country together."

'Because of the Negro Bandits you Foundationals inspired, I lost my father."

'In their absolute savagery, the Negro revolutionaries stormed my family's property and hung my father from an old apple tree."

"That's when my brothers and I joined the Resistance," he said with excitement in his eyes.

'I wanted to become a medical student. However, the Resistance needed Doctors, so they sent me to El Paso to study medicine."

'It was there that I first met Dominic," he further explained. 'She recruited me into a counter-intelligence program run by the CIA named Operation Balboa."

"The CIA sent me back to San Salvador after I graduated. I was assigned to a secret research facility outside of the city that was built by the CIA. At this facility, there were scores of other Doctors, Scientists, and Engineers, but it was Dominic who ran the show."

'She called all the shots. When the bodies of freshly killed Negro Bandits started showing up in our labs, it was Dominic who brought them to us."

Dr. Hernandez scrolled past the photo of himself and found another image. The new picture showed a large grey two-story compound flanked by a rocky dirt road on one side and luscious green jungle on the other. In the picture, I could see armed soldiers in uniform standing outside the building, posted inside a chain-link fence. Whatever this place was, the government of El Salvador thought it important enough to lend soldiers to defend it. As I leaned in to get a closer look, Doc snatched his hand-held computer away, immediately burying it in his pocket.

'So, the CIA had you turn dead Black Freedom Fighters into weaponized transhuman Counter-Intelligence mules," Dennis proclaimed.

"Why am I not shocked by any of this, Doc?"

"Even with all of that withstanding, none of this explains why you killed Dominic or why you participated in Governor Williams and Senator Bean's assassination."

"I didn't give the order for any of them to be killed, Dennis," Dr. Hernandez sternly clarified.

"I want to make that clear to the both of you."

"Everything that happened to those fuckin whores is above me. I'm like every other Hispanic. I'm just a proxy in your shadow race war with white people."

"At the facility, we transformed thousands of Negro Bandits into transhumans," he continued. "Within a few years, the Negro Bandit movements throughout Central and South America were crushed by infighting and treason among their ranks."

"Normalcy returned to my country. Stability was restored, but it was a tenuous peace at best. Small pockets of Negroes that our transhumans could not infiltrate managed to hold out in shanty towns outside of every major city."

"That's when Dominic came to San Salvador to visit us with a special high-ranking military guest. It was during that visit that I first met Admiral Judith Bean."

"Having a U.S. Navy Admiral visit us was very unusual. Everything we were doing was cloak and daggers stuff...so having a U.S. military Admiral openly roaming around our facility made all of us feel like we were merely an extension of the U.S government. Like we were just soldiers ready to take their orders and not proud countrymen fighting to preserve our way of life."

"All of my Hispanic comrades in Operation Balboa and the resistance movement began to question the motives of the CIA."

'Hell, we weren't the only ones upset about the direction of the program. So many of our white CIA counterparts vented their frustration with the ever-changing objectives Dominic and CIA leadership forced on us."

"What was changing within the Balboa Operation?" I asked. "You said yourself that you had mostly quelled the Black uprisings in your country. Why did you still need to pump out so many transhumans?"

Deciphering me with his eyes, Dr. Hernandez reached into his pants pocket and pulled out a box of candy. When I saw the familiar label on the box, my mind instantly went back to the memories of sharing those goodies with Jeremy Woodson. Hours before the Dry Tortugas raid, I had shared one final box of the same candy with him. Dr. Hernandez was trying to send me a message, but I wasn't sure what it actually meant.

'Operation Balboa was too successful for its own good," he continued looking directly at Dennis.

'Scientifically, we advanced by leaps and bounds. Not only could we use transhumans in a counter-terrorism capacity, but we also learned how to manipulate the thought patterns of our transhuman subjects."

'We learned how to control everything about their daily lives. Their cravings...their likes and dislikes. Among other things...we could program their sexual desires, preferred orientations, personalities, hatreds, and aspirations. All of that could be done with a simple syringe injection."

'After those advances, non-Hispanic bodies began showing up at our lab pretty routinely," he described. 'Black Americans, Whites, Asians, Arabs, all kinds of different races."

'My comrades and I didn't ask any questions as long as the funding kept rolling in, but we soon found out why all these bodies were sent to us. Looking back on it, we all should have stopped, but we were too afraid of the Negro Bandits to pull the plug ourselves."

"So, the bodies kept showing up and the money rolled in."

Dr. Hernandez opened the box of candy and poured a small amount into his hand. After stuffing the candy into his mouth, he slowly chewed, and I could hear the crunch echo in the church. The scent of the candy leaving his mouth was almost irresistible. He must have caught the not-so-hidden longing in my eyes because Doc reached over and offered to pour some in my hand. After a long second of deliberation, I shook my head in disapproval and politely declined his offer.

"Just think about it, Nuria," he said, holding up the box of candy. "If you run a company selling candy, how much would you pay to have a percentage of the world population automatically predisposed towards purchasing it?"

"From food Companies, clothing lines, auto manufacturers...hell, even companies that sold gay sex toys. They all paid the CIA high dollar to play in Operation Balboa's sandbox," he explained.

"Everyone made money, and no one was the wiser."

"Operation Balboa ultimately became more about commerce and less about defeating Black Empowerment. Many of us in the program and within the CIA itself hated that!"

"Things only got worse when Dominic and Judith tried to replicate Operation Balboa in Asia and the Middle East. They hoped to use our success as a blueprint to control geopolitics and boost the spread of American Capitalism."

"But there was one big problem Dominic and Judith overlooked," he sighed. "A problem that scared the hell outta all of us. It was a problem that no one could have imagined."

"Let me guess. Somebody found a way to manipulate the bio-programming you installed in the transhumans," Dennis confidently interjected.

275

"And whoever found that out upset the apple cart."

Impressed by Dennis's insight, Dr. Hernandez flashed a broad smile, then slowly clapped his hands in admiration. Now I knew for certain that there was a deadly civil war being waged within the CIA itself. Jeremy Woodson and Darius Royal had not only been transformed into transhumans, but someone had secretly reprogrammed the two men after the fact.

"I see Dennis is starting to see the bigger picture," Dr. Hernandez exalted while wagging his finger.

"In El Salvador, we found out that a good number of our transhuman subjects were malfunctioning. They weren't completing assigned missions. In some cases, they would come back to our facility and end up murdering our doctors and scientists."

"This scared the shit outta Dominic and the CIA."

"One day, the funding the CIA would send to the Resistance, suddenly stopped arriving. Bodies stopped showing up and our request for instructions went unanswered."

"As time ticked by without any explanation from the CIA, the Negro Bandits began to reassert themselves in our countries, gaining political momentum and social capital."

"So, Dominic and the CIA pulled the plug?" I murmured.

"Yes, they did," he confirmed.

"That outraged a lot of my people. Many of us down in El Salvador felt betrayed. Dominic and Judith Bean were basically leaving us to die at the hands of those Negro Bandits. We were left to fight a war we knew we would surely lose."

"We weren't the only ones pissed either...White Extremists within the CIA, business investors, military leaders, certain U.S. Politicians, they all felt the sting of Dominic leaving us high and dry."

"Before your infamous assault at Dry Tortugas, many of our transhuman camps all over the globe were raided by the FBI and INTERPOL. This very church we are sitting in was one of the first to be raided."

"Dominic and her like-minded allies in the CIA were trying to put the cat back in the bag. In her mind, this whole Operation Balboa thing had become a double-edged sword."

"We tried to tell her that if she gave us more time, we could fix the issue. We could develop biological firewalls that would protect our subject from outside manipulation, but Dominic would hear none of it."

"She kept sending the FBI after us, putting most of my colleagues in jail or deporting them out of the U.S."

"That's how I ended up working for the Navy and Admiral Bean," he explained. "They couldn't deport me because I had gained my U.S. citizenship, so the CIA offered me an officer's commission and hid me away in the Navy Special Ops world."

"I believe the CIA knew they would need me later, so Dominic decided to keep me close to her."

"Think about it, Nuria. After all of those FBI raids against us, White Extremists like Bradley Wood suddenly began to attack all of your Reparations Colonies."

"Soon afterwards, you found out about the location of your arch-nemesis, so the Navy helped you to kill him. Isn't that suspicious?" He asked, looking directly into my eyes.

"Patrice Williams wanted you assigned to that mission. She needed you assigned to that mission and she benefited politically because you participated."

"After the Dry Tortugas assault, Patrice became the unchallenged public face for you Foundationals."

'Dominic, a sworn adversary, never attacked nor tried to destroy you like she did to your husband, Quinton."

"Why and how did Judith Bean put a lid on the Kingfish stories about you and Jeremy Woodson? Was it simply because Patrice and Judith asked her nicely?"

"You have to ask yourself hard questions, Nuria."

'Everything you seek to know has always been right in front of you. From Patrice Williams to Judith Bean, to the hardliners in your colony, all the way to Dominic's opponents in the CIA."

'Let's be honest about the Dry Tortugas. Who was actually fighting you at that old fort? Who did you actually kill Nuria? Was it a white man? Was it a White Supremacist?"

Satisfied that he had conveyed his message to me, Dr. Hernandez put his box of candy away and went silent. He didn't need to say anything else. I perfectly understood his message to me. Aside from tricking Quinton, Dominic had also deceived Dr. Hernandez and his allies. She had betrayed Operation Balboa, a covert program she was responsible for giving birth to. Dominic had switched sides in Operation Balboa's secret war. Trading away the mind-altering control of transhumanism to go back to good ole fashioned human manipulation. Patrice Williams had fallen victim to her own thirst for power and status. You didn't need a needle or a dead body to get into her mind. All you had to have was the opportunity she secretly craved deep in her heart. At that fort in the Dry Tortugas, Judith and Dominic presented Governor Williams with that opportunity and she cashed it in on the backs of all of my teammates. She offered us all up as sacrifices in Dominic's panic-filled jihad to erase the hidden remnants of Operation Balboa.

Mental images of that black teenager firing away at us from behind his machine gun nest flashed in my mind. The sparkling blue blood leaking from his moonlit body nearly broke me. Yet, inside, I could feel the disappointment of the moment once again wash over my spirit. Who was that poor child? His black life had been brushed away by circumstances he had no control over. In another world, he could have been a Physician like Dr. Hernandez, or a genius like Dennis. Instead, this boy's life was caught between the crossfire of this messy system of White Domination.

The sting of inner sadness slipped away from me as I looked into Dr. Hernandez's emotionless eyes. It was replaced by a jolt of familiar anger. Dr. Hernandez was Hispanic, but to me, Hispanic was just another word for white. At his heart, Doc was an oppressor. A wannabe that eagerly identified with the sliver of European ancestry tucked away in his lineage. His cosmetic differences with Dominic were meaningless because they both had the same goals at the end of the day. He was just as guilty as Dominic, if not more. Dr. Hernandez was just as deceitful as Judith Bean and as treacherous as Governor Williams. I reached into my pocket, and in an instant, I found myself driving the hard metal barrel of my gun into the soft wrinkled skin on the bottom of Dr. Hernandez's chin. The force of the gun piercing into him caused small droplets of warm blood to squirt onto my hand.

"Get your ass up! You're coming with us, Doc," I said with a hate-filled smile.

"You're gonna tell us who's all involved in this damn thing. You understand!"

Without fear, he laughed at me before leaning his chin into my gun, almost daring me to pull the trigger and end his life. I felt the strength of Dennis pulling my body away before his hands forced me to lower my pistol.

"He knows we can't kill him, Nuria," Dennis explained.

"Darius Royal and Jeremy Woodson are newer versions of his damn transhuman experiment."

"Without him, we won't be able to find a way to neutralize the threat they represent to Black Society."

"Whoever is behind all of this will need to eliminate him. We can use Dr. Hernandez as bait and see who comes after him."

Satisfied with his assessment, I stepped away from him and holstered my weapon. A smile exploded across Dr. Hernandez's face as he wiped away the bloody mess I had created on his chin.

"We can take him back to the colony and lock him up there," I demanded.

"If we let Dr. Hernandez run around out here, anyone could come find him here and kill him."

Out of the corner of my eye, I saw the chubby young child walk back into the church. Turning my head towards him, I noticed his body shaking while he held on to his small toy. His pace was slow as he passed through the front entrance. Then I saw a large shadow looming behind him. It was a white man. He was tall and wearing an unseasonably warm jacket. He held a small metal box in his hands with plastic trigger guards on top of it.

As the both of them closed on us, I was able to see the white man's face. He looked baby-faced, barely out of his teenage years. Tattooed below his right eye were two blue shields. A long dark Satanist symbol dangled from his left earlobe and a thick silver nose ring hung from his nostrils. I recognized the Satanic symbol as iconography associated with several White Extremist groups that dominated the Bay Area's rural outskirts. This man was undoubtedly a terrorist and I knew why he had come here.

"Freeze," I shouted, pointing my pistol at our deadly intruder.

"Whatever's in your hand...slowly put it on the floor in front of you now!"

In silence, the man smiled at me, exposing scores of rotting brown teeth that protruded from his infected purple gums. He lifted his arm so I could see the metal box before gliding his thumb over one of the buttons. In front of him, the chubby Hispanic boy stood completely still, paralyzed with fear as sweat poured down his face. The sudden sound of Riley's voice echoed throughout the church walls.

"Nuria! Sniper! Get down!

I dove forward, tackling the boy while wrapping my arm around him as we hit the carpet. The loud sounds of rifle shots and broken glass accompanied me to the ground. Peering behind me, I saw that Dennis had pulled Dr. Hernandez behind the cover of a wooden pew. Both men lay motionless on the floor as bullets rained inside of the church. I felt something hit my back before seeing it roll out on the carpet in front of me. It was the same small metal box the White Supremacist had in his hands. It was at this point that I recognized that it was a detonator switch. Bullets racked the carpet surrounding me. The body of our would-be white terrorist came tumbling down to earth soon afterward. As I looked at him on the floor, I noticed his eyes were open, but nothing else seemed to be going on within him. Dark blue blood poured from his mangled and disfigured skull. Near his chest, several high-caliber bullet wounds rendered the bomb hiding underneath his thick jacket useless. This man was a transhuman and his suicide mission had been put to an end.

Near the entrance, Riley, Clarke, and Ed all found cover behind pews. All three of them fired their weapons at a small second-story window across from the church. I had every intention of joining them in employing suppressive fire, but the chubby boy underneath me began shoving me away in a hot panic. As the bullets continued to rain down on us both, I tried hard to hold the boy down next to me, but he was strong and managed to slip away from my lonely arm. Everything happened in slow motion as the boy ran towards the church's entrance. A bullet struck the small of his back, but somehow, he was able to continue moving forward. Then I saw Clarke come into view, grabbing the kid and shielding him from the onslaught of bullets. Two loud distinct shots from a handgun rang out from the front of the church. Agent Clarke fell to the ground and the chubby little boy fell motionless beside him.

"Shit!" Riley screamed. "Clarke's hit!"

"Officer Down! Officer Down," he yelled into his radio.

Looking behind me, I saw Dr. Hernandez standing up while Dennis laid motionless on the ground. In his hand, Doctor Hernandez brandished Dennis's pistol. Our eyes met at that moment, and I instantly knew what he had done. The two female nurses opened up a backroom door and Dr. Hernandez made a hasty sprint towards the opening. Pissed at his deception, I aimed at my running target, squeezing off two shots that missed high and to the right. As the door shut behind Dr. Hernandez, I knew he had escaped. Ed tried to take off after him, but the sniper quickly forced Ed back to the floor. Riley attempted to crawl towards his wounded partner, but the sniper's well-placed bullets detoured him. As Agent Clark lay helpless on the floor, I could hear him struggling to breathe. Red blood poured from Clarke's neck and the sound of Riley's high-pitched screams into his radio made all of this into the perfect nightmare. From my pinned-down position on the ugly carpet, I was forced to watch Agent Clarke go motionless and succumb to the silence of post-life. Despite being removed from Dry Tortugas for ten years, I had once again found my way into another death trap.

CHAPTER EIGHT

MAY WE PRAY

IN THE BACKGROUND, I COULD HEAR the bay's dark blue waves splashing up against the jagged shoreline. Heavy-looking rain clouds dominated the depressing overcast sky above us. The sad grey clouds seemed to serve as a constant reminder to us all. This was a solemn event. Yet, there was a maddeningly familiar purpose for this respectful gathering, and it wasn't a celebration. In front of Clarke's shiny red casket sat his two overwhelmed children and his mourning wife. One's heart could not help but be crippled by the scene. A husband was gone forever. The dad of two young black boys would not mentor his children into manhood. It was one of those moments when the cruelties of this earthly life hits you suddenly. At this moment, Agent Clarke was not just a Black Zebra that shunned Foundational Society. At his funeral, Clarke was much more than that to the people who knew and loved him.

Next to me, I noticed Ed solemnly wiping a few tears from his eyes. Quietly, I knew that he and I were sharing the same thoughts as the FBI's Honor Guard slowly folded the American flag into that ominous triangle before handing it to the new widow. Clarke's white wife looked up at the men in their impeccably decorative uniforms. Her eyes were bloodshot red, as was the tip of her nose. Taking the flag from their gloved hands, I could see the toll of it all suddenly defeat her as she pressed the folded flag up against her chest. Everyone in the funeral precession went quiet in sympathizing agony. The soft and exhausted sounds of her grief touched everyone's spirit.

The Black Zebra Pastor leading the ceremony walked over and comforted Clarke's wife with a tender hug. Slowly raising the widow to her feet, he held her firmly and whispered into her ear before gazing out at us in the crowd.

'Let us bow our heads and offer a prayer for this mourning family," the Zebra Pastor instructed in a loud booming voice.

'Let us ask the Lord to provide us all with the strength required to support each other with empathy and compassion."

As everyone bowed their head and shut their eyes to our world of pain, I noticed that Agent Riley failed to do so. In silence, his eyes mistrustfully examined the Zebra Pastor. It was obvious that Riley and his husband were both restraining their inner disgust at the notion of having to pray to God. As the pastor began to pray aloud passionately, Riley leaned his head into the flabby chest of his husband and wiped away tears of discomfort with a small brown handkerchief. The two men held each other in a tight embrace, vainly engaging in a rebellious tongue kissing session as the entire precession around them focused on a much higher power.

'Let them be," Quinton whispered into my ear.

'Don't let them take your focus away from what's most important, my love. That's what they want."

I reached over and grasped Quinton's hand, and gave him a knowing squeeze before closing my own eyes and offering the Lord a humble request for strength. The Zebra Pastor finished his prayer and asked several FBI officials to speak. Their words were short and somber. Each of the men described the years of selfless service Agent Clarke had contributed to the FBI. Only one of them had the class to acknowledge his grieving wife, which didn't go unnoticed by us Foundationals. After each man had spoken, the Zebra Pastor looked over at our group. His eyes reviewed our group, examining us until he found the exact person he was looking for. I watched nervously as his eyes bucked wide when he stared at Gary Freeman.

"Like me," the Pastor started.

"Mr. Clarke also had Foundational heritage."

"I can unequivocally testify from my own experience that deciding to forgo the Reparations package that this great country has allotted to Foundationals is an extremely tough decision."

"It goes without saying that it takes a man of virtue to turn away from wealth and stand up for the greater good of maintaining peace in this humanity of racial discontent."

"Our Foundational family and the Blacks that elected to remain in the Dominant Society have famously been at odds with each other for decades now. The bad blood and acrimony between the two groups has been a source of pain for all Black people worldwide."

"Yet today, I am most pleased to see that Governor Gary Freeman, from the Oakland Reparations Colony, has made it a point to come here today and pay his respects to Mr. Clarke...along with a rather large contingent of other Foundationals."

"That too is a sign of virtue and is to be acknowledged and appreciated."

"Governor Freeman," the Pastor continued.

"I would be remiss if I didn't ask you to speak a few words on behalf of the Foundational Black community."

Put on the spot, Gary humbly nodded at the Pastor before slowly walking towards him and Agent Clarke's widow. After exchanging hugs and whispers, a blank-faced Gary scanned the faces in the crowd. Trying to be respectful, he hadn't come to the funeral prepared to speak and I could tell that he was using this precious moment of silence to gauge his audience. In the stillness, nervous Foundational Security agents and plain clothes police officers could be seen in the background shuffling among the mourning crowd. They had been put on the spot and were now looking for anything suspicious. No one involved could afford to allow another political assassination to go down. Despite this being a private funeral, you could literally feel the vastness of federal and local security forces around us. We were all being closely watched and the trained government killers were almost omnipresent.

"As the honorable Pastor has alluded to," Gary began.

"There is, in fact, a deep rift between the Foundational Black Community and American Descendants of Slaves that chose to remain among the Dominant Society."

"This unrighteous mistrust between Black American kinsmen, whose ancestors forged eternal bonds with one another while being held hostage in the inhospitable killing fields and death camps of North America, is a horrendous product of White Supremacist agitation and conditioning."

"Though we proud Foundationals may have our drastic differences with our Zebra brethren who fearfully cling to the untidy coattails of our fiendish white oppressors, the love and eternal bond between us shall never be compromised."

"I knew our Brother, Agent Clarke, personally. His years of service protecting the late Governor Williams and myself during our visits to this city allowed us to break down the barriers imposed upon us by White Racists," Gary continued.

"Although we had our immense political differences. Clear differences in our taste in women. Differences in the way we viewed the living demons that the Devil himself uses to torment us on God's planet."

"Despite those differences, we shared a mutual respect. A respect borne from black men who wholly believed in putting it all on the line to make this place a better world, which is why I'm here today."

Gary paused, once again scanning the crowd to gauge their reaction to his sharp words. I glanced around and immediately noticed the stares of quiet anger from white spectators and Zebra onlookers. Clarke's White widow stood quiet with a blank stare of disbelief plastered across her face as the Zebra Pastor looked downwards, surely harboring thoughts of regret and embarrassment. Turning my eyes back to Gary, his face could barely conceal the joy beaming from within him. He was thrilled with the specter of hurting so many people with his unvarnished black truth. Across from us, Agent Riley and his husband wore an expression that was not so subdued. Instead of hugging Riley, his husband effectively held him back and kept Riley from approaching Gary and causing an even more embarrassing scene.

"On behalf of Foundationals worldwide," he stated while reaching into his pocket.

"I would like to deliver this token of appreciation to our brother, Agent Clarke,"

Pulling his hand out of his pocket, Gary revealed a small shiny gold plaque. Raising it above his head, he displayed it to the crowd who examined the plaque with confused stares. While everyone around him remained in a state of shock, Gary walked over to the gravesite and placed the gold plaque on top of Clarke's casket. A tearful Ed broke from our ranks and walked up beside Gary as the onlookers watched in hushed bewilderment. Both men secured the small plaque onto the casket and walked back towards our group. It was then that I noticed a specific drawing engraved into the plaque, and the spirit of realization suddenly grabbed me. As Ed made his way back to my side, I gave him a quick stare, and without words, our eyes met. He confidently returned my stare and I instantly knew more about Agent Clarke than I had ever known before.

"Thank you for your statement, Governor Freeman," the Zebra Pastor proclaimed with trepidation dripping in his voice.

Hispanic graveyard workers lowered Clarke's casket into the ground as the Zebra Pastor offered the grieving family a final word of encouragement. Onlookers offered their hugs and sympathy to his widow while shooting holes into us Foundationals with their gazes. Sensing the distaste for us, I tugged at Quinton's arm, letting him know it was time to leave and get back to our colony before Gary did something that would get us all arrested.

'So, your gonna leave without saying anything about all of that shit, Nuria."

I stopped walking, turning around, only to find Agent Riley behind me with his husband in tow. From their body language, I could sense that both of these white men wanted to approach and physically intimidate me, but the specter of my tall husband made both men think twice. In frustration, Riley licked his bottom lip before launching into a muted tirade.

"You Foundationals have some damn nerve. You all came to Clarke's funeral spewing Black Supremacist garbage," he lamented. "You people are as low class as it gets."

"You people?" I asked.

"You better check your tone, Riley. We're Foundationals and you know what we are all about. So if you're in your feelings about that, well, you better learn to wipe away those tears sweetheart."

Glancing over at Quinton, Riley cautiously closed the distance before leaning over towards my ear. "We need to know what you people have been hiding. What do you know about this transhuman situation, Nuria?" he asked.

The bodies of the White mercenary and chubby Hispanic kid killed at the church clinic with Clarke were definitely in the custody of the FBI. After the sniper stopped firing at us and Dr. Hernandez escaped, the blue blood oozing from the chubby boy's fatal wounds told us that adults weren't the only victims of the CIA's horrifying experiments.

"I bet you would love to know that, Riley," I shot back sarcastically.

"I wish I had something to hide, but at this point, you know just as much as I do. Plus, it's your people doing all this shit. You figure it out."

"You have both Darius's and Jeremy Woodson's Bodies. It's time you turn them over to us, Nuria. Cooperate with the FBI, or we'll make you cooperate," he threatened.

"Never," I dismissed. "How can I trust any of you?"

"We have just discovered that the federal government had a whole damn transhumanism program geared towards oppressing black people worldwide."

"Go get an order from a judge or fuck off."

"Where is Dr. Hernandez," he followed up? "Where could he have gone, Nuria!"

"Riley, I get the feeling you and the FBI know exactly where the hell Dr. Hernandez is," I shouted!

"You're just trying to find out what I know! I'm on to your fuckin tricks. So, stop playing dumb. It's insulting Riley!"

Ed walked up beside me with Gary and his large security entourage. Riley looked rather tense as they joined us. Sensing my loss of composure, Gary stepped towards Riley, causing him to back away from me in a defensive posture.

"I just talked to the Director of the FBI, Riley," Gary announced.

"Your boss said you have something you need to tell me and Nuria. Now fess up!"

"I sure do," Riley confidently responded. He reached into his pocket, pulling out a small brown legal envelope before tossing it at my feet like he was throwing a treat down to his dog. I kneeled, picking the envelope up off the ground before opening it and reading its content. From my quick scan, I knew Riley and the FBI had just pulled a fast one. The judge had approved their search warrant two days ago. Yet, Riley and the FBI had waited until now, the day of Clarke's funeral, to let us know about it. I intuitively knew why Riley had orchestrated this. While we were all out here in one location, offering our respects to Agent Clarke, Riley's FBI comrades were in our offices, unabatedly searching them.

"It's a Federal search warrant, Gary," I declared. "They're probably searching through all our offices back at the colony right about now."

"The California Circuit Court Judge," I began reading. "Has granted the FBI permission to search the Oakland Reparations Colonies Government entities for any memory cells, electronic and written records that could potentially store evidence of said colonies involvement in the practice of transhumanism."

"The FBI has submitted sufficient Probable Cause for this court to endorse such a request for evidence, limited in scope to the Oakland Reparations Colonies governing body's possible involvement in the illegal and immoral practice of creating transhuman subjects."

"Oh, this is such bullshit, Riley."

"This document is nothing, but I'm White, and I say so rhetoric."

"That search warrant you're holding ain't bullshit, Nuria," Riley mocked. "It's the law."

"Now tell me where you're hiding Jeremy Woodson. Where is the damn body of Darius Royal?"

Riley asking me about Jeremy and Darius raised all kinds of red flags. I didn't know which side the FBI represented in this internal CIA battle, but the fact that Riley needed to question me about the two transhumans he already knew we had in our custody was telling. He was playing a game. Riley knew we had Jeremy and Darius, but if it had been revealed to the Circuit Court how and where we got possession of both of them, that would have opened up a can of worms the CIA nor the FBI could afford to disclose. It was better for the FBI to pretend to have stumbled upon them at our expense, which was likely one of the many aims of this search warrant. Yet having pulled the perfect sleight of hand trick, for some reason, Riley's search teams hadn't found the transhumans they knew were there. So now, he was here asking me questions like I was supposed to help him.

Thoughts of Dennis flashed in my mind as Riley, and his overweight lover gazed at me for answers. Ed and I had tried to convince Dennis to come to the funeral, but he roundly rejected us. His overwhelming guilt over not stopping Dr. Hernandez from killing Clarke caused him to ignore us and instead drown himself in his work at the office. The scenario at play quickly revealed itself to me. Somehow, Dennis had gotten word of the coming horde of FBI officials and had quickly hidden away Jeremy and Darius at an undesignated safe house. If Dennis had gotten that done, there would be no way the FBI search teams would locate them.

"You have your make-believe search warrant, Riley. Go search," I answered.

"Otherwise, talk to our lawyer and go to hell."

"All of this would be much easier if you just cooperated Governor Freeman," Riley jumped in.

"And who exactly am I supposed to be cooperating with Agent Riley?"

"If you can honestly answer that without your tricky bullshit...then I might consider helping you...sir," Gary responded with a smile.

"Hello...we are the FBI!" Riley shouted pointing at his badge. "Governor, you know damn well who we are. Like you just said today... You worked with Clarke, and I've for years...remember!"

"Didn't that god you people were praying to today give you two eyes Gary", he screamed. "Oh, excuse me I forget, your little sky god made you dumb and blind. By the way, doesn't that book of lies you people read command you to obey the orders of the government?"

"How the hell can you claim to practice some religion and not even follow its rules", Riley proclaimed with cocky smile.

"The hell with you," Gary broke in. "I have no idea who or what you are sir."

"Shit, look at you. You're confused as hell. You and that person you have standing beside you. Neither of you wants to acknowledge who you really are, so don't tell me shit about what I should believe or shouldn't believe."

"I'm free to believe what I want, and I'll be damned if I allow you to control my beliefs or tell me the truth is a lie."

Gary coolly pulled a piece of chewing gum out of his pocket and playfully tossed it into his mouth like a teenager. The ease and precision with which he performed the maneuver showed self-confidence as he chomped down on the gum before letting out a low chuckle, almost teasing the two white men in front of him.

"What the hell is that supposed to mean," Riley's husband yelled with a scratchy voice.

"It means I know who you and Agent Riley really are," Gary teased.

"Aside from all that fantasy and make-believe you Liberal White Supremacists pump out to the world like raw sewage. The God-given reality of both your lives remains the same to those who are willing to see it."

"You two are actually ladies; confused ladies who so desperately want to see yourselves as white men. Your real fantasy is to see yourself brutally controlling my black world like your evil great grandfathers once did."

"All of those testosterone injections, chemically induced beards, none of that can hide the Devil's plan that lives within you."

"You're both just as hate-filled, perverted, and demented as your white supremacist ancestors. You are just as deceitful as they were, if not more."

"Yep. I can see exactly who and what you are. You were born women. No lie or pseudo-science you try to pull out your ass is going to change that fact" he concluded.

Enraged, Riley's husband reared back and threw a wild punch at Gary. The swinging blow missed Gary's head by inches as he leaned backwards, avoiding the fist. On instinct, I kicked Riley's husband in the stomach. The sharp end of my pointy high heel dug deep into the blabby flesh of my target. The blow stung, causing the born woman to retreat backwards in pain. Angered, Riley pulled out her service pistol, aiming it directly at my head. It was then I recognized that angry spirit within Riley. The female intuition within me had sensed it, but now I could officially put a name to it. Someone had mortally hurt Riley; the innocent little girl within her was still wounded. Changing herself into a man was just her coping mechanism, a means of protection in a white male world that had delivered cruel blows upon her as a young child.

'Put that damn gun away. Clarke's family is here, Riley," I slowly cautioned.

'Misgendering a transexual is a Federal Hate Crime in San Francisco, Nuria."

'So is experimenting on dead Black people and turning them into transhuman assassins, Agent Riley," Gary shot back.

'Go tell your FBI Director I told you that and see if he still wants to arrest me."

'By the way, tell your team that once they finish searching through my office, I want all my shit put right back where they found it. Especially, my Luther Vandross collection."

Gary and his security team walked away, unbothered by the gun Riley was pointing at us. Riley's lover recuperated, brushing off the effects of my blow before pleading for calm. Riley put the gun away, yielding to her lover's soft whispers. Defeated, both trans men left us, surely soaking in the wounds Gary had given them.

'We better head back to the colony Nuria," Ed reasoned.

'If the FBI is this desperate, there is no telling want we're gonna find when we get back to the colony."

Ed was right; we needed to get back home. We both knew that this was just a momentary victory. Riley and the FBI were actively trying to hide something. My mind raced back to the valuable high school history lessons one of my teachers taught me. Back in the 20th century, a White Supremacist named J. Edger Hoover had used the FBI as a weapon against our Foundational Black ancestors. Brave Foundationals who stood tall in the face of Anti-Black violence weren't looked upon as American heroes but were instead labeled as traitors and Communists. Fred Hampton, Martin Luther King, and Medgar Evers were all criminalized and illegally investigated by the FBI. Many of them were unlawfully surveilled, arrested, and even assassinated. Given their rich Anti-Black history, it wasn't beyond the FBI to plant incriminating evidence on Black people. Without us closely observing them, the FBI could cook up any justification to accomplish their devilish aims.

"Nuria, I'll get a ride back home with one of Gary's security guards. You go with Ed," Quinton chimed in.

"Both of you have a lot of work waiting on you, so there's no need to waste time dropping me off."

"Are you sure, Quinton?"

"Yeah. I'm positive," Quinton confidently replied.

"Go do your job. Little Lindsey and I will be awaiting your return."

Quinton flashed a cute smile and let out a deep chuckle. At that moment, I could sense the beaming pride of being a husband and father within him. This man loved his family, and I was thankful to be a part of it all.

We walked to Ed's car, anxious to leave San Francisco's depressing rain behind us. Ed buckled up and flew into the cloudy gray sky before making a hard turn towards the brown hills of Oakland. I flicked on the satellite radio out of curiosity, searching through the menu until I found a news channel. After some hasty and fast-talking commercials, my ears were suddenly pulled into an attentive state. To my shock, the United States had suspended all economic sanctions on El Salvador. As the white commentators rambled on with their politically driven spin, Ed and I listened intently while details of this new geopolitical relationship with El Salvador were explained.

"Somehow, I'm beginning to think your old friend Dr. Hernandez and his transhuman obsession had something to do with this," Ed commented.

'I guess that those forces within the CIA that were opposing Dominic put an end to those economic sanctions," I added.

"Why would her own people flip and oppose her?" Ed interjected. "That doesn't sound like the Dominant Society at all."

'Because of greed and power, Ed. It's all about greed and power."

'As our great Foundational Philosopher Neely Fuller Jr. put it, White Supremacy dabbles in all sides of every argument. They have to, in order to always come out of every situation with some advantage."

We flew into our colony's air space, arriving at the Force Protection building to find our parking area filled with unfamiliar cars. All of the cars below us sported bright federal markings and were adorned with law enforcement lights. In our absence, Riley and the FBI had brought out the calvary in a quest to secure the intelligence prizes they so coveted. Feeling the urgency of the chaos surrounding us, Ed and I sprinted into our building to find the lobby littered with our employees. All of them were sitting on the cold tile floor as a handful of heavily armed Federal Agents stood over them wearing their trademark dark sunglasses. My first thoughts were not pleasant ones. Our people were quarantined while these FBI agents were allowed to crawl through every space in our damn building. The guarantees of colonial privacy expressly agreed upon during the Great Recompense were now being violated and dismissed openly by the Dominant Society.

Left to their own devices, the FBI could easily plant evidence, install hidden listening devices, hideaway explosives or perform a host of other illegal activities. With this opportunity, there only needed to be one demonic White Supremacist among them. From my life experience, there had to be at least one in this horde of Federal Agents.

'How was the funeral, Nuria?" A soft voice asked from a blind corner.

I turned around, facing the voice to find Mary Ann Haskins walking towards us. She looked dejected, and her spirit was worn, emitting a noticeable vibe of embarrassment. Given the circumstances, I couldn't blame her. Our white rivals had intruded into our sacred space, flexing their muscles in our faces, while we were made to sit back and watch it all. Without words, I offered Mary Ann my lonely arm, giving her a tight hug. I felt her weight as she collapsed into my grasp, laying her forehead on my shoulder. Ed came up to us and wrapped his arms around us while whispering words of comfort.

Her pride was hurt, and I readily understood Mary Ann's unspoken pain. This was our land, and our base of strength from which we waged our war to protect the Foundational Black community. In our minds, this building was holy ground. Sacred soil that was now being sullied and trampled with the monstrous presence of the unrighteous. Mary Ann gathered her strength, and I felt her slowly steady herself before stepping away from my knowing arm.

'How are you holding up, girl?" I asked. 'I'm so pissed!" Mary Ann vented.

"These bastards just interrogated me in my own damn office. They took my handheld computer, my car keys, and all my case files."

'Hey," a deep voice yelled!

'You are to remain quiet and have a seat if you're gonna be in this building," the armed FBI official ordered.

'If you're gonna protest, you people can protest from the floor with your mouth shut like everyone else in here!"

His bold words took a swan dive into my spirit of anger. Out of the corner of my eye, I watched as Ed stepped towards the white man with balled fists. Like me, he was ready to meet white aggression with black punishment.

"You don't have to worry about us. We'll step outside." Mary Ann quickly intervened.

Undeterred by Mary Ann's unspoken prudence, I moved in front of Ed, pulling my badge out of my purse. I shoved the badge towards the white bastard, purposely making him take a long look at it before ripping away the credentials and meeting his blue eyes with my fury.

"I'm Agent Nuria Phillip Sellers, and this is my partner Ed Carter. We are working with the FBI on the assassinations of Governor Williams and Senator Bean. Is Agent Riley here?"

"That's none of your business, lady," the white man condescended. "Now, you can either have a seat, or I can escort you outta here. Your choice!"

"Neither of those options will work for me," I dismissed. "I know the law. Per our Reparations Treaty, the Federal government has to provide me with a written list of evidence collected. Now, who's in charge here? Go find that person and tell them that Agent Sellers is here, and I want an account of what you've collected so far."

From behind his tinted shades, the white man's face began to turn bright red as he bit down hard on his thin bottom lip. Collecting his anger, he disrespectfully turned his back to me and started whispering phrases into his radio. His speaker shot back a quick static transmission before a high female voice answered him back, telling him that Agent Riley would be down shortly.

"Please tell Agent Riley's lying ass to meet me outside." I barked.

Without words, I turned around, walking away from the white man. Ed and Mary Ann followed me outside, and we walked over to the picnic area in silence. We needed a safe space to communicate away from listening ears privately. We all found seats on the picnic table, and Mary Ann broke the ice with a low whisper.

"They took Secretary Vincent into custody," she murmured.

"I saw them put him in a car and fly off towards San Fran."

"Vincent's a dead man now," I replied. "We'll never see him again."

"Once White Supremacy no longer has a use for a black tool, they break that tool, so it can never be used to harm them."

The conviction in my statement and Ed's agreeable silence took Mary Ann aback. By the twitch in her face, I could tell she wanted to ask us why we were so sure Vincent was in danger, but she instead forced herself to continue with another subject.

"Other than Vincent, it feels like they haven't found what they've been looking for."

"Have you seen them collecting any of our memory cells," Ed whispered.

"Hell yeah. Every single memory cell in the building has been taken to one of their cyber vans to be unlocked and reviewed."

"They've been reviewing each of them, and each time they unlock a new memory cell, they come away from the van more and more pissed off."

"I mean...the memory cells they have found are only administrative in nature; nothing operational was stored in them."

"Well, the FBI can have fun reading through our department's payroll and reviewing our yearly holiday budget if they want," I added.

"What we can't allow them to access are files related to operational matters. Have they taken away any stuff like that from our secure vault?"

"Yeah, they got a few," she whispered. "But it's mostly outdated contingency plans and After-Action Reports from old Force Protection Ops."

My face exploded with a smile when I envisioned a frustrated Riley, bouncing from room to room in a full-blown panic. I could almost see the sweat dripping down her beard as she looked for memory cells that would tell the FBI the secrets they hoped to obtain. Then came the next logical question when my eyes found Mary Ann's.

"Where's Dennis," I mouthed.

Mary Ann shrugged her shoulders and purposely gave me a confused look. Then in one swift motion, she whipped out a piece of paper and began to write. She turned the paper towards me, and I looked down to find an address. When she realized I got her message, she took the piece of paper and quickly ripped it into shreds before stuffing the torn trash inside her bra.

"Why there?" I asked.

"I guess somehow, he knew," Mary Ann cryptically whispered.

"I saw him earlier this morning, but around lunchtime, he was gone. So are his two guests. They're not around here anymore."

"When Riley comes out here, demand that she give you a list of the evidence the damn FBI has collected so far," I instructed.

"Tell Riley that we intend to file an injunction with the Circuit Courts to halt this farce of a search warrant. Let her know; I'll be back when the judge grants the injunction."

A bit confused by my pronouns, Mary Ann didn't ask any questions and simply nodded her head in compliance. The potential of an injunction would certainly cause Riley to rush her search, even if the chances of that injunction being approved were minimal. That's exactly what I needed while I located Dennis and the memory cells.

Ed and I left Mary Ann alone at the picnic table, heading directly to his parked car. After a quick visual sweep of the car's exterior, we entered. Ed drove us out of sight towards San Francisco before turning for our actual destination, Little Lindsey's elementary school. When we arrived, Ed saw Dennis's car and parked next to it.

Dennis sat in his car with his arms folded like he had been patiently waiting on us forever. Under the dawning grey sky, Ed and I hustled to Dennis's car. We all exchanged earnest smiles and grateful hugs upon arrival. Without words, Dennis opened a small brown briefcase, showing us dozens of small memory cells before motioning for us to frisk our outer garments. We obediently followed the emergency protocols, dutifully convincing Dennis that we hadn't been compromised.

"How was Agent Clarke's funeral Nuria?" He asked me with remorse in his spirit.

"It was as nice as it could have been, Dennis."

"Riley had to ruin it with this damn search warrant, though," I added.

"What took you clowns so long to get here," Dennis teased, purposely changing the subject. "I've been sitting in this parking lot for two hours waiting on y'all."

"We just came from the Force Protection building after chatting with Mary Ann," Ed replied.

"How is she holding up?" Dennis asked.

"She's holding down the fort over there," I responded.

"Mary Ann is rough and stubborn as a hot mule, but she knows exactly when to turn on those fake tears and fame weakness in the presence of our enemy."

"Good. It sounds like she did her job then."

"Mary Ann is your protégé Nuria. You should expect her to know how this game works. Anyway, here we sit, the last line of protection for our people's interests."

"Why the hell are we at Little Lindsey's elementary school Dennis?" I asked.

"It's funny and ironic that you're asking that question, Nuria."

"If the FBI somehow decided to try and search here...Gary Freeman and the hardliners know every Circuit Judge in the state of California is going to ask that very same question to Federal Prosecutors."

'Just imagine the worldwide media shit storm if the U.S. government is filmed invading Foundational elementary schools. Searching through school lockers and handcuffing black children. The pretense of moral white Americans will forever be erased."

'So...this school is the emergency storage facility for all our secure Intel?" I asked.

'Yep. It has its own secret vault where they store memory cells. This school has saved every assignment, every essay, and every math problem that our kids have ever solved."

'It's the school's policy to store all the kids' work assignments in memory cells. Nuria, all my third-grade homework assignments are somewhere in that damn vault. Just think about that for a minute."

'That's a frightening thought," I sighed. 'I had such sloppy handwriting back then. I'd hate for Little Lindsey to see my old work."

'How did you know the FBI was coming with a search warrant?"

'A couple of years ago, I hacked into California Circuit courts secure network. Every day, my computer conducts keyword searches through their entire database. The keywords I have been using are Foundationals, Colony, African American, etc."

"This morning, Riley's bogus search warrant popped up in my system when the FBI began to execute it."

'What's on all these memory cells? Why is the FBI so hot and bothered over them?"

'Well, Nuria," he began. 'Some of these memory cells contain defensive strategies to defend our colony from White Extremist attacks. Others contain evacuation plans and others, offshore financial information."

"That can't possibly be what the FBI is after," Ed chimed in.

"Realistically, the FBI has probably already stolen all of that information; given Vincent Towns was their insider." Ed lamented.

"They are looking for spy lists. They are looking to see what we know about them."

"I know this is a loaded question, Dennis, but do any of those memory cells have reports of our clandestine operations within the Dominant Society?"

Dennis turned around in his car seat and looked back at Ed with a stoic expression. For a moment, I could see Dennis considering his words before his eyes relented. I knew the truth was about to come tumbling from Dennis's lips, so I braced my ears to hear every word.

"None of these memory cells contain that type of information Ed. I'm sorry." He admitted.

"At this point, I'm not sure if the memory cell the Dominant Society and FBI have seared into their little black nightmares...even exists. It appears these white folks have created a fictional boogieman. Now, they're about to turn over every leaf on the planet to find this mythical figment of their own creation."

"Let them keep searching," I jumped in. "The more they search, the more they expose us to their truths, paranoias, and insecurities. As long as these white bastards believe we somehow have the goods on them, they are more likely to tread lightly with us."

"Where did you hide Jeremy Woodson and Darius Royal? We can't let Riley find them either."

"Both of them are safe and secure."

"I took them to the Royal household. Darius's mother and sister volunteered to hide them away if we permitted them to bury Darius once this all dies down," he explained.

'After this is all said and done, we'll need to do something with your boy Jeremy Woodson." He pointedly stated as he stared into my eyes, looking for any lingering traces of emotional attachment within me.

'He's an important find for us...scientifically; he is a game-changer."

I knew the unspoken motives behind Dennis's statement. On instinct, I turned away from his probing spirit, hoping to hide the natural urge to protect Jeremy that was exploding within me. It didn't matter that Jeremy was already technically dead. I had seen him die, and now fate had somehow brought him back into my life. Once again, introducing him to my existence at exactly the wrong time. I did not want that to happen to Jeremy. I still cared about him.

"We'll address those issues after we deal with this crisis," I instructed Dennis. 'Our objective right now doesn't involve Jeremy. It's getting the FBI outta here."

Visibly unconvinced with my deflection Dennis didn't try to press any further. He simply nodded his head in silence before looking away and pulling out his handheld computer. Dennis scrolled through his computer with intense focus. Finally, he pressed down on an odd-looking icon, and I watched as he logged into a tracking program.

'Dr. Hernandez may have whipped my ass in that church, but there's a reason he had the upper hand on me," he detailed.

Dennis lifted this handheld computer screen so I could get a clear look at it. The screen displayed a map with a pulsing green light somewhere in Central America. When I recognized the country, I knew why Dr. Hernandez had overwhelmed Dennis and killed Clarke. Amidst their struggle, Dennis as able to plant a tracking device on Dr. Hernandez.

"This location for him is about 16 hours old," Dennis, explained.

'He's somewhere in El Salvador. Outside of the capitol."

'How he got there so quickly, I'm not sure, but he's running for his life."

I took the handheld computer from Dennis, examining its readings for myself. If this tracking device was indeed Dr. Hernandez. It was clear that we needed to bring Dr. Hernandez in alive. Evil forces within the Dominant Society wanted him dead, but having him alive was just as good as having a memory cell filled with their dirty secrets.

"We'll need to have a talk with Agent Riley about this, pronto," I shot out.

"Why the hell would we give Agent Riley Dr. Hernandez's location," Ed protested. "The FBI is probably in on all this. They'll kill him once he's found."

"I'm with Nuria on this one, Ed," Dennis proclaimed. "El Salvador is outside of our jurisdiction."

"We're gonna need Riley and the FBI onboard for this. They can open up avenues for us in El Salvador that we couldn't get into otherwise."

"Plus, I think the FBI and CIA will be more than glad to allow us to tie up a loose end for them. We'll just have to find a way to trick them and get Dr. Hernandez back here alive."

"As a weapon in their war on black people, Dr. Hernandez is now useless," I added.

"The White Supremacists will break any tool that is no longer of use to them. Even if that tool is classified as White."

"Just like they eliminated Bingo Dorrell. Just like they eliminated Senator Bean and Dominic."

I turned my head towards him, looking into Ed's wide brown eyes. Emphasizing the importance of the message, I was trying to convey. I felt his spirit open up to me as I felt my words ring in his mind. Then I continued, speaking a painful truth.

"Just like they killed Governor Patrice Williams. We have to be honest about why she was eliminated."

"This isn't just about finding her murderers anymore. It's about stopping a damn system that's destined to kill every human being on this planet."

"No matter what is motivating the FBI, we must stop this transhuman shit before it kills us all."

The inside of the car went silent at my frank admission. Each of us knew what I had said was the truth. We all loved Patrice. She had been a major part of all our lives in one way or another. Yet, the power of recognizing her truth hurt us to our core. Patrice's ambition ended her life. The CIA had elevated her public status, using her political celebrity to promote her as a more progressive, open-minded brand of Foundational. For them, she was the type of Foundational they preferred to deal with. Patrice was less prone to object or analyze the Dominant Society's motives.

Instead of seeking empowerment, Patrice primarily sought a more comfortable co-existence with white society. Hardliners like Gary Freeman fundamentally disagreed with Patrice. In their view, White Supremacy needed to be aggressively attacked. Trying not to offend or provoke White Supremacy simply causes it to view your engrained morality as a flaw to be exploited.

After a brief discussion with Ed, I instructed him to contact Agent Riley and officially ask the FBI to accompany us in our quest to capture Dr. Hernandez. As Ed exited the car to make the offer, I pulled out my handheld computer and tried to contact Gary Freeman. Dennis saw what I was doing and reached over, asking me to hand over my computer to him.

"You're not gonna find Gary at that location. I know where he's hiding," he lamented.

He typed in a code, and after a few rings, the hologram image of Gary Freeman popped up in front of us. He was at the Governor's secret compound, and this time, he was not alone. Around him sat a host of influential figures in the hardliner party. I immediately recognized most of the faces, as the men and women in the room appeared to be lounging while happily sharing cocktails. The event looked festive and almost celebratory at first blush, causing me to wonder why these strict hardliners felt the need to party while the FBI unlawfully violated our sovereignty.

"Nuria!" Gary loudly greeted me.

"I was just thinking about you and wondering how our dear friend Agent Riley might be treating you at this very moment."

"Gary, we need to go to El Salvador to capture Dr. Hernandez, and I want Agent Riley to come with us." I abruptly asked.

My straightforward request seemed to stun Gary as he shifted in his chair. He slowly put his champagne glass down on a lampstand while considering my bold request. I knew Gary needed to collect his thoughts while trying to soak up the shock associated with this revelation. Next to me, Dennis sat quietly as we both curiously awaited any indication of Gary's response.

"We know where Dr. Hernandez is located, and we need to move on him now before he disappears somehow," I added. "If we can bring him back alive, that will give us all kinds of leverage."

"And exactly how do you propose we do that," he asked with sarcasm. "Every CIA, FBI agent and White Extremist mercenary in the Western Hemisphere will be trying to kill this man."

"Plus, how does doing any of that help us as Foundationals?" Gary asked.

"I don't see the direct benefit of going down to El Salvador to chase an Anti-Black terrorist that the FBI themselves will be looking to silence."

"I mean, he did murder Agent Clarke. The FBI, the CIA, they all know he assassinated Patrice, Senator Bean, and Dominic. These white folks' chickens have come home to roost. The problem is none of them will admit that publicly."

"Gary, me and you both know the FBI will never arrest Dr. Hernandez," I began. "He'll never see the inside of a courtroom. When he's killed, our chances of finding out how high up the food chain this plot goes dies with him. We would lose an opportunity to gain advantage that would benefit us."

Gary burst into laughter at my notion of working hand and hand with Dr. Hernandez. After amusing himself, he reached over and took a sip from his champagne glass before crossing his right leg and anxiously dangling it.

"Dr. Hernandez is a White Hispanic that is loyal to White Supremacy. You're a Foundational Black that is loyal to the truth Nuria. There's a big difference between the two of you and how you both view this world we live in. Remember that."

"Unfortunately for Dr. Hernandez, he'll have to pay the ultimate price for that loyalty."

"And I say good! Let them kill their own," Gary forcibly proclaimed.

"Once they get done shaking us down for some damn memory cell that doesn't exist, they'll be able to go back to their business of lying to the rest of the world and leave us Foundationals the hell alone."

"My priority is protecting our colony. Not picking sides in a childish CIA food fight."

"Besides, we have what we need to protect our people. Our goal moving forward will be further separation, not mutually beneficial cooperation."

"Nuria, you will go nowhere. You and your team will stay here in Oakland. We can't risk allowing ourselves to roll in the mud with these people anymore. White folks are tricky, and they'll use every opportunity to make us the scapegoats for their own issues."

With that Gary, pressed the end button and his bright hologram vanished into nothing. I looked over at Dennis, and he gave me a shoulder shrug that betrayed his nervous spirit. Undeterred, I snatched my handheld computer out of Dennis's hands and began to search for the earliest launch leaving our colonies airport for El Salvador.

"What are you doing Nuria," he retorted. "You heard Gary. We have to stand down."

"The hell with him Dennis. He doesn't see the bigger picture. Gary doesn't understand the danger this transhumanism shit is putting us in."

"If they are allowed to continue their transhumanism practices, these white folks will eventually start undermining our colonies. We have to find a way to blow the whistle now so that we can stop them. We're going to El Salvador. We're gonna find Dr. Hernandez and put an end to this transhuman shit." A tension-filled silence dominated the inside of the car as I searched our colonies airport webpage. Unable to find a direct launch to El Salvador, I began searching for launches to any of the surrounding countries, eventually discovering one that was bound for Panama. I booked the launch for us and arranged for transportation to El Salvador upon arrival. When everything was booked, Dennis let out a heavy sigh, and I noticed the conflict still brewing within him.

"Dennis, you're the last one I have left from my Dry Tortugas days," I began.

"You know the sacrifices Pernell and Donovan made. We can't let them have given their lives up for us just to stand back and let these people surround us with racist transhumans."

"I need you with me on this one. I gotta have you onboard."

"Fuck," he yelled. "If we're both going to go down, we might as well go down together, I guess.

I rolled down my window and called for Ed to get back inside the car. We needed to hurry. The next launch going south of the border was scheduled to depart for Panama in two hours. Dennis drove over to the airport, and we landed in the long-term parking area. Agent Riley and several other white FBI officials were on their way, and Ed told us they would meet up with us at the airport's front entrance. As we stood outside, it wasn't long before we saw three white faces approaching us wearing their badges and light rain jackets.

When they neared us, I recognized the puffy white face of Agent Riley. The two other men flacking Riley were new to me. I hadn't worked with nor seen them before. Both had the distinct look of rookies. They were in their mid to late twenties, and their demeanor was overly serious. Despite the gloomy gray clouds above, both men insisted on wearing their heavily tinted FBI issue sunglasses as if it were daytime. The nervous twitch in their body language told me they were armed and ready to kill.

"You can't give me the right memory cell...but somehow you were able to find the location of Dr. Hernandez," Riley bitched.

"This is bullshit Nuria, and you know it."

"It's time to stop playing games and give the FBI what we need. You Foundationals know more than you're leading on."

"I have nothing to hide, Riley. You're searching my building, aren't you?" I replied. "You have your court-ordered search warrant....so search. You don't need my help. If the memory cell is there, you well-trained FBI agents should find it."

Riley scoffed at my sarcasm, only offering me a few barely audible profanities in return. Then Riley's hand reached into a large pouch. When the hand reappeared, it revealed a small recording device. Riley pressed the play button while looking me dead in my eyes and an audio recording of my conversation with Gary Freeman blasted from it. The conversation played on for several minutes before the audio ended, and Riley tucked the device away.

'I'm sorry, Nuria," Dennis explained. 'I didn't know the FBI would be able to find out where Gary was located and tap his communications so fast."

"Well, now you know, don't you, Dennis," Riley gloated.

"We've always known about your Governor's secure bunker. The FBI isn't as stupid as you think we are, now aren't we."

"Anyway, your Governor ordered you to stay here and leave this matter alone. Why do you feel the need to disobey him?"

'Didn't you just listen to your own recording Riley? You know the games your buddies in the CIA have been playing down in South America."

"This whole time, you weren't really looking for the assassins of Governor Williams because you already knew rogue elements in the CIA had her killed. Your job was to keep me away from the real suspects while trying your best to unearth some fictitious memory cell you White folks are so scared of."

"That's crazy talk, Nuria," Riley shot back. 'Senator Bean was also assassinated, remember. I care about finding the assassins just as much as you do."

"You and Gary talked all that conspiracy shit about the FBI and the CIA. None of this has anything to do with us. Your paranoia about racist white people is driving you mad."

"Well, let's go get his ass Riley," I shot back. "We know where Dr. Hernandez is located. What's stopping the FBI from helping us bring Dr. Hernandez back alive to stand trial for his crimes?"

"This is your opportunity to prove hardliners like Gary Freeman wrong. This is your chance to prove Foundationals like me wrong. Are you pursuing the truth or, are you just trying to stack the deck against Foundational Black Americans?"

'Otherwise, I'll go do this shit alone, and if I'm lucky enough to bring Dr. Hernandez back to this colony...The truth will reign, and the heavens will soon fall."

Riley waved away the two men standing guard with a swift hand gesture. The white men demonstrated their wordless obedience, walking back towards their car. I had outmaneuvered Riley. Now the notions of finding some memory card filled with the identity of Foundational spies, or hiding transhuman bodies, paled when compared to the reality of us having access to Dr. Hernandez. As the airport's loud intercom system blasted launch information, Riley calmly walked up to the front entrance and opened the door for us.

"Well, let's go get him, Nuria. We'll see if we can find this truth you're so fond of." He lamented.

I made my way to the launch kiosk and purchased seats in the orbiter for all of us. After showing airport security our force protection credentials, we handed them our firearms and asked them to pack our guns for safe travel. The steward gathered us in a conference room decorated with photos commemorating the Foundationals that participated in NASA's exploration of Mars. The safety briefing began, and we all watched a boring hologram film detailing the various safety procedures for travel in this model of space orbiter. Once the brief was completed, a steward ushered us to our smallish seats in the orbiter capsule and ensured we were properly buckled into our seats. We sat in nervous silence as pressurized gases from supercooled fuel began to loudly vent out of exhaust panels on the rocket underneath us. Our orbiters two astronauts arrived, greeting us with warm smiles and friendly questions.

During our brief discussion with them, the two black men told us that they had both served as officers in the U.S. Air Force and seen combat in Southeast Asia. Once they had served their time, both men were honorably discharged from the U.S. military and eventually hired to pilot commercial spacecraft for our colony's airline sector. The Flight Commander was an older gentleman, easily in his mid to late fifties. His accent and manner readily told me he was an east coast Foundational, probably from one of the three colonies situated on the outskirts of New York City. Confident that they had quelled our launch jitters, the two astronauts climbed a steep ladder up to their cockpit, closing a heavy quick-acting airtight door behind them upon entering.

Cabin lights within the orbiter briefly flickered as the ground crew activated our onboard generators before disconnecting us from ground power. The low hum of the ventilated mixture of oxygen and other benign gases rushed into my aching eardrums. I could feel the orbiter's stale-smelling air as the atmosphere around me was instantly pressurized. Annoyed with the increasing pressure, I donned a pair of orange earplugs before coughing hard, purposefully making my ears pop. Then the flight commander's New York accent slowly leaked from a small speaker that hung from the low ceiling above me.

"Good evening, passengers, this is the cockpit speaking," he started.

"We should be lifting off here in about ten minutes, so please ensure your wearing your earplugs and have properly buckled into your launch seat."

"Four minutes after launch, we'll eject our rocket and enter lower earth orbit."

"From lower earth orbit, we'll change our reentry trajectory for a Panama splashdown," he explained.

"From launch to safely on deck at Rodman Space Pad in Panama, should be just under seventeen minutes without any delays."

"Steward, please ensure the cabin is ready for liftoff."

The steward walked by our seats, checking safety harnesses and handing out reading material. She made her way to my seat and leaned down close to me. As she smiled at me with a well-seasoned and professional expression, I noticed that her white teeth were manicured to perfection. Her brown skin showed slight traces of excessive makeup. She was an older black woman, but this Foundational woman looked ten years her junior from a distance.

"Here you go, my sister," she said, handing me a light magazine.

"I think you would enjoy reviewing the section detailing our wide array of colonial wines and whiskeys."

She leaned away, and her professional smile evaporated as her eyes seemed to fish around in my mind. Replacing her smile was a knowing expression that seemingly talked to my soul. Having passed the unspoken message, she again affixed her work smile on her face before continuing to the customer on the next aisle. After the steward carried on, I glanced around to find Ed looking at her with that same knowing stare he wore at Clarke's funeral. I knew then I wasn't crazy or seeing things.

I opened the magazine slowly, browsing through dozens of pages until I came to the section advertising black-owned spirit companies. Two pages into the section, I found a yellow note tucked away in between advertisements for Woodson Bourbon and Whiskey products. Grabbing the note, I discreetly unfolded it and read.

"Nuria, if you're reading this," It began.

"You're on the right track. You have my support."

"You'll have helpers when you arrive in El Salvador; I have arranged for them to assist you."

"There will also be enemies monitoring your every move, so be careful and trust no one, even those close to you. If our enemies reveal themselves, eliminate them without prejudice. God's speed."

I took the note and refolded it into a small square. The steward walked up to my seat with an open trash bag. "Ma'am, do you have any trash you need to dispose of before we launch and enter zero gravity?" she asked.

"Once we hit our orbit, we can't have any loose trash floating around our cabin," she explained with her seasoned smile.

I tossed the note into her trash bag, and she continued past me as if my actions were an afterthought. The steward put away her small bag of trash, locking it in a small garbage compartment. Before strapping herself into a seat, she made a call up to the cockpit, confirming the readiness of the passenger cabin. The bright lights in the cabin suddenly dimmed. Our launch countdown began over the loudspeaker. When the countdown hit zero, I felt the rocket underneath us shutter. We seemed to tilt sideways slightly before the loud eruption of the rockets super-cooled fuel suddenly ignited. A storm of ear-blistering noise assaulted every single one of my senses. For what seemed like forever, our cabin shook violently as we rose from the launch pad and raced towards the heavens. The heavy forces of gravity pinned me to my seat as the rocket's rapid acceleration continued skyward. My seat restraints automatically tightened around my chest as we increased in speed. When the sky around us began to turn dark, I felt our rocket perform its roll maneuver, hanging us upside down in the orbiter. In the rush of the moment, the loud roaring rocket suddenly fell silent. Several muffled pops could be heard outside of the orbiter, each cascading in uniformed succession. Through the orbiter window, I watched as our exhausted rocket booster began to slowly fall back to earth. When it was safely away from us, its small landing thrusters ignited, propelling the rocket back down to our launchpad.

As the blood-pulsing thrill of the launch began to subside, my adrenaline started to wear off. Then came the strange sensation of being completely weightless. We had arrived in space. Looking out the window once more, I used my hand to clear away the floating ends of my hair while I stared down at the greenish-blue curvature of our planet. The pitch-dark background of deep space around earth hammered home the true power of the Lord. Out in this abundance of lonely darkness, the Lord had seen fit to create this wonder of comforting light for us.

Hearing cheerful laughter, I turned my head and examined the cabin. Everyone in the orbiter was smiling. Even Riley and Ed were both sharing a rare moment of tranquility as they playfully watched Riley's FBI badge spin endlessly in the air in front of them. Dennis amused himself and a few other passengers by pointing out small islands in the vastness of the Pacific Ocean. Up here, away from earth's halting gravity, we were all just human beings eager to consume our universe. Out of nowhere, the orbiter's small speakers delivered a blaring sound of reality.

"Attention Passengers, this your Flight Commander."

"We are three minutes away from our reentry trajectory to Panama."

"Please stow and secure all floating objects and ensure your safety harnesses are properly buckled in."

"Steward, please conduct one final round about the cabin."

The Steward floated by us, inspecting our harnesses and collecting any floating debris. The expression on everyone's face began to change from the wonderment of God to the somberness of having to return to the strict realities of the world below us. Glancing over at a sitting Riley, I wondered within myself if I could indeed kill her if it came down to it. If it were just her standing in between justice and the decaying lies of this world, eliminating her was something I would have to prepare myself to do. I paused in my inner conflict, closing my eyes and silently asking the Lord to guide me.

I felt a light tap on my lonely shoulder while I prayed, swiftly pulling me off my moment of reflection. I opened my eyes and looked up to see the Steward's pearly white teeth and soft brown eyes examining me. After gently adjusting my harness, she floated close to my ear and began to pepper me with her soft words.

"Is there anything you might need before we start our reentry?" She cleverly asked with her professional smile.

"No, Ma'am." I politely replied. "I actually believe I've got all I need at the moment.

CHAPTER NINE

DANGEROUS TOURISTS

IT WAS AWE-INSPIRING TO TAKE IN the rich dark green canopy surrounding San Salvador. The tropical rainforest looked luscious and refreshing as the clear light blue sky dominated the background behind it. Pulling down my sunglasses to shield my eyes from the bright sun, I discovered that my sweaty forehand had smeared the lens. Taking the shades off my head, I used the bottom end of my shirt to wipe away the wet mess before donning them. The heat in San Salvador was brutal. Being outside felt like walking on a smothering oven.

The humidity alone was enough to dissuade even the most adventurous tourist, yet here we were, taking our chances in the stifling heat in pursuit of a man who knew this city better than we did.

The historic beauty of the buildings in the downtown area were almost enough to distract any sweaty visitor away from the fact that this city was one of the most dangerous places on the planet. There was barely a moment that we didn't hear the loud sirens of the police cars buzzing above us. Earlier in the morning, our chauffeur had driven us by a police station that had recently been bombed by Negro Bandit guerilla forces. From the looks of the debris pattern, I immediately concluded that the explosion had come from inside the building, meaning the Negro Bandits had gotten inside somehow. Like the rest of Central and South America, the country of El Salvador was in the grips of a brutal racial civil war. The Negro Bandits and members of a Mestizo-backed sect called the Resistance were in open conflict. Extremists in both Mestizo and Afro-Latino sects had all but paralyzed the small country that was caught in the crossfires of their mortal combat.

The Resistance organization had the unofficial backing of the government. Many members of the El Salvadorian government were members of the Resistance themselves. Illegally using their status as government officials, these proxies were able to funnel money and military hardware to the Resistance movement. The entire Resistance organization barely clung to its thin claims of legitimacy. Worldwide, many foreign policy experts readily identified the Resistance as the government-funded terrorist cell that it truly was. The Resistance had kidnapped rebellious Afro-Latinos, murdered their Pro-Black collaborators, and illegally confiscated property owned by Negro Bandits sympathizers.

In San Salvador, the quiet presence of the Negro Bandits was everywhere. Posters with clinched black fists were plastered on the sides of abandoned or burnt-out buildings. Young black children roamed the streets wearing shirts with the logos associated with the Black Empowerment Matters movement. While walking the streets searching for clues, I caught several onlookers studying us intensely. As I captured their stares, I certainly knew they were curious about who we were and why we had this funny-looking Blanco with us. After the first day, it became obvious to me that we were being followed. In an effort to quail the concerns of my followers, I made sure that we all spent our money at local black-owned businesses, even if it meant having to suffer the inconvenience of traveling across the city. Remembering the note, the steward had given me in the orbiter, I needed to relay my unspoken message to my potential helpers.

At one restaurant, a young black bartender greeted me with a curious smile before offering me a hushed "B1." Catching his signal, I quickly returned his smile, responding with "B1 to you as well, my brother." After our meal, I wrote him a flowery handwritten note and left him a very generous tip for all his troubles.

We all stopped to have lunch at a local restaurant located in a particularly sketchy part of town. The food was delicious and our hosts were fabulous, but unfortunately, Riley discovered that someone had relieved her of her wallet during our visit. To me and Ed's embarrassment, a pissed-off Riley stormed back into the small restaurant, yelling and cursing at the black owners. Incensed, Riley accused our gracious hosts of stealing, almost causing a physical altercation. After tampering down everyone's temper, we were allowed to search the restaurant but couldn't find Riley's belongings. We backtracked our route for about an hour before finally deciding to bring a merciful end to our search. We relented to the scorching heat, seeking the forgiving comforts of our air-conditioned hotel rooms.

It had been three days since we arrived in San Salvador, and we hadn't found one trace of Dr. Hernandez. On our first day, we visited the last known location of Dennis's tracking device and found the beacon buried underneath a rusty trash can outside of a public swimming pool. Using satellite imagery, we were able to identify the CIA compound that was once the main hub for Operation Balboa. The compound was located several hours outside of the city, near several small villages out in the middle of the rainforest. When we got there, the compound looked just like the photo Dr. Hernandez had shown me inside the Church Clinic, aside from the broken windows, and missing doors. The compound had been deserted. Local farmers had commandeered the vacant building, using it to keep their fresh produce away from greedy insects.

On our second day, we visited several of Dr. Hernandez's distant relatives and old associates. None of them claimed to know where he was. Many of them were under the impression that Dr. Hernandez had been killed years ago. When we showed them recent photos of him, with his wrinkles and greying hair, I saw genuine shock blitz across their faces. It was almost as if they were looking at an old ghost. Dr. Hernandez had lived a life so immersed in secrecy that his closest friends and relatives hardly knew anything about him. Both the Resistance and the CIA had swallowed his entire earthly existence. Everything about his life seemed to be cleverly orchestrated CIA skill craft.

"Ok, Ma'am," Our elderly chauffeur declared with a heavy accent.

"What time do you need transportation tomorrow." He asked as he slowly lowered his van down in front of our hotel.

Our chauffeur was a slick-haired Mestizo who liked to wear long-sleeved button-up shirts with perfectly ironed khaki pants. The scent of his spicy aftershave dominated the inside of our van. Today, his olive-colored button-up was totally drenched in sweat. His van's air condition had failed us during the early morning hours and this afternoon just so happened to be a record high temperature-wise.

"We'll start a bit earlier tomorrow, Hector. Let's get going around six in the morning," I ventured.

The chauffeur let out an annoyed sigh and wiped the sweat from the back of his neck, betraying his frustration as he put the car into park mode and killed the ignition. All of us were starting to feel the fatigue of today's search, but this man had to be feeling a different sort of discomfort. In the middle of a racial civil war, he was driving around three American Negroes and one strange-looking Blanco. I low key noticed his fellow Mestizo brethren giving him looks of disgust when they saw him with us. Yet for Hector, playing the happy tour guide for this group of uppity Foundational Negroes was lucrative. Given the lackluster state of the country's economy, the shame of catering to a group of blacks was outweighed by the specter of experiencing poverty's hunger pains. Content with my early morning instructions, Hector nodded and popped open the van's door locks. Before any of us knew it, a whiny Agent Riley exploded out of his back seat, storming out towards the hotel's entrance.

I reached into my pocket and handed Hector his daily paycheck. His sweaty face widened with an appreciative smile when his eyes saw the stack of Foundational bills adorned with the magnificent portrait of our elder, Dr. John Henrik Clarke. Black lives may not have mattered to Hector, but Black currency was a completely different story.

The three of us in the van exited and made our way to the hotel's entrance. Ahead of us, we all watched as Riley angrily maneuvered his way around a group of black panhandlers who were attempting to sell him cigars and knock off liquor. A few in the group broke away upon seeing us, approaching with hopeful smiles and aggressive solicitations.

"My sister. My brothers." They greeted while displaying small boxes of hand-rolled cigars.

I politely declined their offers as the group followed alongside as we closed in on the hotel entrance. Riley made it to the front door and flung it open in a fit of anger. Then I noticed Riley suddenly fall backward. She struggled to catch balance before ultimately landing hard on the ground. Above Riley stood a black man with charcoal-colored skin, wearing a tight black tank top and sporting a beefy muscular frame. His eyes were fixated on Riley lying below him. In his hand, he held a long glow rod. A bluish-green current pulsed around the bitter end of his weapon, and before I could utter a word, the man plunged his glow rod into Riley's chest.

Stunned by the assault, Riley's body stiffened as the electricity jolt sent her into a state of shock. Beside me, I heard Ed scream out in distress, loudly demanding that someone back away or he would shoot. I turned my head and noticed that all the black panhandlers had surrounded us. Gone were their hearty smiles and solicitations, as they all wore serious and menacing expressions, almost like a pack of hungry wolves. Throwing back the end of my shirt with my lonely hand, I reached into my waistband and pulled my service pistol. As I raised it, I felt someone from behind pulling my arm. Unable to shake away from his grasp, I clinched my pistol with an iron grip and turned my body towards the aggressor. I violently tried to pull away from his hold, but he was able to maintain it easily. For a brief second, I looked into his brown eyes and noticed that it was Dennis.

"Stop, Nuria!" he yelled.

"Their Negro Bandits!"

"Look at the tattoos on their hands."

Confused, I turned to look back at Riley and heard the buff black man barking orders in Spanish. Several young panhandlers obediently lifted Riley's body off the ground and began carrying Riley towards us.

"How can you be sure they aren't Dr. Hernandez's transhumans, Dennis?"

The buff black man walked up to me and Dennis. Reaching into his cargo pants pocket, he pulled out a sharp blade. Displaying his hand to me, I could see the label B1 imprinted on the web of skin between his thumb and index finger. He then took the blade and sliced open a healed wound on his pinky finger. When the bright red blood started oozing out, a smile of satisfaction washed across his shiny black face. Then our eyes met, and he focused in on me.

"We are all humans," he stated in perfect English.

"And we are all Black First, my Queen."

"What is all of this," I asked while motioning towards the men holding Riley.

"We don't have time to waste," he loudly interrupted.

"I just attacked a white man. The race soldiers posing as police will swarm here shortly with every intention to kill any black person they find. I need all of you to come with us. We are your helpers."

"Quickly! Come now." He waved.

The buff black man jogged ahead, leading us away from the hotel's entrance. We turned down a narrow alley, running behind a rusted-out storage facility. The alley's uneven walkway was made of slippery cobblestones. Our brisk pace caused me to trip more than a few times on the unfamiliar footing. Above us, I heard sirens and saw several police cars circling the sky. Voices from loudspeakers barked commands in both Spanish and English, ordering any Negroes on the premise to halt and make ready their papers for inspection.

The buff black man and several would-be panhandlers opened a door into a sewage facility. With the door flung open, they began waving their arms at us, hurrying us inside. We all ran inside the facility, and the smell of hot simmering sewage immediately ruined our senses. The buff black man ran towards a capped manhole, prying off the heavy cover with a long crowbar. The men carrying Riley sprinted to the open space, lowering an unconscious Riley down into the smelly darkness with a manilla rope.

"We must escape using the drainage tunnels," the buff black man instructed.

"The fuck we do," Ed shot back. "Is it even safe down there?"

"You will find that this primitive tunnel is much more hospitable than a Mestizo-controlled prison cell, my brother," he responded.

"It's extremely dark and wet in the tunnel. All you need to do is hold on tight to the shirt of the person in front of you."

"If you get lost down there, don't yell or scream; just remain quiet and stay where you are."

"If the race soldiers hear any noise, they will open all the manholes in the area. They like to toss tear gas down here to smoke us out. The Police will shoot anyone they find climbing out of the holes without question."

Outside of the storage building, I could hear dozens of police officers barking orders to random citizens. Loud pops accompanied the smell of gunpowder, followed by the distinct feeling of pepper spray assaulting my vulnerable eyes. The buff man grabbed my lonely hand and pushed it against his thin black tank top.

"Get your hand accustomed to the feel of my shirt," he ordered. "I'll be waiting for you at the bottom of the manhole."

"When I feel your hand grab my shirt, we'll start moving together."

As best I could, I forced my eyes open, watching the man climb down before me. When the burning sensation became too much, my eyelids slammed shut and I felt Ed's encouraging hand touch the small of my back.

"It's your turn Nuria," he stated. "Let's get the hell outta here."

With my one arm, I slowly descended the twenty or so feet to the bottom. When my feet hit the cold water, the lingering effects of the pepper spray were replaced by the sensation of slimy feces bouncing off my exposed ankles. The smell of stale urine overpowered the lingering pepper spray in my sensitive nostrils. I opened my eyes wide to discover absolute darkness. Unsure of where my guide was, I made a small circle, holding out my hand a few feet in front of me, hoping to brush up against him. Halfway through my circle, I felt his thin black tank top and immediately grabbed a handful.

I felt him tow me forward into the abyss, where the hard breathing of the caravan ahead of us only rivaled the sudden explosions and gunfire from the streets above. We swiftly moved through the ankle-deep sewage, trampling several screaming rats to death in the process. Behind me, Ed held on to the back of my shirt. I heard him unholster his pistol and click the safety off as we passed underneath a beam of light from an open manhole. After five minutes of walking, the gunfire and sound of sirens began to sound distant.

Ahead of me, I heard the splashes of feet moving through sewage water come to a stop. My face bounced off the hard back of my guide, nearly causing me to fall backwards. Hanging on tight to his tank top, we slowly rounded a sharp turn, and the dim light from above replaced the darkness surrounding us. I was able to see an open manhole and ladder up ahead with a long rope dangling from the street. The men carrying Riley walked up to the open manhole and tied several knots around Riley's underarm and crotch. After a thumbs-up signal, someone from above began to lift Riley's body out of our smelly tunnel.

"Ok. Let's go," the buff black man barked.

Each of us climbed out of our odorous bastion of waste, finding our feet back on the sunny world above. Two large service vans were parked and waiting. The buff black man ushered us into one of them and hopped into the front seat. Without words, the two black men in the front compartment handed us hot towels and sprayed us with several bursts of very strong air freshener. Within minutes, we were airborne, heading away from the downtown chaos.

The driver drove us eastbound before hovering over a scattered neighborhood of sheet metal shacks. Below us, several black men waved their arms towards the sky while circling two burning logs. When the van began to lower to earth, the men drenched the burning logs with water, sending white steam into the air. Our landing on the uneven red dirt was rough, making the van bounce hard as it settled onto the ground. The buff black man opened the van door and hustled outside, waving for more men to come and help handle Riley's limp body. Men with long guns trotted to the open door, pulling Riley out and laying her body on a crude-looking wooden backboard.

"Come on family, let's go," the buff black man ordered.

We stepped out of the van, following the buff black man towards a long metal shack. The portion of the shack facing us was open-ended, aside from makeshift blankets that acted as entrances. On the blankets, I saw that portraits of Marcus Garvey and Dr. Claude Anderson had been sewn into them. For several moments, our guests examined us, looking at their American visitors in a fit of curiosity. Then a young black man, no doubt a teenager, walked over to Riley's still body. He held an electronic device in his hands, which he activated as he took a knee beside Riley.

His device emitted a dense green light that illuminated the red dirt beneath him. Confident that his device was functional, the teenager slowly waved the device around Riley's skull, making several deliberate passes near her temple.

"Is he searching Riley for bugs?" Ed whispered.

"No," Dennis responded. "It looks like he's making sure Riley isn't a transhuman."

The buff black man motioned towards us, sending the teenager our way. The teenager reset his device and approached each of us. Using his very broken English, the teenager asked us to remain perfectly still while he scanned our heads and reviewed his readings. Satisfied with his results, the teenager hit a switch and deactivated his machine.

"It's comforting to know we only have human beings with us today," the buff black man stated.

"Your white friend will be OK," he continued. "The effects of the shock should begin to wear off soon, and he will awake, but before he does, we need to have a private conversation."

"Wait here; I have someone who has been waiting to meet all of you."

The buff black man swiftly walked towards the open-ended shack, dismissively brushing the large blanket aside before disappearing behind it. All three of us looked around and took in our surroundings in his absence. Using the moment to examine the scenery, I noticed that everyone in this neighborhood was heavily armed. I could see that the black people here wore combat body armor under their tattered clothes. Most of them looked like they had missed more than a few meals. As I watched them in silence, I could feel their eyes examining us, reviewing our presence with a spirit of prudent caution. For some reason, I couldn't figure out if that caution came from a place of admirable respect or irrational fear.

The blanket swung open, and the buff man walked towards us with another black man behind him. As the two men neared us, I got a good look at the young man and immediately recognized his familiar face. It was the black B1 bartender I had tipped and written a note to. He was wearing a white hospital coat and neat blue jeans that were a bit snug. I noticed the small silver nametag on his coat. It read Student Physician, Juan H. Delgado. In his right hand, he was holding Riley's missing wallet. Stopping several paces in front of me, he held up the wallet and gave us all a coy smile.

"I'm sorry it took so long for us to introduce ourselves." He stated in perfect English.

"We noticed you arrived in San Salvador with this white man."

"When we got word that you were coming down here to visit us. We didn't expect you to bring the FBI along with you."

The questions in my mind began to sound off like a blurring foghorn. Who exactly had told him I'd be coming, and why did they neglect to inform him about Riley coming along? Had the Negro Bandits been following us the whole time? Why did they wait so long before contacting us? Instead of rattling off those questions, I decided it would be better if I kept my concerns close to the vest until I got a better gauge of what was truly going on here.

"Hi, I'm Agent Nuria Sellers from the Oakland, California Reparations Colony," I introduced. "Next to me is my partner Agent Ed Carter and my technical expert, Dennis Winslow."

"My name is Juan. I am the lead scientist for the Negro Militia in San Salvador."

"You have already met my cousin George," he declared while motioning towards the buff black man.

"George is just like you, Nuria. George is in charge of all security matters for our militia here in San Salvador. It's his expertise that keeps the Resistance and their police thugs at bay."

"By the smell of raw sewage on your clothes, I see that George has already shown you how competent he is."

George puffed up visibly, swelling with pride upon hearing his cousin make a glowing comparison between the both of us. From the glint in his eyes when he heard my name next to his, I knew all these people watching me were watching with an air of respect.

"We all admire your sacrifice at Dry Tortugas," he continued.

"And we are honored to have you with us today, Agent Sellers."

"I assume you all are members of the Negro Bandits?" Ed asked.

"Negro Bandits is a term the Resistance, and Blanco Supremacists like to use for us, my brother," he laughed.

"Around here, we go by the name El Viento."

"The Wind," Dennis softly translated. "El Viento means the wind."

"Yes, we are like the wind, my friend. We are a powerful force that can't be seen nor touched, but it's definitely felt and feared. The wind is everywhere."

"George and I have been part of El Viento since we were young boys," he explained.

"My father was a founding member, as were my two uncles. All three were kidnapped and tortured to death by the Resistance. Now, it's just us left to fight this war against the oppressive Blanco's and their Mestizo wannabe's."

Juan reached into his coat pocket, pulling out an old photo. It was an ancient digitally printed image, the type of photo that was all the rave back in the early 21st century. Juan leaned over towards me to present the photo.

"This is a photo of my father, his two brothers, and George and I," he explained. "The photo was taken about eight years ago when your husband Quinton came to El Salvador on a church mission."

I took the photo from his hand and examined it. The first face that caught my attention was Quinton's. He looked a lot younger as he stood in the center of a large group of people with his hands wrapped around his bible. From the lack of grey hairs on his head and his still chiseled physique, I knew the photo had been taken not too long after his retirement from boxing. Around Quinton were three adult men with their arms lovingly draped over two children that stood in front of them, flashing smiles of innocence. The children were spitting images of the three men towering over them. It was easy to recognize the resemblance between a doting father and a proud son.

331

"To the Black people of El Salvador, your husband is a hero," George proclaimed.

"When he won the Heavyweight Championship, it felt like we all won too. It inspired us. We were all big fans growing up."

"Back when we posed for this photo," Juan interjected. "We were winning this war."

"Dr. Hernandez and his Mestizo brethren were starting to lose their grip on the El Salvadorian government. The citizens were tired of this war, and they believed that the Americans were using this conflict to make money for themselves."

"El Salvadorians of all races resented seeing our stores flooded with expensive American products. They were unnerved to see both sides fighting with American-made weaponry. El Salvadorian's were dying, and far left propaganda about gender, sexual orientation and religion were being taught to our children."

"El Salvadorians, who had once been devout Christians and Catholics, seemed to begin to deny the beliefs they once held."

"Rumors of CIA mind control experiments started spreading around the countryside. More and more, black leaders of The Wind were assassinated or went missing."

"Entire families were split or torn apart with mistrust. Strangely, Mestizo government officials began to pour more energy into promoting American commerce. Prominent leaders within The Wind suddenly began to disavow Black Empowerment."

"Our country was in a state of mass confusion...and my father took advantage of the lack of leadership."

Juan leaned down and picked up a small piece of rusted sheet metal off the ground. Walking over to Dennis, he handed him the rusty metal and motioned towards the sea of rusty sheet metal shacks surrounding us.

"Gary Freeman informed my father about the CIA's transhuman operation years before Quinton Sellers came down here on his church mission."

"Doctors that were sympathetic to our movement discovered that Gary Freeman had told us the truth. So, through trial and error, my uncles figured out a way to determine if a person was transhuman or not."

"It's the rust!" Dennis suddenly declared.

"The chemical reaction of rusting makes the bio-mechanical equipment installed in transhumans malfunction."

"Very good, brother," Juan complimented. "I see you've been doing some experimenting yourself."

"Too much rust intake will pollute the bloodstream of a transhuman subject."

"Whether they are breathing the rust particles, swallowing water from rusty pipes, or eating from rusty plates, a certain level of rust in the transhuman blood stream causes their bio-processors to automatically reboot... clearing out any orders that the CIA or Resistance may have downloaded into their consciousness."

"We were able to lock away suspected transhumans," Juan continued. "Right here in this neighborhood of rusty shacks."

"Members of The Wind that were prone to long absences or suspected of being agents of the Resistance...we lock them away right here."

"It only takes a week or so. Eventually, the transhuman body will start to shut down, attempting to preserve itself. From there, we figured out how to map and download our missions into their consciousness."

"So, you created double agents," I opined.

"The term double agents sound so sinister Agent Sellers," Juan rebuffed.

"I'd like to think of them as our very own highly competent

operative class. Transhumans who we can get on the inside and bring about our own brand of chaos."

Several men picked up the backboard holding Riley, ushering her towards a long shack, labeled with a first aid emblem. Juan broke away from us and began walking towards the open blanket, waving for us to follow him.

"Come on now. Your white friend will be awake soon, and we still have much to discuss."

We all walked past the blanket into the inside of the main shack. The inside was well lit, spacious, and cool. Wood flooring covered with sections of plastic tarp lined the ground beneath our feet. Men wearing white coats, gloves, and masks were busy looking through microscopes or typing away on computers. The quiet buzz of a generator was only masked by the constant hum of cool air being pushed through the shack's many vents. This was a well-disguised research facility, hidden away in the midst of what looked like abject poverty. I peeked over at Dennis and saw the wonderment that had consumed his curious spirit.

"How long have you been researching transhumanism?" Dennis asked.

"Personally, I started when I was fifteen, but The Wind has been researching transhumanism for more than a decade."

"When members of the Resistance started disappearing or were assassinated, the CIA suspected we had turned the tables on them."

"The Mestizo Resistance began to lose the war, and the White Americans in the CIA didn't want to be on the wrong side of that political equation. So, the CIA pulled the plug on Operation Balboa, taking away the Resistance's funding, resources, and manpower."

"My father always told us that the white Americans would betray the Mestizos. Abandoning Operation Balboa when it was clear their transhuman war against us Afro-Latinos was no longer in their interest."

'But not everyone in the CIA went along with that program, did they Juan?" Dennis chimed in.

'Dr. Hernandez told us that there were hardcore White elements within the CIA who wanted to continue with Operation Balboa despite the setbacks."

Juan nodded at Dennis, and then walked over to a small dinette area near the shack's entrance. He opened a long brown cabinet positioned against the wall, pulling out a tin can of tuna fish, a small bag of white rice, and two bottled soft drinks. Juan handed each of us an item before opening his warm soda and drinking the bottle down to half.

'That's because there is big money to be made down here, my friend."

'Operation Balboa was bankrolled outside of the CIA and U.S. government. The funding sent down here was almost all private-sector money. It had to be in order for U.S. politicians to maintain a flimsy veneer of plausible deniability. All of this stuff is in clear violation of international law."

'CIA operatives like the white woman Dominic and the Mestizo Resistance heavily recruited American businesses to fund Operation Balboa."

"They sold the business owners on the idea that in the process of creating this submissive Afro-Latino transhuman class, they would also program us Afro-Latinos with addictions, obsessions, and unique cravings for American products."

"The way they saw it. If both sides were in a perpetual state of war against each other, both sides could never grow their own rice, process their own fish, or create their own soft drinks."

Taking the bottle of soda in my hand, I flipped it around to its back label and scanned past the ingredients until I found the answer I was looking for. Sure enough, this bottle of warm orange soda had been produced in Rapid City, South Dakota. I peered over at Ed, who was examining the bag of rice. We found its label and saw that it had been produced in the U.S. as well. The rice came from a small town called Cow Island in Southern Louisiana.

'With the help of Gary Freeman and you Foundationals, we were able to discover the existence of Operation Balboa and not only negate its effectiveness but use it against the Resistance," Juan lamented.

'CIA operatives like Dominic recognized that they had lost. Dominic knew we would win this war, and there was no way the CIA or the Resistance could stop us. Moreover, if Operation Balboa's details leaked to the public, it would be a national embarrassment of epic proportions. Sort of like the Bay of Pigs back in the 1960s."

'So, Dominic betrayed Dr. Hernandez and the Mestizo Resistance. They eliminated the Balboa program, arresting its participants, and even killing scientists to ensure details of the program were never publicly leaked."

'But there was one problem," I interrupted.

Juan looked at me and flashed a smile before motioning with his hands, encouraging me to continue with what was on my mind. I held up the bottle of soda, slowly waving it in the air for everyone to see. I had come to El Salvador to find the truth. Ultimately, finding that truth plastered on the back of a 24-ounce bottle of nasty soda.

'Not everyone was thrilled about leaving the Mestizos high and dry. I can imagine that if I had dedicated my entire CIA career towards combating Black Empowerment, I'd be pissed if my bosses somehow lost their nerve and surrendered to Black interests."

'The same can be said for members of the Mestizo Resistance. The feeling of betrayal must have certainly cut deep when you've relied so much on the CIA to save you."

"More importantly, this is all about those businessmen who profited off of Operation Balboa," I stated while shaking the bottle of soda.

"They must have felt a certain way about ending Transhumanism. I'm sure those greedy businessmen were more concerned with being able to sell their products."

"Combine all three of these groups.... and you have the money, you have the knowledge and the motivation to stage a coup d'etat...All three groups have the key ingredients for a hostile takeover of the CIA itself."

"Three different groups with three separate interests, and one mutual problem, Dominic Bamber."

I paused to collect my thoughts. Everyone around me watched while I tried to gather the words of truth buried in my soul. The forever memories of blue blood shining under the moonlit sky began to come back to me. The visions of that black child firing away at us from behind his machine gun nest felt real again. Within my soul, I was reliving the moment I aimed my rifle and pulled the trigger. In my mind, I could hear that same old annoying question Dr. Wiseman would always ask me during her sessions. Now I finally knew the answer.

"Dry Tortugas," I began. "Was a setup. It was a damn setup from start to finish."

"I'm not a hero. I'm just lucky as hell to have survived. Even before all of this, I somehow knew that, and the memories have sort of tortured me."

"Like Donovan, Pernell, and Jeremy Woodson, I was supposed to have been killed that day."

"Dominic was using us to eliminate remnants of Operation Balboa. She was playing God and manipulating Foundationals to advance her own motives."

"In the Fort, I killed a young black boy," I admitted.

"For all I know, he might have been a member of The Wind. He looked like you Juan. Maybe he was an immigrant from Panama, Honduras, or Belize. Wherever he came from, he was there waiting on us at Dry Tortugas, and I believe that's exactly what our friend Dominic was banking on."

"You're beginning to understand...Agent Sellers," Juan proclaimed. "After Dominic and the CIA pulled the plug on Operation Balboa. The Resistance and rogue CIA elements moved their operations to the United States. They strategically relocated in the Southern states, near the border."

"In the south, they targeted Afro-Latino immigrants crossing the border illegally. Transforming them into transhumans before the U.S government deported the black migrants back to their countries."

"When Dominic and her political allies found out about these crimes, they had the FBI raid all Operation Balboa outposts and arrest the conspirators."

"Angered by Dominic's actions, rogue CIA elements coordinated terrorist actions against your reparations colonies in order to stoke up racial unrest inside the U.S."

"They hoped that the perceived racial violence would ignite an open race war, making any effort to suppress the Mestizo Resistance unpopular among your White population."

"The move backfired badly. Dominic and her politicians ignored White public sentiment and made the unpopular decision to honor their Reparations agreement with you Foundationals. This paved the way for Dominic to use your Anti-Terror FP teams and the entire might of the U.S. military to hunt down members of the Resistance. Dominic had secretly declared war against the rogue elements within the CIA."

"It was a bold power move, that pit one half of White Supremacy against the other."

"That old fort at Dry Tortugas was one of the locations that the CIA rogue elements used to download missions into their transhuman subjects. That's why they allowed you to discover it, Agent Sellers."

"The terrorist you were hunting at Dry Tortugas, his real name is not Bradley Wood, it's actually Javier Ortiz," Juan admitted.

"Javier Ortiz is a Blanco member of the Resistance from Argentina. Bradley Wood is just one of the many false identities he has used over the years."

"Ok, say all of this is true," Ed began. "Why does Dr. Hernandez go out of his way to assassinate Governor Williams and Senator Bean? He could have just killed Dominic and gotten his revenge that way."

"Now you know everything I know brother," Juan answered. "That's a question you're gonna have to ask Dr. Hernandez."

Suddenly, an ear-piercing blast came from outside the shack. A loud blast of rifle fire followed the explosion. Alarmed, Juan trotted over towards the entrance and peered out from behind the thick blanket. The instant his head was exposed outside, the sheet metal shack surrounding us shook as a flood of bullets cut holes into the thin walls.

"Juan's been hit!" George screamed while running towards the entrance.

In front of us laid a wounded Juan, bleeding from his left shoulder area, just above the heart. Another salvo of high caliber gunfire racked the hardwood floor near Juan, barely missing him by only a few feet. His cousin George grabbed him by his arm in a panic, pulling Juan away from the kill zone. When he made it behind the concealment of a long metal desk, I watched as George fell to his knees and tried to stop Juan's bleeding.

"Someone's at the entrance," Ed screamed.

I turned my attention towards the now battered blanket barely hanging at the entrance. At first, I only noticed several sets of boots, but the entire situation came into crisp focus as the seconds rolled by. I could make out the faded black uniforms of an El Salvadorian SWAT team through the small bullet holes. My lonely hand instinctively reached and unholstered my service pistol. In my mind, I made note that I only had one spare ammo magazine, so an extended gunfight was not an ideal option. Next to me, both Dennis and Ed unholstered their handguns as all three of us trained our barrels at the entrance, waiting to let loose on anyone who tried to enter.

Then I heard the unmistakable sound of a cheap metal can bouncing off the hardwood floor. I could see two canisters of tear gas hurdling toward us from the entrance. The first canister rolled over towards Ed, who quickly grabbed the can, tossing it back outside. The second canister came right at me. Using my pistol like a tennis racket, I cocked back and hit the canister, sending the can streaking back at the entrance. Both canisters erupted, releasing their gas among our group of assailants. Over my lonely shoulder, I felt the loud percussions of an assault rifle blasting away above my ear. Empty shell casings began to rain down on my arm. The casings were hot, burning my exposed skin and causing me to wince in pain.

It was George. He towered over me, wearing an expression of pure hatred as he sprayed the entrance, wounding scores of police. Among the dense cloud of tear gas, I could see several dead bodies. George stopped firing to eject a spent magazine. While grabbing a spare, he reached down and slapped my back to get my attention.

"Nuria, grab your people and get your asses out of the back exit," he said while motioning towards a small door in the rear.

"The Resistance and their pals in the police have launched a surprise attack. Follow our personnel to our defense post behind this building."

'I'll stay here and give you all covering fire. Hurry now!"

I looked towards the exit and saw all the Doctors and Scientists fleeing outside. Several of the Doctors were slowly walking alongside Juan as he labored to move. After barking at Dennis and Ed, I sprinted towards the exit with both men close behind. Before exiting, I looked back towards George and saw him firing away at scores of militarized police from behind a metal desk near the back exit. I aimed my pistol at two Race Soldiers attempting to advance on George's exposed flank and pulled the trigger, letting loose three rounds at each man. My aim had been true and deadly, popping both men in their heads and chest, causing each of them to fall harmlessly to their deaths in a pool of blue blood.

I jogged out of the back exit, finding myself in a large open space behind the long shack. About one hundred yards away stood a three-story complex made of dark grey cinder blocks. I could hear mounted machine guns peppering the earth below from reinforced positions in each corner on its roof. Just below the roof, young black teenagers fired rockets and sniper rifles from windowless perches. Several militarized police rovers circled the area in the sky above, indiscriminately firing their canons into metal shacks. Black women and children were sent running for their lives, all heading towards the safety of the large cinder block building directly in front of me. Everything was pure chaos. Gunfire and death dominated this realm.

In this ocean of confusion, I noticed a group of black Doctors escorting Juan into the cinder block building. Not far behind them, Dennis and Ed followed, sprinting towards the open front entrance as volleys of bullets hit the dirt around them. This cinder block building had to be George's defense post. From the gunfire coming from the air and surrounding buildings, I knew the Resistance had us encircled. They had the tactical advantage and definitely would attempt to siege the vulnerable defense post.

I took off towards the building, purposely focusing my eyes on its open entrance. Bullets began to rain down on the dirt path ahead, causing me to swerve several times. From just inside the building's front door, I saw Ed screaming for me to keep moving while Dennis and several black teenagers fired in all directions. My erratic movements spoiled our enemy's aim until I got close, then I made a straight line for the entrance. I was closing on it fast. I was so close that I could see the whites of Ed's panicky eyes. Before I entered, the world around me seemed to tumble and turn upside down.

I felt my back bounce off the ground before my body rolled over my head. Ed's hand grabbed my leg in a tight vice grip, and he dragged me the rest of the way into the building. In a fit of shock and concern, I leaned myself up against the cinder block wall, dropping my pistol on my lap. My lonely hand automatically performed a crush and feel around my chest and neck. Within seconds, I felt the hands of Dennis and Ed combing every limb on my body. Both men's faces looked hyper-concerned as they examined me for any injuries.

"You're alright, Nuria," Dennis screamed, almost as if he was trying to convince himself.

To my relief, there was no blood, no wounds, and I hadn't been hit at all. In a moment of realization, all three of us shared a blessed smile that was interrupted by another earth-shaking blast of mortar fire.

"The police are weakening us with their military-grade artillery. Then, they will charge in here to execute us all." Juan informed us.

Juan slowly raised himself from the floor, struggling to move through the pain of his sucking chest wound. Physically mustering all of the strength that remained in his already thin body, Juan walked over to a wooden closet, pulling it open and retrieving a shotgun from inside.

"We are all in for the fight of our lives," Juan continued. "The Resistance is putting it all on the line. We only have two choices."

"Either we all die fighting these racist bastards, or you die on your knees like cowards. The choice is yours."

Feeling the unbroken spirit within him, I jumped from the floor and walked over to Juan. After exchanging head nods, I reached into his closet and pulled out an automatic rifle. Without words, Dennis and Ed walked over and did the same. As we all loaded our rifles, I finally noticed that Riley had been hovering in the room among us. Riley looked exhausted, as if she had just finished a grueling workout. When I looked into her eyes, I immediately knew that this assault wasn't Riley's doing. In fact, the bonus of killing her may have given this Resistance raid an extra bit of incentive. For the Resistance, eliminating another FBI agent would surely send a healthy jolt of self-preservation into the politicians back in Washington D.C. The politicos could not afford for this entire embarrassing affair to be made public. The CIA had secretly funded and supported the Mestizo Resistance. If the illegal transhuman practices were exposed, America's undeserved role as the world's moral authority would be utterly compromised.

"Are you just gonna sit there and let us do all the heavy lifting, Riley?" I jokingly offered.

"You fuckin people created this mess. How about you help with the cleanup, for once."

"I wasn't sure if I was invited to this party since you folks tasered me into unconsciousness," Riley shot back.

"If you trust me, I'm damn sure not going to die on my knees like Dominic. I'd rather get a bit of revenge for Clarke."

Riley walked over towards me, and I obliged her by tossing Riley a loaded shotgun. Ed and Dennis looked at me with horrified stares, unconvinced of the decision I had just made. After a silent head nod at both men, they relented and submitted to my objective. Agent Riley was still our hated adversary, but a temporary alliance of convenience was essential in this case. Dr. Hernandez and his rogue allies were making a global power move. If they were not stopped, the demonic practices of transhumanism would go unchecked. Black people worldwide would be under serious threat, as would anyone in the Dominant Society that opposed them.

All of us took defensive positions on the first floor of the building. Juan and several armed Doctors opened a hatch to a tunnel, ushering all of the women and children into the safety of San Salvador's underground sewage complex. Positioning my rifle on top of an open window ledge, I used my lonely hand to chamber a round before focusing my eyes outside. For a brief moment, our entire world went silent. The quietness of it all was spooky. Nothing outside of our building moved, and I knew what was about to happen next. My spirit could almost taste the beginning of their siege.

Then came the loud explosions. An intense barrage of mortar fire broke the silence as the inaccurate shells were walked towards our building, one by one. Finally, our building took a direct hit, and I felt the world around me shake from a percussion that sucked the wind from my lungs. I rolled into a ball, hugging the floor for dear life as shell after shell shook the building to its foundation. Large pieces of cinder block fell as a cloud of thick dust filled the air. In the midst of violent noise, I swallowed my fear and used the only weapon I had left. I channeled my concentration and pressed my eyes shut. Screaming at the top of my lungs, I humbly asked the Lord to spare us if it was his will to do so.

Before I could finish my prayer, the noise stopped, and the world around me went still. The mortar fire had ceased, and I was still alive. In this new silence, I could hear distressed men coughing and fighting to gasp for air. Refocused, I grabbed my rifle out of the rubble and repositioned it on what remained of the window ledge. Above the hovering cloud of smoke and dust, I saw two militarized rovers descending to earth. I knew this playbook all too well. Next would come deadly waves of assaults meant to finish us off.

The rovers opened their deployment doors, and several race soldiers glided down, disappearing into the dense cloud below them. I put my finger on the trigger, aiming my rifle at one of the open doors before delivering a three-round burst inside. Looking up from my rifle site to assess my accuracy, I was unsure if my bullets had struck anything. Despite my doubt, the rover began to wobble in midair wildly. Several race soldiers jumped from the rover in a panic without using the repelling rope. Around me, what remained of our building erupted in gunfire, all aimed at the two vulnerable rovers hovering in front of us. The heavy machine guns on the floor above us shot the rover to shreds. One rover flipped upside down in the air before crashing into the ground in a bright orange fireball. The other lifted out of its hover, trying to make a run for it before dark black smoke began to pour from its engines. The rover's nose pointed down at a row of metal shacks and plowed into them, disappearing from my view.

Around me came loud cheers and roars of victory from the mouths of men that were all but defeated only a few moments prior. Riley and Dennis exchanged high fives as if they had just won the Super Bowl. I felt that same energy and let out a scream of joy upon realizing the blessings of the Lord. Amidst our celebration, scores of armed race soldiers appeared from within the clouds of smoke, running towards us with guns blazing. Above me, the heavy machine guns returned fire, laying waste to the approaching line of hostile enemies. Joining in, I let loose a whole clip from my rifle. Blue blood poured from the heads of my targets, and I knew transhuman race soldiers were attacking us. The swarm of transhumans was a mix of White, Asian, Mestizos, and a few of African descent. All of them heavily armed, wearing El Salvadorian police uniforms with military-grade combat armor.

"Aim for their heads," I shouted!

Something in my spirit told me to look behind me and check my six. I glanced over my shoulder and noticed our rear line had been compromised. The back of the building had been completely blown away, and there was little to no cover for the few black teenagers charged with protecting our rear guard. Ed was among the group as they engaged several transhumans in brutal hand-to-hand combat. Alarmed, I bolted up from my window ledge and ran toward the back of the building to help secure the breach. My abrupt movement caught Riley's attention, alerting her to the impending danger. Without words, Riley followed close behind me as we sprinted into the melee, swinging our long guns like baseball bats.

I cocked back and struck a small Hispanic transhuman in the back of his head with my rifle. The blow barely seemed to register as he pushed me aside with a powerful shove that was terrifying in its ease. His green eyes looked possessed, almost like he was staring through me. As I fell to the ground, the transhuman punched a male-looking Riley in her face, causing Riley's nose to bust open and bleed. Fighting for her life, Riley pointed her shotgun at the stocky man and pulled the trigger. The shotgun pellets peppered the stomach of the transhuman. It was a shot that would have quickly incapacitated a normal human being, but the wounds barely slowed the transhuman. He reached out, grabbed Riley's neck, and squeezed hard. Riley's face turned bright red as she struggled to breathe. I jumped up from the ground, picking up a long rusty piece of rebar with my lonely arm. I dove forward using all my strength, piercing the transhuman in his wounded belly with the sharp rebar edge.

Annoyed by my assistance, the transhuman released Riley's neck, and her exhausted body crumbled to the ground in a pathetic display of personal weakness. Now I had his full attention as the enraged Hispanic pulled the rebar out of his belly, then reached out to grab me. I felt the strength in his hand as he squeezed my lonely arm, pulling me towards him as I fought to get away. With one big yank, the transhuman overpowered my meager resistance. Both of his hands held me tight as I felt my body lift off the ground like a ragdoll.

Out of the corner of my eye, I saw him arrive like an angel delivered to me from the heavens. His bulky black frame, with its bulging muscles was unmistakable. In his right hand, he held a long blade, and on his face was the look of a killer. I saw George cock his arm back before I heard the sound of the long blade cutting through the air. The Hispanic transhuman let out a loud cry of agony, releasing me from his grip and letting me fall on top of a pile of rubble. When I landed on the pile, I could hear bones in my ribcage pop and felt an instant streak of mind-numbing pain. The transhuman ignored me and turned around to face George instead. That was when I noticed the loaded pistol laying idle near me. I immediately grabbed it, chambering a round before aiming at the back of his head. Noticing I was about to pop this fucker, George ducked to the ground to stay out of my line of fire.

The gun went off, and the back of the transhuman's skull started to pour out blue blood like hot lava from a volcano. Slowly, the Hispanic transhuman fell on his stomach and went motionless. Looking towards the back of the building, I saw that Ed and the few remaining black defenders were about to be overrun. A new wave of transhumans was advancing upon us while raking our position with small arms fire. At some point, I knew we would all run out of ammunition and end up unable to continue to defend ourselves. When that inevitability occurred, it would be game over for all of us.

'I have orders to get all you American's out of here safely," George barked. "

We will stay and fight these transhumans off, but you and all your people must leave now."

'No fuckin way," I shouted!

'I'm not about to leave you here to die. I have never ran from a fight, and I never will. We are all gonna stay here and fight. No matter the damn outcome. We are Foundationals. We don't run. We aren't cowards."

Ignoring me, George crawled over to the hidden tunnel Juan had used. He brushed away the heavy rubble and popped open three external locks. Rising to his feet, George strained hard as he removed the heavy cover that hid the tunnel's entrance. After a quick scan inside, George turned towards me before pointing at Riley, who now had a face filled with tears.

'Nuria, Dr. Hernandez has lured us into a setup. The Resistance believes that your hardliners have secretly hidden your colonies memory cells inside your subconscious. They brought you out here to get that information, and we can't allow them to have it."

'You and your group must leave," he reiterated. 'This isn't about cowardice, Nuria. It's about control."

'If you fall into the hands of Dr. Hernandez, Black people worldwide will be in danger. They will unlock all your hidden memories and gain a treasure trove of secret intelligence. I will lose this battle today, but we as a people, all must live to fight the war."

'Gather your people now and get inside the tunnel," George ordered.

'Juan and our Doctor are awaiting you. They will get you all out of the city and escort you across the border to Guatemala."

Feeling the steel in George's stare, I knew his intentions and concern were sincere. He believed that Gary Freeman and the hardliners had somehow embedded secret intelligence inside of my brain. I had come to El Salvador to get closer to the truth. Thus far, I had only discovered more confusion, lies, and death. Now I had to make a decision. Was continuing to pursue this elusive truth worth the agony of cowardice, or was fighting and dying for my own truth the right thing to do? Rising from the pile of rubble, I quickly came to a decision. I crawled over to Riley and shook her with my lonely arm, gaining her attention.

'Come on, Riley! We gotta go now," I shouted.

My words barely seemed to register with the shell-shocked transexual. She was completely spaced out and consumed with paralyzing fear. We were in a dire situation, and this was no time to coddle the weak. With my lonely hand, I slapped Riley's still cherry red cheeks, bringing her back to some form of reality. Riley finally crawled over towards the tunnel and sat next to George, swimming in a pool of fear in a silent malaise. I turned towards the front of the building and looked over at Dennis, who was still firing away at a wave of advancing transhumans. I had to scream his name several times before I got his attention. With the wave of my hand, I motioned for Dennis to come my way. Dennis acknowledged me with a head nod before returning his attention to his rifle and sending several bursts into two transhuman attackers bearing down on his position.

Just as I turned around to locate Ed, I saw him sprinting towards us with a pistol in his hand. I ordered Ed to grab Riley and take her down into the tunnel. Ed ignored my command and stood over a kneeling George. Time seemed to slow as I watched Ed's eyes focus on the back of George's head before raising his pistol. With the pull of the trigger,

George's body slumped forward, falling to the ground. Before I could process the moment, Ed pointed his pistol at a shivering Riley. Riley looked up at Ed, letting out a pitiful plea for mercy. Instead of mercy, three loud bursts followed, hitting Riley in the chest.

"What the hell are you doing Ed," I shouted!

Ed walked towards me with a light smile, as transhumans seemed to flood my view, overrunning our position. While pointing his gun down at me, Ed grabbed me by my hair and pulled me up to my feet. I looked towards Dennis and screamed for help, but I saw him and a group of Black soldiers retreating with transhumans chasing behind them. I was all alone now, and I felt the helplessness of it all in my spirit.

"You're coming with me, Nuria Phillip Sellers," he uttered angrily. "When we kill Dennis, I promise to bring his body back to lay next to yours."

"I can't fuckin believe this," I yelled. "Ed...You're a damn traitor!"

Ed laughed before punching me in my stomach. The weight of his blow made my broken ribs scream. I felt my lunch spray out of my mouth. The half-digested pork enchiladas didn't feel as good coming up, as it had going down.

"You fuckin bitch," Ed yelled. "

You threw up on my only good shirt. Now I'll have to wash it in your blood."

"Look at you Nuria. Your weak and pathetic. You and Patrice are the real traitors in our community", Ed screamed. "Both of you whores worked together to keep me off of the FP teams. You both hate black men and I see you for what you really are. I'm tired of your shit and if Gary won't put you in your place, I will."

Ed yelled orders at several transhumans, instructing them to go down the tunnel to locate Juan and the group of doctors. Pulling me by my hair, Ed led me out through the back of the building towards a parked rover. The cargo doors swung open, and Dr. Hernandez stood inside the rover staring at me as I neared.

"All this time, Agent Riley and Agent Clarke tried to nicely convince you to reveal the secrets the hardliners hid away inside your consciousness," Dr. Hernandez started.

"Well, Nuria. Unfortunately for you, I'm not so nice."

"You will give me what I'm after, one way or another."

Ed picked me up with both hands and tossed me inside of the rover. After my crippled body bounced on the hard metal deck, I screamed in pain as my fractured ribs dug deeper into my muscles. Dr. Hernandez walked over to me and pressed his foot down on my throat. While leaning his weight into me, he kneeled closer to look into my eyes. I struggled to breathe, and my lonely arm's attempt to knock away Dr. Hernandez's foot were worthless. Panicking, I felt my body begin to lose strength. My vision became blurry. Every second felt like a century as the smiling brown face of Dr. Hernandez hovered above me.

"If you need to breathe...then you better talk, Agent Sellers," he whispered.

"I need to know every spy you Foundationals have embedded in the Dominant Society. Who are your sources! Who was it that gave you Foundationals all our transhuman science?"

As he leaned more of his weight into me, I heard a faint thump in the background of the rover. Distracted, Dr. Hernandez looked behind his back, and I felt him slowly ease his foot off my throat. Tears rolled down my face as my air-starved lungs tasted the welcoming feel of oxygen. Within a few seconds, my blurry vision cleared up, and I cleaned myself up to see what God sent interruption had saved my soul.

My eyes found the interruption and discovered that it was Agent

Riley. Ed had carelessly tossed her bullet-riddled body into the rover next to me, and Dr. Hernandez was clearly upset.

"What the fuck man!"

"Why did you have to shoot him so many times? You only needed to shoot him in the heart!"

"All these chest wounds are gonna be real fuckin hard to conceal!"

"Doc, you wanted a dead FBI agent," Ed sarcastically responded. "Well, now you have it, so shut the fuck up and stop whining."

"You better be glad I didn't shoot this freak in the damn mouth. God knows I wanted to. It was hard enough remaining silent for so long and keeping myself from just killing both of them. I've done all the hard work here, so I'm not entertaining your tears right now."

A look of frustration washed across Dr. Hernandez's face as he turned away from Ed and loudly barked in Spanish. I heard two different voices respond to Dr. Hernandez from the cockpit behind me, and a short conversation I couldn't follow ensued.

"Where is their Black nerd?" Dr. Hernandez asked Ed.

"Do we have him?"

"We have Dennis surrounded," Ed dismissively responded.

"His ammunition should be getting pretty low. Dennis will be dead in a matter of minutes for sure."

Satisfied with Ed's response, Dr. Hernandez made his way back to me. He grabbed my lonely hand and handcuffed me to the rover's deck. With a light rumble and the slightest vibration, I could feel the pilots turn on the rover's engines. Dr. Hernandez exchanged a few words with Ed before he closed the cargo doors halfway.

He donned a pair of headphones and began whispering commands into a small microphone. Taking a seat behind the cockpit, he pulled out a small handheld computer, and a virtual image of the entire area was displayed in front of him. Small blue figures moved like flowing water, encircling a small shack at the center of the hologram image. Dr. Hernandez was playing General, and I could see the excitement in his eyes as he instructed his transhuman subject to toss grenades at the group of combatants still holding out.

While he was engrossed in commanding his troops, I searched my surroundings, looking for anything that would help me turn the tables on this bastard. Near me, I found a distress flare mounted on the wall. I tried to use my feet to kick it free, but the flare was just outside of my reach. I was helpless, and my fate was sealed. The feeling felt worse than death. Dr. Hernandez had not only outsmarted Federal government agencies, but he had also outsmarted us Foundationals. If the Foundational secrets had somehow been buried into my deep consciousness, when Dr. Hernandez began the process of turning me into a transhuman, he would certainly have access to that intelligence. Like Ed, Riley would be the perfect double agent for the Resistance. The Mestizos would have a covert ally in the FBI and have access to all the counter-intelligence they needed to reinforce their newly found power. The Dominant Society had betrayed them during Operation Balboa, and now the Resistance was about to return the favor in spades.

"How did you and the Resistance get to my partner Ed?" I blurted out. "Did you make him a transhuman?"

Hearing my question, Dr. Hernandez deliberately hit the off button on his handheld computer and looked into my eyes. His half-smile could not hide his thinly veiled arrogance as he searched for the right boastful words that would proclaim his glory.

"Hell no," he replied.

"As a scorned Black woman, I truly thought you would have easily figured Ed out by now."

'Some of your people's minds are so weak; they don't require any bioscience to control them. For black males like Ed, their internal self-hate is so much more powerful than any injection from my needles."

'Hell, you're old, bestie. That racist whore Dominic made her living off of Black men's self-hate and self-denial."

'A kiss or some sexual attention from any non-black woman is enough to confuse them forever. Black men like Ed convince themselves that because the women they idolize are Hispanic.....that it isn't the same as your husband, Heavyweight Champion Quinton Sellers, sleeping around with white women."

'Black men like Ed are just as controllable as any transhuman subject I've ever made. When Ed looks at you, he doesn't see himself, he sees trash. When he looks at my women, he sees everything in life that he desires."

Dr. Hernandez rose from his seat and stood over me. He was deep in thought as he wiped his chin with the back of his hand. Then he slowly fell to one knee beside me. I felt his fingers gently caress my cheek as his face wore a faint look of sympathy, almost as if he viewed me as his very own child.

'Black men like Ed...are much more devout and zealous in their loyalty to my people. They have a loyalty that is genuine and uncorrupted, all because they harbor this sexual attachment to our women."

"They will happily deny your people if it means helping the Hispanic community. Certain things in life are much more potent than any of my laboratory experiments. Dominic knew this. I know this, and now you should understand this as well."

'Are you telling me that Ed betrayed Foundationals for interracial sexual access?" I bluntly asked. 'Because that sounds a bit off. I've known Ed for years, and I don't believe he is capable of being that childish."

"Nuria, I'm telling you that transhumanism is not the only thing at the center of all of this fuckin shit," he explained. "And that, my old friend, is part of the truth you claim you're seeking."

"Finding the truth you seek is one thing. Accepting that same bitter truth is completely another."

"Your old bestie Dominic failed to accept her own truth, and for that, she is now dead...and you will soon share that same tragic fate because you denied Ed's truth when it was right in front of you the entire time."

Dr. Hernandez rose to his feet and walked forward towards the cockpit. Before he could make it, the entire rover shook violently, causing him to stumble and fall to the floor. High pitched rumbling pulses and bright orange flashes followed the disturbance.

"What the fuck was that?" A puzzled Dr. Hernandez shouted.

Seconds later, the half-closed doors of the rover were slammed open, revealing the panicked face of my wayward partner Ed Carter. He carried a duffle bag in his hands, and behind him, I could see scores of transhuman bodies scattered about the ground.

"We gotta leave Doc," he screamed.

"Gary Freeman has tricked us!"

Ed began to leap up into the rover, and as his foot hit the deck, a single rifle shot pierced through the quiet moment of chaos. I watched in horror as Ed fell forward, and red blood took flight from the back of his head. He crumbled to the floor next to Riley and twitched for a few seconds before going motionless..

"What the hell!" Dr. Hernandez screamed while looking out of one of the rover's cargo windows.

Before Dr. Hernandez could elaborate, a series of rifle shots rang out. The cockpit windows shattered, and pieces of thick glass seemed to float like confetti before landing on the chests of the two pilots. The two pilots had been shot dead, and both men sat motionless, soaked in their blood.

Dr. Hernandez hit the deck and unholstered his handgun before crawling towards the rover's emergency exit. He spun the latches lever and pushed open the exit. With fear in his eyes, Dr. Hernandez grabbed a smoke grenade, pulling its pin and tossing it out outside before attempting to run for his life.

"It looks like you're about to find out some hard truth's today, Dr. Hernandez," I teased. "If you wanna live, you need to surrender and submit yourself to me."

"The truth is, I'm the only person who can keep you alive. You either accept that fact or fuckin die."

"I'd rather die than to submit to you people!" He shouted back.

"Well, you better get ready to submit to God if you won't submit to me, asshole," I answered.

Dr. Hernandez aimed his pistol at me and uttered a few curse words. Undaunted, I stared back at him, confronting his weakened spirit with my own uncompromising will. A shadow appeared outside of the cargo door. In front of me, I saw Dr. Hernandez instantly turn both his eyes and his pistol towards the figure. I heard the sound of his gun clicking as he pulled the trigger several times, with no response. Frustrated and panicked, Dr. Hernandez racked the slide back, trying to clear a misfire. The ringing pops of an automatic assault rifle flooded my ears as the gunfire riddled Dr. Hernandez's body with bullets.

"You can never outsmart God's justice, Dr. Hernandez. One way or the other, God's will shall be done."

I turned away from his dying soul. Looking outside of the cargo doors, I saw a pretty black woman with very low-cut hair. Her dark skin seemed to shine under the hot sun. The sight of her majesty made me think of the Spanish-speaking dark-skinned Black woman Jeremy Woodson had confided about. After a tactical reload, the woman whispered into a microphone and reached into a pouch on her body, pulling out a pair of handcuffs. She leaped into the rover and made a straight line towards Dr. Hernandez's body, handcuffing the dying man without a drop of remorse. As she handcuffed him, two more figures appeared outside of the cargo bay doors. They were two black men that I immediately recognized.

"Jeremy!" I shouted.

Hearing the distress in my voice, both Jeremy Woodson and Darius Royal climbed into the rover. Both men came to me in total silence, almost like they didn't know who I was. Jeremy unlocked the handcuffs and pulled me up to my feet. I looked up into both men's eyes and didn't see that spark of recognition within them. Feeling a bit disappointed, I thanked both of them for helping.

"Agent Nuria Sellers," Jeremy responded. "Dennis is outside waiting on you. He said he needs to talk to you in private."

Jeremy's voice sounded different, and the lack of feeling behind his words was telling. Without responding to him, I exited the rover and walked towards Dennis, who stood alone while looking at a large group of black men putting out fires. Hearing my footsteps, Dennis glanced over his shoulder at me and nodded his head. I positioned myself in front of him and looked up into his eyes, staring him down. Dennis nervously cut his eyes away from mine and blinked in embarrassment. Unable to contain my angry spirit, my lonely hand cocked back and slapped Dennis. The force of the loud blow nearly made him stumble, and soon after the sting wore off, I saw the remorse well up in his eyes.

"You and Gary just had to fuck with those men, didn't you?"

"Does Jeremy even know who I am, Dennis? How about Darius... does he even remember his poor family? You two took away everything that made us different as Foundationals. How the hell are we different from Dominic and Dr. Hernandez? Because of what you've done, we aren't any better than them at this point!"

"Nuria, I'll tell you what makes us both different from those White Supremacists." He quickly refuted while stiffening up to me.

"They're dead...and we're alive."

"We're alive because we are actually fighting for something righteous and correct."

"After Jeremy talked with you, he begged me to reprogram him. He knew you would never leave Quinton and he wanted his suffering to stop. I showed that man way more mercy than you ever did by relieving him of the burdens simmering in his heart."

"We all know he could never have you, Nuria...You're just too chicken shit to tell the man the truth."

Dennis turned away from me and looked at the rover. Outside of the rover, Jeremy and Darius were zipping up a plastic body bag that contained Riley. The dark-skinned woman held a bright red gas can and was drenching the hull of the rover with fluid. She was quiet and completely consumed with the task, making certain every portion of the rover got wet. Curious, I walked closer and found the bodies of Ed and Dr. Hernandez. Their corpses were also wet and neatly stacked on top of the two dead pilots. The strong scent of kerosene punched me in the nose, causing my eyes to water.

"Darius's family wanted revenge", Dennis proclaimed. "I promised them I would deliver that revenge upon our opponent's necks."

"The black woman that saved your life, her name is Alexis, and she's a decorated scientist from London. It was Alexis that reprogramed Jeremy after Juan and his militiamen captured him."

"Her father is a Foundational brother from Chicago and her mother is Nigerian. Alexis is one of our leading experts in transhuman science, which is why she is stationed here in El Salvador."

Dennis pointed at the scores of black men dutifully cleaning up the wreckage of the battle. They all were silent and seemed focused. As I continued to examine the group, I finally noticed Juan among them. His chest wound was now heavily bandaged, and he walked with the aid of a long brown cane. I could barely hear the faint sounds of his voice as he gave orders to the group of men surrounding him.

'Like Alexis, Juan has contributed mightily to our mission. These two are the quiet heroes, that can't be celebrated, but make vital contributions to the well-being of our people. Without either of them, black people will lose this war."

'Do you believe that Juan isn't any better than the White Supremacists?" Dennis softly asked. "That young man has devoted his entire life towards fighting for his people."

'Juan and his family have paid the ultimate price in this battle for humanity."

'Look at him, Nuria."

'He's surrounded by transhumans. Black transhumans gave up their human lives in this fight against White Supremacy. These are brothers that the Resistance killed, tortured and tried to weaponize against Black people."

'Now, they are still fighting against White Supremacy beyond their living days. Do you really believe that any of those men would object to what we had to do to them, Nuria?"

Dennis flipped up the end of his shirt and unholstered his pistol. After pulling back the slide and chambering a round, he handed me the loaded weapon. I took his gun, and my eyes met his. I could feel the intensity in his spirit as he looked at me.

'If you believe that any of those men out there would object to us doing whatever it took to justify their sacrifice, then you can go ahead and kill me right now."

'I will tell you that if Donovan and Pernell weren't dead. They would be right here. They both would understand that this is ultimately a battle of commitment and not morals."

Dennis barked out an order in Spanish, and the dark-skinned lady quickly moved away from the rover. He then looked at Jeremy and waved his hand towards the rover. Without uttering a word, Jeremy walked up to the open cargo door. He reached into his pocket and pulled out a cigarette lighter. Jeremy sparked a flame with the flip of a finger, tossing the lit lighter onto the fuel-soaked bodies inside. Orange flames engulfed Ed, and his body disappeared from view as dark grey smoke began to consume the inside of the rover.

'May God forgive his soul," Dennis mumbled.

CHAPTER TEN

THE GOOD BOOK

IT HAD BEEN TWO MONTHS SINCE I had last visited her, and this was not what I expected. Dr. Wisemen had barely asked me anything this morning. For some reason, she seemed preoccupied and unconcerned. Instead of probing with her normal array of annoying questions, Dr. Wisemen was content with the cold moments of silence as she filled out an endless stack of paperwork. I let out a loud sigh in frustration, crossing my legs before laying my purse down on my lap.

'In your time off, have you been keeping up with the news Nuria," she finally asked.

'I've been spending time with my family," I shot back. 'I don't give a damn about the media."

'Since you're so concerned about it, maybe you can waste our time and tell me what's happening in the world. I'll just sit here quietly and listen to you run your mouth for once."

Hearing my words, Dr. Wisemen began to scribble on a sheet of paper before neatly tucking it away into a brown folder. Ignoring my sarcasm, she rose from her seat and flipped on the TV screen. As the screen came to life, the volume was way too loud, causing a ringing echo throughout the half-empty room. Caught off guard by the noise, Dr. Wisemen quickly pressed down on the volume button and lowered the sound down to a reasonable level.

"I hope your family time has been productive, Nuria." She stated as she flipped through the channels.

"The productivity of my family time isn't your damn business," I responded. "

Stay out of my marriage Dr. Wiseman and stay the hell away from my husband."

Sensing she had touched a nerve, Dr. Wiseman refocused on the TV, flipping through the channels until she stopped at one of our colony's more popular news outlets. The two black anchors sat in a well-lit studio, offering the world fake smiles as they led into their next news segment. My full attention was captured when I heard my name blast through the TV speakers. Focusing my eyes on the screen, I watched as the image changed from the studio to a video of Agent Riley. Her beard was neatly trimmed, and her FBI issue Formal Dress Uniform looked sharp. Riley stood next to the Director of the FBI as he spoke out to the gathered crowd, while Gary Freeman could be seen behind her deceptively smiling at the white scene in front of him.

There were tears building in Riley's eyes, and even through the detached lens of the video, I could sense the pride beaming from within the woman. The FBI Director turned towards her, placing a gold ribbon on her uniform before clapping enthusiastically with the standing audience. Riley smiled graciously, and I watched as the tears flowed down her blushing cheeks. The camera cut to a visual of Riley's husband clapping proudly while wiping away her own tears, as the news anchors honored the historic heroism of Agent Riley Simmons.

"It's good that our true heroes get their just rewards, isn't it Nuria?"

Dr. Wiseman commented.

I ignored Dr. Wiseman's cleverly loaded question and instead delivered her a light smile with a rushed head nod. I knew she was trying to find a key into my mind, attempting to fish around in my inner thoughts. I had decided to keep those thoughts to myself. No one outside of my new circle of power needed to know the truth about Agent Riley, our newly minted transhuman informant. Although I truly hated what Gary and Dennis had done, I respected why he chose to do it, so it was better for me to remain silent about our truth and stay on code.

"Yeah, Agent Riley saved the Dominant Society and our colony. Without her expertise, that crazed Hispanic Doctor would have assassinated more politicians," I deflected.

Dr. Wiseman turned around in her seat and looked at me with a shocked expression, almost like she could sense I was serving her a bullshit sandwich. With a button push, she killed power to the TV before tossing the remote onto her desk.

"Nuria. How do you see your heroic actions at Dry Tortugas compared to the killing of Dr. Hernandez by that white FBI man?" She asked.

"I'm no hero," I quickly shot back. "Dry Tortugas was God's will and not my own."

"In this life, I've learned to accept that the Lord's plan for us will always prevail. These days, I feel blessed and grateful to have survived this whole ordeal. Now, it's just a matter of doing the things that God left me here to do."

"Well, that's a very mature way of looking at things, Nuria," Dr. Wiseman replied.

"In fact, you sound just like a politician, which strangely enough, might be appropriate."

I felt my watch vibrating on my wrist. Gazing down at its small bright screen, I noted that my hour-long session was over. Eager to get back home, I zipped up my purse and rose from the couch, fully expecting Dr. Wiseman to issue me my prescription card. Instead, she stared at me with a confused expression, almost as if I had forgotten something important.

"Nuria, this session is scheduled to run a bit longer," she informed me. "Two specialists will be joining us today. I believe they may be outside; please have a seat and wait for a second."

Pissed, I tossed my purse back on the hard couch and slumped back into my uncomfortable seat. The last thing I felt like enduring was another hour of bullshitting with two annoying specialists that would ask me repetitive questions. Dr. Wiseman bolted up from her desk and walked into the hallway, slamming the door behind her. After a few minutes, she opened the door and reentered her office. I was surprised to see who was following her inside, and I immediately knew this had nothing to do with mental health.

"Good afternoon, Agent Sellers," Gary declared.

Gary and Dennis grabbed two chairs from a conference table and sat across from me. It had been weeks since I had last seen either of them. Both men looked relaxed and sharp, wearing designer tuxedos. Their handsome elegance in this plain and stale hospital felt out of place.

"You two tricksters look ready for a big night. Why put on your fancy monkey suits to come to visit lil ole me," I asked?

"Because we're headed to a big press conference Nuria," Dennis responded. "We gotta represent and make sure we look good for our people."

"Really," I laughed. "Well, dabbling in transhumanism like a lying racist isn't a good look, no matter how much the suit you wear costs."

"Is this how you gonna treat an old friend Nuria," Dennis shot back?

"No, Dennis. This is how I treat a person who abused my trust."

My not-so-subtle jab stung him, and I could feel his spirit absorb the verbal punishment. Dennis leaned back in his chair in pure frustration, failing to offer a response. For weeks, Dennis and his wife had tried to communicate with me. I had ignored all of his virtual calls. When he came to my house, I left him outside to ring the doorbell without bothering to answer. Quinton had tried to mediate between us, reminding me that Dennis had saved my life. Yet, despite that fact, I felt I could no longer trust a man that purposely kept secrets from me. He held tightly to secrets that would have saved the lives of people close to us both, and for that, I hadn't yet forgiven him.

"Damnit, Nuria," Gary broke in.

"This man did what he had to do to not only save you but the rest of Foundational Black America."

"Can't you see past yourself for one minute and recognize that!"

"Well, Gary, how about you host some fake ass ceremony and pin a meaningless metal on Dennis's chest, just like they did for that dead bitch Riley."

"If you're here to take away all your little secrets you hardliners stored in my subconscious, you can go fuck yourself, Gary."

"In part, my two best friends died because you and Dennis kept the truth to yourselves. Two other Foundationals that I trusted with my life secretly turned on me. You both knew I was in danger and allowed me to remain around traitors."

"How exactly am I supposed to trust you two after that?"

Gary chuckled to himself and turned around to face Dr. Wiseman in exasperation. As usual, her expression was stone-faced, betraying no trace of emotional reaction. Leaning back against the hard couch, I readied my ears to decipher his excuses. Now it was Gary's turn to try and explain himself while allowing us into his soul.

"There are no secrets hidden away in your mind Nuria," Gary explained.

"That's misinformation we used to flush out Ed and Dr. Hernandez."

"You don't have to trust a word I say Nuria," Gary began while gazing down at the white tile flooring. "

I don't need you to be my trusted friend. I'm not here to make you like me. I'm here to destroy White Supremacy."

Gary stood up from the chair and walked over towards the small window, peering out into the grey overcast sky with fire in his eyes. For several seconds he stood there motionless, taking in the scenery before slowly lowering himself next to me on the couch.

"What our people need is for us to win Nuria. We must destroy White Supremacy at all costs. Either we win, or they kill us all. Those are our only two options."

"I am a warrior. Victory trumps friendship when the lives of our people are on the line. I'm a ruthless asshole who will sacrifice anything for the pleasure of looking in the eyes of our enemy and watching his blue eyes fade away into the gates of hell."

"On this earth's battlefield, your faith shouldn't be given to warriors like Dennis or myself."

"Nor should it be given to flawed comrades like Patrice Williams or Ed Carter. Not even the blessed souls of Donovan and Pernell should warrant your complete faith."

"For us to not only win this race war, but also secure peace for humanity, we need your faith to be given to something far greater than us corrupted mortals. I need you to be just as ruthless as me, in service of something much higher than my limited aims."

With his rough-looking hands, Gary clumsily unbuttoned his tuxedo before reaching inside his jacket pocket. He pulled out several high-definition photos and gently laid them on the couch next to my knee. Looking down at one photo, I saw the bright smiling face of Patrice Williams, and an instant feeling of longing familiarity gripped me. Her fresh eyes and silky black hair gave the appearance of her late twenties, as she proudly wore an oversized Yale sweater. Patrice was inside a dark tavern holding a half-empty cocktail glass while leaning against the bar. Surrounding her were scores of jubilant innocent-looking White faces. The crowd around her looked like fellow college students, all of them glossy-eyed and exuding that unique presence of privilege.

"Nuria, despite my differences with her, I respected Patrice."

"She was intelligent, hardworking, and devoted to our people. Her family name carried a lot of weight within our Foundational community, which unfortunately put a lot of pressure on Patrice to achieve great things."

"I don't think any of us could identify with the pressure that came with upholding that Williams name. After the lynching of her grandfather, we all were rooting for her and her family, so carrying all that hope was a heavy burden for her."

"But I'd be lying if I told you that the hidden demons within the Williams household weren't of a concern to me."

"Her grandfather was an original hardliner. A black man who sought to combat White Supremacy directly, which made him an icon for us Foundationals."

"When I look at photos like those. I see a young woman still struggling to live up to those lofty expectations."

I picked up the photo, examining it closely. Within Patrice's hazy eyes, I finally noticed a tint of red that worried me. Her smile was full, and Patrice's comfort around this group of white associates was pronounced. Grabbing the other photos, I slowly flipped through them, finding one image of Patrice sniffing white lines from the trunk of a car. In that particular photo, awkward-looking white women hovered over her, displaying duplicitous grins and smiles. The final image was the most egregious and shocking. It was a photo of Patrice, passed out on a bed in a small dormitory. She was partially naked, and next to her, the empty remnants of several bottles of vodka were visible. In the top corner of the photo, I could make out the image of a white man. His skinny legs were hairy, and his crotch was exposed. Three pairs of men's underwear and pants laid on the floor next to the bed, while Patrice lay atop blood-soaked sheets.

From the limo rides that ended with plenty of empty wine bottles to Patrice's private getaways into that secret office space after our meetings, I had suspected that her indulgence into intoxication was merely Patrice's brand of escapism. I fancied it all as her way of dealing with the stress of leading our colony. Now I realized that Patrice had been hurting inside, and that pain pushed her into a state of quiet addiction. Along with the family name, Ivy League education, and expectations of political stardom came the pressure of fending off White Supremacy while somehow holding our people together. Carrying that load must have felt like an impossible journey. My heart ached for her soul as I silently sympathized with her plight.

"If you want me to put my faith in something," I began. "I need to truly know what it is, Gary."

"No lies. No bullshit. No omissions."

"The truth stays in this office, between all four of us."

"Tell me about our counter-intelligence operation named Surge, and why is everyone outside of this colony so dead set on finding this mysterious memory cell."

"Nuria, Surge has been around for decades. Hell, Surge began before the Great Recompense was even signed into law." Gary began.

"After we were awarded our Reparations, many Foundationals chose to move to our colonies and start over."

"Yet, there were some that remained loyal to the Dominant Society, choosing to become Zebras."

"Our hard liner ancestors decided that some of our own ought to hang around within the Dominant Society and mix in with the Zebras. We would use the opportunity to infiltrate all facets of life within White Society, with sleeper cells, ready to be activated at a moment's notice."

"The Intel surge sleeper cells provided us has been invaluable."

"Only the most dedicated and devout were selected for Surge. We needed folks who wouldn't go cold on us and could sustain their passion behind enemy lines."

"The strategy wasn't unlike what the Russians and East Germans did during the Cold War. Before the Berlin Wall went up, they made sure that spies were sent to live among the West Germans. Many of our sleeper cells became high achievers within the Dominant Society."

"By sleeper cells, you mean brothers like Agent Clarke," I interrupted? "It sure is nice to have one of your own inside of the FBI. Am I right?"

Gary's head tilted back slightly, and his eyes briefly widened at my words. Unable to contain his regret, Dennis simply bowed his head in silence, surely blaming himself for Clarke's death. His remorseful spirit more than confirmed my inner suspicions. My question caught them off guard, and now they had to finally admit what I had already figured out. Agent Clarke had been one of us, one of our most dedicated and loyal servants. The life Clarke lived within the Dominant Society was nothing more than a clever ruse. Clarke was a black man who had put everything on the line for his people, and in the end, he was not alive to receive the recognition he so richly deserved.

'Losing Clarke Bernard was a tremendous blow for us," Gary continued. "

Because of the status that came with his FBI badge, we had access to all kinds of Intel."

'Clarke flipped a lot of informants for us. Surge isn't just about sleeper cells Nuria. More than half of our Intel comes from disillusioned White people, greedy Asians, and ambitious Immigrants. Most of them were paid snitches, folks with some sort of personal vendetta or criminals looking to beat a federal case."

'Our grandfathers quickly discovered that with our newfound wealth, we were able to secretly buy all kinds of help from people who didn't give two damns about us before the Great Recompense."

"The White Supremacist instantly became less popular than they had been before we received our reparations. For these opportunists, we were simply viewed as new money."

'So, that's why the FBI was so hot about finding that memory cell," I jumped in. "

The FBI knew they had a leak, and they wanted to find out who it was."

'Right," Gary confirmed.

'But Agent Riley and the FBI weren't the only ones looking to access our memory cells and identify Surge sleeper cells within the Dominant Society."

'Dominic and the CIA also wanted to know who our sources were as well."

'Agent Clarke was able to recruit money-hungry doctors and scientists, having them deliver us a stream of raw intelligence about Operation Balboa. From the very beginning of the program, we were already onto the CIA."

'With this information, we were able to assist our black brothers and sisters in Latin America, helping like-minded blacks turn the tide against the racist Mestizo Resistance."

"We reverse engineered all of their transhuman projects, which scared the shit out of the CIA. We had the ultimate advantage over our opponent and could counter every chess move they made."

"This is a threat the White Supremacists cannot tolerate," Gary emphasized.

Gary pointed at the photos in my hand and motioned for me to review them again. Thumbing through them once more, I could not help but re-examine all of the white faces in them and ponder. Then I saw a young white woman with an unmistakable scar below her left eye and knew it was Dominic. Her long stringy hair was blonde instead of dirty blue. The absence of her large silver nose ring was noticeable. Dominic was well-tanned, and her unwrinkled face looked smooth, portraying a sense of youthful innocence as a goofy smile dominated her expression. She could have easily become a fashion model or an actress if the life of a CIA operative hadn't been her calling. In the photo, she stood behind Patrice with her hands tucked behind her waist, watching gleefully while posing as Patrice hovered over several lines of cocaine. The image was horrifyingly depressing.

"Dominic and the CIA tried to use these photos to blackmail Patrice, but the attempt went wrong, and that's what set the course for where we all are today." He explained.

"So, Surge is the reason for all this mess Gary?"

Gary rose from his seat and again faced the window, pausing to collect his thoughts. I couldn't tell if Gary was misleading me, but something in his spirit told me that he wasn't calculating his words. Having looked at the photos myself, I could tell that Gary and I had come to the same horrifying conclusion. A woman we all thought had been the strongest, and the smartest among us had actually been one of our weakest and in most need of assistance.

"Weeks before the Dry Tortugas raid," Gary continued. "Our Surge operatives followed Patrice to Boston."

"Back then, this sorta trip wasn't particularly unusual for Patrice."

"Patrice would periodically travel to Boston and meet with old college friends. White folks in the Dominant Society that she trusted and valued, along with a Zebra couple she liked to have threesomes with."

"When she'd go to Boston, Patrice had somewhat of a routine."

"She'd meet boring friends in the morning for coffee or breakfast. Visit with old professors over lunch and cups of tea...then party hard with her close friends for the rest of the night," Gary explained.

"During her last trip, everything was going well. Patrice ate breakfast, and then went to lunch. Our sleeper cells didn't notice anything out of the ordinary until that evening."

Gary turned away from the window, walking past me and the couch to Dr. Wiseman's desk. While staring her down, Gary lowered himself on the desk in front of her before reaching out and caressing the side of Dr. Wiseman's face. Gary's intimate display was strange, and done without even the slightest objection from my physician. Gary mumbled a few words to her, and the stoic expression I had been all too familiar with disappeared.

Dr. Wiseman slowly stood up from her lounge chair with watery eyes, taking off her glasses as she rose. With a few mumbles of encouragement from Gary, Dr. Wiseman silently walked towards the couch and lowered herself next to me. It felt so strange having her uncomfortable presence that close. For years, Dr. Wiseman had made sure to keep her professional distance from me. Now I knew that whatever she was about to say was immensely personal.

"My late husband and I met up with Patrice for dinner that evening, just like we normally would," she began.

"Patrice had reached out a few days before arriving, asking if my husband and I wanted to hang out. I could tell by the detachment in her voice that she was a little stressed and needed a change of scenery."

"My husband and I knew her very well, having first met Patrice at an exclusive swingers club in Newport, Rhode Island. That night, she walked into the club among a group of snobby-looking white kids and started nervously glancing over at our table."

"Finally, I made my husband wave at her, and Patrice's face lit up with a soul-consuming smile. After a few more welcoming gestures, this sexy black woman gathered her courage and decided to walk over to our table to drink with us. That night, things between us kicked off real fast. It all felt magical."

"From that first night on, whenever Patrice came to Boston, she would always contact us. We'd drink bottles of wine and buy a little powder before going back home for the night."

"She became part of our family. My husband and I treasured the moments we shared with Patrice. She added life to any room she was in, and her infectious smile could melt an iceberg."

Dr. Wiseman's watery eyes were now a flowing river of clear tears. I could feel her soul suddenly reliving the memories that had surely been buried away deep within her. Feeling a spirit of compassion, I reached my lonely hand into my small purse and found a handful of napkins. As Dr. Wiseman composed herself and gathered her words, I offered her a few napkins to clean her face.

"Two days before Patrice was scheduled to arrive, my husband and I ate dinner at an Asian restaurant. It was our wedding anniversary, and we were only looking to share a quiet dinner to celebrate our eight years of marriage."

"Halfway into our meal, a well-dressed white lady sat at a table next to ours. The white lady complimented me on my high heels, so we began chatting with each other."

"After my husband bought her a few drinks, she moved over to our table and sat with us. She let us know that she was an editor for the Kingfish publication, and we told her that we both worked as mental health counselors."

"As the conversation wore on, the lady complained that her date for the night had stood her up. She confided that my husband buying her drinks and the both of us being so friendly had considerably softened her disappointment."

"One thing led to another, and all three of us ended up in her plush townhouse naked, smoking weed in her king-sized bed."

"From the passion in his eyes, I could tell my husband enjoyed the encounter. For us both, it was all about the forbidden thrill of it all. Yet, the whole night, I had this lingering feeling."

Dr. Wiseman gently took a photo from my hand and gazed down at it. Following her eyes, I noticed that her stare locked in on the image of young Dominic. I watched as Dr. Wiseman's bottom lip shivered, almost like the cold temperature of her freezing office had finally subdued her.

"I can still remember looking into her blue eyes," she continued. "All of her flirting glances mixed in with those smiles filled with sexual curiosities, sort of entrapped me."

"I should have told my husband to stop. It was our wedding anniversary. I should have told him that the night was about the both of us and not anyone else. Part of me wanted to leave Dominic at the restaurant because I knew we were being too greedy."

"Yet, seeing my husband's barely hidden sexual excitement lured me in, fueling my desires with raging thoughts of burning satisfaction."

'After we passed out in her bed," she continued. "We both woke up in the morning and found ourselves alone. My husband and I searched around the townhouse looking for Dominic, but she was gone."

'Scared and not knowing what we had gotten into, we got ourselves dressed, rushing out of the front door and locking it behind us. When we made it to our car, my husband unlocked the doors, and we found that someone had gotten inside.' Dr. Wiseman described.

'Hundreds of photos were scattered inside the car, revealing photos of my husband and I with some of our clients. All of them very incriminating and professionally embarrassing."

'On the dashboard, there was a long brown envelope. In it was a short unsigned letter addressed to us along with the photos of Patrice you're holding in your hand. The letter was offering us a deal. Either we convinced Patrice Williams to sabotage your virtual wedding with Quinton Sellers, or all the photos in our car would be released to our employers."

Understanding where this was all heading, I took the photos in my lonely hand and threw them in Dr. Wiseman's face. I felt my soul come to a boil as the hot spirit within me scorched every ounce of sympathy I had left for the bitch. As Dr. Wiseman sat beside me, balling in tears, I raised my clenched fist in the air. Just as I was about to swing at her with all of the burdensome weight from the past decade of my life, the strong hands of Dennis grabbed me.

'No, Nuria," he softly whispered above my screams of anger.

'Calm down. Please. We need you to calm down."

I fought hard against the arms of Dennis and Gary. Both men had me pinned down on the ice-cold floor, pleading for me to compose myself. As my strength began to waver, I looked up to see both of them breathing hard in their own exhaustion. Gary pleaded with me to hold my peace.

Relenting to his words, I laid my head down on the cold tiling, feeling each tear of anger as it rolled from my eyes.

'Let her finish, Nuria,' Gary panted. 'You wanted the truth, well you gotta be ready for it. Lies are really easy. The truth is hard, and we still have a lot more of it to go.'

Sensing my surrender, Gary rose from the floor and walked over towards Dr. Wiseman. He picked up a few napkins lying next to my purse and handed them to her. Dr. Wiseman took them, clearing away the bubbles from underneath her snotty nose.

'We met Patrice at a nightclub,' Dr. Wiseman continued.

'From the hazy look in her eyes, I could tell that Patrice had started a little earlier than us this time. So, we didn't stay long before we left the club to go buy a bundle of dope and head home.'

'As soon as we got home, Patrice was really frisky. She wanted to get right to it, but neither of us was in the mood. We wanted to work things out first, hoping that Patrice would somehow be on board to help us.'

'Without uttering a word, my husband pulled out the letter and the photos of Patrice, handing them to her. After pleading with her, she opened the letter and looked at the photos.'

'We all must have sat there in that living room for at least five whole minutes, in complete silence and fear. None of us knew what to say to each other. It was the strangest moment of my life.' Dr. Wiseman explained.

'Patrice broke the silence and asked who had given us the pictures, and we told her. Then she let out a strange laugh that really spooked me. I'll never forget that look on her face. There was no panic, fear, or remorse.'

'Patrice cut open the bundle of dope and took several large sniffs. She told us she could get us close to Quinton Sellers.'

'She began to ask us how we intended to set up Quinton in New York. My husband told her about a young client he knew. A white girl that was bipolar, suffering from hypersexuality."

"My husband opened a cabinet and retrieved her photos. The photos were all headshots. She was a brunette white girl that looked older than her age, although she was barely sixteen."

Dr. Wiseman closed her eyes, letting out a heavy sigh. The office went totally silent. None of us needed her to explain the details of what happened in New York. After Quinton's arrest, the whole world had a minute-by-minute timeline of the events. I looked at Dennis, who was still lightly holding me down. With a few whispers, I asked him to let me up, and he did. I didn't need to hurt Dr. Wiseman. I knew her conscience was already giving her the reward that bitch deserved. After standing up, I walked over to Dr. Wiseman's desk. I lowered myself down in her lounge chair and stared at my last name, printed on my brown patient folder, reading it over and over again in my mind with thoughts of Quinton. We had been through a lot together. In that split second, I determined that nothing would come between us.

"What happened to your husband, Doctor Wiseman?" I asked.

"He was murdered," Gary answered. "After Dry Tortugas, Dr. Wiseman and her husband both took a trip back home to Jamaica. One day he rented a boat, went out sail fishing, and was never seen again."

"At least that's the official government version of what happened," he added. "The unofficial account is that the CIA assassinated him."

"Dr. Wiseman here narrowly escaped death. Our sleeper cell in Boston was able to convince her to join our witness protection program, so we brought her here for safekeeping."

"Safekeeping," I laughed. "So, whose bright fuckin idea was it to make her my doctor?"

"It was mine," Gary admitted. "We had to hide her in a place that Dominic and the CIA would never think to look. They'd never believe she'd be your doctor, let alone live in the same colony as Governor Williams."

"We changed her name and appearance, gave her a new life, and assigned her to look after you. From what I understand, the sessions you two were having have been pretty therapeutic for the both of you."

"Fuck you Gary!" I shouted.

"You knew that they had turned Patrice into a traitor, and you didn't do a damn thing about it."

"My team walked right into an ambush, and you didn't utter one word to save our lives. My wedding was ruined, and you couldn't even warn us."

"This isn't about you, Nuria," Gary shot back. "Please don't take any of this shit personally, Ok." "I decided to wait. We had to be really careful about using our secret information to protect your virtual wedding or stop the Dry Tortugas ambush."

"Doing either would have surely revealed our covert Intel sources, so I decided to wait for the right opportunity to strike. Nuria, the truth of the matter is...neither events warranted exposing our advantages and capabilities to our enemies."

"So, you sat back and allowed your own people to die and suffer," I blasted. "What the hell makes you any better than Patrice!"

Gary walked over towards my lounge chair and the long desk in front of me. Stopping at the desk and reaching into his tuxedo pocket, he pulled out another photo, tossing it down on the desk. The momentum of the toss made the photo briefly spin in a tight circle. When it stopped spinning, I recognized that it was an old photo of Donovan, Pernell, and myself. All three of us were smiling while holding each other in a tight embrace. Our uniforms were soaked in mud and our sweaty brown skin shined under the hot North Carolina sun. It was an old photo of one of our joint training evolutions with the U.S. Army Rangers. Looking at the image bought back a lot of closely held memories.

"There's a big difference between me and Patrice, my sister," Gary calmly replied.

"Just like you, I loved and admired both Donovan and Pernell."

"Hell, part of me still loves Patrice and Ed, despite their obvious shortcomings."

"But I have an awesome responsibility to our people. Above my emotional attachment to individuals in my life, is my commitment to our people's agenda and interests. As cold-hearted as that may seem, it's a responsibility that tortures my soul."

"I carry that photo of Donovan and Pernell with me every day," he softly explained. "It reminds me that I'm not, in fact, a monster."

"Before Dry Tortugas, I had a private conversation with Donovan. Given the weight of Patrice's betrayal, transhumanism, and the CIA's thirst to sabotage your virtual wedding, I found myself torn."

"Despite the risk of outing any of our vulnerable operatives living among the Dominant Society, I discreetly told Donovan everything we knew."

"After Donovan heard it all, we both shed a few tears. Just like me, Donovan understood that in life, doing what is hard and not what is easy is almost always the correct course of action."

"Everything about this was hard," Gary explained. "Every damn decision we could make would hurt people we loved and cared about. Do we save you and Quinton's marriage from outside meddling? Doing so would expose our secret sources within the CIA, ultimately endangering our ability to fight White Supremacy."

"Donovan agreed that it was better to preserve the identity of our spies. We couldn't risk losing that tactical advantage."

"We both knew Dry Tortugas was a trap. A well thought out CIA ambush meant to deliver maximum benefit to the Dominant Society, no matter the outcome."

"Yet, on the flip side. How do we morally justify canceling the raid and not helping the CIA destroy transhumans that the Resistance would surely use against our like-minded brothers and sisters south of the border?"

"Donovan convinced me that he could keep you all alive. The threat from transhumans was a bigger threat than any media narrative the Dominant Society would be able to spin."

Gary picked up the photo of my team from the desk in front of me, abruptly shoving it back into his pocket. Turning away, he walked over to the couch and sat down next to a now numb-looking Dr. Wiseman. When he looked up at me, I could tell he was fighting to hold in all the emotions. His manly pride wouldn't allow him to display his pain for the world to see. If I asked Gary a question, I knew the weakening dam holding back his tears would burst. He didn't need me to witness that, and I knew I didn't need to see it. A long moment of silence followed him to his hard seat on the couch, only to be interrupted by a thoughtful sigh from Dennis. Then Gary collected himself, giving me a stare before diving back in.

"Donovan and I also discussed Patrice Williams," he began. "That was one of our hardest decisions."

"After talking with me, Donovan asked Patrice to send you home, Nuria. He made up a story about you and Jeremy Woodson having this long-standing affair that had finally gotten out of control."

"Donovan embellished your affair, telling Patrice a lie. His lie was a ploy to see where her heart truly was."

"When Patrice still wanted your FP team to press forward with the raid, Donovan and I knew Patrice Williams was unsalvageable. She made the fatal decision that salvaging her family name was more important than her people."

"Donovan made me swear that I wouldn't kill Patrice. He told me it was best if we waited to reap our revenge. He believed that if we knew who among us were traitors, knowing exactly who they were would go a long way towards winning this war."

"Donovan was right. In this thankless war against these Demonic Racists, it's best to play dumb, yet hold every card you need to win the game, in your hands."

Gary rose from the hard couch and exhaled in relief before slowly buttoning up his tuxedo. After a head nod at Dennis, both men gathered themselves to depart. I looked into Dennis's eyes and saw his determined spirit. They were about to leave us and do something important.

"Gary, I'm sorry about your cousin Ed," I offered. "I know how it feels to have betrayal living so close."

"When Clarke Bernard was killed, I knew it was Ed Carter who told Dr. Hernandez about him being a sleeper cell. For that infraction, Ed had to lose his life." Gary explained.

"His crazed addiction to non-black women could no longer be tolerated among the decent."

"I'm sad my cousin is gone." He affirmed. "But I'm blessed to have found you in this painful journey. Ed was a weak man, but you were strong. Your husband was strong. Your family is strong, and our community needs that strength more than ever, Nuria."

"Gary, did we assassinate Patrice, or was Dr. Hernandez the assassin," I asked?

"True power, moves in silence, Nuria. Never forget that fact," Gary replied.

"I kept my promise to Donovan," he cleverly answered. "Dr. Hernandez and his secret allies orchestrated her demise, but in truth, the Patrice we all knew actually died in Boston that night."

He hadn't answered my question, choosing to instead talk in riddles that clouded the fundamental purpose of my inquiry. I already knew the answer without him verbalizing it, so Gary didn't need to speak it. We may not have planted the bomb in that couch, but knowing it was there, waiting to explode did gave us our own measure of quiet justice.

"The FBI believed we killed Patrice, which is why they were after our memory cells," He explained.

"The racists understood that if we Foundationals have the power to reward or punish those among us, that we essentially have the power of the Lord at our disposal. They also understand that once we punish or reward our own, it's only a matter of time before we use that very same power on them."

"They are determined to fight against God's will. This is what all of this boils down to Nuria."

"Thank you for finding the truth and protecting us. Our colony will be forever indebted to you and your husband."

"What about that memory cell Gary. Does it really exist?" I followed up.

Gary chuckled to himself after winking at me. Turning towards the exit, he walked away from us without words. I felt Dennis tapping on my lonely shoulder. The earnest smile on his face almost distracted me from the note he had in his hand. After taking the note from him, he quickly followed Gary out of the office without saying goodbye. I opened the note and began to read it as the door slammed behind them. Gary was about to resign, and Dennis would be our colony's new Governor. The note asked for support, inviting Quinton and I to a formal function that evening that would celebrate the official transfer of power. The words

Gary stated rung in my head as I folded the note in half and stuffed it into my purse. True power moves in silence, and Gary Freeman wanted no part of being loud.

"You should go home to your husband," Dr. Wiseman blurted out.

"I'm sure you and Quinton have a lot to talk about."

"Remind yourself to never take your moments with your husband for granted," she whispered.

After grabbing my purse, I walked to the door. Once again, feeling the chill blowing from the vents above, my thoughts wandered to Quinton. I missed him and wanted so very much to let him know that I appreciated him. For some reason, that emotion felt strangely welcome. I quickly zipped up my light jacket, determined to fight off the abrasive cold that was invading Dr. Wiseman's office. On instinct, I stopped before exiting, having the faint notion of asking Dr. Wiseman about refilling my prescription. As I looked at her sitting all alone on the couch behind me, part of my soul wanted to warm her defeated spirit. Dismissing the thought of needlessly worrying a remorseful woman, I slipped out of the office and quietly made my way out of the hospital's back entrance.

I sat in my car and lifted off into the clear blue sky, soaking in the beauty of my colony from above. As I neared my home, I slowed down at the playground and took in the sight of young black children running on the beautifully cut grass. Tears rolled down my face when I thought of the amount of faith our ancestors had displayed to continue fighting for the day when the green grass was in our neighborhoods. I made it home and walked through the front door. Warmth and the sweet smell of an apple cobbler baking in the oven, greeted my senses. Locking the door behind me, I walked into the living room to find Quinton sitting alone on our soft couch. His hairline was freshly edged, and his beard was perfectly groomed. Quinton looked handsome in his dark blue tuxedo.

It had been years since he had worn it, and I was amazed that it fit him so well. Next to him laid my dark brown formal gown, neatly dangling from its small wooden hanger. I hadn't worn it once, and it still had this gloriously new look to it.

"Hey baby," Quinton greeted.

"Well, I suppose Gary and Dennis must have already given you our invite." I teased.

"Yep. I figured we could use a night to ourselves, so I called the pastor's wife and made arrangements for little Lindsey to spend the evening at their house."

Quinton stood up from his seat and walked into the kitchen. As I leaned down to pick up my gown, I could hear Quinton open the stove and pull a pan from the oven. Pressing the gown up against my stomach, I wondered if I could still wear it. I had gained a few pounds since I'd bought it, and I knew it would definitely be a tight squeeze.

"You wanna bowl of apple cobbler," Quinton shouted.

"No," I quickly rebuffed.

"I better not eat anything before I put this on. I'm going to need every damn inch I can spare to wear this thing."

Worried, I placed the gown back on the couch and immediately felt Quinton come from behind, wrapping his arms around me in a warm embrace. As he held me, I could see the hot bowl of cobbler drowning in a sea of melting ice cream in his hand. He was teasing me, so I playfully delivered my sharp elbow to his ribcage.

"You can afford to enjoy a few spoons of this," he pleaded. "Don't worry about that gown."

"You won't be wearing it too long anyway," he playfully teased.

Meeting his flirty words with my eyes, I turned around in his arms and kissed his lips. The sensation sparked my desire, so I pulled his head

384

down towards me. I felt him lean down further to place the worrisome bowl on the coffee table, next to my mother's Bible. Something about the sight of my mother's old Bible, sitting there in front of the couch, captured my attention. It brought back the childhood memories of my momma laying in her bed, dutifully highlighting scriptures during her midnight study sessions.

"Were you reading that Bible before I came home, honey?" I asked while gently pulling away from Quinton.

I reached down to pick up the Bible and fell onto the couch before aimlessly flipping it open to the book of Job. Looking at the words, I remembered the painful plight of Job and immediately pondered upon his powerful testimony of faith. The words Gary had spoken in Dr. Wiseman's office began to ring in my spirit. Through all of the hardship, Job maintained his faith, submitting himself to God's will.

Quinton sat down next to me and pulled out his reading glasses. Instead of donning them, Quinton placed them in my hand and motioned for me to put them on. In my confusion, I held my tongue and put the glasses to my face. Looking down at the page, I saw something completely different. The scriptures were no longer there. Replacing them were states, cities, towns, counties, and parishes. Following each location, there was a list of names, various addresses, and bank accounts. Alarmed, I snatched the glasses away from my eyes, blinking several times before looking down at the pages to find the familiar holy scriptures again.

"Were you able to see the names and locations Nuria," he softly asked me?

"What is this Quinton", I asked? "Is this Bible what I think it is?"

"It's an old forgotten spy trick," Quinton lamented. "Invisible ink and clear tinted glasses. It worked like a charm during World War II.

There is a reason your mother gave me her Bible. She told me to read it to understand. So, I did."

'Nuria, your mother, wanted to preserve this secret intelligence and pass this down to you, so she entrusted it to me for safekeeping until you were ready."

'It's the reason Donovan chose you for his FP team and fought to save your life at Dry Tortugas. It's the same reason your grandfather passed down so many life lessons to you as a child."

'My mother was a spy," I sighed.

'No. Your mother was a hardliner," Quinton corrected. 'She was a Foundational woman of faith; and was dedicated to our cause."

'Our enemies are evil and clever, but we Foundationals are blessed with skills of discernment. The memory cell these White Supremacists are after exists, but it doesn't require some computer to access it. It just needs an open mind and spirit."

'So, the hardliners hid their most valued Intel inside of this Bible," I chuckled. 'The Dominant Society would never think to read this book in a million years."

'A book they would scorn and most likely burn before even examining it," I continued. 'That is absolutely brilliant."

'This is why I retired from boxing." Quinton confided. 'I gave up my championship belt for something far more important. I didn't need to climb into a boxing ring to fight our enemies. I can defeat them with the knowledge of who we are, what we can do, and the powerful truth we live in."

'True power makes moves in silence, Nuria. It doesn't need the flaws of being flashy or grabbing all of the attention. It simply gets things done and doesn't care if it hurts its opponent's feelings. Our truth will seek loud enough for us, and our enemies can do nothing but submit to our will."

Quinton took the Bible and glasses from me, placing them on the coffee table. He grabbed his bowl of apple cobbler and put a large spoonful in his mouth. I watched as joy rippled through his spirit upon tasting the savory goodness. As he chewed, I finally figured out the real reason my husband had visited El Salvador, the church in the Mission District, and why he had taken Darius Royal back to Dominic in Bodega Bay. To our enemies, Quinton was simply a washed-up black athlete. A black loser treading the waters of life in his self-pity while carrying around his Bible and proclaiming his faith to the world. In a selfish world obsessed with grandiose titles and perceived success, our enemies never saw Quinton coming, sort of like a lowly carpenter that once walked the humble soil of Nazareth.

The Foundational community had fashioned me into this hero after Dry Tortugas, but the power of heroism could never replace the efficiency of our people's faith. The quiet diligence of my mother. The uncompromising sternness of Gary. The loyal dedication of Dennis and the loving patience of Quinton. All of them had given Foundationals an advantage. I had always sought this precious truth and now I could honestly say I had found it. With my lonely hand, I grabbed my gown and rose from the couch. As I went upstairs, I heard Quinton shout up from the living room.

"Riley is going to be there tonight, so make sure you look nice baby. We can't have him outdoing you in front of the cameras." He stated with a mouth full of cobbler.

"She could never outdo me," I proclaimed. "I'm a proud Foundational and God has blessed me with you. Those two things are more than enough for me, my love."

UPCOMING PROJECTS FROM SPIRIT OF 1811 PUBLISHING LLC:

"God Love Us: An Achim Jeffers Novel" – Achim Jeffers Counter-Racist Hitman, returns in Josiah Jay Starr's much anticipated sequel to the groundbreaking hit novel "War of The Heart". Read this hair-raising plot twister and experience Achim's ruthless form of black justice as he unapologetically eliminates blood thirsty White Extremists. (Thriller, Drama, Espionage)
Tentative Publishing Date: August 2022

"The 13th Floor" – Donald London is a black man that seemingly has it all. He's well-liked, highly educated, good looking, and has all the right connections to win the upcoming Louisiana Senate Race. His election day victory appears certain, as the white media has showered him with adulation and national prominence. Suddenly out of nowhere, comes a polarizing racial scandal that disrupts the momentum of his campaign, presenting Donald with a critical life changing decision that tests his loyalties. How does Donald reconcile his political ambitions, while advocating for the Empowerment of the black community he comes from? (Urban, Romance, Drama)
Tentative Publishing Date: Winter 2022 or Spring 2023

"Spirit Of The Trembling Prairies: The New Orleans Slave Revolt of 1811" – The 1811 Slave Revolt was one of the most captivating moments in Foundational Black American history. Sadly, it is also one of the most forgotten and racially suppressed moments in American history. Relive the revolt and feel the revolutionary spirit of the "trembling prairies" in New Orleans, Louisiana. (War & Military, Black Historical Drama)
Tentative Publishing Date: TBD

Visit our website for more details at: www.spiritof1811publishing.com

RELEASED NOVELS ON SALE NOW

"War Of The Heart: An Achim Jeffers Novel" – Mold breaking debut novel of the Achim Jeffers Counter-Racist series. Rated 4.7 out of 5 stars on Amazon/Goodreads. Available in Ebook, Print book or Audiobook, at Amazon, Google Play or any place books are sold.

Visit our website at www.spiritof1811publishing.com and sign up for books specials, newsletter updates and exclusive offers. Follow Spirit of 1811 Publishing on Instagram, Facebook, Twitter and TikTok. You can also contact Spirit of 1811 Publishing and its authors at www.6zeros.net.

AUTHOR'S PLAYLIST WHILE CREATING 'NOTHING WILL COME BETWEEN US'

"Nothing Can Come Between Us", Sade, Stronger Than Pride

"Rain", SWV, Release Some Tension

"Love Is Stronger Than Pride", Sade, Stronger Than Pride

"Couldn't Love You More", Sade, Love Deluxe

"If I Could Change", Master P, I'm Bout It Soundtrack

"Free", Deniece Williams, This Is Niecy

"Remind Me", Patrice Rushen, Straight From The Heart

"Everybody Loves The Sunshine", Roy Ayers Ubiquity

"Keep Looking", Sade, Stronger Than Pride

CPSIA information can be obtained
at www.ICGtesting.com
Printed in the USA
LVHW010529180122
708583LV00003B/30

9 781953 102058